ONCE UPON an *Irritatingly Magical* KISS

#3 The Whickertons in Love

BY BREE WOLF

WOLF PUBLISHING

Once Upon an Irritatingly Magical Kiss by Bree Wolf

Published by WOLF Publishing UG

Copyright © 2021 Bree Wolf
Text by Bree Wolf
Cover Art by Victoria Cooper
Paperback ISBN: 978-3-98536-009-3
Hard Cover ISBN: 978-3-98536-010-9
Ebook ISBN: 978-3-98536-008-6

WOLF Publishing - This is us:

Two sisters, two personalities.. But only one big love!

Diving into a world of dreams..
    ...Romance, heartfelt emotions, lovable and witty characters, some humor, and some mystery! Because we want it all! Historical Romance at its best!

Visit our website to learn all about us, our authors and books!

Sign up to our mailing list to receive first hand information on new releases, freebies and promotions as well as exclusive giveaways and sneak-peeks!

WWW.WOLF-PUBLISHING.COM

Also by Bree Wolf

The Whickertons in Love

The WHICKERTONS IN LOVE is a new series by USA Today bestselling author BREE WOLF set in Regency-era England, portraying the at times turbulent ways the six Whickerton siblings search for love. If you enjoy wicked viscounts, brooding lords as well as head-strong ladies, fierce in their affections and daring in their search for their perfect match, then this new series is perfect for you!

#1 Once Upon a Devilishly Enchanting Kiss

#2 Once Upon a Temptingly Ruinous Kiss

#3 Once Upon an Irritatingly Magical Kiss

#4 Once Upon a Devastatingly Sweet Kiss

More to follow!

Prequel to the series: Once Upon A Kiss Gone Horribly Wrong

ONCE
UPON
an Irritatingly Magical
KISS

Prologue

Whickerton Grove 1794 (or a variation thereof)

Nine Years Earlier

Mistakenly, the door to the drawing room had been left ajar, allowing voices to carry out into the corridor...

...to the ears of Lady Christina Beaumont, daughter to the Earl of Whickerton, presently thirteen years of age. She stood hidden behind said door, her ear almost pressed to its smooth wood, as she tried to peek through the minuscule gap that allowed her this unique glimpse of adult life.

"Please, Beatrice, you need to help me!" Aunt Francine pleaded with Christina's mother, her voice choked with tears. "I cannot stay! You of all people must surely understand!"

"Must I?" Christina's mother replied, her voice tinged with disbelief. Christina heard the soft sound of footsteps as her mother began to pace around the room. "Why do you believe so? Why would I—?"

"Because you did the same!" Aunt Francine exclaimed, pride and awe ringing in her voice as she surged forward, hasty steps carrying her toward her older sister.

Christina held her breath, waiting for her mother to reply. She did not know what had happened, what had brought Aunt Francine to Whickerton Grove in the middle of the night, nor did she know why her aunt was so agitated. Had there been some kind of accident?

"What are you doing out of bed?" came a sleepy voice from behind her, and Christina spun around.

When her eyes fell on her little sister Harriet, only two years her junior, she exhaled a breath of relief. "Shhh!" she urged, pressing her finger to her lips and beckoning Harry forward.

With her green eyes squinted, Harry tiptoed to her side, her fiery-red hair unruly as always. "What is going on?"

"Shhh!" Christina urged again. "Listen." Side by side, the two youngest sisters of the Whickerton clan stood outside the door to the drawing room, quieter than they had ever been in their lives, straining to hear the drama that was unfolding only a few paces from where they stood.

"Let's try to remain calm," their father suddenly spoke out, and Christina flinched, her hand clamping about her sister's mouth to keep her from making a sound. Christina had not known their father was in the drawing room as well. Until this moment, she had only believed it to be her mother and aunt.

Christina felt her heart skip a beat. This was serious! If her father was there, it had to be, did it not?

"What do you mean I did the same?" came their mother's voice, filled with incredulity. "I never—"

"You chose your own path," Aunt Francine interrupted. "You married Charles against our parents' wishes. You did not care what they said, how they objected. You chose your own path." A deep sigh left their aunt's lips. "As I wish to do."

"But you're married!" Christina's and Harriet's mother exclaimed. "Surely, your husband would not want you to—"

"Of course not!" Aunt Francine exclaimed, and Christina could not help but think that her voice resonated with deep-seated anger. "He demanded I abandon all *foolish thoughts* of being an artist and only concern myself with providing him with an heir." A choked sob fell from her lips. "He threatened to lock me away." Again, footsteps echoed to the girls' ears, and Christina could all but imagine her aunt grasping their mother's hands, her eyes full of tears and pleading. "I cannot live this life. Please, will you not help me?"

For a long moment, silence lingered. Christina looked down at Harriet's face and saw the same kind of confusion she, too, felt. Always had Aunt Francine been a cheerful and carefree, lighthearted person, her smile radiant and her laughter infectious. Now, however, she seemed completely changed, despair in her voice and fear ringing in every word she spoke.

Christina clutched Harriet's hand, and together, they inched closer to the door. As much as this conversation unsettled Christina, she could not imagine turning away from it.

"Let's try to remain calm," Christina heard her father's voice say, the way he spoke not betraying the deep kind of emotions she had heard in her mother's and aunt's voices. "Of course, we will help you, Francine. But what is it that you have in mind? As you surely know, your options are severely limited." Caution rang in her father's voice, and Christina felt an icy chill inch down her spine.

"I want to leave."

"Leave?" their mother demanded, incredulity in her voice. "What do you mean *leave*? Go where?"

Aunt Francine inhaled a deep breath, and Christina could picture her straightening and lifting her chin. "To France."

Shocked silence stretched from one heartbeat to another as Christina held her breath, waiting for either one of her parents to reply. Surely, Aunt Francine could not be serious. She could not leave behind the life she had here and go to France. She was married. She had been married only a few months ago. Was she not happy? Was that not why all young ladies were encouraged to seek husbands? Did marriage not mean happiness?

"France?" Christina's father asked in that calm voice of his while her mother remained quiet, perhaps too shocked to reply at all. "Why France?"

"I'm an artist," Aunt Francine replied, her voice gaining strength as she spoke. "My whole life, I have been complimented upon my artistic excellence, but it is only now that I realize that none of the words spoken to me ever truly meant anything. Yes, painting is considered an accomplishment for a young lady, but she's never truly expected to become an artist. At some point, I crossed that invisible line, that line that exists between acceptance and outrage. Of course, I'm not meant to be an artist. A woman is only ever meant to be a wife and mother. But what if that is not enough?"

Christina's mother drew in a deep breath, a heavy sigh falling from her lips. "Have you spoken to your husband? Perhaps there is a way for you to—"

"I've tried more than once," Aunt Francine replied, resignation weighing heavily upon her voice. "He is a kind man, but he wants a wife, not an artist. He is ashamed of my aspirations. He does not understand."

"Are you certain you want this? Do you understand what you would be giving up?" Christina's mother counseled, her voice softer now, kind and soothing.

Christina held her breath, her blue eyes dropping down to meet Harriet's green ones. Was this truly happening? Was Aunt Francine leaving them? Leaving England? Would she ever return?

The tall grandfather clock in the drawing room struck three in the morning, and Christina flinched, almost losing her balance and falling against the door left ajar. Harriet's hands, however, shot forward and clamped over her arms, pulling her back.

With their arms wrapped around one another, the two girls remained where they were, listening.

"I know what I would be giving up," Aunt Francine finally replied, "if I were to stay. This is who I am. This is who I want to be, who I need to be. I suppose I was a fool to never see this coming, to not understand that women are never meant to do anything noteworthy beyond marriage and childbearing. Yes, I should've seen this coming." She exhaled a slow, long breath, agonizing in the way it spoke of all the disappointments she had suffered so recently. "You took a chance," she said to Christina's and Harriet's mother, "and you found happiness. It was a risk, but it was worth it, was it not?"

In her mind's eye, Christina could see her parents look at one another, her mother's eyes misted with tears, a devoted smile upon her father's lips, as they nodded, silent words passing between them, words no one else ever understood but them. "Yes," her mother finally replied. "It was worth it. I have no regrets, and I do not want you to have any, either."

First, a relieved sigh and then the rustling of skirts drifted to Christina's ears. "Oh, thank you! Thank you so much, Beatrice!" No doubt embracing their mother, Aunt Francine began to sob with joy. "I promise I shall write. I promise this shall not be the last time we see each other."

"I will hold you to that," their mother replied, tears now choking her own voice. "I shall miss you so much."

Christina felt tears sting her own eyes as the truth began to sink in. Aunt Francine would be leaving, and they could not be certain when she would return. Christina wished she understood what exactly had happened, what had made her aunt daring and desperate enough to make such a choice. Yes, her aunt loved to paint. She had always been a formidable artist. Yet it seemed not to be enough. It seemed her husband suddenly disapproved of her artistic ambitions. Why? Christina wondered. Was this merely the way of the world? Something children could not understand. Something that simply happened sometime down the line.

Closing her eyes, Christina thought of the countless notebooks up in her chamber. Notebooks her mother had given her, urging her to write and express herself. Notebooks all the Whickerton siblings had received. Not all of them filled them with the same content. Leonora wrote about observations of the world around her. Louisa enjoyed copying poems that touched her heart. Harriet had not yet decided quite what appealed to her while their brother Troy had never bothered with them in the first place. Christina, however, had begun writing down stories, fairytales about magical creatures and faraway lands, about dauntless knights and fierce princesses. Always had her musings brought Christina joy, and perhaps not unlike her aunt, she had somehow expected it to always be so. Would the day eventually come when she would have to choose? Between her passion and her family? Did husbands not appreciated it if their wives possessed creativity, ambition and talent?

Harriet tugged on Christina's arm. "We should go to bed," she whispered before a wide yawn stretched across her face, "before we're found." Something thoughtful lingered in Harriet's eyes as well as though she, too, had found herself confronted with a part of the world she had never known existed until today.

Nodding, Christina followed her little sister back up the stairs. Yet the moment they had overheard kept her awake for the remainder of the night. She remembered the sound of desperation in her aunt's voice. She remembered her sadness and her regret. Most of all, though, she remembered that her aunt had been forced to make a choice.

Choices had always rung with possibility for Christina. Choices had always been highly valued in their family. Now, however, they spoke of loss. After all, at their core, choices spoke for one thing and against another.

Christina could not imagine leaving her family. She could not imagine ever being away from them, perhaps even separated by the sea. She could not imagine ever making such a choice.

Perhaps, the time had come for fairytales to be laid to rest. After all, she was already thirteen years of age and fairytales were only for children, were they not?

Chapter One

NEW TO LONDON

London 1803 (or a variation thereof)

Nine Years Later

Mr. Thorne Sharpe stood on the edge of the ballroom, hands linked behind his back, eyes sweeping over the assembled guests. Although his heart beat in a steady rhythm, he could not deny the slow crawl of anxiety along the back of his neck.

He was well aware of the looks cast in his direction. How could he not be? After all, London's high society did not exactly try to hide their disdain for him and his profession. In fact, they stared at him quite openly, whispering behind fans and glasses filled with imported liquor.

Yes, here he was standing among them, the *ton*, the crème de la crème of society. Of course, Thorne was not ignorant of why he had been invited. For one, he was a peculiarity, something fascinating to gaze upon and gossip about. For another, by now, all of London was aware of his lucrative business dealings, aware that he had amassed a fortune most could only ever dream of, aware that he was looking for a wife.

"Mr. Sharpe, how good to see you this evening," Lord Hartmore greeted him with a friendly nod, the look in the man's eyes, however, spoke of the same sense of superiority Thorne could see in the eyes of all those around him. "I hope you're settling in well."

Thorne nodded, doing his best to act accordingly, to display the sort of manners expected by people of Lord Hartmore's station. "Quite well. Thank you." He allowed his gaze to sweep around the room, taking in the lively playing orchestra as well as the many dancers crowded upon the dance floor. "It is a most entertaining evening."

Trivial chitchat followed, giving Thorne the opportunity to assess Lord Hartmore more thoroughly. The deep wrinkles upon the man's face made him look more aged than the gray in his hair. They spoke of strain and concern, burdens that weighed upon his shoulders day and night as Thorne now knew was true. As far as he was aware, Lord Hartmore enjoyed more than the occasional gamble, which had lost him most of his fortune. Recently, he had even been forced to sell the townhouse his family had held in London for generations. Indeed, the situation was growing more dire by the minute...and from the looks of it, Lord Hartmore knew that Thorne was aware of it.

Indeed, it was a barely concealed look of disdain that lingered in the older man's eyes. He knew he needed Thorne's fortune, yet he could not help but hold it against him. Lord Hartmore like so many others considered themselves superior, expecting the world to be laid at their feet, and were outraged when they discovered it not to be so.

"Shall I introduce you to my daughter?" Lord Hartmore asked, a polite smile upon his tense face. "She is most eager to make your acquaintance."

Thorne inclined his head courteously. "I would like nothing more, my lord."

Yes, finding a wife among English high society was part of Thorne's plan. It was necessary in order to be accepted into their circle. Never would he be considered an equal; however, with a society wife at his side, his chances of finding favor would increase. Thorne knew that he needed society's support in order to make a difference. He needed those who shaped the land with laws and regulations to listen to him, to hear his words and heed them.

Thorne knew that he and Lord Hartmore had much in common in this regard. They both had aspirations and needed the other in order to obtain them. Hartmore needed Thorne's fortune, and Thorne needed Hartmore's influence and standing. If only the man's poor daughter, innocent in all of this, need not be involved.

In truth, Thorne did not cherish the thought of marrying a stranger. He knew how the *ton* conducted their marital affairs, and he could not say he approved of it.

He himself had grown up with nothing, with neither fortune nor family. His parents had died when he had still been young, but old enough to survive on the streets. He could not recall how many siblings he had lost. He could neither recall their names nor their faces. That life seemed so distant now as though it had not been his own past but someone else's instead. Still, the emptiness of his childhood still lingered, and deep down, Thorne had always wanted what he had never had.

Not truly, at least.

A family.

Following Lord Hartmore's gaze, Thorne paused when his eyes fell upon a golden-haired beauty. She stood with a friend, her sparkling blue eyes animated as they spoke and laughed. Her cheeks shone rosy, complementing the light blue of her gown. Although she looked like a dozen other debutantes around the room, there was something fierce in her gaze, something wild and untamed that spoke to Thorne.

Was she Lord Hartmore's daughter? Would he find himself married to her in a matter of months? Weeks perhaps?

At the thought, Thorne's apprehension turned to something else, something warm and delicious. Anticipation coursed through his veins, and he barely managed to still his feet before they could carry him across the room and to her side. Never before had he experienced such an overwhelming reaction to a woman. Perhaps not all hope was lost after all. Perhaps for once, the world would work in his favor.

His heart sank a moment later when it was not the golden-haired beauty who reluctantly moved toward them, but her friend instead.

Heeding her father's beckoning gesture, Miss Mortensen whispered a few words to her friend and then hesitantly moved across the ballroom toward them. When her gaze fell upon him, she seemed to draw in a shuddering breath as though she had to force herself to continue onward. Soft blond curls danced upon her shoulders, her skin pale and growing paler in the warm glow of the chandeliers above. For all intents and purposes, the young woman looked frightened.

Thorne frowned. Of course, he had expected Miss Mortensen to be somewhat displeased with her father's choice for a husband. However, he had not expected her to look at him like a frightened deer. What was it about him that inspired such fear?

"Mr. Sharpe," Lord Hartmore addressed him when Miss Mortensen had reached their side, offering a polite, but somewhat strained smile in greeting, "may I present my daughter, Miss Sarah Mortensen? Sarah, my dear, this is Mr. Sharpe."

Offering the frightened girl a formal bow, Thorne smiled at her. "It is a pleasure to make your acquaintance, Sarah."

The moment her name left his lips, Thorne realized his mistake. He saw her eyes widen before they fell from his as though his blunder, the intimate use of her name, had somehow proven to her that he was to be feared.

Miss Mortensen exhaled a shuddering breath, her eyes still glued to the floor as she clamped her hands together to keep them from trembling. "How...How do you find London, Mr. Sharpe?" Her voice was no more than a whisper, and she glanced up at her father in desperate need of reassurance.

Lord Hartmore's jaw seemed tense, but he nodded to his daughter. His shoulders straightened as he regarded Thorne in a way that made Thorne think that he held no more importance in their world than a tool that refused to function. It was in its essence what was wrong with the world...at least in Thorne's opinion.

"It is most diverting," Thorne replied to her question, trying his best to put her at ease. Perhaps somewhere beneath this shaking exterior existed a kind and warmhearted, young woman. "A beautiful and important city to be sure, historically as well as economically."

At his reference to his trade, Miss Mortensen tensed, casting another pleading look at her father.

Lord Hartmore nodded to her, urging her to continue the conversation.

"Where do you hail from, Mr. Sharpe?" Miss Mortensen inquired, forcing another strained smile onto her face.

"Manchester," Thorne replied, pride ringing in his voice. He knew that the *ton* despised him for his origin and upbringing; yet he himself felt nothing but pride for all he had accomplished. It only fueled his desire to continue on and change the world not only for himself but also for others. People Lord Hartmore and his peers would barely even glance at if they were to cross paths. "It is a most inspiring city, changing rapidly, new businesses stamped out of the ground every day. It holds the promise of the future, lives changed and living conditions improved by machines to aid us in our daily struggles." Thorne inhaled a deep breath, urging himself to slow down. Always when he spoke of his plans, of his vision for the future, did he find himself carried away as though he was not the one holding the reins.

Again, Miss Mortensen smiled at him, and again, it looked strained. "Do you plan to...to return to Manchester?"

"Of course," Thorne replied without a thought. "Most of my business is there. I've already opened one cotton mill, and I plan to open another sometime in the next year."

Another shuddering breath left Miss Mortensen's lips, and her cheeks seemed to pale even more.

Thorne frowned as Lord Hartmore stepped forward, that indulgent smile back on the man's face. "Let's leave the details to be sorted out later," he said with a marked look at his daughter. "This evening is to be entertaining. *Business* has no place at a societal ball." Lord Hartmore spoke the word as though it was something dark, disgusting and repugnant.

Thorne wanted to strangle the man more than anything, but he held himself in check. He was not one to be led astray by his emotions. He knew what needed to be done, and he would see it through. "Of course." He offered Miss Mortensen his most charming smile; unfortunately, the young lady seemed utterly immune. "May I ask you for the next dance?"

For a moment, Thorne feared Miss Mortensen might faint on the spot. Then, however, she straightened her shoulders and met his gaze. "Certainly." Although she held herself rigid, Thorne could feel her muscles trembling as she accepted his arm. He led her onto the dance floor, asking simple questions, trying his best to set her at ease. Unfortunately, Miss Mortensen's mind seemed made up. She replied politely, but more often than not, offered him only monosyllabic answers.

Before long, Thorne's attention shifted from the woman sharing this dance with him to those standing on the fringes, watching them, their faces contorted in disapproval and distaste. Anger stirred within Thorne until his gaze fell upon the golden-haired beauty he had seen earlier.

Indeed, her face, too, was scrunched up in a way that clearly signaled disapproval. Yet her blue eyes shone with a fierceness that spoke of anger. Something protective rested in her gaze, and Thorne realized that she was upset with him for dancing with her friend. Did she know that Lord Hartmore intended to marry his daughter to him? Was that why she was glaring at him, her eyes all but shooting daggers in his direction?

Thorne could not deny that he enjoyed looking at her. She was indeed beautiful, but it was the wild look in her gaze, that unimpressed way she regarded him, that made him want to know her, know who she was. Yes, she was a woman worth knowing. Thorne was certain of it for she would not cower or drop her gaze. No, she faced him with open eyes and a lifted chin. Thorne realized he would have liked such a wife. Indeed, if he had the choice, if there was any chance of her accepting him, he would have proposed to her, his golden-haired fury, this very moment.

But it was not to be. He needed to remember why he was here. He needed to do what was right. He needed to protect his people, all those who had no one who spoke for them.

No one but him.

And he would not fail.

Chapter Two
STRONG OBJECTIONS

"What happened?" Christina asked as she thrust Sarah's hat and gloves into a footman's face. "You look pale. Is something wrong?" Her hands reached for Sarah's, her heart beating faster as she took note of the strain lingering upon her friend's face.

Sarah heaved a deep sigh, and her eyes closed briefly as though she needed a moment to comport herself. "I don't even know where to begin." The words tumbled from her lips on a rushed breath, and for a moment, Christina worried that her friend might collapse in her arms.

Sarah had never been bold and daring, every step she took measured by her parents' demands and expectations. Yet Christina had never seen her so...frail and resigned as she had seemed lately. Something was most definitely wrong.

Grasping Sarah's hands, Christina pulled her friend into the drawing room and closed the door. Her eyes darted to her grandmother, seated in a cushioned armchair near the fireplace. Her eyes were closed in slumber, and her chin rested upon her chest, a mild snore filling the room.

"Tell me what happened," Christina urged her friend, pushing her down onto the settee and then sitting down next to her, their hands still entwined.

Sarah heaved another deep sigh. "It seems I am to be married," she told Christina with an almost anguished look in her eyes before her gaze fell and she bowed her head in defeat.

Christina felt anger bubbling up in her veins. "Who? Who did your mother choose this time?"

Not long ago, Sarah and her family had lived in the townhouse next door. For many years, the families had been close, Sarah coming and going as one of them, through a gap in the hedge between the two properties, an easy gateway. Blissful years had been spent like that, but had come to an end when Sarah's father, Lord Hartmore, had been forced to reveal his severe gambling debts. The family had had no choice but to sell their townhouse and move to a more affordable neighborhood.

Ever since, Sarah's mother had been most devoted to finding her daughter a wealthy husband in order to pay back her husband's debts. Even Sarah's dowry had been used for this purpose, leaving her with nothing, no prospects on the marriage mart. All she now had to recommend her were her father's position as well as her beautiful face and kind character. Unfortunately, it seemed those were not enough to tempt an honorable gentleman.

As far as Christina knew, Sarah had not yet received any offers of marriage. In turn, it had made her mother desperate, going to great and somewhat questionable lengths in order to see her daughter married.

Earlier this year, Lady Hartmore had arranged for her daughter to be compromised by Lord Barrington in order to force them into marriage. However, by that time, Lord Barrington had already been in love with Christina's elder sister Louisa, a fact which had rendered Lady Hartmore's attempt unsuccessful.

Sarah's hands tightened upon Christina's. "His name is Mr. Thorne Sharpe," her friend replied on a trembling breath. "He is from the North. As far as I know, he owns a cotton mill in Manchester and intends to open more. He says, it is a thriving town that—"

Christina stared at her friend. "A cotton mill? He is in trade?" It was unthinkable! "Was he the man your father introduced you to the other night?" Christina remembered him well. He had struck her as...

misplaced, for lack of a better word. With one glance, she had seen that he did not belong, that he was not one of them.

Not a gentleman.

Sarah nodded, tears glistening in her eyes. "He intends to return to Manchester."

Her friend's words cut deep. "Manchester?" In Christina's mind, it was a place of factories, smoke-filled skies and dirt roads. "But he cannot!" The thought of losing Sarah was unbearable. They had known each other since before she could remember. Always had Sarah been there.

Always.

Straightening her shoulders, Sarah lifted her chin. "I admit he seemed fairly...decent and—"

"It does not matter!" Christina exclaimed, feeling her heart beat painfully in her chest. "You cannot leave. Your parents cannot make you marry him. Who knows what kind of man he is! He could be—" Words failed her, and for the first time in a long time, Christina realized that her knowledge of the world was severely limited. It had never bothered her before, but it did now.

Sarah's eyes hardened. "I do not have much of a choice," she told Christina gently as though her friend were the one in need of comfort. "Debtors keep knocking on our door, and—"

"That is not your fault! Your father should—"

Sarah's hands tightened upon Christina's, cutting off her words. "My family needs this. I need this." Her chest rose and fell with a deep breath. "You know that I have no other choice. No gentleman wants to marry me, considering our reduced circumstances. It is the way of the world, is it not? Perhaps I ought to consider myself fortunate that Mr. Sharpe has come to town and is willing to marry me despite my father's debts, despite the fact that he cannot give me a dowry."

"Do not think like that, Sarah. You have so much to offer. You're kind and devoted. You're beautiful. You are—"

Sarah smiled at her sweetly. "You know as well as I do that that does not matter. Marriages are arranged for mutual benefit. It has always been thus." Her smile deepened and took on a wistful note. "Not everyone can be as your parents are. Not everyone can marry for love." Again, her shoulders rose and fell with a deep breath. "I shall be fine. Mr. Sharpe appears to be a kind man, no matter his birth or standing. There is no reason why I should not be happy with him." Still, Sarah's voice faltered on the last words, and Christina knew that her friend harbored doubts she was not willing to admit to.

"You cannot know that," Christina replied, torn between cautioning her friend with regard to preventing such a marriage and giving her comfort and strength in order to see it through. Yes, Christina knew that not everyone was like her parents. Indeed, she and her sisters were fortunate that their parents insisted they marry for love. It was a Whickerton tradition despite the fact that they were only the second generation to uphold it.

"You're right," Sarah admitted. "But what I do know is that my family needs this. We shall be ruined if I don't make an advantageous match, and whatever Mr. Sharpe may be, his fortunes will save us. It is as simple as that." Tears burned in her eyes, and Christina could see that Sarah was holding on by a thread. Before Christina could say another word, Sarah pushed to her feet, dabbing a handkerchief to her eyes. "I better leave. My mother is expecting me home. She says there is much to be done before..." A tight smile came to her face as she stepped toward the door. "Thank you for listening. You are the dearest friend I've ever had." And with that, Sarah turned on her heel and left.

"What will you do?" came Grandma Edie's voice from behind her.

Christina sighed, turning to look upon her grandmother. "I knew you weren't sleeping. Why did you pretend to?"

Grinning in that mischievous way of hers, completely unbefitting her age, Grandma Edie said, "Would you not say it proved to be a good idea? Would you and Sarah have spoken as freely as you did had you known I was listening?"

Christina chuckled, then sat down in the armchair opposite her grandmother. "Any pearls of wisdom?"

Grandma Edie leaned forward and gently patted Christina's hand. "I cannot tell you what to do or what not to do, my dear. However, generally I find that listening to one's instincts is never wrong."

Looking at her grandmother, Christina nodded. "I feel I should stop this from happening." She held her grandmother's gaze, waiting for her to say something. When she did not, Christina continued, "As angry as I am with Sarah's mother, I understand why Lady Hartmore is pushing for this marriage. Yes, they are in debt, severely, and without this marriage..." She shook her head. "Still, there must be some other way. She cannot marry this man."

Grandma Edie's brows drew down into a frown as she regarded Christina carefully. "Why do you object to the man? Judging from the way you speak, I suppose you have other reasons aside from his upbringing in the far north as well as his occupation?"

Christina nodded, remembering the evening a few days ago. "I've seen him here and there at a ball," she replied, drawing upon her memories, trying to see his face the way he had looked across the ballroom at her and Sarah. "I've never taken much notice of him as I've merely seen him pass by. However, a few days ago, I was there when Lord Hartmore introduced Sarah to him. I watched and I..." Somehow, Christina knew that Sarah ought not marry Mr. Sharpe; however, it seemed she did not possess the words to explain why exactly she felt so strongly about it.

"What impression did you get of him?" Grandma Edie asked as she tapped her fingers upon the armrest of her chair. "Did you speak to him yourself?"

Sighing, Christina shook her head. "I did not. However, I..." She could not quite say what it was, but something lurked in her memory, far back, whispers she had heard, but had not been meant to. "Men of trade," she began, looking at her grandmother, "are they different from gentlemen?"

Her grandmother's eyes narrowed in a way that whispered of intrigue. "Different? Well, I suppose it's safe to say that each man is different from any other. The same holds true for women, would you not agree?"

Christina nodded, feeling her grandmother's eyes upon her, aware of the way she was watching, waiting for Christina to explain herself more fully. "I've heard it whispered," Christina began, uncertain what precisely it was she wanted to say, "by gossips, of course, that common men make different husbands. I've heard matrons speak quietly about it to one another, about the way they treat their wives, that they are not considerate and aware of a lady's sensibilities."

Grandma Edie chuckled. "My dear sweet child, Mr. Sharpe may not possess the same manners as the gently bred men of your acquaintance; however, that does not mean he's not capable of kindness and respect." She cocked her head to the side, a quizzical expression coming to her eyes. "Is that what you believe? That somehow some people are simply better than others? Born better?"

Frowning, Christina shook her head. "Of course not, Grandmother. However, the way we grow up shapes who we are, does it not? If Mr. Sharpe grew up among thugs and thieves, what does that make him? Is he truly capable of treating Sarah with the kind of respect she deserves? What would a marriage to him be like for her?" Christina shook her head, unwilling to picture such a possibility. "She's too... gentle and kind and...a man like that would crush her spirit. I am certain of it."

"And you?" her grandmother inquired, a daring gleam coming to her eyes. "Would you consider yourself up for the task? Would you expect to see your own spirits crushed as well?"

Christina snorted, knowing it was not ladylike, but also knowing that her grandmother would not mind. "Of course not!" Although she could not be certain for she did not know what it would mean to be married to such a man.

Throughout her life, every once in a while, Christina had observed moments between a husband and his wife—at a ball or a picnic—that had made her wonder. She had seen a man grasp his wife's arm and tug her toward him, angry words falling from his lips. The wife's eyes had been open wide, her skin pale, and she had stood before him, bowing her head, accepting defeat. Christina knew that some husbands dominated their wives, that some even raised their hands to them. She had never seen it, but she had heard the whispers, and she could not help but wonder if Mr. Sharpe was such a man.

"I know that look," Grandma Edie remarked with a grin. "Tell me."

Smiling sweetly at her grandmother, Christina rose to her feet. "I have not the slightest inkling what you are speaking about."

Her grandmother laughed. "I may be old, but I've known you since the day you were born. You cannot fool me, nor do you seem to wish to." Her eyes twinkled. "Good luck."

Christina smiled at her and then slipped out the door, knowing that she could not simply stand back and see her friend sacrificed to her parents' ambitions. No, she needed to do something. She needed to—

Somewhere in the back of her mind, Christina remembered the pleading sound in her aunt's voice as she had begged her older sister for her assistance. Aunt Francine had found herself trapped in a marriage she had been unable to bear a moment longer. However, Aunt Francine had always possessed a daring spirit, not unlike Christina's.

Christina smiled, remembering her aunt. Years had passed since she had last seen her, and now that England and France were at war yet again, many more would pass before they would ever lay eyes on one another again. Still, what mattered was that Aunt Francine had found happiness after all. Not in the way demanded or expected of her. But in her very own way.

Always had Christina known herself to be different from her aunt, that she would not choose her passion over her family as Aunt Francine had. No, all those years ago, Christina had decided that her stories were to remain a secret, a secret she would only ever share with those closest to her—her sisters. However, beyond that small circle, no one would ever know that a writer's heart beat in Christina's chest, that she sometimes spent the evenings writing page after page, her imagination running wild.

And yet, over the years, Christina had often found herself wondering what would have happened to Aunt Francine if she had not taken the risk she had that night. Indeed, her aunt had been daring and she had found happiness because of it. And now, here, in this moment, Christina knew that she needed to be daring as well. This was not about her, but it was about someone dear to her. Sarah was like another sister, and Christina would not see her married to a man who did not appreciate the treasure she was.

"No matter what," Christina mumbled under her breath, "I will find a way to prevent this marriage from happening. No matter what."

For Sarah's sake.

Chapter Three
ARRANGEMENTS

Thorne was tired of discussing the terms of his marrying Miss Mortensen with Lord Hartmore. The man seemed utterly heartless and greedy at the same time. All the stipulations were only with regards to Thorne's fortune and the gains he desired in exchange for his daughter's hand in marriage. Not one word concerning her welfare and happiness passed his lips, and Thorne began to feel like a villain because he was beginning to see that his agreement to Lord Hartmore's terms would force Miss Mortensen's hand.

She did not wish to wed him. That much was crystal clear. No matter what he said to her or how kindly he spoke to her, she always seemed ill at ease, barely meeting his eyes and fleeing his presence the first opportunity she got.

Lord Hartmore did not seem concerned. In fact, he did not even seem to notice. Even when Thorne addressed the issue plainly, Lord Hartmore merely waved it away. "There is no reason to worry. Young women are always a bit apprehensive when it comes to marriage. It shall pass," the older man replied, not even casting a glance at his daughter, who once more stood across the room with her golden-haired friend.

The fury!

Thorne smiled. While Miss Mortensen was eyeing him with no small measure of apprehension and anxiety, the fury beside her seemed to burn with anger. Thorne could see her all but bouncing in her slippers, a muscle contracting as though she wished to charge across the room and slap him hard across the face. What he had done to deserve such hatred, Thorne did not know; however, he had to admit he found it most intriguing.

He could not help but wish to speak to her for he fully expected the exchange to be life-altering. He did not know why, but he was certain of it. Perhaps it was those expressive eyes of hers, revealing how she felt quite openly while at the same time concealing something he could not quite grasp.

Indeed, the most intriguing woman!

Glaring at the man across the dance floor, Christina felt her hackles rise when he flashed her a teasing smile. The nerve of that man! Was he completely unaware that his mere presence caused her friend deepest unease? In fact, Sarah looked ready to faint, her face pale with a tinge of green as though she were moments away from casting up the contents of her stomach. It all the more proved to Christina that Sarah would not survive such a marriage. Something had to be done.

But what?

"What did he say to you earlier?" she asked her friend, placing a gentle hand upon Sarah's arm.

Sarah blinked, her breath coming quickly. "Pardon me?"

Christina smiled at her reassuringly. "When you spoke to him before, what did he say?" Indeed, she had watched Lord Hartmore and his daughter approach Mr. Sharpe with great care, tension lingering in her shoulders as she had been well aware of her friend's reluctance.

Shaking her head, Sarah blinked, refocusing her thoughts. "I...He... I believe he asked about my favorite pastime." She frowned, then shook her head again. "To be honest, I don't quite remember exactly what he said. Whenever I see him, all I can think about is leaving London, leaving my family, leaving you." Her hand reached for Christina's and held hers tightly within her own as tears began to mist her eyes. "I never thought I would one day find myself marrying a man outside of the social circle I've always known. Manchester will be a completely new world, no doubt terrifying and overwhelming." She swallowed hard. "I'm not certain I can do this."

"Then don't," Christina urged. "There must be another way. Perhaps..." She gritted her teeth, trying to think of something, anything.

A defeated look came to Sarah's eyes. "There is not. The only solution is for me to marry a man of wealth and no one else has offered."

Christina's head snapped up, hope tingling through her limbs. "But if we could find someone, not anyone, but a gentleman who would—"

Sarah shook her head. "My father's situation is well known, and this is my third season." A sad smile came to her face. "I have not received a single proposal in all this time."

"Neither have I," Christina pointed out, determined not to allow Sarah to give up so easily. There had to be a way! There simply had to be!

Sarah chuckled. "It is not the same. Everyone knows that the Whickertons marry for love and nothing less. No man simply seeking a connection would propose, knowing it would be a waste of time if he did not also possess the heart of the one he was offering for." She shook her head. "No, Chris, it is not the same."

Christina huffed out an annoyed breath, unable to argue with her friend. Yes, the Whickertons married for love. Everyone knew that. It was like a law of nature. Something written in stone.

"Then perhaps..." Christina thought out loud, uncertain what she wanted to say, but knowing that there had to be a solution. There simply had to be!

Gritting her teeth, she turned to look across the room at Mr. Sharpe. Yes, he was not unpleasant to look at. Those teasing eyes of his might even seem appealing to some women. And that smile...

Christina whirled around and grasped her friend's hands. "I know what to do!"

Sarah tensed, her eyes widening ever so slightly, hope as well as the fear to give into it mingling there.

"It's simple," Christina explained, eagerness bubbling in her veins. Never had she been able to bear being idle. It gave her a feeling of helplessness, powerlessness. "We'll see him married to another. That's the solution. If he marries another, he cannot marry you."

The spark of hope vanished from Sarah's gaze. "You know as well as I do, that only someone desperate would accept him. Someone like me." She looked around the ballroom, then shrugged her shoulders. "Everyone is hoping for a great match, and he is simply not that. The only reason for anyone to accept him aside from his fortune would be to save face."

Christina's eyes widened as a new thought formed in her head. "We could see him compromised with another."

Sarah cast her an indulgent look. "Would you truly do this to another? A young woman like us? Would you trap her into a marriage to a man you're so determined to keep from my side?"

Christina could have groaned as her newly formed plan slipped from her fingers, and she closed her eyes. "No, of course not." Again, that feeling of helplessness washed over, and Christina felt like retreating from the harshness of the world and curling up into a ball, ignoring all that was and might be. Yet if she did so, she would find herself forever running. No, she was not that kind of person. No matter what, she would face what was coming head-on.

Casting a smile at Sarah, Christina reached out to squeeze her hand. "If you'll excuse me for a moment. There is someone I need to speak to." And with that, she spun on her heels and began to march across the ballroom.

Toward Mr. Sharpe.

"Chris, please don't do this!" Sarah hissed under her breath, a frantic tone in her voice as she tried to dissuade her friend. "My parents will be furious."

Christina could not have cared less. She could not simply stand by. She had to do something.

Anything.

Perhaps Mr. Sharpe would turn out to be a reasonable man after all.

Miracles did happen upon occasion, did they not?

Chapter Four

A LADY & A SCOUNDREL

The golden-haired fury was heading toward him!

Surprised, Thorne noticed his heart skipping a beat, an altogether unexpected reaction. Few things surprised him these days or affected him in a way that would be considered noteworthy. Nevertheless, something about her was different.

While speaking to Lord Hartmore, Thorne had continued to glance in her direction out of the corner of his eye, unable to ignore that almost magnetic pull he felt deep down. There was something about her. Something he had never encountered before. Even from across the room, he knew that something alluring rested in her gaze. He could all but sense her fierce glare, no doubt put there by a sense of loyalty to her friend. If she despised him—and it seemed quite reasonable that she did—then it something had to do with Miss Mortensen.

A part of him realized, that now, there was another reason why he no longer thought it a good idea to marry Miss Mortensen. Still...

"Good evening, Lord Hartmore," the golden-haired fury greeted Miss Mortensen's father with a kind smile. "It is a most enjoyable evening, is it not?" Although she kept her gaze fixed upon Lord Hartmore, Thorne thought he saw impatience in the way she stood before them as though she wished to do away with this polite chitchat and address Thorne in a more open and honest way.

Thorne almost chuckled, realizing that without anyone to overhear, this woman was not one to hold her tongue! He had to admit he rather liked that about her.

"Indeed, it is," Lord Hartmore replied, a hint of annoyance coming to his face at being interrupted in his business negotiations.

Thorne could not help but want to slap him!

A sweet smile came to the golden-haired fury's face, one that told him she was being the opposite of genuine. "I'm afraid I require your assistance, my lord. You see, Sarah doesn't seem quite well. A turn about the terrace would do her a world of good. Would you be so kind?"

Thorne listened curiously, wondering if Lord Hartmore would ask why she could not simply take Miss Mortensen for a stroll through the gardens herself. However, the old man did not, although he did look a bit perplexed. Perhaps, once again, it was some kind of societal etiquette Thorne knew little about.

"Certainly. Thank you for alerting me," Lord Hartmore said although he looked far from pleased. "Lady Christina. Mr. Sharpe." And with a nod of the head, he strode across the room toward his daughter.

"Lady Christina, is it?" Thorne addressed her the moment Lord Hartmore was no longer within earshot. Why he felt comfortable speaking to her as though they were confidants, he did not know. However, it felt perfectly natural.

Lady Christina turned to face him, her gaze narrowed and the smile upon her face all but absent. "Mr. Sharpe, I presume."

Thorne laughed. "You presume right. However, I do believe you've known my name for far longer than you care to admit. The more interesting question is, why?"

Her gaze narrowed even further as she regarded him, the right corner of her mouth curling upward in a sign of displeasure. "You are most direct, *Sir*." From her lips, it sounded like an insult, and it bothered Thorne more than he liked to admit.

"As are you," he countered, enjoying the dark blue sparks that came to her eyes, proof that at least on some level he affected her as well. "Is it not true that you came here to speak to me?"

Lady Christina chuckled. "How presumptuous of you!" Her brows rose in a daring gesture. "I came here to alert Lord Hartmore to his daughter's...unease. Nothing more."

Thorne chuckled. "Is that so? Indeed, here I thought you had only used it as a distraction to rid us of his company." He cocked a brow at her. "Or am I wrong?"

Her lips thinned. "*Us?*" she demanded, a highly disapproving tone in her voice. "You speak as though we share confidences when in truth, I only learned your name a moment ago." Something sparkled in her eyes that momentarily made Thorne's breath falter in his chest.

They both knew that she was lying. She had learned his name long before today. He could see it in her eyes. Yet she denied it. Why? Was she teasing him? But why would she when the very sight of him seemed to make her blood boil?

"Then, pray tell, why are you here?" he demanded with equal boldness, taking a daring step closer to her. "Why did you seek me out? Is my company so desirable?"

Instead of acting offended, Lady Christina smiled, a brief spark of appreciation flashing in her eyes before she crossed her arms in a defiant gesture. "I must inform you that it is highly untoward of you to speak to a lady in such a way," she told him with no small measure of condescension. "I assume you are ignorant of society's ways?"

Thorne grinned at her. "I might be ignorant in some ways," he said quietly, lowering his head as though he were whispering secrets, "but not in others. Despite my...rustic upbringing, I am quite capable of reading between the lines." He lifted his brows and held her gaze. "You are stalling. Why did you come here? What is it that you seek? That you hope to uncover?"

A touch of annoyance came to her blue eyes. "Your behavior is most unusual. Has no one ever instructed you on how to speak to a lady? To pretend in order not to offend?"

Despite her chiding words, Thorne got the impression that she was not terribly disappointed with his reply. "Yet you seem to linger in my presence longer than need be, *Lady Christina*. Why is that? After all, you could simply tell me why you sought me out and then leave." Again, he cocked an eyebrow at her in challenge.

Her lips thinned, and for a moment, she looked severely tempted to scratch his eyes out. Her nostrils flared, and she glared at him in a way that Thorne found most endearing. "I came here to make out your character," she finally replied, her gaze sweeping over him as though it would only take one look for her to see to the very core of him and know the person he was.

"And what have you found?" Thorne asked lightly, belatedly realizing that despite the fact that they had only just met her opinion mattered to him. He swallowed hard and waited for her reply.

Again, Lady Christina seemed to survey him, her blue eyes trailing over his features as though wishing to commit them to memory. Thorne could all but feel her gaze like a caress upon his skin, and a shiver danced down his spine. "Well?"

"You are a most unusual man," Lady Christina remarked, her nose crinkling slightly as her eyes continued to peruse him.

Thorne laughed. "Is that supposed to be a compliment or an insult?"

Her eyes snapped up to meet his, and she glared at him as though chiding him for daring to ask such an inappropriate question. "Why are you here? In London?"

Thorne paused, hesitant to discuss his business dealings, reluctant to stray away from this comfortable banter between them. Though, what else was he to say but the truth? "Among other things, I came in search of a bride." He waited, looking deep into her eyes, seeing another spark of resistance flash to life.

Her jaw tensed, and she inhaled a slow breath. "And your choice has fallen on my friend?"

Thorne shrugged, pretending to be free of concern in this matter, knowing that it would unsettle her. "The union between us would be most beneficial to both parties, would it not? Is it not precisely how the *ton* conducts their *business*?"

Her nostrils flared. "Sarah is not a sheep to be bartered off to the highest bidder," she hissed under her breath, casting a careful glance around them, ensuring that no one stood too close to overhear. "She's sweet and kind, and she deserves someone better than the likes of you."

Thorne gritted his teeth. "The likes of me?" Anger flared in his veins as all the moments of easy dismissal resurfaced, moments when eyes had swept over him but had not seen him, moments when pain had been ignored and suffering had been disregarded. It had not always been his own suffering, but also that of others.

Yet in this moment, it did not matter.

"Common men," Lady Christina explained as though he did not know. "Men who do not know how to treat a lady. Men who –"

"What precisely have I done," Thorne demanded, anger now etched into his voice as he leaned closer, "that offended you? Or your friend? In what way have I treated her ill?" Challenge lit up his gaze, and he could see that she was regarding him with new eyes.

"You discussed marriage with her father without even once addressing her," Lady Christina huffed, now eyeing him with as much disdain as he himself felt in that moment. "You do not even possess the decency to—"

"Is that not how marriage is conducted in your circles?" Thorne demanded, aware that his pulse was quickening with each incremental step he took toward her. "How precisely have I given offense? From what I understand, I have conducted myself in a most appropriate manner." He grinned at her. "Why then do you object? Why are you so determined to see me as a villain?"

Her teeth gritted together, and a barely audible growl fell from her lips. "You are rude and ill-mannered and—"

"Are you not also?" Thorne teased. "Or would you consider it good manners to judge me in such a way for behaving in the very same fashion as any other man here?"

Her arms unfolded, and he could see her hands balling into fists that she clenched at her sides. Although her eyes still shot daggers at him, no words left her lips.

"Why did you come here?" Thorne inquired, inching close enough to feel a faint brush of her breath against his skin. "You said to make out my character, but that is not all, is it? What is it that you want... from me?" The last two words made his question feel strangely intimate, and he could see the slight widening of her eyes, clearly stating that she had not failed to notice.

Lady Christina inhaled a slow breath. She clearly wished to lash out at him, but held herself back, knowing that if she did so, whatever she wanted from him would be outside of her reach. "I want you to retract your marriage proposal." The words fell from her lips in one rushed breath.

"Truth be told, I have not yet proposed. I've merely entered into negotiations with—"

"Then step away from them," Lady Christina urged, her fists now trembling with barely concealed eagerness. "Leave London and return to where you came from. You do not belong here, and Sarah does not belong in Manchester."

Thorne regarded her carefully. "But what then? What if I do as you ask? We both know why Lord Hartmore is more than willing to give me his daughter's hand in marriage." His gaze narrowed as it swept over her features. "You are no fool. You know as well as I do that Lord Hartmore has no choice but to barter off his daughter's hand in marriage. The real question is, why do you object to *me* so strongly?"

"Sarah does not wish to marry you," she replied in her haste when it became clear to her that he would not simply comply with her request.

"Is there a gentleman she wishes to marry? A gentleman who also wishes to marry her?" Thorne demanded, enjoying the way she all but fidgeted where she stood. "If that is not the case, then this conversation is moot. Lord Hartmore requires funds, whereas I require a bride of noble birth. This union is of mutual benefit. Again, I ask you, is this not how marriage matters are conducted among *your* people?"

Lady Christina did not miss the mocking tone in his voice, and the look she gave him could have frozen the seas. "You are a most horrible man," she exclaimed, returning to insults when all arguments failed her. "I only wish..."

Thorne grinned at her. "You only wish what? That you could take her place?" Where the question had come from, he did not know, but it seemed to make the air around them sizzle with heat and temptation. His pulse quickened, and he saw her eyes widening as she drew in an unsteady breath.

Yes, he would accept her as his bride in a heartbeat.

No questions asked.

But how far was Lady Christina willing to go in order to save her friend? Now that was an extremely interesting question, and Thorne could not help but wish that he knew the answer. He was not fool enough to believe that Fate would grant him such a woman. That somehow he would be meeting not Miss Mortensen, but Lady Christina at the altar.

Still, in that moment, Thorne dared to dream.

Chapter Five
WRONG TIME, WRONG PLACE

Sarah's face paled in a way that made Christina reach out and grasp her hands, concern quickening her pulse as she stared at her friend. "What is it?"

Sarah swallowed hard, but then quickly regained her composure, a polite but somewhat intense smile coming to her face. "It is nothing. I was merely—"

Christina frowned, then turned to look over her shoulder, wondering what her friend was staring at or rather trying not to stare at so intently. "What is it? What did you—?" Christina's insides tensed at the very sight of him. "What is he doing here?"

Sarah shook her head. "I don't have the faintest idea. I never expected to..."

Indeed, what *was* he doing here? At her sister's wedding reception? In her sister's new home?

Craning her neck, Christina spotted Leonora and her new husband speaking to a few other guests, their eyes aglow with happiness, her hand resting upon his arm as she leaned into him. "Why would they have invited him?" she mumbled more to herself than anyone else. Then she turned to look at Sarah. "Do you think it was your mother?" Christina felt the frown lines upon her forehead deepening. "No offense, but I would not put it past her."

Sarah waved Christina's concerns away. "Neither would I. However, I do not believe she would invite him without permission from your parents or your sister."

Together, they turned to look toward the pianoforte where Lady Hartmore stood in a small circle of elderly matrons, a glass of ratafia in her hand. Truth be told, she did not look particularly conniving at the moment. If she had, in fact, invited Mr. Sharpe, the expression upon her face did not betray her. Indeed, she looked completely unperturbed.

"Do you think he could've invited himself?" Sarah asked, keeping her gaze fixed upon anything but Mr. Sharpe. Clearly, the man upset her deeply. Whenever he was near or was merely talked about, Sarah seemed uneasy.

Christina understood why. The man was most irritating! In fact, he was most likely the most irritating man she had ever met. When she had spoken to him the other day at the ball, he had been most direct and impolite. No gentleman would have spoken to a lady the way he had spoken to her.

A small voice whispered that neither would a true lady have addressed Mr. Sharpe the way Christina had; however, Christina silenced that voice immediately. "Honestly, it would not surprise me. He has no manners, no sense of decency, no—" Her words broke off when the man's gaze met hers from across the room.

Mr. Sharpe smiled at her in greeting, which infuriated Christina even more. What was he thinking? They were not friends! They were not even acquaintances! In fact, he was her nemesis. Granted, that might be a bit extreme. Still, Christina loathed him with every fiber of her being for the role he was currently playing in ruining her friend's life.

"Who are you glaring at so intently?" Harriet's voice chirped up a moment before she appeared in Christina's field of vision. Her fiery red curls bounced upon her shoulders and then flew sideways as she quickly turned her head in Mr. Sharpe's direction. "Oh, him." Her green eyes narrowed as she looked at Christina. "Honestly, I never understood why you dislike him. He seems quite amiable."

Christina snorted in derision. "How can you say that?" She glanced at Sarah, not wishing to upset her friend further. "Do you know why he's here? Did Mother and Father invite him? Did Leonora?" She frowned and cast a quick glance at her new brother-in-law. "He's not a friend of Drake's, is he?"

Harriet threw back her head and laughed. "Oh, can you imagine that? They are like day and night, one dark and skulking and the other cheerful and teasing. Now, if he's anyone's friend, I think he must be Phineas'. They are a lot alike, wouldn't you say?"

Christina frowned, then looked at Sarah, somewhat relieved to see an equally confused frown upon her friend's face. "Harry, honestly, I don't know how you cannot see it. He is so—"

Harriet lifted a hand to stop her. "If you insist on yelling and ranting on our sister's wedding day, then please let me get away first." She made to turn away, but then stopped and looked at Sarah. "Would you care for a stroll through the gardens?" Her eyes darted to Christina, then did a quick little roll before she held out her hand to Sarah. "You look like you could use a little fresh air."

Christina tried her best not to be offended by her sister's remark. "Go ahead," she told Sarah, well aware that she was truly poor company at the moment. "I need a moment to myself."

With a bit of a sigh, Sarah took Harriet's arm, cast Christina a small smile and then, together, the two crossed to the terrace doors and stepped outside into the warm air of early summer.

Inhaling a deep breath, Christina tried her best to calm her nerves. However, the slight tingling sensation trailing down the back of her neck made her once more glance over her shoulder at Mr. Sharpe.

To her utter surprise, the blasted man was still looking at her. Worse! He was watching her. Why on earth was he watching her? After all, there was nothing she *could* do to protect her friend, and he knew it. Was it boastful pride? Did he delight in letting her know that he would win eventually?

Merely thinking about it stirred Christina's blood. She felt the need to curl her fingers into tight fists. Her teeth gritted together, and her eyes narrowed. She could see that *he* saw that she was angry. She could see the teasing smile that came to his lips as well as the slight arc of his brows as though daring her to lose her temper.

Here.

In front of everybody.

Oh, no! She would not play into his hands. She would not explode. She would hold her temper until she was alone.

Straightening her shoulders, Christina lifted her chin and met his gaze head-on. Then she did her best to imitate a genuine smile, one that spoke of confidence and self-assuredness, and did her utmost to maintain that smile until she had counted to three in her head. A moment later, she shot him a challenging glare, turned her back on him and walked away.

Her heart was hammering in her chest, and Christina wanted nothing more than to stomp on his feet and scratch out his eyes. It was a childish and immature desire, but it was one he had only himself to blame for.

Leaving the assembled guests behind, Christina stepped out into the deserted corridor, the cheerful voices echoing after her a taunt, a reminder of how different she felt from those around her. If only she could have enjoyed her sister's wedding day! If only she could have simply joined in! But no, *he* had to ruin everything! What was he doing here in the first place?

"Who stepped on your toes, my dear?"

At the sound of Grandma Edie's voice, Christina whirled around. "How is it possible that you always manage to sneak up on us? And with your cane no less?" She drew in a replenishing breath, her gaze moving from her grandma's chuckling face to her cane.

"I doubt it had anything to do with me, dear," her grandmother replied with an indulgent smile. "You seemed rather lost in thought. Anything on your mind?" With her right hand leaning heavily upon her cane, Grandma Edie slipped her other hand through the crook of Christina's arm as they proceeded down the corridor. "Speak to me, child, and I promise I shall not breathe a word of it to anyone."

Christina shook her head. "Oh, it is nothing."

Her grandmother snorted. "Chris, I have seen *nothing* countless times—although admittedly not as often as I have seen *something*—and I can tell you that *nothing* rarely leads to flushed cheeks and an accelerated heartbeat." She grinned up at Christina. "Will you truly pretend that it is nothing?"

Christina heaved a deep sigh. "Oh, very well. There is no point in trying to hide anything from you, is there?"

Again, her grandmother chuckled. "Of course, you are free to try; however, I doubt you will succeed."

Christina smiled at her grandmother, then gave her a quick hug, grateful to have her in her life. Although often quite intrusive and annoyingly tenacious when it came to knowing other people's business, her grandmother had the kindest heart Christina had ever known, and she liked the thought that her own tenaciousness had come from her darling grandmother, passed down to her like a precious gift.

"What is it, dear? Is it Sarah's soon-to-be-betrothed?"

Christina drew to a halt and turned to stare at her grandmother. "How do you know?" A deep frown drew down her brows. "Have you been watching me?"

Her grandmother chuckled. "How else would I know what I know?" Her pale, watchful eyes looked over Christina's face. "He upsets you," she remarked thoughtfully. "He upsets you deeply."

Christina felt a surge of anger at her grandmother's words. Yes, he did upset her! He irritated her! He—! "I don't know what to do," Christina admitted, realizing that Mr. Sharpe upset her so deeply because his insistence upon marrying her friend made her feel helpless. Never had Christina felt helpless. Never had she found herself confronted with a problem she could not solve. And now, here she was dependent upon his cooperation, which he stubbornly refused to give! "Sarah cannot marry him. She simply cannot."

Her grandmother's head cocked sideways. "Why not? Would he truly be such an awful match for her? You have to admit, he looks quite dashing with those teasing green eyes and those dark brown locks." A youthful twinkle came to her eyes.

Christina threw up her hands. "You sound like Harriet," she accused. "He looks like a blackguard, a scoundrel, a rogue, a...villain! Yes, he looks like a villain, the kind of villain the hero has to defeat in order to save the damsel in distress." She heaved out a deep breath and crossed her arms over her chest. "That's what he looks like!"

Grandma Edie chuckled, and for once, that sound deeply annoyed Christina. "So, he is the villain, and I suppose it is safe to assume that Sarah is the damsel in distress. Then, who is the hero?" She asked, grinning at Christina. "You?"

Christina rolled her eyes. "Since we're lacking a dashing gentleman, yes! Who else?" Oh, how she wished there were a man—a gentleman, to be precise!—who would swoop in and sweep Sarah off her feet. A man who would marry her. A man who would be good for her. A man who would be good *to* her.

"Well," Grandma Edie began, once more slipping her hand through the crook of Christina's arm, "even a hero needs a moment to breathe every now and then. Come." Together, they slowly made their way a little farther down the corridor before Grandma Edie used her cane to point at a door. "I believe the library is through there."

Christina nodded for she had known this house what felt like all her life. After all, it had been Sarah's former home!

Stepping forward, Christina pushed down the handle and stepped inside, her eyes darting from the tall floor-to-ceiling windows to the many rows of books along the walls. A fireplace was nestled in one corner with inviting armchairs set around it. Indeed, the room looked peaceful with the warm sun streaming in through the windows, touching the dark mahogany wood of the shelves and the floor.

"Rest your thoughts a bit," Grandma Edie instructed from the door. "I shall see to Sarah."

Sighing, Christina nodded, suddenly feeling utterly exhausted. "She went outside with Harry. Please, make certain that Mr. Sharpe does not approach her. He upsets her whenever he draws near."

A gentle smile came to her face. "Of course. Do not worry. I promise all will be well."

"I wish I had your faith in the future," Christina mumbled, then turned to head toward the most comfortable-looking armchair. After a single step, though, she stopped and turned back around. "Do you know who invited Mr. Sharpe here today?"

Grandma Edie shrugged her shoulders. "I haven't the faintest idea." Then she smiled and closed the door, her hobbled steps echoing down the hall as she moved away.

Chapter Six

WITHOUT HESITATION

Long before Thorne stepped into Lord Pemberton's townhouse, he knew what was to come. With each step, more whispers drifted to his ears, and he could almost feel the other guests' stares like little pinpricks on the back of his head. Indeed, they barely tried to hide their shock and outrage at his presence. Of course, they did not need to. They were the top of society, looking down on all those they considered beneath them, him included. No one ever held them accountable for their deeds nor sought to correct them for their conduct. As far as they were concerned, they were portraying appropriate manners.

As far as Thorne was concerned, they were being rude.

Nevertheless, Thorne was determined not to respond. He held his head high, an appropriately polite smile upon his face, and entered the drawing room. His gaze swept over the many guests, and he ignored their pointed stares as best as he could before he retreated to one side of the room, a vantage position from where he could overlook most of the goings-on. While he was being watched by everyone else, he himself continued to observe the people he had come here to see today.

Indeed, the *Wicked Whickertons*—as the *ton* had come to call them

—were a rather unusual family; however, Thorne could not say that he disapproved. Quite on the contrary!

While Lord and Lady Whickerton were conversing with their daughter and new son-in-law, the Marquess of Pemberton, the other five siblings were mingling with friends and acquaintances around the room as well as in the gardens, Thorne supposed. Out of the corner of his eye, he glimpsed the dowager countess snoozing in an armchair, the eldest Whickerton sister never far from her side. The youngest, a redhead, was standing by the windows, her gaze fixed on a flock of birds crossing the light blue sky, their calls echoing indoors.

Where *was* she?

A tempting tingle snaked down the back of his neck, and Thorne turned around, his gaze falling on his golden-haired fury, Lady Christina.

She had yet to take notice of his presence as she stood with none other than Miss Mortensen—of course!—in a corner of the drawing room. Had they only just entered? Or had he truly overlooked her before?

Thorne doubted it.

His pulse quickened as he looked at her. She was beautiful—there was no doubt about it! Still, what captivated his attention were neither her golden tresses nor the enticing curves of her figure. Indeed, Thorne found himself trying to catch her eyes, trying to make her look at him and see him. Those deep blue eyes often flashed with sparks, some speaking of joy and exuberance while others—particularly when she was looking at him—revealed annoyance, fury even. She loathed him; that much was clear.

And it bothered him.

It bothered him a lot.

On some level, of course, he could understand why she felt about him the way she did. She was clearly protective of her friend. For some unknown reason, Miss Mortensen seemed all but terrified of him. Never had he raised his voice to her or spoken unkindly in her presence; her eyes, though, never quite dared to meet his, and she seemed pale whenever he stepped into a room. Thorne was mightily tempted to address the issue; however, he gathered that it would once again show poor manners and most likely send her into retreat once more, leaving him without answers yet again.

Perhaps Lady Christina would be more forthcoming. Indeed, she had not struck him as someone who would hold back. Her directness and unflinching approach had been impressive to watch. He had enjoyed their conversation the other day, and it had lingered upon his mind far longer than he had anticipated.

All the Whickerton siblings seemed rather dauntless and unflinching in their approach to the world. While some, like the newly married sister, Lady Pemberton, seemed to be of a quieter disposition, she still did not strike him as one who would ever bow her head. Neither did the eldest daughter, who constantly hovered around her grandmother. Although she remained in the shadows, her watchful eyes saw more than he supposed others ever suspected. She seemed quite assured of herself, conversing easily with others, her chin raised and her eyes never fearful.

It was a family with great respect for each individual member. Thorne could see it in the way the parents' eyes constantly swept the room as though needing to assure themselves that all their children were well and accounted for. The six siblings often seemed to drift toward one another, never straying far from each other's side, always aware when one was leaving or in need of counsel or comfort.

Thorne had to admit observing them made him yearn. It made him remember what was lacking in his life. It made him wish his parents and brothers and sisters had lived. It made him wish he had had a chance to get to know them beyond the few years they had shared.

His gaze moved back to Lady Christina, and as though she could feel him looking at her, her head turned in that moment and those flashing blue eyes looked into his.

Thorne felt it like a punch to the gut. That moment when they connected, when she was seeing him. Her eyes shot daggers, of course, but they were looking at him.

Him.

And no one else.

Thorne offered her a little smile, and it seemed to rile her even further. Behind her, Miss Mortensen seemed paler than before, her eyes darting to him and then quickly away again, never quite lingering. Words were exchanged between the two young women before the youngest Whickerton sister appeared, her red hair bouncing on her shoulders, as she turned to see what her sister was glaring at.

Her eyes came to fall upon him for a moment, and Thorne saw the corners of her mouth curl upward. Clearly, she did not share Lady Christina's aversion to him.

The three conversed amongst themselves as Thorne continued to watch, delighting in each and every loathing glare Lady Christina cast his way. He could not help but think that she did not despise him nearly as much as she wanted to. There was something in those blue eyes of hers that whispered of other emotions, emotions she desperately wanted to hold in check. Indeed, he could not help but think that on some level she, too, was enjoying this rather unexpected connection between them.

It was precisely what had brought Thorne here today.

A moment later, the youngest Whickerton sister pulled Miss Mortensen away and the two of them stepped out into the gardens. Lady Christina remained behind, but only for a moment before she cast him another menacing glare and then turned on her heel and disappeared out into the corridor. Thorne could not be certain where it led; however, he was certain he needed to follow.

Willing his feet to remain still for another few heartbeats, his gaze fixed upon the arched doorway through which Lady Christina had disappeared. Thorne then moved forward, feeling his heart quicken inside his chest with anticipation.

Always had he known what he wanted. Always had he been one quick to realize his ambitions and desires. And always had he been one to pursue them with single-minded purpose, never hesitating, never questioning.

The corridor lay deserted, and with each step he took forward, the voices at his back began to dim. His gaze swept over the many doors lining the walls on each side, and he wondered how to proceed when suddenly his gaze caught movement up ahead.

The door opened, and he could hear voices. He was yet too far away to make out what they were saying; however, he was certain that one of the voices belonged to Lady Christina.

In the next moment, the dowager countess stepped out into the corridor, paused for a moment, more mumbled words leaving her lips, before she chuckled and then closed the door. She turned down the corridor and her gaze fell upon him.

For a heartbeat or two, the elderly woman simply looked at him, something curious and determined in her gaze. Then she moved toward him, her right hand leaning on her cane; nevertheless, she moved with surprising agility. "Mr. Sharpe, I presume." Something almost wicked twinkled in her pale eyes as she regarded him.

Thorne chuckled. "You presume right, my lady." *As though she did not know!* His gaze moved down the corridor and came to linger upon the door she had closed behind her.

"These events can be somewhat tiring," she told him, casting a glance over her shoulder. "If you are in need of a temporary retreat, I would suggest the library. It is a most peaceful place." A devilish grin came to her face. "It might be precisely what you're looking for." Her brows rose in what seemed like a daring challenge before she nodded to him and then began to continue making her way back toward the drawing room. Her hobbled steps made him wonder which of the impressions he had gained reflected the truth.

"Are you certain?" Thorne asked by the time she had almost reached the end of the corridor. "I know that...doubts can be a hard thing to live with."

The dowager countess turned to look back at him. "Truer words have never been spoken," she said to him, her eyes now thoughtful. "However, doubts can be had for more than one reason. The choice is yours as it will be hers."

"As it was yours?"

The dowager countess nodded. "As it was mine, and I never once regretted it."

Thorne smiled at her. "Never?"

She shook her head. "Never." Then she turned and slowly walked away.

Inhaling a deep breath, Thorne marched down the corridor toward the door she had closed behind her earlier. He hesitated for a moment, thinking that perhaps it would be wise to think things through more thoroughly. Nonetheless, deep down, Thorne knew what he wanted.

He had known since the first moment he had seen her. He had never expected to feel anything remotely like what he felt, yet it did not alter the truth, did it?

A smile came to his face as he reached for the handle and then pushed the door open.

Indeed, he knew his choice, and he would not hesitate.

Chapter Seven

THE PLACE OF ANOTHER

Despite the emotional upheaval that made her heart beat frantically in her chest, Christina felt herself breathe more easily as her gaze swept over the rows upon rows of books in the library. After discarding her slippers, she had snuggled into the armchair, pulled up her legs and rested her head against the soft upholstery. Warm light streamed in from the windows, casting a soft glow around the large, vaulted room.

Christina breathed out a sigh of relief, feeling her muscles relax and her mind quiet. Always had the library been her favorite place in the world, ever since she had been a child. Although she had given up writing down her own musings and imaginings long ago, Christina still enjoyed diving into another's. Few books remained in her father's library that she had not yet read for she enjoyed being carried off to another world, to see the world through another's eyes, to experience things far removed from her own, comparatively cloistered life.

Indeed, it felt good to retreat from the world every once in a while. Her grandmother had been correct to suggest it. Her heartbeat slowly calmed, and she felt the tension of the past few moments slowly leave her body. A familiar smile came to her face as her gaze continued to sweep across the long rows of books, and her mind began to urge her to tiptoe across the carpet and snatch a volume from the tall bookshelf across from her.

"Only a page or two," Christina whispered to herself as her legs slipped off the armchair, her stockinged feet coming to rest upon the floor. "No more than a page or two, then I'll return to the drawing room." A soft giggle drifted from her lips as she rose to her feet, leaving her slippers behind, and stepped toward the promise of retreat her eyes were fixed upon. She had taken no more than a few steps when a soft *creak* had her whirl around, eyes snapping to the door.

Her heart jumped into her throat, and she felt her body tense as the door swung open, revealing none other than Mr. Sharpe.

For a seemingly endless moment, Christina simply stared at him, certain that he was some kind of mirage. Perhaps her mind was torturing her with the image of him, punishing her for retreating into the library on her sister's wedding day. She ought to be out there, congratulating Leonora and assisting her and her husband in tending to their guests. Instead, she had fled, all thoughts focused upon herself and that sense of powerlessness that always came over her when she thought of Lady Hartmore's intention to see her daughter married to Mr. Sharpe.

That same feeling seeped into her bones even now as she looked into those bright green eyes of his. A small smile lingered upon his lips, and her gaze swept over him, taking note of his slightly tousled hair and his less than perfectly tied cravat. In fact, it looked as though he had been tugging upon it repeatedly, unfamiliar with wearing such a piece of clothing.

Lifting her chin, Christina fought down that overpowering sense of inevitability—as though she had no say in who would win her heart—and steered her thoughts toward more worthwhile emotions. "What are you doing here?" she demanded, crossing her arms over her chest and glaring at him in a way that would have made a true gentleman immediately retreat from the room.

However, Mr. Sharpe was not a gentleman, true or otherwise, was he? Christina had known this long before this day, and so it came as no surprise that instead of leaving, the blasted man closed the door and stepped toward her. "I came here in search of a moment of solace," he told her in a tone of voice that made her doubt his every word. "And you?"

Christina lifted her chin another fraction as he continued to move toward her, for the way he was looking at her stirred a deeply unsettling feeling in the pit of her stomach. "Leave!" she instructed haughtily. "You are not to be here! If we are found together—" She clamped her lips shut, momentarily thrown by the way the right corner of his mouth curved upward as though...as though... "This is not proper!" she shot at him, trying her best to ignore the slight flutter coming to her heart.

The man's smile deepened as his gaze dipped down to touch upon her shoeless feet. "You seem to be the expert on such matters, or am I wrong?" Leisurely, he strolled closer, his gaze sweeping over her in a way that made Christina shiver. "May I ask you a question?"

Christina's gaze narrowed as she regarded him curiously, upset with herself for wanting him to speak. Why was it that she cared what he thought? "If you must."

Again, that irritatingly endearing smile danced over his lips. "Do you ever not say what you think?"

Christina felt her nostrils flare. "Oh, believe me, I am holding back. If I were to say what I thought then—" Her sense of decorum fought with an almost desperate need to lash out at him, tearing at her and making her indecisive. Christina hated being indecisive!

"Why is it that you seem to hate the very sight of me?" Mr. Sharpe asked rather unexpectedly, another stride carrying him closer, close enough that Christina could see flecks of gold dance in his green eyes.

Christina huffed out an exasperated breath. "How dare you ask me that? You know very well why!" Staring at him, she shook her head. "Have I not made my sentiments on this subject abundantly cl—?"

"You have, indeed," Mr. Sharpe interrupted her, another step bringing him ever closer, his eyes fixed upon hers, something daring and challenging twinkling in their depths. "Yet why this hatred? I can understand your displeasure with my presence here in London as well as my intentions of offering marriage to your friend; however, the way you're looking at me right now tells me that there is something else that fuels you."

Christina swallowed as he looked down at her in a way no one else ever had before. It was as though he could see inside of her and knew precisely what she thought and felt.

"Something you refuse to admit to," Mr. Sharpe continued, now barely an arm's length between them. "Tell me now," he dared her, that irritating smile once more upon his lips as though he knew precisely what she would do. "Tell me what you're thinking of when you look at me."

Christina swallowed hard, desperately trying to recover her voice. "When I look at you," Christina told him, hardening her voice as much as she could, surprised to find it a task far from ease, "I see a man undeserving of my friend. I see—"

Mr. Sharpe scoffed. "For how much longer do you intend to hold onto that excuse?" he teased, leaning closer as his gaze drilled into hers as though he could dig out the truth despite her lack of cooperation.

"Excuse?" Christina snapped, welcoming the wave of anger that washed through her at his condescending words. "You might not possess any sense of loyalty, which, of course, is not surprising considering your upbringing; however, Sarah is my dearest friend. She is almost like a sister to me, and I will do whatever I must to ensure that—"

"Whatever you must?" Mr. Sharpe echoed, his lips stretching into a teasing smile. "That reminds me; you still owe me an answer."

Christina frowned. "An answer? An answer to what?"

He chuckled. "Do you not recall our conversation the other day?" The smile upon his face told Christina that *he* recalled every detail of it, and she could feel a slight flush steal onto her cheeks. "Perhaps you do," he mused, his eyesight clearly impeccable.

Ignoring the urge to rush from the room, Christina squared her shoulders and held his gaze, refusing to be intimidated by a man of low birth. "You have no right to be here. This is my sister's wedding day, and I doubt that anyone in my family has invited you. Leave! Leave this house! Leave London! Go back to where you came from!"

Holding her gaze, Mr. Sharpe slowly shook his head from side to side. "Not until you've answered my question," he whispered, making his words sound much more intimate than they otherwise would have. His gaze continued to linger, daring her to answer him, stating loud and clear that he would not move unless she did. "Answer me, and I shall leave. Not London, mind you, but this room."

Christina did her best to cast him an exasperated look, one meant to hide the irritating flutter in her chest. "Very well then. What was your question?"

Grinning at her, the blasted man chuckled. "As though you don't remember," he whispered in that low tone yet again.

Of course, Christina remembered. After she had all but fled his side that day at the ball, his question had continued to echo in her mind, keeping her awake night after night for a reason she did not dare dwell upon. "I'm afraid I do not," she said, and even to her own ears her words sounded hollow.

Mr. Sharpe's grin deepened, and Christina's breath caught as he moved closer still, his eyes fixed upon hers as though they could hold her in place. He inhaled a deep breath, and the moment between them stretched from one heartbeat into another and another. "How far would you go?" he asked, echoing his words from the other night. "Would you take her place?"

Christina knew what her answer should be. She had known it then and she knew it now. All of a sudden, though, her voice deserted her. The words simply would not come, would not leave her lips and put him in his place. Why? Why could she not simply say it?

Angry at herself, Christina opened her mouth, determined to say something, to reply, to give an answer that would make it unmistakably clear that she despised him...when Mr. Sharpe suddenly closed that last bit of distance between them.

Christina inhaled a sharp breath at his sudden nearness, completely taken aback, only to feel her heart all but still in her chest a moment later when his arms swung forward, and his hands settled almost possessively upon her waist. "What are you—?"

"Would you sacrifice yourself to save her?" Mr. Sharpe asked, and his breath fell against her lips. "Would you take her place...at my side?"

Christina could not stop her breath from quickening as she stared up at him. She felt his warm breath mingling with her own, and she knew that she ought to stop him. She ought to step out of his embrace. She ought to chide him for taking such liberties. She ought to—

"It seems I have found a question without an easy answer," he chuckled, and his hands upon her waist tightened, pulling her closer against him.

Christina held her breath. "Release me!" A wave of relief swept through her at the rediscovery of her voice. "I demand that you release me this instant!"

He grinned at her. "And I demand an answer." His head lowered toward hers, his eyes not veering from her own. "Would you?" he whispered. "Or is there a reason why you're not answering me? Are you stalling yet again? Are you so enjoying my company that you're hoping if you refuse to answer," his gaze briefly dropped from hers to touch upon her lips, "that I will kiss you?"

Christina's eyes widened as shock slammed into her. Indeed, what was most shocking was not the threat—or perhaps the possibility—of a kiss, but instead to have the truth revealed to her in such an unexpected way. Yes, Christina had been on the brink of a kiss before. However, never before had she been indecisive. She had always known without thought what she had wanted. Or rather what she had *not* wanted.

Now, however, she had to admit—at least to herself—that the thought of kissing Mr. Sharpe was irritatingly appealing. She should not want his kiss. She should not, and yet somehow, someway, inexplicably so, she did.

Before either one of them could make up their mind to act, the door to the library was suddenly flung open and in poured a small group of guests, their voices echoing through the vaulted room that Christina found herself momentarily wondering how she had not heard their approach. Perhaps, the truth was, that she had simply been too caught up in the moment. Whatever the reason, it did not change what was.

And what was was that Lady Christina Beaumont, daughter to the Earl of Whickerton, found herself in an intimate embrace with a gentleman—scratch that, man!—his head lowered to hers for a kiss, her slippers discarded a few paces away, and a group of onlookers staring at them as though they were on display at the museum.

Indeed, the day could not have gone worse, or could it have? What were they to do now?

Chapter Eight

WHAT IS TO BE EXPECTED

Thorne had to admit that he, too, had gotten lost in the moment. Although he had planned every step so carefully, the moment he had drawn near, he had acted on instinct alone. She had that effect on him. Whenever those flashing blue eyes looked into his, he seemed to forget everything that was or should be. One word from her lips upended his most carefully laid-out plans, and he found himself giving in to desires he had not quite expected.

Of course, he knew the effect a beautiful woman could have on a man. He had felt himself get lost in the haze of desire before. Still, this was different.

She was different.

Granted, he wanted to kiss her, but it was not all that he wanted or longed for or cherished. Indeed, he loved the way she lied to his face, pretending that she did not feel that sizzling attraction between them. It was utterly endearing to watch her fight for control and not give in, to see her hold her head high and pretend that she truly despised him. Perhaps she did, but most likely because of the effect he, too, had upon her. He knew that she did not like losing control or being at the mercy of another, and so she fought him.

She fought herself.

Her own desires and longings.

Nonetheless, with each breath, he had sensed her begin to yield a bit more. Her resistance had waned. He felt her muscles begin to relax, and he had seen sparks of temptation flash in her blue eyes.

He could see she was displeased to find herself drawn to him, something deep inside telling her to resist him, to resist this unexpected allure between them.

Yet the moment before the blasted door had opened, Thorne had been certain that she had been close to acquiescing.

Now, he would have to wait.

Wait for another chance.

But his moment would come.

Their moment would come, and he would not allow it to slip from his fingers again.

"I'm afraid we are no longer alone," Thorne whispered, seeing her eyes widen in shock as the impact of their situation slowly found its way into her mind. Neither one of them had yet turned to look upon those who had entered without even the courtesy of a knock; however, they both knew what would happen now.

Lady Christina swallowed, then dropped her gaze, and he could feel her retreating from his embrace. Thorne removed his hands from her, allowing more distance between them than he would have preferred. Still, this was not the moment. Now, here, their thoughts needed to focus elsewhere.

Thorne did not know any of the people who stood in the doorway gaping at them. One by one, they moved inside instead of back out into the hallway. Curiosity urged them onward as hushed whispers flew from their lips. With each one stepping inside, another followed as though an endless supply of guests remained outside in the corridor, only waiting to be allowed entrance.

Hushed words of *compromised* and *a most indecent situation* as well as *a marriage to swiftly follow* drifted to his ears. Although he could not say that he minded, his gaze moved to his partner in crime, noting the paleness of her cheeks, and he felt a small stab of shame at what he had done.

He could only hope that she would forgive him one day.

"What is going on here?" came a deep, masculine voice before the small crowd began to part, making way for Lord Whickerton and his wife, closely followed by today's bride and groom. Their eyes moved from Lady Christina to him and back again, puzzled and somewhat suspicious expressions coming to their faces.

"If you would allow us a moment of privacy," the master of the house said in a commanding tone as he turned to face the assembled wedding guests. He gave a swift nod of the head, his tall stature and authoritative tone no match even for the most curious tattletale. Reluctantly, one by one, they retreated back out into the corridor, their whispers flying frantically back and forth, new rumors spreading far and wide as they hastened back to inform others of what they had just unearthed.

And then, finally, the door closed behind them.

"Christina, what happened here?" Lord Whickerton asked as he stepped toward his daughter, concern instead of reproach in his voice. "Are you all right?"

Lady Christina nodded, her face pale, but her eyes as luminous as always. Despite the look of shock that seemed to linger upon her face, she seemed as agile as always. Thorne wished he knew what she was thinking in that moment.

What Lord Pemberton was thinking in that very moment seemed abundantly clear, though, for the man glared at him in a rather hostile manner. The pulse in his neck beat rapidly, and despite his outward calm, Thorne thought to see anger begin to boil under the surface. It seemed only his bride's calming presence as she placed a hand on his arm, her eyes seeking his, managed to dispel all thoughts of retribution.

Thorne had met Lord Pemberton once before, not long ago, and the man had struck him as one who adhered to his conscience rather than public opinion. A commendable quality, as far as Thorne was concerned, and he was not in the least put off by Lord Pemberton's dark glare. After all, the man was merely looking out for his family.

"Father, it is nothing," Lady Christina said all of a sudden, her features reviving as she took charge of the situation. "It was a misunderstanding. No more."

Her parents exchanged a look before her mother stepped toward her. "Chris, dear, you were found alone with a gentleman. That is not nothing. Surely, you must know that."

Lady Christina heaved a deep breath, then nodded. "Yes, of course, Mother. I'm not a simpleton. However, it truly was...a misunderstanding." She cast him a meaningful glance, one Thorne could not quite interpret. "Nothing untoward happened."

"What kind of misunderstanding?" the new Lady Pemberton asked, a somewhat suspicious glimmer in her blue eyes, eyes that looked a lot like her sister's.

Lady Christina hesitated, casting another, somewhat irritated glance in his direction. "I came here to seek a moment of solace and found myself not the only one with that intention. That is all."

Her father frowned. "May I ask what your shoes are doing over there?"

Lady Christina quickly explained how she had rested in the armchair by the fireplace and then had intended to fetch herself a book when *he* had entered unexpectedly. Thus far, Thorne knew her words to be completely truthful. However, her further explanations barely scratched the surface of it.

"If that is the case," Lord Pemberton began as he turned to look at Thorne, "then why are you still here? Why did you not leave the moment you discovered yourself alone with her?"

Thorne cleared his throat. "Quite frankly, the lady and I had something to discuss."

"To discuss?" the new Lady Pemberton inquired, exchanging a look with her sister. "What did you have to discuss? And alone no less?"

Lady Christina heaved a deep and somewhat exasperated sigh. "I wanted him to cease pursuing Sarah. I thought if I could speak to him, perhaps I could convince him to set his sights elsewhere." A rather exasperated sigh left her lips, and the look she cast in his direction was far from favorable. "Unfortunately, it seems I was less than successful."

Again, Lord and Lady Whickerton exchanged a meaningful look before their eyes moved to him, sizing him up from head to toe. "You are still set to marry Miss Mortensen?" Lord Whickerton inquired with a sideways glance at his daughter.

Linking his hands behind his back, Thorne straightened and met the other man's inquisitive gaze. "As I explained to your daughter, I am merely in negotiations with her father, Lord Hartmore. Beyond that, no understanding has been reached."

Lord Whickerton nodded. "I see." A thoughtful expression came to the man's face as he looked around the room, his thoughts no doubt lingering upon the implications of the situation they found themselves in.

Thorne knew precisely what was expected and could not deny that he was curious to see how Lord Whickerton would react. Would he demand or counsel or suggest? What kind of a man and father was he? Thorne had his suspicions; however, he could not be certain if he would see them confirmed.

Turning, Lord Whickerton looked at his daughter. "Christina, where do you intend to go from here? You know as well as I do what course of action is expected now. No doubt, the news of what happened here has already spread through the guests present here today and will be carried through London in the days to come." His jaw moved, and his wife stepped up to his side, her arm coming to rest upon his. Again, they looked at one another, one of those silent exchanges Thorne had observed here and there. Then Lord Whickerton turned to face him. "Mr. Sharpe, what are your intentions? What will you do now?" Tension rested in the man's voice, understandably so; his expression, though, remained calm.

Thorne exhaled a deep breath, allowing his eyes to sweep over the people looking most curiously at him before they came to rest upon Lady Christina for a long moment. In truth, his decision had been made long before this moment. Things had been set into motion and could not be undone. He knew what he wanted, what he *still* wanted, and he would not back down now. The only question was, what did she want?

Meeting Lord Whickerton's gaze, Thorne nodded. "Although I am considered an outsider to your circles, I am aware of what is expected in such a situation. If that is what you wish," he looked at Lady Christina, aware that her blue eyes were all but glued to him, a hint of apprehension in her gaze, "we shall be married."

As expected, her eyes widened, and it looked as though her jaw would drop to the floor. She stared at him, completely taken aback by this turn of events. Had she truly not seen it coming? What would her answer be? Clearly, Lord Whickerton would never force his daughter's hand; so, the decision was hers.

Hers alone.

Would she choose him?

Chapter Nine

IN SERVICE OF A FRIEND

For a moment, Christina felt as though the room was suddenly spinning. Her vision blurred, and a strange rushing, gurgling sound echoed in her ears. She continued to stare at Mr. Sharpe like a simpleton, as though she could not make out the words he had said. Yet they echoed within her mind over and over again.

We shall be married.

Yes, his reply had taken her aback. She had not expected him to respond in this manner. Had he not seemed rather obstinate before when it came to his impending union with Sarah? Why now the sudden change of heart?

Of course, from a rational standpoint, it should not matter to him whether he married Sarah or her. In fact, objectively speaking, Christina would be the better match. After all, her father would bestow a generous dowry upon her—which considering his own fortune would perhaps not have much sway with Mr. Sharpe—and her family's connections would no doubt see Mr. Sharpe elevated in position, opening doors for him and assisting his business ventures. So, yes, she understood why he was so ready to agree to this marriage.

Blasted man! Had all this been nothing but a ruse to secure her hand in marriage? Had it not been a coincidence that he had stumbled upon her here in the library? Indeed, with each passing second, that scenario seemed more likely than any other.

Fury once again burned in her veins, and for a split second, Christina was tempted to fling herself at him, determined to inflict physical pain however she could. Who did he think he was? Coming here, to London, into her sister's home and manipulate her in such a way? Had everything been nothing but a ploy? The way he had...looked at her, reached for her?

Christina still felt the warmth of his hands upon her waist. She still remembered the fleeting brush of his breath against her lips. Indeed, she had lost herself in that moment. She had *allowed* herself to be manipulated. She had been so cautious and suspicious of him from the start, and yet in the very moment when she had needed her wits about her, his mere presence had robbed her of every rational thought.

Angry at herself, Christina felt her hands ball into fists, and she quickly hid them in the folds of her skirts. She did not want him to know how deeply he unsettled her, angered her. She did not want him to know that he had outsmarted her.

He had, had he not?

Shame sent heat to her cheeks, and Christina held onto the thought that at least now she would have the chance to refuse him. To put him in his place. To reject him. Never, no matter the circumstances, would her parents force her to accept a man she did not wish to marry. Yes, her reputation would be in tatters; however, there were worse fates than—

Christina paused as a new thought slowly found its way into her mind. Indeed, she did not want to marry him. No woman in her right mind would want to marry him. Neither did Sarah. Nonetheless, if he were to marry her, Christina, Sarah would be safe.

Aware that everyone in the room was staring at her, waiting for her reply, for her answer, Christina turned away and began to pace, her gaze falling on her slippers, still lying by the foot of the armchair she had sat in before...when the world had still followed its usual rotation.

"Nothing has to be decided right now, does it?" her sister Leonora asked, her eyes slightly widened and deep concern in her voice as she looked toward their parents.

Not long ago, Leonora had almost been blackmailed into marriage for the sake of her sisters, worried that her ruined reputation might harm them all. Ultimately, however, all had ended well, and Leonora had married a man she genuinely loved, a man who had come to her aid without a moment's hesitation. Still, Christina could see that the threat of a forced marriage still lingered in her heart, giving her voice that touch of fear as though she were the one standing at this crossroad.

"Of course not," their father replied, his face tense as he was no doubt torn into various directions. Of course, everyone knew that recovering from such a scandal was almost impossible for a woman. Nonetheless, their parents had always insisted their children make their own decisions, for better or for worse. Free will: it was the only way to live one's life and find happiness. Her parents had always believed that to be a universal truth.

Never would Christina have thought that only days after Leonora, she herself would find herself in a similar situation, forced to decide between her own wishes and what might be best for those she loved. Indeed, if she married Mr. Sharpe, it would certainly protect her family's reputation as much as it would protect Sarah.

Christina turned and looked at Mr. Sharpe, trying to imagine spending the rest of her life at his side. Yes, he was a nuisance of a man. Teasing and mocking, and those sharp eyes of his saw more than she would have liked. However, as far she could tell, he was decent enough for her not to worry about her well-being as the man's wife. Indeed, she had always been made of sterner stuff than Sarah or even Leonora. Yes, she would be able to handle him. She would not allow him to bully her into submission. No, she would hold her head high and perhaps she would even be able to teach him how to treat a lady. God knew, he needed the lesson!

"Mr. Sharpe," her father addressed him, "I have heard it said that you hail from the North?"

Mr. Sharpe nodded and provided a quick overview of his business dealings, including the cotton mill in Manchester.

"And what brings you to town?" Leonora's husband, Drake, inquired, that look of protectiveness in his gaze that Christina had come to appreciate. Before it had only ever been directed at Leonora. Now, it seemed he was extending it to the rest of her family. Indeed, her sister had made a wise choice.

Christina looked at Mr. Sharpe, wishing that she, too, would have had such a chance. Even if she refused him, no decent gentlemen would now seek her favors. If she refused him, she would be worse off than Sarah.

"I believe," Mr. Sharpe began, the look upon his face determined as his gaze moved from Drake to Christina's father, "that fair labor should be a requirement in all business dealings. I have seen far too many workers injured or killed because of unsuitable working conditions. It is something, I believe, needs to be regulated by the law."

The expression upon her father's face relaxed, the look in his eyes becoming intrigued. "You seek to rally support?"

Mr. Sharpe nodded. "Quite frankly, I feel very much at home in Manchester. However, London is the place where one must travel to see any changes made to labor laws. I came here to see those I am responsible for, as well as others in their position, better protected. Thus far, it rests within each mill owner's discretion to determine working conditions. Unfortunately, few take this responsibility serious-ly." His voice darkened, and Christina was surprised to see his teeth grind together, his jaw tensing, as he spoke of something that clearly stirred anger within his heart.

Her father nodded in approval, and it was obvious that Mr. Sharpe had risen in his opinion. "That is very commendable. I would like to hear more of this issue," he glanced at Christina, "at another time."

Christina was not certain whether or not she liked the fact that hearing Mr. Sharpe speak with such compassion about the needs of others somehow endeared him to her...at least a little. It seemed he did possess a kind and caring side, somewhere below that obnoxious surface he generally portrayed in her presence. He was perhaps not the worst sort of man after all. However, he was not a gentleman. A gentleman would not have done what he had. A gentleman would not have maneuvered her into a position where she had no choice but to comply with his wishes.

Christina frowned as she realized her own thoughts were far from accurate. Yes, somehow, she wanted there to be good people and bad people. People who could be trusted, and people who could not. Would that not make the world a simpler place? Only the truth was far from simple. Indeed, there were those who were considered gentlemen who would surely commit deeds most heinous in order to achieve their goals. Had she not just learned that very lesson when Leonora had been blackmailed by a *gentleman* of the *ton*? Indeed, he had possessed breeding and standing, fortune and connections, and yet he had been the vilest sort of man.

He *still* was a most vile man.

Perhaps Mr. Sharpe, in comparison, was indeed the lesser of two evils. Perhaps, Christina thought, she simply ought to see this as a challenge. After all, she possessed strength and daring and no small measure of forthrightness.

"Very well," Christina said into the momentary stillness, her eyes drifting from her parents to her sister and then to Mr. Sharpe.

"Very well?" she heard her sister ask, her voice slightly trembling with anxiety. "What do you mean?"

At her words, Mr. Sharpe's gaze narrowed, yet a slow smile teased the corners of his mouth as he looked at her, watched her and waited. She could see amusement and curiosity dancing in those eyes of his, teasing her and mocking her as he always did. However, she saw nothing that frightened her or made her worry about her well-being. Perhaps, just perhaps, he was a more or less decent man after all.

And *she* would certainly be able to handle him. How hard could it be?

And Sarah would be safe.

At least for now.

"Yes," Christina replied to her sister's question; her gaze, however, never veered from Mr. Sharpe's. "I will marry him."

Silence fell over the room before all their voices seemed to erupt at once. While her parents urged her to delay and think this through, her sister objected outright to her decision. Mr. Sharpe, on the other hand, smiled at her, the look in his eyes reminding her of his earlier question.

How far would you go? Would you take her place?

Never would Christina have expected this day to end in such a way.

Yet here she was, all but betrothed to a man she had only yesterday considered a scoundrel and the worse sort of man imaginable. Today, well, she had to admit that he was not...all bad. To her utter shock, it seemed they shared certain similarities. They both had a way of speaking their minds that was rarely appreciated by those around them. In fact, Christina could not say that she appreciated *his* outright manner. Still, perhaps, with time, they would learn to get along.

And perhaps a kiss would be worth the bother of teaching Mr. Sharpe proper manners.

If only she did not have to wait!

Chapter Ten

REPERCUSSIONS

Angry footsteps echoed along the corridor, and Thorne put down his quill and looked toward the door. A moment later, it burst open and in sailed Lord Hartmore, closely followed by Thorne's rather indignant-looking butler. "Sir, I'm terribly sorry, but—"

"How dare you treat my daughter this way?" Lord Hartmore roared, his face turning a dark red as he stormed toward Thorne's desk. His hands had balled into fists, and he waved them around as though wishing to land a punch. "I ought to challenge you right here and now!"

Slowly, Thorne rose to his feet, familiar with the likes of Lord Hartmore. Men who ranted and roared, put up an aggressive front, but ultimately lacked the courage or determination to back it with deeds. "Then do so," Thorne challenged the other man, his gaze steady as he stared across the small expanse of his desk between them.

Clearly taken aback, Lord Hartmore clamped his lips shut. His eyes narrowed in distaste, and his face darkened considerably. Still, he did no more than huff out an indignant breath before saying, "I demand an explanation. What happened last night at Lord Pemberton's wedding reception?" His gaze narrowed even farther, and he looked at Thorne as though he were an insect Lord Hartmore wished to squash beneath his boot.

Thorne squared his shoulders. "I'm afraid I cannot share any details with you, my lord; however, it seemed that a misunderstanding occurred." He chuckled, deviously delighted to see the other man squirm before him. He knew better than anyone that Lord Hartmore considered himself superior to others; nonetheless, right now, here he stood, furious to have been robbed of an advantageous match for his daughter. For himself. After all, his gambling debts were staggering.

The older man's jaw ground together, his muscles tensing violently. "A misunderstanding?" he demanded, outrage in his voice. "We had a deal! Have you no honor?"

Thorne chuckled. "Do you?" Keeping his gaze fixed on Lord Hartmore's, he slowly rounded the desk, noting the way the other man seemed to shrink back, unease coming to his bloodshot eyes. "You gamble away your family's fortunes, risk their welfare and happiness, rob them of everything and then demand your daughter sacrifice her own future in order to save her family. To save you! Where is the honor in that?"

For a moment, it seemed Lord Hartmore would expire on the spot. His face turned a shade of dark violet and his eyes almost bulged from his head as he stared at Thorne in outrage.

"I apologize if I've caused your daughter any unease," Thorne continued, suspecting that Miss Mortensen had been relieved to find that she was no longer to be his future bride. After all, whenever her eyes had fallen on him, her face had paled, and she had quickly turned away as though unable to bear the mere sight of him. Clearly, he had frightened her or at least something about their impending union had. Who knew what her parents had told her about him? Or what she might have overheard from others? After all, as far as society was concerned, he was not considered worthy to be among them.

"She'll be ruined now," Lord Hartmore snarled, his fists once more gesturing wildly as though by waving them fast enough he might be able to rewind time and set things right. "How dare you jilt her? Have you no decency? No gentleman will want her now!"

"I did not jilt her," Thorne insisted, unable to curb that small stab of guilt he felt when thinking of Miss Mortensen. Yes, she had been the victim in all of this, and perhaps he should have been more cautious to spare her such humiliation. "We had not yet reached an understanding. Neither had I proposed to your daughter. Indeed, it was you who was presumptuous by circulating rumors of our impending nuptials. Had you been more discreet, none of this would've happened! No one would ever have known." He gave Lord Hartmore a pointed look.

The man's fists shook as he stared at Thorne, dumbfounded to have someone he deemed inferior speak to him in such a way. After all, Lord Hartmore seemed to be of the opinion that none of his troubles were his fault. Therefore, he had never even stopped to consider laying blame at his own feet. In Thorne's humble opinion, that was precisely what had caused all this trouble. If the man had had any sense of responsibility, he would not have gambled away his family's fortunes and future in the first place.

"I thank you for your visit," Thorne said icily. "However, since I am on my way out myself, I must politely ask you to leave." His brows rose into arches as he gestured toward the door.

A huffed breath left Lord Hartmore's lips before he spun around, mumbled something unintelligible, but, no doubt insulting, under his breath, and then stormed from the room, his footsteps thundering down the corridor.

Thorne allowed a small smile to cross his face at seeing a member of the *ton* thus humiliated. Of course, it was petty and spiteful, yet after a lifetime of being looked down upon and treated with no respect at all, Thorne could not help it. In fact, in his opinion, Lord Hartmore deserved far worse for what he had done...for what he would no doubt continue to do to his family. If only there was something Thorne could do to protect Miss Mortensen from her father's next scheme. Who knew, what *solution* Lord Hartmore would concoct next?

Striding from his study, Thorne donned his hat and then proceeded out of the house and down to the pavement in front of the townhouse, which he had let for the duration of his stay in London. The air was warm and soothing, a mild breeze stirring the leaves of the trees lining the street. He moved at a leisurely pace, his thoughts turning from Lord Hartmore's visit to the woman he was to marry.

He smiled, a part of him still wondering if he had merely dreamed her acceptance. In fact, he had expected her to fight him tooth and nail. Nonetheless, it would be foolish of him to think that she had agreed to become his wife because she cared for him. Of course, Thorne knew that Lady Christina had only agreed to marry him in order to protect her friend, to protect Miss Mortensen.

Her devotion to her friend was something that made Thorne hold her in even higher regard. Yes, she had her faults and follies, but deep down, she was a deeply compassionate and loyal woman, willing to sacrifice her own happiness in order to protect someone she cared about. Thorne could only hope that in the end happiness would still find them both.

Thinking of her, Thorne's steps quickened, and a smile came to his face the moment his gaze fell upon her family's townhouse. Indeed, he was looking forward to seeing her.

A lot more than he would have expected.

Chapter Eleven

AMONG SISTERS

Descending the stairs to the ground floor, Christina found a small mob waiting for her at the bottom, their eyes fixed on her and matching frowns upon all their faces. "I sense an intervention," Christina mumbled, unable to help the smile that came to her face as her gaze swept over her sisters. Generally, Harriet was the recipient of these interventions for she was the one with the most outrageous ideas and plans.

Harry laughed, no doubt guessing Christina's thoughts. "I actually have no objections." She ignored the dark looks from her sisters. "I'm just here for the fun of it."

Stopping on the bottom step, Christina turned to look at Louisa, Leonora and Juliet. "Well? Say your piece then."

Louisa shook her head. "Not here. Come." Without waiting, she grabbed a hold of Christina's arm and pulled her forward, their sisters following in their wake. The door to the drawing room was shoved open, and Christina was pulled inside and then pushed down onto the settee. The door was closed behind them before her sisters settled around her, all their eyes coming to rest upon her. It was an eerie feeling, and Christina did not much care for it.

Jules, the oldest and most rational sister of them, smiled at her softly. "Christina, we only wish to speak to you to ensure that you—"

"You cannot marry him!" Leonora interrupted, the pulse at the base of her neck beating wildly as she shook her head. "You simply cannot!"

Christina could understand her sister's concern considering what she herself had been through recently; however, she had made up her mind and would not be swayed.

"Why not?" Harry inquired, a bit of a frown coming to her face as she looked from one sister to the other.

Leonora gaped at her for a moment, then inhaled a deep breath, trying to calm herself down. Indeed, she had never been impulsive, but rather calm and collected, thinking everything through before taking a single step. Every once in a while, it had been rather maddening to wait for Leonora to make up her mind. Today, however, was different. "She hardly knows him," she began, her voice trembling and a bit of hesitancy in the way she spoke as though she did not quite know what she wanted to say. "In fact, she does not know him at all. They have barely said two words to each other. The only reason we are even here discussing this is because they were discovered alone together."

A wide smile came to Harry's face. "Precisely," she teased, her gaze moving to Christina. "How exactly did that come to be?" Something wicked twinkled in her eyes, and Christina knew from experience that her youngest sister more often than not was like a dog with a bone once she had found something that piqued her curiosity.

Christina rolled her eyes at Harry, then turned to look at Louisa and Leonora, deciding that at the very least she ought to try and distract them from this topic. "What are you two doing here anyhow? You've both been recently married, and yet you have nothing better to do than to call on your little sister early in the day? Leonora, you should be on your honeymoon. Does your husband not object to you spending all your time here with us?"

Leonora shook her head. "Of course, he does not. He—" She paused, and her gaze narrowed. "There are more important matters to be discussed here than my marriage. Stop trying to distract us!" She threw up her hands and looked at Louisa for the two of them had always been close in the same way Christina and Harry had.

Louisa nodded, coming to Leonora's defense. "She is right, Chris,"

Louisa said with a bit of a chuckle. "You know we need to talk about this. You did not truly expect us to simply accept this madness and—"

Christina laughed. "What madness? You two are the ones to talk. Have you not both found husbands in...how shall we say it?...most unusual ways? Did you truly expect me to be an exception?"

"We married men we love," Leonora objected, exchanging a knowing look with Louisa. "Are you telling us you're in love with him? How could that be possible?"

Chuckling, Christina shook her head. "Of course, I'm not in love with him. However, I have my reasons as you have had yours. Why can you not respect that?"

Harriet scooted forward in her seat, curiosity sparking in her green eyes. "What exactly happened last night?" she asked, looking from Leonora to Christina. "I admit I am terribly disappointed that I was not there to see it."

Heaving a deep sigh, Christina gave a brief recollection of what had transpired the day before, frowning when she realized that sharing the mere necessities of how she had retreated to the library and how he had come upon her there made it seem quite uneventful.

Yet it had not been.

Not for her.

Had it been for him?

Christina felt her breath momentarily lodge in her throat as she recalled how close they had stood in that moment. She could still feel his hands upon her, those emerald eyes of his looking down at her, seeing more than she wanted him to see. She remembered that teasing smile upon his lips and the way she had all but swayed toward him. More than anything, Christina remembered her regret upon being interrupted. Would he have kissed her if the door had not been flung open? Would she have let him?

"I admit, Leonora has a point," Louisa stated, reaching out to pat her sister's hand, to which Leonora responded with a grateful smile. "Quite frankly, I have never heard you speak well of the man. On the contrary, you seem to loathe the very sight of him." Louisa's green eyes looked deeply into hers, demanding an answer, demanding the truth.

Juliet cast a somewhat placating smile around her small circle. "Is he not the man you thought him to be?" she asked gently, turning to look at Christina. "Or—?"

"Wait!" Harriet interjected, holding up a hand to stop everyone in their thoughts. "Are you only marrying him so he cannot marry Sarah?"

All her sisters' jaws collectively dropped open.

Christina shrugged. "It is a good plan. Frankly, the best one I could come up with."

Leonora stared at her, her cheeks paling. "It is not a good plan! It is not even a plan at all! It is foolishness! It is madness!" Her hands began to tremble, and once more Louisa settled her own steady ones upon hers, offering comfort.

Louisa then turned her inquisitive gaze to Christina. "Are you serious? You're only marrying him to protect Sarah?" Slowly, she shook her head. "Believe me, I, too, want to see her happily married, but not at the price of your own happiness. If this man is so awful that you fear for her, should she be forced to marry him," anxiety darkened her eyes, and she once more shook her head from side to side as though hoping the movement would convince Christina, "how are you not afraid? Are you not worried about yourself?"

Christina swallowed, struggling to maintain the lighthearted, unconcerned expression upon her face. She did not want her sisters to worry. She did not want them to know that, yes, of course, she was worried. Despite the temptation Mr. Sharpe presented, she could not be certain of his character nor of the way he would treat her once she was his wife.

The past night, Christina had struggled to keep her thoughts focused on her accomplishment—she had found a way to save Sarah!—and away from the uncertain future now looming in front of her. A future with a man she knew little about. Of course, she had heard whispers about men of his kind. Whispers that suggested they were far different from the gentlemen she had grown up with. A part of Christina knew that these were only rumors spread by gossips. They were not necessarily the truth. People could not be judged according to superficial aspects. Although she knew so, she could not help but hear those whispers repeated in her head, and they made her wonder.

Were the smiles Mr. Sharpe had thus far bestowed upon her

genuine? Did they speak to his character? Or were they simply a mask, like the one Lord Gillingham had worn? He had seemed like a gentleman, and yet it had been he who had attacked Leonora. Was that not proof that those deemed gentlemen could possess equally dark souls? And that men of Mr. Sharpe's kind could be...decent and respectful and treat a lady the way she deserved?

Christina wanted it to be possible. She wanted it to be true, and yet she knew she did not honestly believe so. Because if she did, would she then not have let Sarah marry Mr. Sharpe? Would then Sarah not have been safe with him? Indeed, the only reason for why Christina had intervened had been because she believed him be a horrible scoundrel, had it not?

Feeling her sisters' eyes upon her, Christina focused her energy upon appearing unconcerned. The corners of her mouth once more drew upward, and she smiled at them, giving a quick wave with her hand, dismissing their concerns. "You all know that Sarah is all but a delicate flower. She would never be able to handle a man like Mr. Sharpe. I, on the other hand, have lots of experience dealing with... challenging personalities." She lifted her brows in challenge and looked at each and every one of them.

Harriet snorted with a grin. "Who are you calling a challenging personality?"

They all laughed, and Christina could see that her sisters were not convinced.

Leonora heaved a deep sigh, her hands still trembling. "Even if you marry Mr. Sharpe, it will not save Sarah forever." She exchanged a knowing look with Louisa. "One of these days, her parents will find a suitor who cannot be discouraged. Who knows who that will be? And what then?"

Christina gritted her teeth, upset with her sister for bringing this up in her moment of triumph. "Don't you think I know that? Of course, I know that. However, this is the best I can do now. Tomorrow, I shall try and find Sarah a suitor deserving of her." She looked at all of her sisters. "I would appreciate your help."

Juliet nodded, that maternal smile once more upon her lips as she looked from one sister to the other. "Of course, we will do what we can. However, today, we are concerned for you. What did Mother and Father say to this?"

"Surely they are not forcing you to accept his hand," Louisa remarked with no more than a slight frown. "They would not do that!"

"Of course not," Christina confirmed. "In fact, they have spoken to me in much the same way you are. They've asked me to reconsider, to take my time and think this through carefully, to not make any rash decisions that cannot be undone." Indeed, speaking to her parents earlier this morning, Christina had felt all but discouraged upon leaving their chambers. Her mother's words had been disconcertingly final as though agreeing to marry Mr. Sharpe was something akin to accepting a death sentence. Could it be?

"And?" Leonora prompted.

Christina gave her an exasperated look. "And I told them what I'm telling you now. I've made my decision."

Leonora shot to her feet and began to pace in front of the window, wringing her hands and casting the occasional disbelieving look at Christina.

"Perhaps we should—" Louisa began when a knock sounded on the door.

A moment later, their butler appeared in its frame and announced that Mr. Sharpe was here to see Christina.

The sisters drew in a collective breath, their eyes slightly widened as they all turned to look at Christina. Leonora seemed dangerously close to arguing with her, but then clamped her lips shut. Louisa hurried to her side and drew her close. "We shall leave you alone to speak to him," Louisa told Christina, a warning look in her eyes. "I suggest you try to get to know the man you agreed to marry."

Christina nodded and then watched her sisters one by one leave the room. She, too, rose to her feet and stepped over to the window, inhaling a deep breath in order to prepare herself to face Mr. Sharpe once more. As before, Christina felt torn in two different directions. A part of her felt a deep sense of unease while another almost tingled with anticipation. This was odd, was it not?

Footsteps echoed to her ears, and then a familiar voice spoke out from behind her. "If I am not at all mistaken, your sisters loathe the very sight of me. I assume, you've shared your own unflattering opinion?" A teasing tone rang in his voice, and as Christina turned to face him, she could not help but smile.

With him, it seemed she never knew what to expect, and she was not quite certain whether she liked that...or not.

Chapter Twelve
IRRITATINGLY TEMPTING

Thorne could not help but stare at Lady Christina as he used his boot to push closed the door behind him. She was beautiful; the early sun shone in through the window and sent golden sparks dancing across her silken tresses. Her eyes were wide and focused solely on him, and Thorne had to admit he quite liked it that way. A hint of nervousness lingered, and he could see the pulse at the base of her neck beating a little faster than he would have expected.

Then her gaze moved from him past his shoulder, and she crossed her arms over her chest in a bit of a chiding gesture. "For propriety's sake, the door is supposed to remain open," she instructed as one would an unruly child.

Thorne laughed and took a step into the room. "As you are well aware I am most ignorant of society's rules. Care to instruct me?"

A smile teased her lips as she did her best to fight it down. "Your behavior is outrageous, Sir."

He moved toward her. "Nevertheless, I cannot fail to notice that you are not *insisting* I open the door. Why is that?" He held her gaze, enjoying the way indecision sparked in her eyes. She regarded him carefully, curiously, quite the same way he was looking at her. After all, they were strangers, and yet they were to be married soon. There was much to learn about the other, much to know and discover.

"Why are you here?" Lady Christina asked instead of answering his question. Neither did she step toward the door in order to open it.

Thorne could not help but chuckle. "I came to speak to my future bride," he teased, delighted to see a soft rosy shine come to her cheeks. Still, she held his gaze unflinchingly, a touch of anger lighting up those blue eyes of hers.

"You've come to tease me?" she remarked, giving him one of those haughty looks he had come to expect from her. Indeed, it seemed it was her way of teasing him.

"I have come to see if you've changed your mind," he said lightly. Nevertheless, he felt a hint of tightness growing in his chest as he waited for her to answer.

She regarded him curiously and then took a step toward him, making a statement and showing him that he was not the one leading this conversation, that she was an equal participant. "Why would you think I changed my mind?"

Thorne shrugged. "Quite frankly, we both know why we find ourselves in this situation, do we not? Had we not been discovered, none of this would have happened." He took note of the slight rise and fall of her chest as she inhaled a deep breath, the way her gaze did not fall from his but...perhaps wanted to? Did he make her nervous? "I willingly admit that I know very little about *your* social circle; however, I have heard that it is not uncommon that in order to save the family's reputation, young women are often forced to accept proposals they would otherwise wish to refuse." He held her gaze, daring her to speak her mind, to be truthful with him. He knew very well that she had not agreed to marry him out of affection. He was no fool! Nonetheless, he was selfish upon occasion. He had been selfish that night. The night before. He knew he wanted her, but selfishly, he also wanted her to want him back.

Of course, she did not.

Not right now.

Not yet.

But perhaps one day she would.

Only he was certain the path to her affections was found in open words. If he was to have any chance of proving her wrong, proving her impression of him wrong, then he needed to speak to her openly. She needed to know that he was not the kind of man Lord Hartmore was. The kind of man he had seen among the *ton* far too often. Men who dominated others through fear. Men who did as they wished with no regard for others. Was that not what had forced Miss Mortensen into this unbearable situation? Was it not precisely the accusation Lady Christina had placed at her friend's father's feet?

Selfishly, Thorne needed her to know that he was not such a man.

"My father would never force my hand," Lady Christina insisted, her voice hard and determined, a whisper of outrage in the way she spoke. Clearly, he had offended her by suggesting that her father would go over her head and decide her future without consulting her. Indeed, Thorne had never believed it to be so, but it was good to know that Lord Whickerton was the kind of man Thorne had thought him to be.

A man he could respect.

"Perhaps there are other reasons?" he continued, allowing a wide grin to show upon his face as he sauntered closer. "In fact, you yourself have more than once described me as the worst sort of man." He stopped an arm's length in front of her, noting the way her eyes followed his every movement. "Why then would you agree to marry me?"

Her jaw hardened, and a fiery glare came to her eyes. "We were compromised," she replied flatly as though he was a fool for asking such a question. "I have little choice in the matter."

Thorne chuckled. "You don't strike me as the kind of woman who bends to societal pressure," he mused, noting a strange shadow pass over her face as though, once, perhaps long ago, she had.

She did not drop her eyes, their deep blue like ice, hard and unbreakable. "Why are you asking me all these questions?"

"To make out your character," Thorne echoed her words from their first conversation, delighting in the slight eye roll she gave him. "After all, how am I to know if you're the kind of woman I want for a wife?"

Lady Christina laughed. "That you should have thought about before cornering me in the library."

He frowned. "I did not corner you."

"Yes, you did." She stepped toward him, indignation in her tone as she shook her head at him. "You could have left, but you didn't."

He grinned. "Neither did you." He looked down at her, noting the exact moment when she realized how close they were standing. Her eyes widened ever so slightly, and she drew in a somewhat unsteady breath. "You stayed as well."

She swallowed, and for a split-second, her gaze moved from his. "I did not have my slippers, so I—"

"That is nothing but an excuse," Thorne accused, enjoying this small back-and-forth far more than anything else since coming to London. He had thought the city dull and full of pretentious people. He still did. Only now, he had found a ray of sunshine in the fog and he would hold on to her for as long as he could.

Her mouth dropped open in outrage. "An excuse? How dare you—?"

"Then why did you stay?" Thorne demanded, lowering his head no more than a fraction. Still, it was enough, and he could see the effect of his closeness upon her face. Could she see the same in him? For his own heart seemed to be doing somersaults as well. Never before had he known anyone this...exciting.

Tempting.

Irritating!

"You knew even better than I," he continued when she opened her mouth, no doubt to contradict him, "what consequences there would be should we be discovered. Yet you stayed, accepting the risk. Why?"

"I told you why!" she snapped, then inhaled deeply, a hint of annoyance in her gaze. Not with him though, but with herself.

A moment later, the anger vanished from her features, and Thorne was surprised to see even a small smile curl up her lips. Ought he to be wary? Was this some sort of trick or manipulation?

"Let us be clear about something," Lady Christina said sweetly. "The only reason I agreed to marry you is to protect my friend, and the only reason you wish to marry me is to gather support for your ambitions. Let's not pretend this is anything else than what it is." She fluttered her eyelashes at him teasingly, then turned and walked over to the settee and sat down. "Shall I call for tea?"

Ignoring her question, Thorne laughed, then sank into the armchair opposite her. "You think you know exactly what this is?"

A slight furrow came to her forehead. "This? Do you mean our impending nuptials?"

Grinning at her, Thorne nodded, certain she knew exactly what he was talking about. It seemed his future wife enjoyed playing games. Indeed, the look in her eyes told him so for he could not help but think that she was not at all opposed to the idea of marrying him. Perhaps this thought was a bit presumptuous of him. Still, Thorne could not help but think that despite the circumstances of how they had found themselves tied to one another, the union would be a successful one.

"Of course," Lady Christina replied rather haughtily. She folded her hands in her lap, her gaze meeting his openly as she spoke with a calm he doubted she felt. "Marriage like most things in life is governed by rules. Two parties finding mutual benefit in such a union agree to—"

"Is this truly the kind of marriage you wish to have?" Thorne interrupted as he leaned forward resting his elbows upon his knees. "You cannot tell me that as a little girl you dreamed of a mutually beneficial agreement." He laughed, eyeing her curiously.

Lady Christina cast him a bit of a glaring look, but momentarily refused to answer. Was it that she did not wish to lose her temper in his presence? After all, the pulse at the base of her neck beat as rapidly as before.

"If that were the case," Thorne continued, wondering how far he could push her before she erupted like a volcano, "then why did you seek to protect your friend from me? After all, our agreement would've been mutually beneficial. Why did you interfere?"

Her lips thinned, and she lifted her chin a fraction, giving him the impression that she was suddenly looking down upon him. "You simply do not deserve her," she said calmly; still, a touch of anger resonated in her voice that she could not quite seem to quell. "We are not all equally capable to treat such a union as a business agreement." Her brows rose pointedly.

"May I ask," Thorne began, curious to see what she would say, "what precisely do you object to? Yes, I know you despise my upbringing and my lack of manners. That much we have already established. However, I doubt it is enough to persuade you to think so ill of me. What then?"

Her lips parted as though she wished to respond immediately. Then, however, she paused, her soft blue eyes trailing over his features as though suddenly uncertain that she knew the answer to his question. A deep sigh followed, and then she spoke, "Did you not notice? Not even once?"

Thorne frowned. "Notice what?"

Sighing, she shook her head. "Of course not," she mumbled more to herself than to him. "Whenever you drew near," she continued, her voice no harder than before, "Sarah paled, her hands began to tremble and she all but tried to flee your presence." Her gaze held his for a long moment, challenge lighting up those blue depths. "Did you never notice?"

Thorne swallowed, sensing how deeply his answer mattered to her. "Of course, I did. Despite what you may believe, I am not a heartless ogre. I did not set out to ruin your friend's life."

"Then why did you not retreat?" she asked, another furrow adding to her forehead. "Once you knew that she did not wish to marry you, why did you insist upon the union?"

Thorne shook his head. "I did no such thing. Yes, I entered into negotiations with her father, but that was all. No agreement had been reached yet and, quite frankly," he inhaled a slow breath, "I was beginning to have doubts. Yes, I did notice her reluctance, and, of course, I wondered why. However, as you said it, most times she all but seemed to flee my presence."

A slight chuckle drifted from her lips. "Did that truly surprise you?"

Thorne threw up his hands. "Am I such a hideous monster that it would be only natural for me to expect any woman to run from me?" To his surprise, at his question, Lady Christina's gaze fell from his. Only briefly. Only for a split-second. It was enough, though.

A slow smile spread over Thorne's face, and he could see that she knew he had noticed. He pushed to his feet, his gaze lingering upon her slightly downturned head, and stepped around the coffee table until he stood next to her. Then he slowly lowered himself onto the settee beside her, his gaze seeking hers. "Look at me."

The muscles in her jaw worked as she fought to maintain her composure. Moments ticked by, and then she moved her gaze to meet his, something unflinching and determined in those blue eyes of hers. "Well?"

Thorne smiled and inched closer until barely a hair's breadth separated his knee from hers. "Do you *not* consider me a hideous monster?" he teased, delighting in the soft rosy glow that darkened her cheeks.

She huffed out an exasperated breath, then rolled her eyes at him for good measure. "I would not call you *hideous*, no. Monster, however—"

Thorne laughed. "Not hideous. My, what a compliment!" He shifted and his knee briefly bumped against hers. Her eyes narrowed, and Thorne's grin deepened. "Does that then mean that you think me strikingly handsome?"

This time, it was Lady Christina's turn to laugh, the look in her eyes growing livelier as she shook her head. "Strikingly handsome? Please, do not flatter yourself."

"Extremely good-looking then," Thorne offered, not for a second thinking she would agree with him. Yet he was quite certain he did not even want her to.

Her brows rose and fell in that way of hers that made it look as though a little wave had rolled over her features. "*Barely passable* would be closer to the truth." Thorne could see that she was lying and also that she knew him to be aware of it. Still, she continued, "Your eyes are too close together, and their color..." She leaned closer, softly shaking her head. "It seems pale and unimpressive. What a shame!"

"Even if that were the case—"

"It is!"

Thorne nodded. "Yes, let's pretend you're right and assume my features are *barely passable*, would that then be reason enough for you to think me a monster, unworthy of your friend? Indeed, what is it that you fear? That I would devour her? That I would lock her up in the highest tower and never let her go free again?" He chuckled.

Lady Christina, however, did not smile or laugh. Indeed, an oddly serious expression came to her face, and she scooted away from him on the settee. "My objections are not with your features, but with your conduct."

Thorne frowned. "What precisely are you accusing me of?"

To his surprise, Lady Christina shot to her feet and quickly put a few paces between them. "Of course, you wouldn't understand. Only a gentleman would—"

"Yes!" Thorne hissed as he rose to his feet and followed in her wake, his eyes fixed upon hers as though he were a predator and she, his prey. "I am not a gentleman, so you have said many, many times."

"It is the truth," she defended herself, and he could see that his approach unsettled her. Was it his nearness? Nonetheless, only moments ago they had sat next to one another upon the settee. Or was it perhaps the look in his eyes? Was she worried? Worried that he would do...what?

Stopping an arm's length away from her, Thorne lowered his head a fraction to better look into her eyes. "Whatever does that mean? What is it that makes me *not* a gentleman? My common background? My—?"

Lady Christina shook her head. "It is not that!" she snapped as though he had just insulted her. "However, it all pertains to how you were raised, how you grew up and what values and morals you were taught. You do not even know which way you give offense. You do not know how to speak to a lady. You do not know how to treat a lady. You are not the kind of man I could abide marrying my friend." She swallowed and then lifted her chin, holding his gaze without flinching.

Thorne smiled at her as he inched closer, seeing the minuscule widening of her eyes. "Yet" he whispered softly, "*you* agreed to marry me."

Chapter Thirteen

A FAR CRY FROM A GENTLEMAN

C hristina felt her stomach do flip-flops and somersaults until she felt queasy and slightly lightheaded. He stood so close, so very close, and his eyes were such a deep shade of green that she could have lost herself in them. Nonetheless, his words were teasing and challenging and put her on her guard. Despite his easy smile and quick humor, Christina was certain that Mr. Thorne Sharpe was a dangerous man.

Perhaps she truly ought to reconsider.

Perhaps.

"You cannot intimidate me," Christina snapped, only her voice sounded all but strong. In fact, she could not help but despise the slight tremble she heard with her own ears.

That slow smile once again curled up the corners of his mouth as he inched another fraction closer, no doubt fully aware of how deeply his presence unsettled her. "I have no wish to intimidate you. Far from it." He exhaled a slow breath, and she could feel it brush against her lips. Faintly. Just faintly. And it sent a thrilling shiver down her back. A shiver *he* was also fully aware of for the right corner of his mouth quirked upward in acknowledgment.

"Why did you come here today?" Christina asked simply to have something to say, something that would fill the quiet and the strange sizzling in the air between them as though something were on fire.

"Did I not already answer that question?"

Christina sighed exasperatedly. "And that is precisely why you are not a gentleman."

Mr. Sharpe frowned. "Because I refuse to answer the same question twice?"

Once more, Christina felt her anger flare and she gritted her teeth to tamp it down. "Because you refuse to play along in order to protect a lady's sensibilities." Indeed, saying it out loud made it sound almost nonsensical.

That irritating grin of his returned. "Are you saying you, my dearest Christina, have sensibilities? That is indeed a shocking notion and quite removed from the truth, would you not agree?"

Christina wanted to sink into a hole in the ground. Never before had she encountered a man as blunt and unaware of society's unwritten rules as him.

Before she could say anything, Mr. Sharpe laughed. "I did it again, didn't I?" His gaze searched hers. "Before, you did not truly wish for me to answer your question *again* but were merely using it as a distraction." His eyes remained on hers as he spoke, searching, contemplating. "A distraction from what?" he mused before that knowing smile once more returned.

Heaven help her, but this man was infuriating!

"I believe you should leave," Christina hastened to say before he could read more on her face. Never before had she noticed how expressive it had to be. Could others do the same? Read her thoughts on her face? Or was it only him?

She made to turn away, but his hand closed over her arm, holding her back. His touch made her head snap back around, her eyes wide as she looked up at him, uncertain what she feared, or perhaps wanted, to see.

Looking down at her, he pulled her closer, something annoyingly victorious flashing in his green eyes. "I'm making you nervous, not because you fear me, but because..." He broke off, and his brows rose meaningfully.

For a long moment, they simply stood there, his hand wrapped around her arm, keeping her in place. In truth, it was wholly unnecessary for Christina had no wish to be anywhere else. Yes, Mr. Sharpe frustrated her to no end. She despised him...or at least tried to. Nevertheless, there was something...

She could not help but think that...

He almost looked as though...

"Will you change your mind?" Mr. Sharpe whispered gently, his gaze holding hers as he waited patiently. Or did he? Out of the corner of her eye, Christina took note of the rapid beating of his pulse, speaking against the inner calm he was portraying.

"No."

A small smile began to form upon his face. "Are you certain?"

"Yes," she replied without hesitation, wondering how she could for her own pulse was beating as fast as his.

His smile deepened. "Good," he said as though her answer had truly brightened his day. "Then I suppose we will be married soon." His voice was soft and teasing, and Christina could sense hidden meaning dancing upon each and every word.

"I suppose so." Despite the shiver that danced down her spine, Christina did not drop her gaze. He made her nervous. He made her feel all kinds of things she had never experienced before. He also made her want to stand tall. It was as though every word from him was a challenge, and to her surprise, it seemed as though he did not wish for her to back down. Indeed, he did not seem like an ogre, determined to get his way, to intimidate others into submission.

Perhaps she had been wrong about him. Perhaps he would prove to be a somewhat decent man. The thought had occurred to Christina before; only it was always swiftly followed by doubt because if Mr. Sharpe proved to be a decent man after all, should she then not allow him to marry her friend? Would he then not be a good husband for Sarah?

"I shall speak to your father," he told her, his eyes still lingering upon her face as though expecting her to faint or lose her temper at any moment. "Are you hoping for a grand wedding?"

"Not at all," Christina replied, uncertain what exactly she was hoping for. Yes, she had often heard other debutantes gush about elaborate wedding celebrations. Christina herself, though, had never entertained such ambitions. She had always kind of pictured her future husband, imagined the kind of man he would be, the way he would look at her. Was that not what was important? To find oneself married to someone who...

Her thoughts trailed off, and a deep sigh left her lips. The Whickertons married for love, did they not? Her parents had. As had her grandparents. And now, Louisa and Leonora were both happily married as well, married to men they genuinely loved.

I'm breaking with tradition, Christina thought to herself, feeling a pang of guilt, of remorse. Always had her parents encouraged her to follow her heart.

Again, Christina recalled the day Aunt Francine had come to Whickerton Grove all those years ago. The day still seemed as clear to Christina as it had back then. She remembered well Aunt Francine's despair over the decision forced upon her. Yet Aunt Francine had chosen herself, her own will, her right to be the master of her own destiny. She had not bowed her head, and Christina could not help but feel as though she was disappointing everyone by agreeing to a marriage she did not genuinely want. She had given up her passion in order to find happiness in marriage, had she not? To ensure that her family would never be lost to her? Still, she was marrying Mr. Sharpe for fairly rational reasons, was that not so?

She was marrying him to protect Sarah.

She was marrying him to avoid a scandal.

She was marrying him to—

Christina blinked, finding those expressive eyes of his searching hers. How long had she been standing here, staring at nothing? Had he said anything to her? Had she failed to respond?

"Are you all right?" he asked gently, reaching out a hand to brush a curl from her forehead. The tips of his fingers never brushed her skin, but she could feel their soft pressure as he trailed them along her hair, his fingers curling downward behind her ear. Still, he withdrew his hand before his fingers reached the slope of her neck.

Awareness trailed down Christina's spine, and her gaze remained fixed upon his, her breath lodged in her throat as she continued to wonder if perhaps a small part of her *did* want to marry him.

Christina cleared her throat. "Yes, I'm perfectly fine. What were you saying?"

The teasing smile once more appeared upon his face, and she could not help but think that he was rather delighted with her distractedness. "I was asking you how soon the wedding should take place. I've heard that sometimes a special license is procured in these situations; however, if you would rather wait three weeks..." His voice trailed off; but the way he lifted and arched his brows, his mesmerizing eyes sparking with something wicked, made Christina smile.

"You're impossible," she laughed, shaking her head at him.

He grinned. "Am I? Careful or I might come to think that you do not loathe me nearly as much as you would like me to believe." Again, his hand reached out and he captured the end of a curl between thumb and forefinger, giving it a slight tug. "When you look at me like that, someone who does not know you might even think you're beginning to like me."

Christina closed her eyes, for she could not help the smile that stretched traitorously across her face. "Like what?" she demanded, meeting his eyes once again, knowing that not doing so would only encourage him, give him the wrong impression.

Again, his fingers gave her curl a soft tug as though he wanted to urge her closer. "Well, I did not fail to notice that your eyes are no longer shooting daggers at me. Instead, there is a very fetching soft glow upon your cheeks, and I cannot help but wonder if perhaps...I put it there." His brows lifted into arches, the look in his eyes conveying even more than his words had.

Christina could not deny that in all likelihood Mr. Sharpe was correct. Still, that did not mean she had to say it out loud. Instead, she chuckled, pulling her curl free. "I must say for a man who is generally considered not to be a gentleman you certainly think quite highly of yourself."

Grinning, he shrugged. "Well, you cannot deny," he whispered, slowly lowering his head closer to hers, "there is something between us, can you? You feel it too, do you not?"

Christina pressed her lips into a bit of a thin line, feigning ignorance. "Feel what?"

Holding her gaze, he waited. Then he said, "Honestly, it would make everything a lot easier if you simply admitted to it."

Christina frowned; yet her pulse seemed to quicken. "Admit what?"

His grin deepened, and his hand suddenly reached out, slipped around her waist and pulled her against him.

Christina exhaled a sharp breath, her eyes locked onto his. "You... You should not be doing this." She had meant to chide him, to put him in his place, yet her words came out breezy and hesitant.

"Because it is not proper?" he asked, and she could feel his breath against her lips. "Or because you do not like it?"

Christina gritted her teeth. "Why do you always tease me so? Why do you demand an answer when you can see that—?" She clamped her lips shut, afraid to say too much, to reveal too much. Indeed, his closeness was addling her mind. She could not think clearly. If she was not careful, she might admit that she—

That she what?

"You're trying to be upset with me," Mr. Sharpe whispered as one hand slipped from her waist and reached up to grasp her chin. He gave it a soft pinch, another teasing gesture, another challenging gesture. "Yet you're failing miserably."

Christina hated that daring gleam in his eyes, that victorious glimmer as though they had been opponents locked in battle and he knew her to be weaker, he knew she would eventually admit defeat. "I was right," she snapped, lifting her hands in order to push him away. "You are the most infuriating, irritating and—"

"And you like me," he whispered, his fingers holding onto her chin, resisting her attempts to push him away. "No matter what you're trying to tell yourself, to convince yourself of, you like me."

In shock, Christina stared at him as his words continued to echo in her head. Was it true? Did she? Yes, perhaps, there was some kind of redeeming quality in him, something that made him *tolerable*, something that—

He chuckled. "Don't look so shocked." Then a soft frown came to his face. "You truly didn't know, did you?"

"No!" Christina exclaimed before she could stop herself. Instantly, she felt heat rush to her cheeks, finally giving her the strength or rather the determination to break free, to remove his hands from her body and step back. "I mean, no, I do not. I didn't mean to say that I did not know because I cannot know what is not..." Clamping her lips shut against the embarrassing babble that came out of her mouth, Christina felt her hands ball into fists.

"I like you as well," he said rather unexpectedly.

Christina's head snapped up and she stared at him. She could not deny the warmth that began to fill her heart at his words, wondering why it was there when it had not been before. Did she seek his affections? "You... You like me?" She wasn't quite certain what she was asking or why. The moment itself seemed strangely surreal, and she did not quite know what to do with it.

Taking a step toward her, he nodded. "Is that wrong of me? Do gentlemen not *like* the women they are to marry?" That teasing grin returned to his face. "Would you not consider that foolish? To find yourself, gentleman or not, betrothed to a most exceptional woman and not be glad for it?"

Focusing on evening her breathing, Christina looked at him, wanting to believe his words, wanting to believe that despite everything he was glad to marry her.

Her.

Not her family or her family's connections.

But her.

Again, his hand reached out and tugged upon one of her curls. "I cannot help but think that we shall get along splendidly, you and I."

Christina could not help but agree, at least quietly. Was she a fool to do so?

A soft chuckle drifted from his lips. "Goodbye, until we meet again, Chris."

At the sound of the nickname her family used for her, Christina felt her eyes narrowing almost reflexively. "Do not call me that!" she chided, once again feeling the sudden need to put him in his place and uphold her own. Mr. Sharpe had a way of distracting her, confusing her even, that she could not help but feel that she might lose herself if she were not careful. Indeed, he was a dangerous man!

"Why?" he demanded in that casual way of his that Christina was slowly coming to expect from him. "I've heard your sisters call you that. Do you not like it?"

Christina shot him a challenging look. "They are my sisters. You're not."

He chuckled. "But I am to be your husband." Again, he inched closer, another challenging look lighting up his eyes. "Am I not also permitted to use it?"

Christina could not deny that a part of her, deep, deep down, did not oppose his suggestion. She had always liked being called Chris. It was unconventional and daring and unique for a woman to have such a nickname. At least, outside of her family. Only she was not certain if it would be wise to allow him to use it...just yet. Perhaps she ought to make him work for it. "I shall think on it," she finally told him in a rather haughty manner.

As expected, he seemed to find her reaction amusing, another one of those infuriating chuckles leaving his lips. "By all means." He grinned at her, and then...

...then he leaned forward and gently brushed a kiss onto her cheek.

It was fleeting and brief and utterly chaste, and Christina felt as though any moment now her heart might jump from her chest. A strange sensation rolled through her body, teasing her skin and almost drawing the air from her lungs. Never before, had she felt so overwhelmed.

And Mr. Sharpe knew it. The dreaded man knew it! The teasing grin upon his face attested to it as he pulled back and his eyes once more met hers. "See you soon, Chris," he whispered, issuing yet another challenge before he stepped away and left the room.

With her knees suddenly feeling beyond weak, Christina sank down onto the settee, trying her best to restore her sense of balance and composure. Was this what the rest of her life would look like? Married to such a man? Would they forever be teasing and testing one another?

In the back of her mind, an annoyingly honest voice whispered, *would you mind?*

Chapter Fourteen

TWO PEOPLE

Only a day had passed since Thorne had last seen his future bride; yet something within him was beyond impatient to see her. He had not felt this sense of restlessness in a long time. In fact, he had spent years taming that impulsive spirit that lived within him. Day by day, he had struggled with himself, urged himself to think first and act later, to not rush into things. Over time, he had felt himself calm, his pulse no longer spiking in the way it used to.

Indeed, it had been a long time since anything had brought him this kind of thrill as though fire burned in his veins, making it impossible for him to remain still.

"May I ask why you have come?" Lord Whickerton asked calmly as he eyed Thorne across the expanse of his desk. The man's eyes portrayed the same calm as Thorne's no doubt did, while a sense of apprehension lingered in his voice.

"I apologize for any faux pas I may have committed," Thorne replied, allowing an easy smile to spread over his face. For a reason he could not name, he did not feel the need to uphold any sort of pretense with Lord Whickerton. "As you may know, I am not well acquainted with society's rules. However, I assure you it is not intended as an insult to you or your daughter."

Although the other man's face remained rather impassive, Thorne could not help but think that his open words were well-received. "Thus far, I cannot find fault in you." He paused, and his brows rose meaningfully. "At least not today."

Thorne nodded. "Yes, it would seem my conduct the other night was far from appropriate." Nevertheless, Thorne could not deny that if he could change the night he had compromised Christina, he would not. "However, now I am here to do what is considered honorable."

Lord Whickerton regarded him carefully, fingers steepled. "Is that the only reason you are here?"

"Quite frankly," Thorne replied after a moment of consideration, "I do not have any regrets. I wish to marry your daughter because she is an exceptional woman, unlike any I have ever met."

Slowly, Lord Whickerton nodded. "I see," he said rather ominously, and Thorne could not help but wonder if indeed the man understood Thorne's motivation. "My daughter has informed me that neither one of you wishes to be married by special license."

Thorne nodded, although he could not deny that the thought of waiting three weeks for her to become his wife was becoming a little more unbearable each day. She had something alluring about her that made him think of her even when she was nowhere around. He kept wondering about her, about what she would look like early in the morning or what dinner conversations they might have. He felt the desire to speak to her countless times throughout the day, feeling a pang of regret when he realized that it was impossible. Indeed, when he had spoken to her the day before, he had returned home with an absolutely elated feeling. However, he had quickly fallen from that height as though only her continued presence was able to lift his spirits in such a way. Even now, he all but hungered to lay eyes upon her again, to hear her voice and see if he had been mistaken the day before.

Thorne doubted it very much. He had felt something between them. Something that she had refused to admit to. Yet it had been there, had it not?

"Very well," Lord Whickerton stated as he leaned forward, his gaze fixing upon Thorne. "As my daughter has apparently made up her mind, I will arrange for this wedding to take place." His voice was tight as a bowstring, and it resonated with something dangerous, threatening even. "However, I want to make it absolutely clear that you are to treat my daughter with the respect she deserves at all times. She may become your wife, but she will forever remain my daughter, and in this family, we look out for one another. Fail her, and you will come to regret ever having laid eyes upon her. I will hold you accountable in all matters. Am I understood?"

Despite the hostile note in Lord Whickerton's voice, Thorne felt his heart swell with something unknown, unfamiliar. It was something warm and soothing, something safe and caring, and a deep longing began to take hold in his heart to have someone, anyone, think of him the same way that Lord Whickerton thought of his daughter. "You have my word," Thorne vowed, pleased beyond words to see that Lord Whickerton was first and foremost a father. A father who cared for his daughter's happiness. A father who would never sell her into marriage. A father who would, in fact, *not* do anything to further his own social standing.

It was a rare trait.

Thorne held the man's gaze. "I myself have never known the meaning of family," he heard himself say without thinking, "and since coming to London, I have only ever observed faint imitations of its true meaning." He inhaled a deep breath, trying his best to hold at bay that sudden longing pulsing in his veins. "I promise that I shall do everything within my power to prove myself worthy of your daughter and the trust you are bestowing upon me."

Silence fell over the room as the two men regarded one another. Although Lord Whickerton's gaze remained contemplative, Thorne thought to see some measure of understanding develop between them. Each had expected or perhaps feared to find the other to be less than they truly were, and each had found himself surprised to discover that he had been wrong in his assumptions. "I am glad to hear it," Lord Whickerton finally said, his voice softening.

Thorne nodded. "Would you permit me to escort your daughter on a stroll through the garden? I admit, I am looking forward to speaking to her again."

Something that might have become a smile flickered over Lord

Whickerton's face; only it passed so quickly that Thorne could not be certain. "You have my permission to ask her."

"Thank you," Thorne replied with a smile of his own as Lord Whickerton reached for the bell rope. Moments later, a footman appeared and was instructed to fetch Lady Christina to her father's study.

Both men rose to their feet, and Lord Whickerton stepped around his antique-looking desk. "Who we are," he said in a voice that made Thorne listen carefully, "is determined by how we treat those deserving of our respect. That, is a man's true worth."

Holding Lord Whickerton's gaze, Thorne felt his heart all but pause in his chest as he fought to draw in a deep breath. Never before had anyone spoken to him in such a way. He had not expected to find such acceptance, such a chance to prove himself, here in London of all places, among people who were known for their shortsightedness when it came to those they deemed unworthy of their attention. Clearly, Lord Whickerton was not such a man, and Thorne's respect for him grew as did his desire to be found worthy. For all he cared, the rest of English society could look down their noses at him, but Lord Whickerton was a man whose good opinion Thorne now desired.

And then the door opened, and Christina stepped into the room, her large blue eyes widening as they fell upon him. Thorne cleared his throat and felt something deep inside hum to life.

"What are you doing here?" his intended asked bluntly before her gaze traveled to her father. "Father? Why did you ask me here?"

A warm smile came to Lord Whickerton's face as he stepped toward his daughter. "It seems your intended would like to get to know you better, my dear." His gaze moved to Thorne.

Smiling at her, Thorne stepped forward, respectfully inclining his head. "It is such a fine day. Would you like to take a stroll through the garden with me?"

Christina considered him with questioning eyes. "I suppose there is no harm in that," she finally said, the tone in her voice held doubt, though.

Indeed, from the first, it seemed that some sort of competition had existed between them. It was a constant struggle, like a tug-of-war, each of them trying to come out the victor, each of them concerned to be yanked forward and stumble into the mud.

Stepping outside into the sunshine, they both remained quiet as they made their way down the few steps from the terrace. Then they turned onto the gravel path that would guide them through the green oasis blooming in the middle of London.

Thorne could feel her glance up at him every once in a while, his own eyes straying to her as often as he dared. A strange sense of shyness lingered about them, something he had not experienced before. It was as though, all of a sudden, they both realized that this was no longer a game. This was their life, their future. It was not about winning or losing, but about finding a way to find at least some semblance of happiness.

"Your father is an impressive man," Thorne finally said, wanting her to know that he cherished the same family values...even if he had never known them. "He made it unmistakably clear that he would end me should I ever dare to cause you any unhappiness."

Whether it was the words themselves or perhaps the lightness that now lingered in his voice, Christina's face brightened instantly, a warm glow coming to those large blue eyes as they turned to look upon him. "He is very protective of us. So, you better watch yourself."

Thorne loved the warm smile upon her lips, and he nodded. "I shall consider myself warned."

"What of your family?" Christina asked unexpectedly, the ease between them suddenly palpable that the words all but flowed from her lips without thought. "Are they still in Manchester? Will they come to attend the wedding?"

Thorne stopped and shook his head. "I'm afraid they will not." Although he barely remembered them, his heart still tightened at the thought. Perhaps it was not even the parents and siblings he could barely recall. Perhaps it was the absence of a family's affections that brought on regret.

Her eyes held his, and Thorne knew that she could sense the change in his mood. "Why not?"

He swallowed. "Because they are dead."

Her face paled visibly as she stared back at him, her lips parted as though she wished to say something, but then thought better of it.

Thorne tried to smile at her. "Do not worry yourself. It happened a long time ago."

Christina swallowed. "I'm so very sorry," she said then, and the way she spoke made it more than a platitude, an offer of condolence that was expected. Indeed, the look in her eyes spoke of deepest regret and sadness as she no doubt imagined what losing her own family would have meant for her. "How did it happen?"

Thorne inhaled a deep breath, finding himself at odds with this rather unexpected situation. Never before had he shared such simple, though intimate words with another. With anyone. "My parents all but worked themselves to death, and my siblings died young as children of the poor often do." Images of their pale faces still clung to the dark corners of his mind, but he had no wish to speak of them, to conjure them. He remembered frail bodies, malnourished and weak, with eyes as wide as Christina's, but without hope or strength.

From the look upon Christina's face, Thorne could tell that his answer was not what she had expected. He could see shock, but also a certain measure of shame. "The struggles the lower classes face on a daily basis are invisible to those far removed from such a life." Although he had no wish to lay blame at her feet, he could not remain silent. Some things needed to be said, especially those that were far too often wrapped in silence.

Her head sank. "I do not know what to say," she whispered under her breath, and Thorne was glad for her honest words.

"It is not your fault, nor should you feel responsible."

Her head rose, and her large eyes found his once more. "Yet?"

Thorne frowned. Despite his words, had there been censure in his voice? Had she somehow heard the anger that still lingered within him, the same kind of anger that had brought him to London?

Turning back down the path, Thorne shook his head. "Nothing."

"It is not nothing," Christina objected, rushing to catch up with him. She placed a hand on his arm and urged him to turn back and look at her. "You meant to say something, I know you did." She lifted her chin. "Then do so."

Thorne could see the challenge in her eyes. He could feel something within himself fighting to be unleashed. Nonetheless, he knew that this was neither the time nor place.

Nor was she the intended recipient of his anger, of his outrage. He had come here today to court her as was expected of a gentleman, had he not? He had come here to get to know her, to tease her as he had the other day, to speak to her and hear her thoughts.

He had not come here today to insult her...only it would seem that he had.

Chapter Fifteen

TWO WORLDS

Christina had not expected this.

As the soft summer breeze tugged gently on her curls and skirts alike, she felt something deep inside her almost wince away from the harsh truth now all but staring her in the eyes. Shame slowly claimed her heart as she began to realize that she had never truly given much thought to those who lived outside of her own social circle. Of course, as the daughter of an earl, she had grown up shielded from the harshness of life that others knew as their daily bread. Yet she had never tried to see beyond the rim of her own little world.

Mr. Sharpe's throat worked as he stood before her, his shoulders tense and his hands moving to link behind his back. Reluctance rested in his gaze; a gaze that no longer quite met her own. Although she could see that he did not wish to discuss these matters, the words he had already spoken told her that anger still stirred within him.

Understandably so.

"It is not something I wish to discuss with you," he finally said, his voice tense and somewhat reluctant.

Christina regarded him carefully. "Nevertheless, it is the very reason why you came to London, is it not? Is that not what you said the night we were discovered in the library? That you wish to garner support? To bring about change?" Despite the slight tremble in her hands, Christina took a step toward him, her eyes open wide and fixed upon his, daring him to answer.

For a long moment, he simply looked down at her, and she could see that he was torn about what to do. The truth rested in his eyes in a way that it was unmistakable. Yet he did not speak. Why? Did he not wish to upset her? Or were common men and gentlemen the same in one regard, namely that they did not care for the thoughts of a woman?

"From the very first," Mr. Sharpe finally said, a muscle in his jaw twitching, "you told me that you held men like myself in low regard. Well, to be quite truthful, I have never thought highly of people of your kind, either." His nostrils all but flared, and Christina almost felt compelled to take a step backward. "I do not blame you, of course not; however, the gentlemen you regard so highly are the very people who could easily bring about change. If only they cared, they could end this useless suffering." Anger darkened his face, and she could see the pulse in his neck quickening like a stampede, increasing its speed as it barreled forward. "In your world, it is as though people too poor to afford food or medical help or firewood in winter do not even exist. You simply close your eyes, and everything is well." Sadness hung in his eyes, his jaw still tense with anger. "I cannot do that because when I close my eyes, all I see are starving children, their bodies battered and bruised from a life that never treated them well. Not once."

When the last word finally left his lips and silence fell over them, Christina knew that her world would never be the same again. In truth, she had known so even before he had spoken a single word. She had read it in his eyes that what he was about to say would change everything. Although she had dreaded to hear it, she had known that she could not ask him to remain silent.

After all, he was to be her husband. If he cared so deeply about this matter, then so should she. It was the way of the world. The way of *her* world. Wives supported their husbands in everything. Yes, Christina could not deny that his words had left her rattled. She could all but see the children he had spoken off, and her heart broke for them. Would she ever again be able to close her eyes and not think of the image he had conjured?

Christina doubted it.

After a long while, she lifted her head and allowed her gaze to sweep over his features in a new way, trying to see him without the prejudices that always clouded her sight. Who was he?

"I should not have said what I did," Mr. Sharpe remarked, a bitter tone in his voice as he fought to banish the look of disappointment from his face. "None of what I spoke of is your fault in any way. After all, you yourself are trapped in a world where decisions are made for you with little regard for your own wishes."

His words instantly conjured the night Aunt Francine had come to Whickerton Grove. The night Christina had learned that sacrifices were demanded of women who wished for something beyond marriage and motherhood. "My father would never force my hand," Christina insisted, remembering equally well how her parents had aided her aunt in her decision.

An approving smile came to Mr. Sharpe's face. "That I know. Indeed, your father made it unmistakably clear that the only reason he would accept me as his son-in-law was because..." His gaze held hers as he took a step closer. "I am *your* choice."

Your choice.

The words echoed in Christina's head as she stared up at him. In a way, they were true; however, Christina had never once thought of it that way. Yes, it was true that she could have refused marrying him. As she herself had said only a moment ago, her father would never have forced her hand. Even now, she was free to change her mind. If she did not choose to, she would not have to marry him.

So, in an odd way, he *was* her choice. Still, Christina had always expected her choice to feel...different. She had always expected...more. Some elated feeling. A feeling of triumph or victory even to have discovered something her heart genuinely wanted. Was he what her heart truly wanted?

Or could he be...one day?

"Have I done it now?" Mr. Sharpe teased as he regarded her carefully, curiously, the dark clouds that had lingered above his head only moments ago suddenly gone as though they had never existed. "Have I convinced you to change your mind and refuse me? You look doubtful, stunned even." He frowned, and his eyes narrowed. "What is going on in that head of yours? I admit I dearly wish to know, for it must be something quite captivating."

Christina shook off the thoughts that lingered, calling herself back to the here and now. "To be frank, I was marveling at the notion of you being my choice. It doesn't quite seem..."

"Appropriate?" he suggested, the grin upon his face widening as he watched her.

Christina nodded. "Yes. I admit I always thought choosing a husband would feel..." She shrugged. "I don't know."

The look upon his face sobered slightly, and she could see his shoulders rise and fall with a deep breath. "Is it true then? Have you changed your mind?"

Christina could not help but think that he was all but holding his breath as he waited for an answer. Yes, he dreaded her answer because he feared that she would confirm his suspicions.

A breath-stealing tingle danced down Christina's spine at the thought that he genuinely wanted to marry her, that he wanted to be her husband and that he wanted her to be his wife. She wished she could dwell upon that feeling and rein in her thoughts, keep them from straying to musings that would cause doubt and regret. Still, her thoughts could not be reined in. She had never been able to do so. They were free spirits, going where they pleased.

The truth was that, yes, he wanted her to be his wife but not because of who she was. Not because he wanted *her*. It was only her family's connections that appealed to him. He would just as easily have married Sarah had she, Christina, not come along, representing a more influential trophy to place upon his mantle.

Focusing her gaze, Christina looked up at him, into his emerald eyes, eyes that sparked with mischief and daring. She saw the slight quirk of his lips, proof of his innate playfulness despite the hardships he had suffered. He had not grown sullen and depressed. Instead, he had risen to the challenge and found a way to overcome every obstacle placed in his way. And he had done so without losing that childlike part of him, that part that still saw joy and had hope despite everything to the contrary.

It was a gift, was it not? To be able to see the world and enjoy it after everything that he knew, that he had seen?

It was humbling.

"No," Christina finally said. "I have not changed my mind." Oddly enough, she could not imagine not marrying him. Although only a few days had passed since the night in the library, the future now slowly taking shape in front of her was one she did not want to turn away from. She could not quite say why, but she knew that on some level at least she wanted it.

Perhaps she even wanted him.

In answer, that devilishly charming smile once again stretched across his face. He leaned closer, too close for propriety's sake, and all but whispered, "Are you certain? Are you not afraid that I am a heartless ogre, determined to carry you off to my black castle up in the North, to lock you up in a tower and keep you there for all the days ahead?"

Shaking her head at him, Christina laughed, loving the way his carefree words seemed to be able to chase away her rather dark and gloomy thoughts. He had a way of looking at the world that made it seem better than it truly was. How did he do it? "You are unbelievable!"

"Thank you!" He all but puffed out his chest.

"It was not meant as a compliment."

Mr. Sharpe shrugged. "Meant or not, I choose to see it that way."

Christina paused, once more regarding him most curiously. "Is that your secret?" she mumbled more to herself than him, completely unaware that she had spoken aloud.

He frowned. "My secret? What do you mean?"

Taken aback, Christina felt heat rush to her cheeks. She quickly turned away and walked a few steps down the path. Still, when she heard his footsteps behind her, she could not deny that she was glad for it. She did not truly wish to escape him or this conversation. In truth, she wanted him to come after her.

His hand settled on her arm, gently but determinedly, and pulled her to a halt. "You're not one to hide," he stated as though he had known her all her life, his eyes searching her face. Although she kept her head averted, lowered, she could feel his gaze like a caress upon her skin. "Do not do so now. Tell me what you meant."

Slowly, Christina lifted her chin, her eyes looking up into his, trying to determine whether or not he spoke truthfully. Still, thus far, everything he had said had been the truth, had it not? He was not one to use pretty words as a means to an end; at least, she hoped that he was not. "Despite everything..." She lifted her hands for a wide sweep that was to encompass everything he had told her. "You...You still smile and jest and..." Staring up at him, she shook her head. "How do you do it? What is your secret?"

The look upon his face sobered at her words, and for a moment, Christina felt regret for being the cause of it. "There is no secret," he finally said, his voice somber. "It is a choice. The choice we all need to make. Perhaps we are not aware of it, but it is the truth. We can all choose not only the path we walk on, but also how we perceive it." He heaved a deep sigh, and for a brief moment, lifted his face to the sky above. Then his gaze returned to meet hers as though he needed that connection to continue on. "There is darkness and pain and suffering everywhere, and yet there is also light and warmth and hope. We need to be aware of the first, but we need to believe in the second. How else are we to live? How else are we to know what is right and wrong? How else are we to find...happiness?"

It was in that very moment that Christina realized that everything she thought she knew about him was wrong. He was not the kind of man she had thought him to be. Yes, he was not a gentleman as far as society was concerned. Yet he possessed decency and kindness in a way she had rarely seen before. While he was not a selfless man, he had made the choice to fight for others. He was here, in London, because of it. At the same time, though, he had not allowed his thoughts to be consumed by that fight. He still knew how to find joy.

"Is that what you seek?" Christina felt compelled to ask. "Happiness?"

He grinned at her. "Don't we all?"

"In truth, I believe that very few people desire to find happiness. At least, I do not believe that they would state it in such a way. They all long for fortune and standing, for certain possessions and experiences, convinced that those things would bring them happiness. Nevertheless, I think very few people truly see happiness itself as their life's goal, their desire and wish. And I think somewhere along the way, they often forget about the happiness they worked so hard to obtain something that ultimately makes them feel hollow."

Christina blinked, surprised by the words that left her lips and found a set of dark green eyes looking down at her. A hint of confusion lingered upon his face as he watched her, no doubt equally surprised to hear her speak in such a way.

Willing a smile onto her face, Christina once more turned down the path. "Will you tell me a bit more about your life? If we are to marry, I suppose we should know a bit more about each other."

A slight chuckle rumbled in his throat, but he did not comment upon her words. He did not explain what thoughts her words had conjured. "What is it you wish to know?" He fell into step beside her, and together, they strolled along the path, the sun shining warmly upon their heads as birds trilled in the trees nearby.

"How did you grow up? Where?"

Mr. Sharpe inhaled a deep breath as though preparing himself to launch into a story that would take all his strength to tell. "I grew up in Manchester. Truthfully, I remember very little about my early childhood. I remember being hungry and cold." A wry smile came to his lips as he looked down at her and their eyes met. "Sometimes, I think I still dream of it although I cannot be certain. Dreams have a way of showing us things in a distorted fashion, do they not?"

Christina nodded, remembering the dream she had had every once in a while since the night Aunt Francine had come to Whickerton Grove all those years ago. In the dream, it was not Aunt Francine who had been forced to make a terrible choice between her own dreams and her family, but Christina instead. She had felt as though invisible forces were tugging on her arms, each pulling her in the opposite direction. She had felt torn and frightened and unable to move, to decide. It always strangely and sickeningly reminded her of people being drawn and quartered in the Middle Ages. Ripped apart by forces they had no control over.

"My mother died in childbirth when I was perhaps six or seven years old," Mr. Sharpe continued, a slight frown resting upon his brows as he tried to remember. "The babe died as well. To this day, I am not certain how many brothers and sisters I once had. They were so incredibly young when they were lost. I remember one or two faces." He turned to look at her, sadness visible in his eyes. Christina was surprised that he did not try to hide it but allowed her to see it so openly.

"I cannot imagine that," she replied, feeling her heart constrict at the thought of losing her siblings. Of course, she had known them all her life. How would she have felt if she had lost them when she had been her younger self? Would she still remember their faces? Would those memories have been lost over the years?

"Perhaps it is better this way," he continued on, his gaze once more directed ahead, his eyes focused on the past, on something deep inside. "Perhaps it is a way the mind protects itself, protects us from suffering too much. Pain needs to wane over time, or it will consume us. How are we supposed to go on if we feel it every moment of every day?"

Christina nodded. "Perhaps you're right. It is simply hard to imagine. Did you not often find yourself wondering who they might have become...had they lived?"

"Every once in a while, yes," he admitted, that wry smile once more upon his face, a testament to his determination to move forward, to not forget the past, but to focus on the future. "However, I must admit I had very little time for thinking about my childhood."

Somewhat glad to see their conversation moved to a less painful topic, Christina looked at him, eager to learn more about the man she was to marry. "Will you tell me more?"

Smiling at her, he nodded. "Well, it might shock you to hear it, but the truth is that the first real money I ever earned was through boxing matches."

Christina felt her eyes opening wide as she tried to imagine him in the ring facing an opponent. Of course, as a lady she had never even caught a glimpse of any such event. She knew that gentlemen occasionally sparred in such a way for fun and exercise. She had even heard that they would place bets on such a match. Still, standing here in her parents' grand garden, a balmy breeze brushing across her skin,

Christina could not imagine the man standing in front of her to engage in such an undoubtedly brutal pastime.

Still, for him, it had not been a pastime, had it?

Mr. Sharpe eyed her curiously; only when she did not portray the expected signs of utter shock, he continued on. "It was a good way to make money, but I knew that it was no way to live, to continue on indefinitely. I knew I needed something more permanent, something more reliable and so I started investing what little money I made boxing. I paid attention wherever I could, listened carefully, tried my best to understand the workings of the world in order to use this knowledge to my advantage." A shadow danced over his face as he spoke, belying the rational-sounding words that left his lips. "I knew I needed to find a way out of living from day to day, never knowing if I would have food the next or not." He turned to look at her. "It is a life far removed from your own, is it not?"

Christina did not know what to say. Of course, his words were true; yet admitting that it was so somehow made her feel...awful. She felt as though she had failed someone.

Meeting his eyes, she took a step back, then let her gaze sweep over his face, the way he stood before her, proud, and yet approachable, something men of the ton generally were not. "I thought you a scoundrel," she told him honestly, deciding that if indeed she was going to move forward with this marriage, she would be honest from here on out. "I thought you a blackguard with no manners and no decency."

Amusement resonated in the chuckle that left his lips as he smiled at her, and Christina realized that she was not at all surprised that he was not offended by her words. In truth, she had not expected him to be. "And I," Mr. Sharpe stated, something daring once more lighting up his eyes, "thought all upper-class ladies to be simpering misses, empty-headed and with false smiles upon their faces." Holding her gaze, he grinned at her. "Perhaps we were both wrong."

Christina could not deny that a part of her still urged her to be cautious, to not place her trust in him and believe that he was the kind of man she wanted him to be. Still, laughter erupted from her throat, and she turned away to draw a deep breath. "Very well! I admit you are in all likelihood not as bad as I thought you to be."

Mr. Sharpe stretched his arms up to the heavens in a gesture of utter triumph. "Yes!" He exclaimed. "The lady grants me a most rare compliment!"

Christina laughed. She did not want to, but she could not help it. "You are impossible, and quite frankly, sometimes I don't quite know what to make of you." Her gaze narrowed as she recalled the night in the library. Taking a step closer, she met his gaze. "That night, it was no mistake, was it? It was no accident. You knew what you were doing. You knew the rules. You knew that if we were discovered..."

"... you would be compelled to marry me," he finished for her, holding her gaze, making it absolutely clear that, yes, he had sought her out that night on purpose.

Christina held his gaze, feeling her heart quickening in her chest. She knew she ought to remain quiet, but she could not. "You wanted me." It was a statement, not a question because she already knew it to be true.

Despite the *little scandals* attached to her family as of late, her father's reputation remained impeccable. The Whickertons were highly sought after, and even now with both Louisa and Leonora causing a bit of a stir, the *ton* had not withdrawn from them. Yes, Mr. Sharpe had wanted her, instead of Sarah. Her family's connections were far superior as Lord Hartmore was widely held in disdain for his inability to manage his family's finances successfully. They were one step away from the poorhouse, and everyone knew it. Poor Sarah!

Perhaps Christina ought to reconsider after all, not for her own sake, but for Sarah's. It turned out Mr. Sharpe was a decent man after all. At the very least, he was not a man her friend needed to fear, as far as Christina could tell. He would make a decent husband.

His hand settled on her arm, warm and tempting, and Christina blinked, her eyes once more focusing on his. "I wanted you," he whispered, the air between them once again sizzling in that strange way as though a fire had been lit. Although Christina could not quite understand it, she knew that it drew her near, like the moth to a flame.

Yes, she ought to reconsider, but she would not.

She was being selfish!

Chapter Sixteen
A MOTHER'S COUNSEL

To her utter shame, Christina found herself looking forward to each and every visit of her betrothed. Although they did not know each other well, an odd honesty existed between them.

With gentlemen of the *ton*, Christina had always experienced somewhat strained conversations, as though both sides were constantly on their guard, considering every word well before speaking it. She had never been certain how much truth lingered in the other's words, wondering even after weeks of conversations who the other person truly was.

Of course, Christina's knowledge of Mr. Sharpe's character as well as past was still severely limited; however, she could not help but feel as though she was slowly becoming acquainted with the man he was at heart...not the man he might be trying to portray. It was a thought that often calmed the rapid beating of her heart whenever Christina thought of her impending nuptials. Despite everything, she was marrying a complete stranger, a man from a world quite unlike her own. Yes, it worried her, and yet part of her was looking forward to this new life that had so unexpectedly opened up to her.

To Christina's dismay, her family was less convinced. Her father had told her in no uncertain terms that should she choose to end the engagement at any time, he would support her. She knew he wanted her to know that she had every option, that as soon as she had doubts, she was free to change her mind. Christina loved her father for his devotion and loyalty, but his own doubts also served to feed hers.

Because, of course, she had doubts. How could she not? Of course, there were moments when she worried she was making a monumental mistake. Still, whenever she thought of changing her mind, there was always *something* that held her back.

She could not quite say what it was, but it was enough to keep her from reconsidering.

Her sisters were no better, constantly urging her to think things through, to not rush into anything. Christina could see that they were worried; however, no objection they brought forth truly unsettled Christina.

Under the circumstances, she was thinking that she was walking into this marriage with her eyes wide open. Far more often than not, women did not know what would await them after their vows were spoken. With Mr. Sharpe, however, Christina believed to have a fairly accurate idea of what life with him would be like. Indeed, his character was not unlike her own. Perhaps that was why they managed to communicate with such ease.

Only Grandma Edie refrained from questioning Christina's decision. Indeed, her grandmother said little on the subject. Every now and then, she would pat Christina's hand, smile at her and assure her that all would be well.

It often seemed as though her grandmother knew more than everyone else. How that was possible she could not begin to fathom. However, over the course of her life, she had learned to trust her grandmother's instincts. It seemed they were rarely wrong, and Christina drew strength from the certainty that lingered in her grandmother's steady gaze.

Christina looked up as a knock sounded on her door. "Come in," she called and set down her quill. She had been in the process of writing to her aunt in France, unable to find the right words, afraid that Aunt Francine would be disappointed in her. After all, her aunt had all but fled England, leaving behind a husband and her entire family, in order to be who she was.

"Do you have a moment?" Christina's mother asked as she stepped over the threshold. A small smile lingered upon her soft features, and the hand that moved to close the door seemed to tremble ever so slightly.

"Of course, Mother." Christina rose from her chair and moved over to meet her mother halfway. "Are you all right? You seem...unwell somehow."

Her mother heaved a deep breath into her lungs before her hands reached out and grasped Christina's. Yes, they were indeed trembling. "There is something I need to speak to you about." Her words came fast, and yet Christina heard reluctance in her mother's voice.

"Is it about Mr. Sharpe?" she inquired, surprised that her mother would seek her out now with barely a fortnight left before the very day. "Will you, too, urge me to reconsider?"

A warm smile came to her mother's face, and the trembles in her hands ceased as she looked upon Christina, her eyes beginning to glow in a way they sometimes did when she looked upon one of her children. "You've become a most determined young woman," she said rather quietly as though more to herself than Christina. "You know what you want, and you're not afraid to go out into the world and claim it." Her eyes settled upon Christina's, truly seeing her now. "I am glad for it, but I also know that there is another side of the medallion for determination can often turn into stubbornness."

Christina chuckled despite herself. "Are you calling me stubborn?"

Her mother sighed. "I am not certain. That is precisely why I'm here. I need to know why you chose to marry him. I've watched you most carefully, and I am uncertain whether you are simply determined to marry him because you genuinely want to or if you are too stubborn to change your mind because you believe you must not." The question, daring and unwavering, lingered in her mother's gaze as she looked at her daughter with those seeing eyes of hers. It was a way mothers often looked at their children as though they could see into their hearts no matter how hard their children tried to shield them.

Christina frowned, trying to ignore the soft shiver that snaked down her back. "I'm not certain I know what you speak of."

Her mother's hands clasped more tightly over her own. "Are you doing this for yourself? Or for Sarah?" Her brows rose meaningfully, letting her know without a doubt that she was well aware of the conflict that existed within Christina's heart.

Christina heaved a deep sigh, wishing she did not have to defend her decision to her mother. Always had her mother had a way of reading between the lines and understanding with perfect clarity what it was Christina did not dare to admit to herself. "Does it matter? Does there need to be a difference? Perhaps I'm doing this for myself as well as her."

"Are you?" her mother pressed, something determined in the way she looked at Christina. Or should it be called stubbornness instead? Where was the difference?

"Why don't you tell me what objections you have?" Christina replied instead of answering her mother's question, uncertain if whatever she might say would satisfy her mother. "Why is it that you do not want me to marry him?"

For a moment, her mother remained quiet. Then she inhaled a slow breath as though she needed strength for what she was about to say. "Come, sit with me." Seating herself at the foot of Christina's bed, she urged her daughter to sit down beside her.

Christina watched her mother carefully as moment after moment slowly ticked by. There was a hint of reluctance and perhaps a touch of mortification upon her mother's face as she tried to find the right words to voice what was on her mind. Christina felt herself grow tenser with each moment that passed, beginning to get worried about what aspect of Mr. Sharpe's character or perhaps of married life itself she had failed to consider.

After a small eternity, her mother finally spoke, her gaze now steady despite the hint of hesitation in her voice. "You may or may not be aware of this—perhaps you've already spoken to Louisa or Leonora —however, there are...certain intimacies shared between husband and wife that you need to consider." Her mother swallowed, and Christina could not help but think that she was relieved to have said what she had.

Christina frowned. "What do you mean?" Of course, she had observed heated looks exchanged between spouses—or even strangers at a ball—as well as passionate embraces and the occasional kiss between her parents as well as her sisters and their husbands. What else was there?

From comments she had overheard here and there, Christina deduced that the marriage bed might be a somewhat different matter; however, would it not be the same no matter whom she married?

For a moment, her mother looked down at their linked hands and inhaled a deep breath. Then she looked up again, the look of hesitation once more upon her face. "My dear, you know that I love your father dearly and, therefore, of course, I do not mind the moments when he pulls me into his arms. Quite on the contrary, I cherish them." A smile full of longing and joy came to her mother's face that Christina felt her own heart skip a beat, a stab of envy distracting it from its normal rhythm. "I married him because I loved him, and I love him still. Every day is more beautiful because he is with me and I am with him." Her mother's hands no longer trembled but were warm and steady upon her own. "That is what marriage is supposed to be. I cannot imagine how it might feel if the person to pull me into his arms were someone I did not care for. I know that most marriages begin like that. It is the way of the world. However, I do not even want to contemplate such a life. I don't want to live with a stranger, always finding myself tensing when he draws near. After all, who would feel comfortable sharing anything intimate with someone one does not hold to heart?"

Christina bowed her head as her mother's words slowly sank in. *The Whickertons marry for love.* It was a family tradition, and quite obviously, it was one based on sound reasoning. The question was, did she care for Mr. Sharpe enough to feel comfortable with him?

Christina did not know. Although she did enjoy his company, she could not be certain how she would feel if he ever...kissed her. Embraced her. Admittedly, in the library, he had drawn close, remarkably close, and as far as Christina remembered, she had not been reluctant. Yes, her heart had hammered wildly in her chest, and yet it had not been out of reluctance, had it? In fact, she believed that she had been tempted in that moment. Did that mean she would feel comfortable being his wife...in every way?

Her mother's hand squeezed hers. "I suggest you speak to your sisters." A youthful smile came to her mother's face. "After all, I am an old woman. I have been married for decades, and perhaps it would be more helpful for you to speak to someone who has only just started upon the journey you, too, are determined to embark upon. Ask them and hear their answers." Her mother's eyes became imploring. "There is no rush. Please, think this through for it cannot be undone once you have made your choice."

Christina nodded, unable to utter a reply. Still, she had given her word, and the wedding was to take place in less than a fortnight. If she went back on her promise now, would she rob herself of her only chance to ever be married? Would this be the final scandal to ruin her family's good name?

"Be absolutely certain of what you want, my dear," her mother urged, something lingering in her gaze as though she, too, had once stood at the same fork in the road. "Marriage cannot be undone, and sometimes we find ourselves swept off our feet by a charming smile and kind words only to discover later that no true bond exists, especially not one that would last a lifetime."

Christina looked more closely at her mother, feeling the sudden need to ask for more details, sensing that there was more her mother was not telling her. Still, whatever it was that lived in her mother's past seemed well shielded, buried almost, and she knew that her questions would not be rewarded with answers.

"Speak to your sisters, please."

Smiling at her mother, Christina nodded. "I will." Perhaps it would be wise to do so. Of course, she had a fairly good idea of what Louisa and Leonora would say. Especially Leonora seemed terribly upset by the idea of Christina marrying Mr. Sharpe. After what her sister had been through, Christina was not genuinely truly surprised. Yes, Leonora had experienced forced intimacy with a stranger, and it had wounded her in ways Christina could not even begin to understand. Only her new husband's kindness and patience had given her the strength to rise above and once again stand tall.

Yes, Christina thought. Perhaps it would be wise to speak to her sisters and find herself better prepared for what might await her.

Chapter Seventeen

A WELL-KEPT SECRET

The world seemed aglow as the sun streamed in through the tall windows of the drawing room. Thorne stood with his hands linked behind his back, his gaze focused out at the grassy hills, the tall stalks swaying gently in the summer's breeze. It was a peaceful view, calm and soothing, and he could imagine living his life out here. Was this the life his future bride had known since birth?

Thorne heaved a deep sigh, wishing that every child in the world could grow up in a place like this. A place full of warmth and kindness, full of space and endless horizons. A place filled with a loving family and guiding hands.

His own life, of course, had been far different from this magnificent place and all it promised, all it inspired. It had been cold and harsh and painful, and it was like that for countless other children all over the country. Never would they know the meaning of undisturbed sleep, of sweet dreams and wonderful awakenings. Too harsh was the reality they faced every day, and it was that thought that never failed to stir anger in Thorne's heart. Yes, he had come to London to do something.

To accomplish something.

For them.

He needed to garner support and influence. New laws were needed.

Laws that would require cotton mill owners to uphold safety measures and take health requirements into account.

That was why he was here.

Only ever since Thorne had laid eyes on Christina, a dormant part of him had reawakened. He could not even recall if that part had ever known life before. Perhaps as a child. Perhaps when his parents had still been alive.

It was a dream.

Hope.

Thorne sighed for although he knew his duty and responsibilities, he could no longer deny that all of a sudden there was something that he wanted.

For himself.

He wanted her.

He had wanted her from the first moment he had laid eyes upon her.

Still, it was not all that he wanted. He did not simply want her in his bed or even as his wife. He knew very well—had observed it count-less times—that marriage was no guarantee for...closeness.

In truth, what Thorne wanted was love and family. People that were his to protect and provide for. A wife and children he could dote upon and whose smiles and laughter would bring him joy.

His gaze swept over the windswept hills outside the window once more, and he heaved another deep sigh, one full of longing and desire.

Perhaps this was the place. Perhaps they could all be happy here.

Thorne knew that Christina was close to her family and always would be. He would not have it any other way for he was beginning to grow quite fond of them as well. They were her family, and perhaps one day they might be his as well.

Only too well did Thorne remember Christina's reaction to the idea of him taking Miss Mortensen away from London and back to Manchester. He could only imagine how upset she would be if upon their nuptials she would find herself whisked away to the north. No, he was certain she would want to stay close to her family.

And this estate—Pinewood Manor—was everything he thought she would want. Although it was sizable, it was not overly large, giving it a somewhat cozy character where it sat nestled among gently sloping hills. It was no more than a day's ride from Whickerton Grove, her family's estate, which would ensure that his future wife could remain close to those she held dear.

Footsteps drifted to his ears, small and swift ones racing with no regard for care or caution down the large staircase in the hall. Happy giggles accompanied those footsteps, immediately followed by words of caution from Mrs. Huxley.

Despite himself, Thorne smiled. "In here!" he called, turning away from the window and toward the door the moment Samantha crossed over the threshold.

Her sparkling eyes were full of mischief and her blonde curls danced wildly upon her shoulders as she came skipping toward him. "This is a wonderful place!" she exclaimed, clasping her hands together as those wide round eyes rose to meet his.

At five years of age, of course, Samantha did not even reach up to his midsection, forcing Thorne to kneel down if he wished to look into her eyes. "Do you like it?" he asked, reaching for her little hands. "Are the stairs in the hall not too steep?"

Her eyes lit up like fireflies. "No, they are perfect. Perhaps another year or two and I will be able to slide down the banister."

Panting under her breath, Mrs. Huxley finally reached the drawing room. "You are not under any circumstances to do that, young lady!" she admonished sternly. However, the effect of her words was somewhat lost considering the heaving gasps rattling from her chest.

"Quite right," Thorne agreed with a quick glance at Mrs. Huxley. However, when he shifted his gaze back to Samantha, he winked at her. "Not under any circumstances!"

Samantha giggled, a conspiratorial gleam in her eyes. "Of course not!" Then her gaze traveled past his shoulder to the window, and her round eyes grew even wider as they swept over the grassy hills. "Is this to be our new home?" she asked, awe tinging her voice as she drew her hands from his and stepped around him up to the window.

Thorne nodded, allowing his gaze to follow hers. "Would you like that?"

With her nose almost pressed to the glass, Samantha nodded. "Oh, yes, I would." She glanced up at him over her shoulder. "Do you think your new wife will like it here?"

Thorne heaved a deep sigh. Then he moved to stand next to Samantha, one hand braced upon the wall. "I very much hope so."

"Tell me her name again."

"Christina," Thorne whispered, cherishing the feel of her name upon his tongue. Thus far, he had only occasionally uttered it out loud. Of course, he had called her Chris as her sisters were wont to do. He had done it to tease her, and he had quite liked the result. As had she, he suspected, despite her objections.

"It's a beautiful name," Samantha marveled, saying it once, twice. "Like that of a princess." With her little hand still resting upon the windowpane, Samantha slowly turned her head to look at him. Something serious rested in those green eyes of hers, something vulnerable, and Thorne found himself drop to his knees once more, his large hands reaching for her small ones. "Do you think she will like me?" Samantha asked then, an almost desperate need swinging in her voice.

Thorne swallowed hard, afraid to raise Samantha's hopes, when, in truth, he had yet to mention the little girl to Christina. "Of course, she will," he told her nonetheless and without delay. After all, when her wide eyes so full of hope and trust looked into his, he found himself unable to deny her anything.

She was a child, one of many out there in the world, who deserved everything. A family. A home. A future without backbreaking labor.

Try as he might, Thorne knew that he would never be able to ensure every child's future. He certainly would do his best to protect them, them and their families, but he knew it would never be enough.

But for Samantha, there were no limits. Nevertheless, all she ever dreamed of was a mother. A mother who would love her, who would soothe her tears and read her stories. A mother who would stay by her side for the rest of her life, provide counsel and loving care.

Could Christina be that woman? Was it possible that perhaps in a year from now they would all be a family?

Looking at Samantha, Thorne knew that that was what she wanted. In truth, though, it was what he wanted as well.

Chapter Eighteen

MEN TO LOVE

Taking her mother's advice, Christina invited Louisa and Leonora for an afternoon visit. The three sisters sat outside in the gardens near the small fountain where two marble benches had been set in the shade of a canopy of tree branches. The sun shone down almost mercilessly; its heat only offset by the soft breeze that stirred the leaves above.

"There is something on your mind," Louisa remarked with a thoughtful gaze, her eyes slightly narrowed. "Something that gives you concern." She exchanged a look with Leonora, and both sisters seemed to scoot closer on their bench as though proximity was key. "Tell us."

Christina smiled at Louisa's blunt words. Her sister had a way of saying out loud what others might simply think, but not voice. Christina often found it made it easier to address certain issues. "Yes, you're quite right. In fact, it was mother who suggested I speak to the two of you."

"The two of us?" Leonora echoed her gaze once more drifting to her elder sister. "Why the two of us?"

Christina inhaled a slow breath. Though she was not generally wont to shy away from addressing uncomfortable subjects, she could not help but feel a hint of unease.

"Oh, out with it!" Louisa exclaimed with an impatient wave of her hand. "I'm not getting any younger!"

This time, Christina and Leonora exchanged a glance before both of them chuckled. "You sound like Grandma Edie," Leonora remarked, gently elbowing Louisa in the side. "Are you suggesting you've become wise beyond your years? You've been married no more than six months, not sixty years."

Louisa feigned a laugh, then quickly turned her gaze back to Christina. "Well?"

"Well," Christina began, feeling a bit more at ease after the short bout of sisterly affection, "I asked you here because there's something I wish to speak to you about." She looked from Louisa to Leonora, wondering how they felt about intimacies with their husbands. Of course, she had observed the occasional kiss between Louisa and Phineas while Leonora and Drake seemed to reserve such displays of affection for more private moments. Was there a reason why their two marriages seemed so different to an outside observer like her?

In all honesty, Christina found it rather annoying that young women were rarely told about marital aspects. They were told to do their duty, certainly; however, intriguing details were conveniently left out. Christina remembered her mother looking rather tense and flustered and surmised that perhaps it was simply a sense of mortification to discuss these matters in the light of day. Still, Christina had heard it whispered here and there that husbands, like people in general, were not all alike. In fact, she remembered hearing some old matron mumbling behind her fan that men like Mr. Sharpe, men who could not be considered gentlemen, often demanded *unspeakable things* from their wives.

Christina wished she knew what those unspeakable things were.

"As I am myself on the brink of matrimony," she began carefully, seeing a somewhat tense expression upon Leonora's face, "I was wondering if you would kindly share your own insights into marriage with me."

Leonora looked down at her hands folded in her lap. "Well, I—"

"That is a heavily worded sentence, little sister!" Louisa exclaimed, those inquisitive eyes of hers lingering upon Christina's face in a way that made her want to squirm. "What exactly are you asking?"

Christina grinned at her sister. "Always straight to the point, aren't you?"

Louisa shrugged. "I find it saves time."

"That is something Grandma Edie would say," Leonora remarked with a chuckle. "Again."

Christina laughed. "It would seem you are becoming more and more like our dear grandmother every day."

Holding Christina's gaze, Louisa shook her head. "Don't even try to distract me. Now, what is it you want to know?"

Christina met Louisa's daunting gaze with an equal one of her own. "Well, if you must know, mother cautioned me to rethink my acceptance of Mr. Sharpe's proposal—if you can call it that." She shrugged. "I know, all of you have more or less done the same; however, she urged me to speak to the two of you about...marital intimacies."

A bright grin came to Louisa's face. "I see," she said in a teasing voice. "What is it that you wish to know?"

For a moment, Christina was at a loss, but then she remembered her mother's words. "Do you mind...being close? How does it make you feel when Phineas embraces you? Kisses you?"

A longing sigh left Louisa's lips and a dream-like expression came to her eyes that said more than a thousand words.

Christina laughed. "You enjoy his affections that much?"

Louisa nodded eagerly, a wide grin upon her face. In all honesty, she seemed rather childlike in that moment; however, Christina did not fail to detect the utter joy that seemed to linger in every fiber of her sister's being.

"And...your wedding night was...?" Christina began carefully, uncertain how to finish her question. Fortunately, she did not have to.

"Wonderful!" Louisa exclaimed, the dreamlike look still upon her face. "Amazing! Marvelous!" She grinned at Christina. "Is that what you wanted to know?"

Christina nodded. "So, it did not make you feel uncomfortable?"

Louisa laughed. "Of course not. Admittedly, I was a bit nervous, yes. But mostly I remember being overly excited and more than a little impatient." She grinned devilishly before the look upon her face sobered. "Is that what you are worried about? That you might not like his...attentions?"

"Mother suggested I might not."

Louisa nodded thoughtfully. "I suppose that can be true if you marry without love."

Christina drew in a slow breath. Of course, she was under no delusions about her union with Mr. Sharpe. There was no love between them, but perhaps one day there could be. However, until then...would he demand intimacies of her that she would be unwilling to give?

"What about you and Drake?" Christina asked Leonora, wondering about how—after the vicious attack upon her a little more than a year earlier—she had experienced her recent wedding night. After all, not even a fortnight had passed since.

Leonora exchanged a look with Louisa before she turned her attention back to Christina. "Quite honestly, I have to say that I was very nervous." Her chest rose with a deep breath as she searched for the right words to explain how she had felt. "You know that I feel completely at ease with Drake. I love him and I trust him, and yet that night, I felt tense and...apprehensive. Not because of him, but because..."

A slight frown came to Leonora's face as her teeth sank into her lower lip. "I think it was different that night because a marriage is to be consummated on the wedding night, is it not? It is not only expected but demanded. It is part of a contract, and the contract is not binding unless..." She broke off and shook her head, her blue eyes shining with an odd mixture of vulnerability and defiance. "Quite frankly, it felt...forced."

Louisa smiled at her, reaching out a comforting hand and placing it upon Leonora's.

Christina frowned. "But Drake did not...? I mean, he...?"

Leonora's eyes widened as she grasped Christina's meaning. "Of course not. I think, he knew before even I did that something was wrong." A small smile danced over her features. "He often does. He pulled me into his arms and...put my mind at ease in that utterly endearing way of his." A longing sigh left her lips. "We did not consummate our marriage that night, but a few days later instead when it didn't feel...forced. It simply happened and was not planned in any way. It felt natural, and it was beautiful."

Christina smiled at her sisters, glad to hear that they both had experienced such wonderful moments with their husbands, that they had found husbands who treated them with respect and kindness. Indeed, Phineas and Drake could not be more different, but they both looked at their wives the very same way.

It was love, was it not? Love that made all the difference. What would a marriage without love, a wedding night without love, be like?

"You need to be certain of what you want," Leonora counseled carefully. "You need to be certain what you are willing to endure. According to the law, Mr. Sharpe will have every right to consummate your marriage on your wedding night."

Christina shook her head as a small shiver ran down her back. "He will not force me," she replied instantly, uncertain where that conviction came from.

"How do you know?" Leonora demanded, her hands once more trembling, no doubt inspired by the memories of a most painful moment. "You hardly know him, and we all know that he came to London to seek influential connections. Yours is not a love match, and only a husband who loves his wife can be trusted to treat her with the necessary consideration."

Louisa nodded in agreement as she squeezed Leonora's hands reassuringly. "You know me, Chris. I am far from cautious. Yet I, too, urge you to consider this carefully. We all know of marriages that are nothing more than a contract. We've all seen the false smiles that hide a sorrowful heart. I dread the thought that you might end up like one of them."

Christina heaved a deep sigh. "I thank you for your concern, and I know I cannot disregard what you said. Of course, you're right. Yes, I, too, have seen these women, these wives, and I have pitied them, sworn that I would never join their ranks." Her gaze moved from her sisters to the horizon, or where it would have been were it not blocked by a tall, leafy hedge. Still, Christina did not see the greenery before her but instead tried to recall her betrothed's face, the moments they had spent with one another. Although it was true that she did not know him very well, a part deep down urged her to place her trust in him. Perhaps that part of her was foolish. Perhaps it was wise. She did not know, and she could not know. What was she to do?

"You will marry him, nonetheless, won't you?" Louisa finally said into the stillness, her inquisitive eyes once more lingering upon Christina's face. "You have that look about you. I've seen it before. It means that while you have heard what we said, you will do what you see fit, nonetheless. Are you not worried? Not in the least?"

Again, that odd shiver snaked its way down Christina's back. "Perhaps a little," she admitted, heaving a deep sigh as a sense of relief swept through her. Perhaps she ought to have spoken to her sisters earlier, to have voiced her concerns and seen her heart lightened by simply sharing such things with those she held dear.

An aghast look in her eyes, Leonora shook her head. "How can you do this? Are you not afraid?"

Christina considered this for a moment. "No, I'm not afraid. I am perhaps...a little nervous, but not afraid." Indeed, Mr. Sharpe had never inspired fear in her, not even when they had stood head-to-head, and he had been reluctant to give in to her demands. Although he was not a gentleman, he was a decent man.

Or at least, Christina hoped that he was.

That she was not mistaken.

That he was not fooling her.

That she was not making a monumental mistake.

Chapter Nineteen

MEASUREMENTS OF A MARRIAGE

A beautiful summer's day drew many people to Hyde Park. They promenaded along the Serpentine, enjoying the soft balmy breeze as well as the sight of shrubs and flowers in bloom. Bees buzzed busily, and birds trilled from every branch. The lawns were crowded with children, racing one another or enjoying a picnic with their families.

Walking side-by-side with Christina, Thorne glanced over his shoulder at her family, situated under a small tent, their eyes following them like those of hawks. "I wish I could read their minds," he mumbled before turning back to look at his betrothed. Then he laughed, "Although perhaps it is better that I cannot, for the looks upon some of their faces suggest rather murderous thoughts."

Christina followed his gaze and chuckled. "I'm afraid you might be correct." Her eyes shifted to meet his. "Quite frankly, with the exception of Harriet, my sisters seem to dislike you." She paused, a slight frown coming to her face. "Perhaps that is not completely accurate. They...do not trust you. They are concerned for me." She lifted her brows in a challenging gesture. "Should they be?"

"Are you asking for them?" Thorne wondered, unable to shake the feeling that something was different since he had returned from Pinewood Manor. "Or for yourself?"

Although the glow in her eyes remained, there was a slight twitch to her lips as though she had to force herself to maintain the smile she showed him. Yes, something was different. "Does it matter? They are a part of me, and I will forever be a part of them. That is what family is, is it not?"

Thorne nodded, well aware that she had not answered his question. "Yes, I'm beginning to see that. Family is priceless." He thought of Samantha and wondered if perhaps one day the Whickerton clan would strive to protect her as much as they were now protecting Christina. He hoped they would!

The smile upon Christina's face faltered. "I'm sorry," she whispered, dropping her gaze momentarily. "I did not mean to cause you pain. I cannot imagine what life would be like without my family. I cannot imagine ever being without them." Her eyes returned to meet his, a question in them that he understood well without words.

"It is lonely," Thorne told her openly as they turned down a somewhat less crowded path, the canopy of the trees overhead shielding them from the almost blistering sun. "You learn to rely on yourself alone because, when you're weak, there's no one else who will be strong for you. That life has taught me to be cautious and self-sufficient, to be distrustful and always expect the worst in order to be prepared and not be caught off my guard." Thorne felt her eyes upon him as he spoke. He all but felt her soft breath as she took in every word, mulled it over in her mind and tried to imagine a life quite unlike her own. She was a thoughtful and empathetic person, and Thorne liked that about her.

He liked her.

Christina looked lost in thought for a long time and just when he was about to ask what was on her mind, she turned to him and asked, "What is marriage to you?"

Thorne had to admit that he had not expected that question, and so he shrugged. "Quite truthfully, I have not yet given it much thought. As I've never been married before, I have no experience to draw upon." He grinned at her, trying to lighten the mood because he sensed that something else was hiding underneath that simple question. "I suppose, marriage means companionship. It means to have someone to speak to and to count on. At least, I hope it will."

Her head bobbed along to his words as though in approval, and he could see a small measure of relief lighting up her eyes. Had she been concerned?

"And for you?" Thorne asked as he moved to step into her path, his gaze seeking hers. "What does this marriage mean for you? After all, you've made it unmistakably clear that you do not approve of me in any way and are only sacrificing yourself in order to protect your friend." He grinned at her, his voice light and teasing. Only he could not deny the sudden tightness that came to his heart.

Christina shook her head at him, but once again refrained from answering. "Are you ever serious? We are to be married in less than a fortnight, and here you are speaking as though this was nothing more than a jest." Her brows furrowed as she regarded him carefully. "Is there no small part of you that is concerned? You will be sharing your life with someone you hardly know."

"Is that what concerns you?" Thorne replied, noting the way her gaze dropped from his for no more than a split second. Although it would have been easy to miss, Thorne could not imagine ever being oblivious to anything that concerned her. It seemed the moment she drew near, his attention, his thoughts and emotions shifted toward her, like a moth drawn to a flame. "Are you worried to be sharing your life with me? If that is the case, then say it."

For a moment, she hesitated, but then nodded. "It is. Does that surprise you? Displease you?" A daring note came to her voice as she held his gaze.

Thorne could not help but think that this was some kind of test to make out his character, to see what he was made of. "No, it does not surprise me. In fact, it would surprise me if you had no reservations at all for what you say is true, we hardly know each other. How am I to know what kind of person you are? Perhaps you have despicable taste, and I will soon find myself living in a home I cannot bear to look at," he teased, and she laughed. "Perhaps your idea of a delicious dish is one I cannot stomach. Perhaps you have a most dreadful singing voice, and yet insist upon entertaining me each and every night with a song."

Christina rolled her eyes at him, then turned back down the path, laughing. "Indeed, you are a most dreadful person. How will I ever tolerate you?"

Thorne liked the easy conversation between them, and he hoped it would always be thus. "Perhaps," he continued, as he fell into step beside her once more, "you snore in your sleep, and I will not have a moment of peace."

Although she did not stop in her tracks or flinch in any way, Thorne could not help but think that somehow his words unsettled her. Was it the intimacies they would naturally share as husband and wife that gave her concern?

"What would you do," Christina asked all of a sudden, "if I were to disobey you? To insult you even?" She took one more step and then turned on her heel and faced him, her blue eyes wide and unflinching, demanding an answer.

Thorne chuckled. "Have you not already done so? You've told me quite honestly what you thought of me, what you still think of me. As far as I'm aware, you never hesitate to speak your mind, and—"

"Is that something that displeases you?" she asked, and from the tone in her voice Thorne knew that there was only one right answer.

Holding her gaze, Thorne took a slow step toward her until barely an arm's-length separated them. He watched her draw in a slow breath, the muscles in her neck and shoulders tightening as she held her ground, her blue eyes as watchful as before. "I am aware," he began, his voice no more than a whisper, "that gentlemen of the *ton* do not favor women who think for themselves. However, as you have so often pointed out, I am not a gentleman."

"Does that mean that it does not displease you if I voice my own thoughts? Especially when they're different from your own?"

Thorne felt the corners of his mouth twitch. "I might not always like what you have to say, but I find that I quite enjoy arguing with you. I suppose, if we always agreed, life would be utterly boring." He could see something sparking in her eyes, amusement and a sense of approval. Perhaps he had answered correctly, the way she had wanted him to. Only a spark of concern remained. "What is it that frightens you?"

Like a whiplash, her brows drew down, and a scowl came to her face. "I'm not frightened," she insisted, lifting her arms and crossing them in front of her chest in a gesture of utter defiance.

Thorne did not reply. He merely lifted his brows in challenge...and waited.

Chapter Twenty

RIDICULOUS NOTIONS

Christina could see the daring gleam in his eyes. It was clear he was challenging her. Hence, he did not seem to wish to see her back down, bow her head and retreat. Instead, she could not help but think that he wanted her to rise to the challenge. Few men wanted their wives to stand tall, did they? Only men in love ever dared. Was Mr. Sharpe perhaps a rare specimen?

Deciding that at least in this instance there was nothing to lose by being blunt, Christina lifted her chin and willed her arms to loosen, releasing them from their tight hold. "Very well," she said, instantly beginning to feel better about herself by accepting this challenge. "If you truly wish to know, then, yes, there is something that...I've been wondering about."

Something mischievous sparked in his eyes for he had no doubt taken note of her inability to use the word *frightened* in her reply. "Do tell."

After her conversation with her mother and then later with her sisters, Christina had spent hours mulling over everything she had been told. In conclusion, she realized that it all depended upon the kind of man Mr. Sharpe was. So far, everything she had learned of him had made her unafraid to enter into this marriage.

Slightly concerned, perhaps, but unafraid.

It certainly would be a challenge, but Christina felt confident that she would master it. Yes, even if time would prove that they would never come to care for one another, separate living arrangements were not unheard of among the *ton*. Some married couples spent no more than a handful of days or perhaps weeks under the same roof with one another.

The only concern that remained was the marital bed.

It annoyed Christina that she had no specific knowledge of what awaited her for it seemed that very few people ever spoke about the marital bed openly. Even her mother and sisters had seemed reluctant as though it was a topic that one should never venture to discuss. All she had to go on were rumors and whispers and overheard snippets of conversations.

Perhaps speaking about this to her future husband would ultimately prove a marvelous idea indeed. And so, Christina cleared her throat, willed her courage not to falter and said, "As we both agree that you do not qualify as a gentleman," he chuckled, "I find myself slightly concerned with...expectations in the marital bed."

His chuckle ceased abruptly, and he stilled, staring at her.

Mortification began to rise up her cheeks, and Christina huffed out an annoyed breath, trying her best not to let it show. "Do not act so shocked!" she chided, fighting the urge to once more cross her arms over her chest. "I have every right to be concerned."

Mr. Sharpe blinked a couple of times, his mouth opening and closing, then opening again. Clearly, her words seemed to puzzle him; for a reason Christina could not even begin to fathom. Then, after a small eternity, he cleared his throat, his eyes once more focusing on her. "Allow me to clarify," he began, grasping his chin in thought. "You are concerned with my expectations in the marital bed because I am not a gentleman?" He said each word slowly as though he needed time to grasp the thought he was trying to convey.

Christina swallowed. "Yes. Why is that such a surprise to you?"

He frowned, that look of incomprehension still clouding his features. "You are concerned because I am not a gentleman?"

Christina huffed out another breath. "Yes!"

"And you wouldn't be concerned if I *were* a gentleman?"

Glaring at him, Christina rested her hands upon her hips. "Have you recently suffered a blow to the head, *Sir*? Or why does it seem so hard for you to grasp this simple concept?" Indeed, with each word, her mortification seemed to worsen. Her cheeks felt hot, and the pulse in her neck hammered far too rapidly. She could only hope he had not noticed.

Beginning to recover, Mr. Sharpe grinned at her, amusement twinkling in his eyes, fueling Christina's desire to sink into a hole in the ground. "May I ask? What expectations were you thinking of?"

"Must you ask?" Christina snapped.

"I'm afraid I must."

She glared at him. "As though you don't know!"

Again, he stilled, and his eyes narrowed as though he was trying to look at her more closely. "Do you?"

Oh, if only she had not begun this line of questioning! She could not retreat now, could she?

Clearing her throat, Christina willed her gaze not to drop from his. "I've heard people whisper of...unspeakable things commonly-bred husbands demand of their wives." There! She had said it. After all, there was no further explanation she could give as she had none. That was the whole point!

Again, Mr. Sharpe chuckled.

"Do you have to laugh at me?" Christina demanded indignantly, wondering if she had been completely mistaken in her impression of him. "It is rather disrespectful."

He shook his head, a hint of apology in his gaze. "I'm sorry. I assure you I am not laughing at you. I am laughing at the ridiculous notions you have overheard."

Christina frowned. "Ridiculous?"

Again, he laughed, rather out loud this time. "I'm afraid so." He inhaled a deep breath, clearly seeking to calm himself, before he stepped closer, his gaze fixed upon hers. "Of course, men are not all the same—neither are women; however, expectations cannot be split along the line of nobility. You say you're worried about what I would want from you because I am a common man."

Christina nodded.

"But you have no notion what that could be? Only that, as a lady I suppose, it should worry you?"

Again, Christina nodded.

Smiling at her, Mr. Sharpe paused. "Have you ever been kissed?" he asked abruptly before his gaze darted downward to touch upon her lips.

Christina drew in an unsteady breath, aware that it was neither indignation nor outrage that sent a tremble through her this time. "I have not."

"Why?"

"I..." She shrugged, remembering the moment Lord Kenton had tried to kiss her. "I did not wish to."

He nodded in understanding. "Has anyone ever *tried* to steal a kiss?" An odd tension rang in his voice as he asked that question.

Christina nodded, and the muscle in his jaw twitched again. "Once," she replied as her mind once more traveled back to the moment Lord Kenton had drawn closer. She had seen the intention in his eyes, and she had intuitively known that she had not wanted his kiss. "He was a perfectly amiable gentleman; however, I simply...I..."

Mr. Sharpe nodded, something soft and kind and understanding coming to his eyes. "That is what matters, is it not?" He smiled at her. "It is not about who we are—lord or commoner; lady or maiden." A quick grin flashed across his face before he inched closer by no more than a fraction. Still, Christina felt his nearness as though he had touched her, and she could not say she minded. "It is about how we feel together," Mr. Sharpe continued in that soft, alluring whisper, his watchful eyes trailing over her features like a caress, "how you feel about me, how I feel about you." The corners of his mouth twitched in wicked amusement. "Perhaps a test would help you decide if there is reason for concern."

Christina swallowed, somewhat displeased with her own reaction to him; still, she could not deny the pleasurable tingle his words elicited. "A test? What do you mean?"

The corners of his mouth stretched into an irritatingly appealing grin as he leaned closer conspiratorially. "I'm speaking of a kiss, of course." He said no more, his gaze watchful upon her as he waited.

"You want to kiss me?" Christina asked for clarity's sake as well as the need to provide herself with an additional moment to gather her thoughts.

"Yes. Does that surprise you?"

She regarded him carefully. "You're teasing me. Why?" Although she could not say that she minded. Somehow, it made it easier to talk to him.

Mr. Sharpe shrugged. "That I cannot say. It seems to come naturally to me whenever I'm near you." He chuckled. "Although I cannot say that you look as though it truly bothers you. You certainly try to pretend that it does; however, I cannot help but think that—secretly—you quite like it."

Staring at him, Christina shook her head. "You're unbelievable!" Never in her life had a gentleman spoken to her in such a direct and straightforward manner. Yet he was not a gentleman. That much they had established countless times by now.

"Thank you!"

"Again, it is not a compliment."

He shrugged. "I choose to see it as one. Is that not what life is about? Our choices?" Those green eyes of his sparkled with something that spoke of a vivacious nature Christina had never truly seen in any of the men of her acquaintance. Mr. Sharpe seemed to have a zest for life that none had ever matched before. Despite all the suffering he had had to endure, he looked at life and saw its beauty.

Christina held his gaze, uncertain about the direction of their conversation, but undoubtedly intrigued. "And what is your choice?"

"You," he whispered without hesitation, daring claiming his eyes as though he knew that his answer would stun her.

Christina wanted to believe him. She wanted to believe that he had chosen her out of his own free will because there was something about her that no other woman possessed. She wanted to be special. She wanted...to be the one.

At the same time, however, she knew that she was not. After all, she knew better than anyone why he had *chosen* her. How they had come to be betrothed. She knew, and yet in some moments, she all but forgot, distracted with hopes and wishes she had thus far never realized lived in her heart.

Steeling herself against the almost magnetic pull of his words, Christina rolled her eyes at him, doing her best to pretend that they did not affect her in the least. "Yes, and we all know why. We all know, equally well, why I chose you," she replied, needing him to know that she did not want him anymore than he wanted her.

Indeed, they were equally matched, each having chosen the other for reasons that had nothing to do with affection. At least, that was what Christina chose to believe.

Mr. Sharpe chuckled, something he seemed to be wont to do. "So, you do not *want* to marry me?"

Christina swallowed. "No. You are merely the lesser of two evils."

He laughed. "But you *will* marry me?"

"Yes."

"Although you're concerned about the marriage bed?"

"Yes." Christina willed her cheeks not to flush.

"And yet you wish to kiss me?"

"Yes." The word left Christina's lips before she could hold it back. The flush she was desperately fighting to hold back shot to her cheeks, and she could feel its heat like the blistering sun. Mortification burned in her veins, and she glared at her betrothed. "You scoundrel! You truly have no manners. You—"

Her voice broke off as he stepped closer, and she could feel his breath fan over her lips. "I wish to kiss you as well," he whispered then, the look in his eyes open and honest and almost vulnerable.

Christina drew in a shuddering breath, trying her best to hold on to the shred of composure she had left. "You do?"

The right corner of his mouth twitched. "Did you truly not know? Have I not made it abundantly clear that I do?"

Her mouth opened and closed before she managed to find the words. "How was I to know? You never said a word about—"

"Of course, I never said a word. People rarely say what they want, do they?" His gaze drifted down to her lips once more; only briefly, but long enough for her to notice, to feel. "Nonetheless, there are other ways of making one's intentions unmistakably clear."

Christina felt her head begin to spin. It was a sensation she had never experienced in this way before. His meaning became abundantly clear, and she quite understood what he meant. Had he not looked at her like this before? That night in the library?

The thought that he might want her in this small way at least brought a flutter to Christina's belly. Was that what people meant when they spoke of butterflies? Yes, it felt odd, but oddly intoxicating.

"Would you mind?" Mr. Sharpe asked, making no move to step away and put a more appropriate distance between them. "If I were to kiss you, would you mind?"

Of course, their rather unorthodox relationship had always been a battle of minds. From the first, Christina had felt the need to outdo him, to triumph over him. Only she had just as easily seen that he, too, felt that very way. In that regard, of course, she ought to decline, she ought to refuse him and put him in his place. Yet that would leave her unkissed, and Christina was quite certain that would bother her even more.

"I suppose, I would be amenable to the kind of test you proposed earlier," she finally replied in her most condescending voice.

Although she expected it, Mr. Sharpe's laughing reply was no less irritating. "Oh, you would be *amenable*. How very flattering!"

"Well?" Christina prompted, slowly becoming aware of a slight pinch in the back of her neck. After all, they had been standing like this for quite some time, forcing her to tilt her head upward to hold his gaze. How she had not noticed this before, how very tall he was, Christina could not fathom? Indeed, she suddenly felt dwarfed standing so close.

"Well, what?"

She regarded him with a chiding look. "Will you kiss me, or not?"

His smile brightened, and something deeply tempting came to his gaze. "As much as I would like to kiss you here and now, I do not dare."

To Christina's surprise, a deep sense of disappointment welled up in her chest. Heaven help her, but she seemed far too eager for his kiss. "Why?"

His gaze slowly moved from hers and traveled to something beyond her shoulder. "It would seem that your family's nosiness knows no bounds, which is—I suppose—precisely why they are right over there, watching us closely." He chuckled, no sign of alarm in the way he spoke. "Indeed, if I am not at all mistaken your brother as well as brothers-in-law are presently entertaining rather murderous thoughts toward me." Grinning, he looked down at her. "I am not fool enough to encourage them to put whatever plans might be forming in their minds into action." He inhaled a slow breath and looked at her for a long time, something thoughtful in his gaze. Then he whispered, "Later," something irritatingly magical in the way he was looking at her.

Despite her best intentions, Christina felt herself respond, felt herself begin to yearn and regret the lack of privacy that prevented him from kissing her here and now. "Later."

He nodded in agreement, then reached out to hold her back as she made to turn away. His gaze once more settled upon hers, and Christina could see that what he was about to say would not be negotiable. "Call me Thorne," he demanded, the hand upon her arm steady and relentless. "Chris."

"That would not be appropriate," Christina replied instantly for it was part of the dance they had been engaged in since the first time they met, was it not? He made a demand, and she refused him; and vice versa. Those were the rules, were they not? The rules that had somehow developed between them.

Thorne laughed, clearly amused and even delighted with the way she always sought to resist him. "I don't care." His brows rose teasingly. "Do you? Truly?"

Christina regarded him carefully. "Thorne," she murmured, trying out his name and finding herself surprised at how natural it felt to say it. Of course, he was not to know that! "The name suits you for you seem to be a thorn in my side, constantly irritating me."

A wide smile came to his face. "Oh, Chris, I've grown quite fond of you as well." Then his hand fell from her arm, and Christina found herself wishing it had not.

Indeed, it seemed that she was finding her future husband far too appealing. A most inconvenient development!

If only she knew what to do about it!

Chapter Twenty-One

SHIELDED FROM PRYING EYES

Thorne found himself looking forward to every moment he was able to spend in Christina's presence. She was a delightful woman, bold and yet caring although she was far from admitting any amiable emotions toward him. They seemed constantly locked in some kind of competition, always trying to outdo the other, to come out on top.

Still, Thorne could not say that he minded.

Quite on the contrary.

As Thorne stood in the hall of the Whickertons' townhouse, waiting for Christina to meet him, the dowager countess stepped out of the drawing room and came toward him, once again leaning heavily upon her walking stick. "Mr. Sharpe," she greeted him, an almost youthful spark in her pale eyes. "Here, again." Her brows rose in a mocking gesture.

Thorne smiled. "Yes, I am here to see my betrothed."

The dowager countess nodded. "Yes, it would seem you are unable to stay away from her." The corners of her mouth crept upward into a grin. "I find that quite interesting. Quite interesting, indeed."

Thorne knew that she was teasing him; only it was not out of malice. Far from it. There was affection in her eyes, and Thorne marveled at the thought that the dowager countess truly seemed to approve of him. Of course, she had not said so. As he had pointed out to Christina only a few days earlier, people rarely said what they thought. Still, if one looked closely, there were always signs that betrayed another's true intentions.

Soft footsteps drew Thorne's attention, and he turned to look toward the large staircase and found Christina slowly descending it to the ground floor. She wore a pale blue summer dress that made her look like an innocent maiden; although the shrewd expression in her deep blue eyes proved any such assumption wrong. Yes, she was a sheltered young woman, but one who was not afraid to explore the world.

Thorne quite liked that about her.

"Mr. Sharpe, I admit I'm quite surprised to see you here again," Christina greeted him, the look in her eyes more pointed as she addressed him by his last name. "Did you not come to visit only yesterday?"

Thorne chuckled. "Are you saying you're tiring of my company?" Yes, they had spent a lot of time with one another in recent days. Unfortunately, her family seemed to be almost aware of their desire to find some time alone and conduct their test. In consequence, one of them was always nearby, be it a sister or brother or even brother-in-law, their eyes watchful and concerned. Although Thorne could not help but be a little annoyed with them, he still loved the affection he knew to be the reason for their diligence, for their disapproval. They loved Christina, and they would protect her, no matter what.

That was family.

That was what Thorne wanted.

For himself as well as Samantha.

For all of them.

"Perhaps a little," Christina replied, the tone in her voice belying her desire to tease him, but not wound him. It was a fine line, and yet somehow they managed not to cross it.

Stepping off the last step, Christina ventured toward them, her gaze sweeping from side to side as though she were looking for someone. "Where is everyone?" she asked before her eyes came to settle upon her grandmother.

Thorne turned and saw a bit of a wicked smile coming to the

dowager countess's face. "It is such fine weather," she replied in answer to her granddaughter's question, "that I suggested they take a stroll through Hyde Park."

Christina frowned. "They left without me?"

"They may have been under the impression," the dowager began, "that you had a headache and needed some rest." Thorne barely managed to hold back a laugh, understanding the dowager's words with perfect clarity.

"Where would they have gotten that impression?" Christina asked as her gaze moved from him to her grandmother.

"From me," the dowager replied with a chuckle. Then her pale eyes turned to him. "Would you assist me onto the terrace? I believe, I would like to sit out in the sun for a little while."

Thorne offered her a formal bow, grateful for the old woman's interference. "Of course." He held out his arm to her, and she took it, leaning upon him as they made their way to the terrace doors.

"Are you coming, my dear?" the dowager called over her shoulder, and a moment later, Thorne heard Christina's footsteps catching up to them.

Once the dowager was comfortably settled in one of the terrace chairs, she waved her hands in a rather dismissive gesture at the two of them. "Now, leave and give an old lady some peace." She inhaled deeply, momentarily closing her eyes in bliss. "What wonderful weather! If I felt up to it, nothing would please me more than a stroll through the gardens." She all but cracked open one eye and looked at Thorne, something meaningful and rather insistent clearly visible in her expression.

"I quite agree." Thorne turned and offered Christina his arm. "Would you care to join me?"

Her eyes met his, and he could see without a doubt that she, too, understood what had just happened here. Still, she accepted his offer and they proceeded down the few steps onto the lawns, not bothering with the gravel path, but instead finding their own way.

"My grandmother has a bit of a meddlesome streak," Christina said with a chuckle as they headed deeper into the garden. Trees cast a welcoming shade, and the soft gurgle of a fountain nearby complemented the chirping of the birds somewhere above them. "One can never be quite certain what she will be up to next or what she might have already done."

Thorne laughed. "But she means well."

Christina nodded. "Yes, she does, and she has a way of...seeing the truth, I suppose you could say." She turned her head to look at him, her blue eyes finding his. "I am not certain any of my sisters—or even my cousin—would be married today without her interference. She has a way of seeing when two people belong together." A question seemed to linger in her gaze, yet she refrained from asking it.

"So," Thorne began slowly, his gaze moving to a thick hedge up ahead, "your brothers and sisters are in Hyde Park?"

"So, it would seem."

He quickened his step, pulling her along. "And your parents?"

Christina frowned at his increased pace. "I am not certain. Perhaps they joined them. Or they went to call on someone. Why?"

With a last glance over his shoulder at the terrace, Thorne urged her around the corner of the hedge. "I doubt your grandmother will follow us into the garden."

Christina chuckled. "You would be correct in that assumption. Why? Why are you—?"

As soon as the hedge shielded them from curious eyes, Thorne abruptly turned to face her and all but caught her in his arms for her steps were still wide as she continued to try and keep up with him.

His arms slipped around her, and he could feel her breath against his lips as the distance between them shrunk to nothing in a matter of seconds. Her eyes widened, and he felt her lean back, momentarily overcome by the sudden closeness between them. "What are you—?" She broke off, and he could see understanding come to her eyes.

Thorne grinned at her, enjoying seeing her thrown off her guard. Clearly, she had not expected this; yet he could see temptation in her eyes. "Any objections?" he whispered, pulling her closer, holding her tighter, wanting her to know what he wanted and how desperately he wanted it.

Her breath faltered, and for a moment, she did not reply, her eyes wide and overwhelmed. Then she swallowed, and one little word emerged from her lips. "None."

Thorne felt a somewhat primitive sense of triumph that she did not refuse him especially when she had—as she had told him the other day—been unwilling to accept a kiss from a gentleman before.

Abandoning that thought quickly, though, Thorne lowered his head to hers, eager to feel the brush of her lips. Her eyes fluttered shut, and he smiled the second before his mouth claimed hers.

Never had he wanted anyone more, and he could not imagine for that to ever change.

Chapter Twenty-Two

A SCOUNDREL'S KISS

The moment his lips touched hers, Christina knew she was making a monumental mistake. She knew she ought not have allowed him to kiss her because now she knew. Now, she knew how wonderful it felt.

How intoxicating!

How...almost magical!

Irritatingly magical!

After all, had she not agreed to marry him to protect her friend? What precisely was she protecting Sarah from? From stolen kisses that made her breath catch in her throat? From sinking into his arms and feeling the whole world fall away?

Guilt swept over Christina, warring with the teasingly wonderful sensations she had never known existed. Yes, she had imagined a kiss to be...pleasant, perhaps.

But not this!

Never this!

In truth, she lacked the words to do it justice, to explain how it made her feel, how *he* made her feel.

His arms held her close, keeping her from stepping away—not that she wanted to. His lips moved over hers in an utterly possessive way. She could feel that he wanted to kiss her as much as she longed for him to do so. Passion simmered in her veins, and a new sense of curiosity sparked somewhere down low.

At the same time, Christina began to feel lightheaded, her limbs growing weak as she sank deeper into his arms. She felt his knuckles brush along the line of her jaw before his hand moved to the back of her head, holding her to him and deepening the kiss.

Did all men kiss like this? She wondered somewhere in the back of her mind. Did gentlemen? Or was this kiss among those unspeakable things she had heard old matrons whisper about?

If so, Christina could not understand their objections to common men. To her utter shame, she had to admit that now that she knew how he could make her feel, she would be hard pressed to keep her distance from him.

His teeth nipped her lower lip, and Christina gasped, her hands reaching up to settle upon his shoulders. She needed something to hold onto lest her knees were to buckle, which they threatened to do any moment now.

How was she ever to face Sarah again?

It was a thought Christina did not want to think, especially not here and now. She tried to banish it. She tried to keep her attention focused on the man holding her in his arms.

Her betrothed.

Her future husband.

Because she had stolen him from Sarah, had she not? As much as Christina wanted to believe that it was not so, that she had done what she had done in order to protect her friend, the truth could not be denied.

How was she to ever face Sarah again?

Balling her hands into fists, Christina twisted out of his embrace, her heart hammering in her chest in a way that made her think it would stop any moment. She staggered backward, unable to look at him, her heart and mind utterly confused.

"Is something wrong?" Thorne asked, his breathing coming as fast as hers. She could hear him moving toward her and then felt his hand upon her arm, urging her to turn and look at him.

"It's nothing," she shot back, walking a few steps away, trying her best to regain some measure of composure. If only her pulse would stop beating with such force!

A chuckle echoed to her ears as he came after her. "Do not tell me you find your concerns confirmed!" Again, his hand seized her arm and this time spun her around, his eyes seeking hers. "You cannot tell me that that was not..." He drew in a panting breath, passion still darkening his eyes.

"Magical," Christina whispered despite herself. She felt tears beginning to brim in her eyes so overcome was she with emotions, good and bad ones. What would she not give to be able to embrace this marriage? This man, and allow herself to be swept away on this tide?

Thorne pulled her into his arms once more, a wide smile coming to his face. "Indeed, utterly magical."

Staring up at him, Christina shook her head. "No, it cannot...I cannot." She pushed his arms away and took a step back. "It wasn't supposed to feel like this."

He frowned at her. "You're upset because our kiss felt magical?" He shook his head. "You did not want it to be good? Why?"

Christina felt her head continue to shake from side to side as she began to pace along the length of the hedge, her thoughts and emotions hopelessly jumbled. "I'm a most despicable person. How could I have done this? How—?"

His hand closed over her arm and pulled her to him. "What are you talking about?" Anger lingered in his gaze, and Christina wondered if she had hurt him with her reaction. Was that possible? "Why are you so determined to dislike me? To discount what is between us?" He shook his head at her again. "Are wives not supposed to care for their husbands? Is it in poor taste among the *ton*?" Contempt swung in his voice as he stared down at her.

Christina's breath still came fast as she found her gaze caught by his. She could not look away; neither could she answer, though. Part of her urged her to make it unmistakably clear that their marriage would be nothing more than a marriage of convenience. Had that not been his intention from the start?

Christina knew that it had. Still, the way he was looking at her right here, right now did not speak of a rational mind. The look in his eyes burned into hers, demanding an answer, demanding the truth. Could he see in her eyes somehow how deeply he affected her?

Closing her eyes, Christina could only hope that it was not so. "I believe it would be best for you to leave," she whispered weakly, taking a step back, surprised and equally disappointed to find his hands fall away, releasing her.

Somewhere, deep down, the traitorous part of her heart had hoped that he would not allow her, that he would insist she answer him.

Blinking, she lifted her chin and looked up at him, praying that her emotions were not written all over her face. "You should leave."

His gaze held hers, and she saw his lips pressed together into a tight line. "Is this what you want?"

Christina swallowed. "It is."

Reluctance showed upon his face, and that traitorous little part in Christina's heart rejoiced at the sight of it. What was she to do? Never had she expected herself to come to care for him. Not like this! It was a complication she had not foreseen. What was she to do?

In silence, they walked back to the house, the tension lingering between them in stark contrast to the lighthearted banter that had carried them outdoors earlier. Christina could sense waves of anger rolling off him. She could feel them brush against her skin. Out of the corner of her eye, she could see the tension in his shoulders and could not help but think that he was exercising great restraint. It seemed clear—even to her, someone who knew him so little—that he wanted nothing more but to confront her. Yet he did not. He respected her wishes, her own emotional state. Could he truly see how she felt?

In an odd way, his reaction frustrated Christina even more. She wanted him to be the villain. She needed him to be the villain! If he was the villain, she was the hero, saving the damsel in distress. But what if he was not the villain? What would that make her then?

The villain, a quiet voice whispered in her head.

Christina almost flinched for she knew it to be true.

As shocking as it was, Christina had to admit that Mr. Thorne Sharpe—gentleman or not—was a good and decent man and would in all likelihood have made a good and decent husband for Sarah.

If Christina had not interfered, that was.

Accepting his hat from a footman, Thorne stepped toward the door, then turned back around to look upon her. His eyes fell upon hers, and she could see that, yes, she had hurt him. Oh, she was truly making a mess of things!

"I will leave then," he said calmly although the tension in his voice still lingered. "I will leave," he took a step closer, and slowly lowered his head to hers, "for now."

Christina felt a shiver dance down her spine. Had his words been a threat or rather a promise? Either way, she could not deny that something inside of her rejoiced, knowing that her reaction had not driven him away.

He would return.

He was still her betrothed.

He was still hers.

Christina swallowed, doing her best to hold his gaze and not let him see how deeply those few words had unsettled her, stirred her heart. "Very well."

The footman moved to open the door as Thorne turned toward it, casting a last look at her over his shoulder. Unfortunately, the moment he made to depart, he pulled up short as someone else appeared on the front stoop, her face pale and her eyes wide.

Sarah.

Chapter Twenty-Three

A HEART'S TRUTH

Never in her life had Christina experienced a more awkward and painful moment. From the looks of it, neither had Thorne. He offered Sarah a polite greeting and a short bow and then quickly took his leave, undoubtedly relieved to escape the moment ahead.

Sarah, too, looked as though she was ready to faint. Her eyes were wide, and her cheeks were pale. Her gaze remained all but fixed upon Christina as though she did not dare look at Thorne. She never had, had she? Whenever Christina had seen Sarah with Thorne or near him, Sarah had always pointedly avoided eye contact as much as possible. She had always seemed frightened of him, the unease she felt in his presence written all over her face. Was that not what had prompted Christina to interfere?

Yes, initially she had been concerned for her friend. That had been her motivation, had it not? She had not set out to steal Sarah's intended because she wanted him for herself. That had simply happened somehow over time.

When the door finally closed after Thorne, Christina slipped an arm through Sarah's and pulled her away toward the drawing room. She could not help but wonder why Sarah had come because following the night Christina and Thorne had been discovered in the library, Sarah's parents had been far too furious with the Whickertons to allow their daughter to visit. The friends had exchanged the occasional note, but there had been no more contact than that. What was Sarah doing here now?

"Are you all right?" Christina asked as they seated themselves. She offered Sarah tea, praying that her hands would not tremble.

Sarah heaved a deep sigh and wrung her hands in her lap before looking up and meeting Christina's eyes. "I apologize for not seeing you sooner. My parents are still furious." Confusion and regret lingered in her voice, and Christina could see the same torn expression she suspected showed on her own face as well.

"Do not worry yourself," Christina assured her friend, trying her best to offer her a comforting smile. "I do understand, and I would never hold it against you. Your parents have an exceptionally good reason to react the way they do. I'm sorry for what happened."

A frown drove down Sarah's brows. "Never have I heard you speak with such understanding about my parents. You were always so furious with the way they used me in order to solve their own problems." Her gaze swept over Christina as though she were looking at someone she had never seen before. "What changed?"

Christina felt her hands begin to tremble, and she quickly folded them in her lap. "I do not know what you mean," she quickly said, glancing out the window so Sarah could not look into her eyes. "Perhaps it is simply that the threat of a forced marriage between you and...Mr. Sharpe is no longer looming upon the horizon. You are safe now." The words felt like ash in Christina's mouth.

Sarah's features softened, and a deeply affectionate smile came to her face. "You truly are the dearest of friends," she exclaimed in a relieved sigh. "The moment I learned of what had happened, I could not help but feel..." She broke off and bowed her head, then glanced up at Christina. "I'm a most despicable person, am I not?" She swallowed, then raised her chin determinedly. "I came here today to tell you that I cannot allow you to sacrifice your happiness for mine."

Christina froze. "Whatever do you mean?"

"I cannot allow you to marry him," Sarah burst out, her features tense with reluctance despite her exclamation to the contrary. "I cannot allow you to ruin your life for me. I've thought about it long and hard, and I have come to accept that me marrying Mr. Sharpe is the best solution for everyone."

Not for me, Christina thought to herself, desperately searching for some kind of argument that would convince Sarah to allow things to go ahead as planned. Or was this Christina's chance to step back? Was this the moment when she ought to admit to Sarah what a good man she had found Mr. Sharpe to be? Was this the moment that she ought to tell Sarah not to be afraid, but happy instead?

Was this the moment she ought to let him go?

"It would most certainly appease my parents," Sarah continued in a hushed voice. "They are so furious with me for—"

"Furious with you? Why would they be furious with *you*? You didn't do anything!"

Sarah's gaze dropped to her folded hands. "I...I failed to secure his affections."

Christina gritted her teeth lest she be swayed to voice her outrage with regard to Lord and Lady Hartmore's latest failure as parents. "You have nothing to blame yourself for, Sarah." Christina reached out a hand and gently placed it upon Sarah's. "Please, do not torture yourself. You are a good and kind person, and any man would be fortunate to call you his wife."

A small smile appeared upon Sarah's face. "You are kind to say so, but we both know that it is not true. Otherwise, I would be married already, would I not be?"

Christina shook her head vehemently. "I know no such thing. What I know is that your father's interest in gambling and your mother's need to re-furnish your family's estate three times a year have chased away most eligible suitors. It had nothing to do with you. You must believe me, Sarah. Your parents are the problem, not you."

Sarah's hand squeezed hers gratefully. "Be that as it may; I cannot let you marry him. I want to see you happy. I want to see you find love, like Louisa and Leonora did." Tears misted in her eyes whereas a wide smile stretched across Sarah's face. "The Whickertons marry for love after all. Everyone knows that."

Christina heaved a deep sigh, her heart twisting painfully at her friend's kind words. She knew she did not deserve them; yet she also knew that if she were to give up Thorne, she would regret it for the rest of her life. "And what about you? Do you not also dream of finding love?"

Sarah shrugged, once more averting her gaze. "Not everyone is lucky enough to find love. I've been out for too many seasons already, and yet I have never truly lost my heart to anyone." She looked up, blinking back tears. "Perhaps it is not meant to be for me."

Christina tightened her hold on Sarah's hand, more for her own sake than her friend's. "Do you truly wish to marry Mr. Sharpe?"

A brave smile came to Sarah's face. "Not everything in life is about what we wish."

Christina frowned. "Whenever you look at him, I see you tense. Why? How can you contemplate marrying someone who clearly makes you uncomfortable? Has anything happened between the two of you? Has he done something to you that—?" Christina felt the breath lodged in her throat as she contemplated something she did not dare believe. Still, sometimes the world had a way of shocking one that went beyond one's wildest imaginings. Could she truly have been wrong about Thorne? About the kind of man he was?

"What?" Sarah's eyes widened before she quickly shook her head. "No! Nothing ever happened. We barely spoke two words to each other."

Christina breathed a sigh of relief, surprised by how deeply she felt it. "Then why?"

Sarah bowed her head. "I cannot say for certain. I've heard...whispers." She glanced up at Christina. "You yourself have spoken harshly about him, about men of his kind. I cannot help but think that..." She broke off, clearly unable to finish the thought. "He makes me nervous. I don't know why, but I cannot help it."

Christina closed her eyes, remembering her own apprehensive thoughts only too well. She remembered how Thorne had laughed when she had spoken to him of unspeakable things common men demanded of their wives. Had their kiss been such an unspeakable thing? If so, Christina could not help but think that the world at large was very mistaken about common men.

Or perhaps simply about Thorne.

Giving Sarah's hand a gentle squeeze, Christina smiled at her friend. "I'm afraid I was severely mistaken about Mr. Sharpe's character," she said honestly, unable to lie to her friend, to *keep* lying to her friend.

Sarah frowned. "Whatever do you mean?"

"I mean," Christina began, dreading every word she was about to say, knowing equally well that it needed to be said, "that over the past fortnight I've had the opportunity to spend some time in Mr. Sharpe's company, and I have come to realize that...he is an incredibly good man." Her voice caught on the last word, and she swallowed hard, trying her best to remain strong.

Sarah's eyes were wide as they searched Christina's face. "Do you truly mean what you say?"

Christina nodded. "We've spoken about...many things. He's told me about his past, about his motivation in coming to London. He truly seems to care about those he's responsible for. He's one of those people who seek to make the world a better place. He has ambition, but not for himself. He's kind and caring and devoted. He knows how to laugh about himself. He does not hold a grudge, and he treats others with respect, no matter the foolish things they might have said." A wistful smile flickered across her face at the many wonderful memories she had acquired recently in Thorne's company.

Sarah's hand tightened upon hers, and Christina found her friend all but staring at her the moment her gaze refocused on the here and now. "You care for him," Sarah breathed, shock marking her features. "Is it possible? Have you truly come to care for him?"

"No!" The word flew from Christina's lips without thought, not because she intended to withhold the truth from her friend, but because she was not quite ready to admit it to herself.

Sarah's eyes narrowed, a bit of a chiding look coming to her face.

"Perhaps," Christina mumbled under her breath, unable to hold her friend's gaze. "A little."

"Look at me," Sarah instructed, her voice surprisingly steady. "Christina, would you please look at me?"

Christina lifted her head. "I'm so deeply sorry. I should never have interfered. He is a good man, and I'm certain he will make you a good husband. I think you will be happy with him." Her heart throbbed painfully as the words left her lips, and she could not recall ever having felt this wretched.

A look of awe came to Sarah's face as she slowly shook her head from side to side, her eyes still wide with shock...or rather surprise. "If you want him," Sarah whispered, a smile in her voice, "then marry him."

Thinking her ears had deceived her, Christina stared at her friend. "But I cannot! You were to marry him, and I should not have interfered. Who can say who your parents will settle on next? Sarah, you will continue to remain in danger to be married off to someone, anyone with a full purse if you do not marry Mr. Sharpe now." She looked imploringly into Sarah's eyes. "He is a good man. You will be safe with him."

"And what of you?"

"My parents will never force me into an unwanted marriage. You know that. I shall be safe. Always."

Sarah nodded. "Safe, yes. But is that enough? What will become of us if I marry the man you care for?" Slowly, she began shaking her head. "No, the only reason I came here today was to prevent you from throwing away your happiness for me. But," her hands grasped Christina's more tightly, "if marrying him makes you happy, then I want you to do it."

Christina's heart beat wildly in her chest. Hope made her smile, urging her to accept her friend's offer. Still, guilt and fear lingered, concern for Sarah's future, compelling her to insist otherwise. "I could never be happy as long as you are miserable."

"We do not know what the future will bring. Perhaps I shall find love after all. But not now. Not with Mr. Sharpe." Deep longing rested in Sarah's eyes, and Christina could understand that she did not want to marry a man who might never love her. "Has he spoken to you of love?"

Christina shook her head, feeling that blossom of hope slowly whither. "He has not." Only had he not said that he liked her? And had he not said so in a way that had made her insides dance with joy?

Perhaps one day...

"I do not wish to make this decision for you," Sarah stated clearly, a new determination in her eyes that Christina had rarely seen before. "It is yours and only yours to make. However, I urge you to think on it. Do not throw away something that could mean your happiness. Think it through and tell me what you decide." Giving Christina's hands a last encouraging squeeze, Sarah rose to her feet. "I need to return home before my parents realize my absence." She moved away, and then stopped at the door, looking back once more. "Ask yourself what you want, and don't be afraid to reach for it."

Then the door closed behind Sarah, leaving Christina alone with her thoughts. All those many thoughts, now more contradicting than ever. What was she to do?

Despite Sarah's urgings, Christina could not disregard her friend's future. No, Sarah was not her responsibility. Still, they had been friends since childhood. As Sarah had said, neither one of them would be happy if the other were miserable. What was she to do?

In truth, Christina could not say if she would ever come to love Thorne. Certainly, she had come to care for him, but what did that mean? Would she still care for him a year from now? Or would time teach them that they did not suit after all? How could she be certain?

A deep sigh left her lips as she sank deeper into her seat, her shoulders slouching as her head rolled back and her eyes closed.

What on earth was she to do?

Chapter Twenty-Four

IRRITATINGLY MAGICAL

The day had finally come. It was the night before his wedding day, and Thorne found himself seated at the Whickertons' large dinner table, surrounded by Whickertons left and right, his somewhat sullen-looking betrothed across from him.

Ever since their kiss roughly a week ago, something had changed between them. Thorne could not quite say what it was; however, whenever they had seen each other since, she had reacted in a rather peculiar manner to his presence. Sometimes she had seemed rather hesitant and even displeased with his visit. Other times he could have sworn she had all but longed to see him. Unfortunately, no opportunity to be truly alone together had arisen since, and so Thorne kept wondering what had happened.

Had it truly been their kiss?

"Three granddaughters married in one year," the dowager countess chuckled from one end of the long table. "Shall we make a wager?" She looked around the table, something mischievous sparking in her pale eyes as they came to linger upon her as of yet unmarried grandchildren. "The year is barely half over. Perhaps enough time is left to seek matches for all of you."

The youngest Whickerton Harriet laughed and shook her head. "You are too sweet, Grandma, but there is no need to play matchmaker for me. I have," she glanced down at her lap, "other plans." Then she lifted her hands and set a toad onto the tabletop.

Thorne stared as did many others, completely caught off guard by the youngest Whickerton's unusual behavior.

"Harriet!" the eldest Whickerton Juliet chided, her cheeks darkening as she cast a quick glance at Thorne. "I had hoped you would portray better manners in the presence of a guest."

Harriet chuckled. "He is not a guest, is he?" She grinned at him. "He and Christina are all but married, which makes him our brother." Her gaze darted to her two other brothers-in-law, Lord Barrington and Lord Pemberton, each seated next to his wife. "I think it about time he knows our true colors."

While Lord and Lady Whickerton exchanged a knowing look, the dowager countess chuckled loudly. "That is too true, my dear. There should be no secrets among family, do you not agree, Mr. Sharpe?" Her eyes twinkled wickedly, and Thorne felt a slight chill crawl down his back as he thought of Samantha.

"Most certainly," he replied, then turned his gaze to Christina, wondering about her quiet demeanor. Never had she been one at a loss for words; however, recently, it seemed she had nothing left to say.

Thorne wondered if he should have told her about Samantha. He had considered it. Only he had worried that it might be a reason for her to change her mind, and he had not wanted to give her any such reason. Still, he wondered what would happen if Christina did not welcome the little girl into their lives. Perhaps it would have been wiser to part ways instead of force them together against Christina's will.

Perhaps he ought to have given her a choice.

Yet the truth was that he wanted her. But did she want him as well? Was that what their kiss had taught her? That she did not want him? That day, though, she had called their kiss magical, had she not? It had seemed as though she had been overwhelmed...yet strangely displeased to have found passion in his arms. Why would that bother her? Was she truly afraid of what else he might demand of her as her husband? Perhaps he ought to address the issue.

Although Christina remained somewhat quiet for the remainder of the evening, Thorne watched in delight as the rest of the family conversed easily. Laughter echoed through the room countless times. He saw glowing eyes and rosy cheeks as food was passed around and stories were shared. Everyone spoke without restraint, Harriet in particular, her toad returned to her room upstairs only after it had found its way into the bread basket, causing a shriek to escape Juliet's lips.

It was a wonderful night, quite unlike those at home with Samantha. Of course, Thorne loved the girl dearly. Yet the house was rather quiet with only the two of them in it. How would Samantha feel living amongst a large family such as the Whickertons?

A smile came to Thorne's face for he knew that she would adore it. Her little eyes would light up and she would shriek with delight.

When the evening finally drew to an end, Christina escorted him back out into the hall. At first, some of her siblings as well as her two new brothers-in-law intended to follow; however, a few words from the dowager countess held them back.

Thorne had to smile yet again, surprised to have found an ally in the old lady and appreciating it more than he would have thought.

The slowly setting sun shone in through the tall glass windows and cast a warm glow over the main hall. No footman lingered nearby, and Thorne wondered if that, too, had been the dowager countess' doing, allowing Christina and himself a moment alone.

"Good night," his betrothed whispered, turning to face him, a somewhat strained smile upon her face.

Casting another glance over his shoulder, Thorne assured himself that they were indeed alone. Then he stepped toward her, his gaze insistent as it sought hers. "Did you lie?"

Her head snapped up, and a frown came to her face. "Why? What do you mean?" Her hands seemed to tremble before she balled them into fists and forced them behind her back as though seeking to hide them from him.

Thorne frowned, trying to understand what he was missing. "The other day, when I kissed you, you seemed to like it." An unsteady breath left her lips. "Was that not true?"

Instead of answering him, Christina bowed her head in an oddly submissive gesture he would never have expected from her. He could not say he liked it. In fact, it troubled him.

"Why are you acting so strangely?" Thorne inquired, placing a hand upon her arm.

Her eyes rose to meet his, and he was relieved not to see anything akin to fear. Rather it was something that spoke of a torn heart. But why? "Who are you to say I am acting strangely," she shot back, a hint of anger in her voice. "You barely know me. We've spoken once or twice, no more than that. We are all but strangers. So how would you know—?"

Thorne pulled her toward him, cutting off her words. Her eyes widened, and she lifted her hands to his chest. Still, he did not release her, but looked down into her eyes, daring her to keep contradicting him. "Do not lie to me," he whispered quietly, feeling the soft puff of her breath against his lips. "You're not shy and coy and insecure. You are none of these things. You're bold and dauntless and...impertinent." He grinned at her.

Displeasure came to her features as she glared at him. "Are you accusing me of—?"

"I'm not accusing you of anything," Thorne replied, very much aware of the fact that she was not trying to free herself from his grasp. "I like it." He lowered his head even further until his forehead almost touched hers. "I like you, the real you." He searched her eyes. "I don't know who you've been these past few days. Tell me what happened. What has changed?"

Christina swallowed, that torn look once more in her eyes before they darted lower and touched upon his lips. He could see the memory of their kiss resurfacing in her mind. He could also see that she was upset with herself for remembering. "Nothing happened." Her hands pushed against his chest. "Would you please release me? This is most inappropriate."

Thorne chuckled and instead held her closer. "Do you still wish to marry me?" He demanded, uncertain whether or not it was wise to ask this question. What if she said no?

Her eyes widened, and she stopped struggling as she stared up at him. "Why would you ask me that?"

"I simply am."

Her gaze hardened. "Have you found a more advantageous match? Someone else who suits your purpose more fully?" Bitterness lingered in her voice.

Thorne could not help but enjoy himself for her reaction was quite telling. If he was not at all mistaken, then she was jealous, was she not? At least, a little. "Do you still wish to marry me?" he asked yet again, holding her tightly in his embrace.

"Tell me!" she snapped instead of replying to his question. "Is there another you would prefer to marry? Another family whose connections are superior to ours? Are you hoping I will cry off?" Thorne could see that she tried to appear rational as though they were truly discussing no more than a business contract. However, emotions flared in her eyes, and he could see that it was not her mind asking these questions, but her heart.

The knowledge brought him joy. "Do you still wish to marry me?" he repeated, his right arm tightening upon her back.

Christina gasped and drew in a sharp breath. "Why won't you answer me?"

Thorne chuckled. "Why won't *you* answer *me?*" His left hand slipped into her hair, moving to the back of her head. "Do you still wish to marry me?"

"Release me!"

"Answer me!"

Her eyes burned with anger...as well as something else. "I told you to release me!"

Slowly, Thorne shook his head. "Answer me first."

Christina rolled her eyes at him. "You are a most insufferable man!"

"Do you still wish to marry m—?"

"Yes!"

Her swift reply stunned them both for it was not merely a rational statement, but instead a deeply emotional answer.

Thorne did not hesitate in his own response. Drawing her ever tighter against him, he lowered his head and kissed her.

He kissed her the way he had kissed her that day out in the gardens. He kissed her the way he wanted to, the way she wanted him to because after an initial moment of stunned surprise, Christina sank into his arms as she had that day. Whether she wanted to admit it or not, there was something between them. She felt something for him, and although she might not like it, it was true, nonetheless.

Her hands snaked upward and came around his neck as she pushed herself closer, returning his kiss with a boldness that stole his breath. Yet he reveled in it and allowed his own hands to travel over her in a way that would be considered most inappropriate by anyone's standards.

Still, Christina did not object.

Only when the dim cacophony of voices from the dining room seemed to be drawing closer did Thorne remember that they were indeed *not* alone. A disapproving growl rose in his throat as he forced himself to break their kiss, urging her back down onto her feet before he took a step back.

Her cheeks were flushed as she stared up at him, confusion swirling in her blue eyes. Still, he knew that she had enjoyed their embrace as much as he had.

Thorne grinned at her. "Good," was all he said before he quickly inclined his head to her and then took his leave lest he succumb to the need to pull her into his arms all over again.

Stopping in the doorway, he turned back to look at her. "Until tomorrow, *Wife*."

A slight tremor seemed to dance down her spine as she inhaled a deep breath and forced her chin back up. "You should not have kissed me."

Thorne shrugged. "Perhaps not. Yet I cannot bring myself to regret it. It was magical, was it not?" He lifted one brow in a teasing manner.

Although Christina shook her head ever so slightly, she could not prevent a smile from showing upon her face. "Irritatingly so."

Chuckling, Thorne tipped his hat and then left, his feet carrying him down the few steps to the pavement as though he were walking on air. He felt different.

Better.

Lighter.

Was this happiness?

Chapter Twenty-Five

A WEDDING DAY

Thorne's wedding day dawned bright and early. He felt an eagerness in his limbs he could not even remember from his childhood days. Whatever today would bring, it was the first day of the rest of his life.

A life he had always wanted, but never dared to dream of.

And then Lord Hartmore appeared on his doorstep the moment Thorne made to leave.

The other man seemed rushed, his eyes wide and his breathing more rapid than Thorne would have expected. Still, the look upon his face was one of imminent triumph, a smile curling up the corners of his mouth the second he beheld Thorne. "Ah, you haven't left yet. How marvelous!"

Of course, Thorne found nothing marvelous about it. "I'm afraid I have no time," he replied, making to stride past the other man and down to his waiting carriage. "You might not be aware of it, but today is my wedding day."

A dark chuckle left Lord Hartmore's lips. "Believe me, I'm very much aware of it. As it is, I would have sought you out much sooner. Unfortunately, the needed information only reached me this morning." A self-serving grin came to his face.

Thorne felt a cold shiver snake down his back. "What information?" he asked frowning, wondering what Lord Hartmore was up to. After all, the man seemed sickeningly confident. It did not bode well.

"Shall we speak inside?" the other man asked, gesturing across the threshold. "You might not like for others to overhear what I have to say." His brows rose meaningfully.

Thorne inhaled a slow breath, steeling his features so as not to let on how deeply the man's words unsettled him. Had the man dug into his past? His life? "If you insist," Thorne finally said, a bored expression upon his face that was not easy to maintain. "But make it quick." They stepped inside, and Thorne gestured for the footmen to leave before turning to Lord Hartmore. "What is it then?"

The man's grin widened. "I am here to insists that you marry my daughter as you promised, Sir." His eyes seemed to sparkle with utter delight, and it gave Thorne pause. "I am aware it will cause quite the scandal; however, a man of your kind should not concern himself with such trivial matters."

"Out with it!" Thorne snapped with an annoyed huff, which in turn gave Lord Hartmore pause, his eyes narrowing in mild confusion. "You clearly believe to have some kind of damning information and are here to blackmail me, is that not so?"

For a moment, Lord Hartmore seemed taken aback, his confidence wavering. Then, however, he seemed to remember that Thorne's accusation was after all the truth and that he would walk away from this the victor.

"Well?" Thorne pressed. "I haven't got all day as you're well aware."

Lord Hartmore straightened. "As you wish," he conceded, the look upon his face one of deepest enjoyment. "I have recently learned that you, Sir, are the father of an illegitimate daughter. A child that lives in your household and bears your name." The man's grin widened for he clearly expected Thorne to break down, perhaps even beg for mercy or at the very least give in.

Thorne, of course, had no such intention. While he could not deny that the thought of Lord Hartmore revealing Samantha's existence to the Whickertons—especially today of all days!—was deeply unsettling, he knew better than to allow that emotion to show upon his face. He had been in far too many confrontations to reveal his hand so easily.

"Yes, and?" he asked nonchalantly, allowing the hint of boredom upon his face to deepen.

Lord Hartmore paused, his gaze once more narrowing in confusion. "If you do not call off this marriage and uphold the promise you made to my daughter, I will be forced to reveal her existence to Lord Whickerton. I cannot imagine he will allow his daughter to marry a man of your questionable character."

Thorne snorted. "But you would?"

The man's lips pressed together. "What will it be?" he gritted out, his expected triumph far less glorious than he had expected.

Thorne heaved a bit of an impatient sigh. "What makes you think the Whickertons are not aware of her?" he asked with as much confidence as he could muster. "After all, there is a reason the *ton* refers to them as the Wicked Whickertons. Believe me, I was not concerned for a second to share news of my daughter with them, and I was right to do so. They were delighted to learn of her, and if my darling girl had not caught a cold, she would be here with us today to join in our celebration." He held the other man's gaze as he took a step forward. "In fact, my new bride and I will travel to Pinewood Manor tomorrow so that Samantha can meet her new mother." He allowed a slow grin to spread across his face. "But, please, if you feel the need to embarrass yourself, my lord, then feel free to accompany me to my wedding. In fact, may I offer you a ride in my carriage?"

With his look of utter indifference in place, Thorne all but held his breath, praying that Lord Hartmore was a greater fool than he had initially thought.

To his great relief, Fortune smiled on him that day.

Twice.

Within moments, Lord Hartmore's face began to turn a darker shade of red, his hands balling into fists at his sides. Fury burnt in his eyes, and yet Thorne could read deepest shame in the man's gaze. His mouth opened and closed a few times as though he wished to vent his anger, but then thought better of it.

A moment later, he spun around and stalked out, his footsteps thundering down the steps to the pavement.

Thorne heaved a deep breath, praying that he had been successful in fooling Lord Hartmore and that the man was not at this very moment rushing over to the Whickertons. Although Thorne could not believe that the Whickertons would reject Samantha, there was a better place and time for them to find out.

Indeed, he ought to have said something much sooner! Now, however, it was too late. Now, all he could do was proceed as planned and hope that Christina would forgive him.

If only he could be certain of that!

As it had been his bride's wish to hold the festivities at her family's townhouse, Thorne soon found himself striding across the Whickertons' threshold instead of awaiting her arrival at his own rented townhouse. Fortunately, Lord Hartmore seemed blessedly absent.

The Whickerton home seemed like a beehive that morning. Maids and footmen dashed every which way, carrying items to and fro. Flowers were everywhere, all the curtains pulled back to allow in the early summer sun. It was a beautiful house; more than that, it was a home. Thorne spotted paintings of each of the siblings as well as their parents and grandparents here and there, along the wall leading up the staircase or down the corridor toward Lord Whickerton's study.

Yes, it made him wistful. It made him realize what he had lost. What childhood joy had been denied him. The same childhood joy he now wanted for Samantha. Thorne could only hope that all would go according to plan. He had never been one to deceive others; only considering Christina's flaring temper, he had felt rather uncertain about whether or not it would be safe to reveal his own family situation to her at an earlier moment.

Perhaps he had judged her wrongly. Still, he had not dared risk it and could now only hope that all would go well and his plans would not come crashing down around him.

"You look happy, Sir," the dowager countess remarked from behind him, a slight chuckle in her voice.

Allowing a smile to steal onto his face, Thorne turned to face her. "I suppose I am. Are you genuinely surprised?"

Her pale eyes were watchful, but she, too, was smiling. "Not at all. We both know it is the outcome I had hoped for."

His brows rose. "You hoped for my happiness?" He chuckled. "I would rather have thought you would hope for hers."

Giving him a rather indulgent look, the dowager countess hobbled a step closer, leaning heavily upon her cane. "Perhaps my hopes extended to you both. Is that not what a marriage is? A union of two into one?" Her eyes swept over his face. It was a fluid motion, and yet at some point it seemed as though her gaze jarred to a halt. Her eyes narrowed as though she had detected something she had not expected. "What is it?"

Thorne swallowed. "Pardon me?"

Hobbling closer, the dowager's eyes squinted even farther. "You are concerned," she remarked as though reading him like a book. "There's a frown line upon your face. It has deepened." Her eyes met his. "Is it the child?"

Thorne almost doubled over as he stared at her. "You...You know of—?" Was Lord Hartmore here after all?

The dowager chuckled, gently patting his arm in a comforting way. "Do not worry yourself. All will be well. I guarantee it."

Not knowing what to say, Thorne stared at her. "Does everyone else know?" His gaze moved down the corridor toward the front hall, his thoughts straying to Christina. Had she already called off the wedding?

"Not if you have not told anyone," the dowager countess replied, once more giving his arm a reassuring pat.

"How do you know?" Thorne asked, coming to believe that the dowager had not learned what she knew from Lord Hartmore. No, it seemed she had known for some time.

The dowager grinned. "I have my ways."

Thorne sighed deeply. "She will be furious, will she not?" Somehow it felt good to say it out loud, to have someone who would listen and not judge.

Christina's grandmother grinned at him. "Of course, she will be...at first." A warm smile came to her face as her thoughts no doubt settled upon her beloved granddaughter. "She is headstrong and determined, but she's also kind and compassionate. She will be furious, yes, but in the end, she will love her because she simply won't be able to help herself. You ought to know what that feels like."

Thorne nodded, wondering at the same time how much the dowager truly knew about his past and about Samantha. "Thank you." Indeed, speaking to her had lifted a heavy weight off his heart. As had knowing that Lord Hartmore was nowhere around!

"That is what family is for, is it not?"

Thorne nodded, smiling at her. "So, I have heard. I am glad to see that for once gossips were right."

The dowager countess chuckled. "I suppose it does happen upon occasion." She gestured down the corridor. "Now, go and speak to your betrothed. I imagine she is about as nervous as you are."

Thorne frowned. "Who said I was nervous?"

Shaking her head at him, the dowager once more pointed her cane down the corridor and then turned and walked away, still chuckling.

Indeed, when Christina finally made her way down the stairs and met him in the front hall, Thorne could see that her nerves were about as unsteady as his own. It was a significant day, and they still knew so little about each other, no doubt each of them afraid to have their hopes disappointed.

"You look beautiful," Thorne told her in a whispered voice as he offered her his arm the moment she stepped off the last stair. His gaze held hers for another second before it once more dipped down and swept over her light blue gown. It shimmered like the sky on a bright summer day, complementing the deep blue of her eyes and the golden glow of her curls.

She returned his smile weakly. "Thank you." Her hand trembled as it came to rest upon his arm.

The ceremony was thankfully short-lived. It was held at a nearby church, and Thorne was relieved that he had decided to visit the Whickertons' home beforehand.

Indeed, the dowager had been right. He was nervous, and he could see that Christina was as well. They sat seated next to one another in the carriage, the dowager across from them. Not many words were spoken on the way there or on the way back. Still, Thorne could feel Christina beside him. He heard her breathing, took note of the stolen glances she cast in his direction, saw the slight tremble in her hands as she willed herself to maintain her composure as best as possible.

It was these few moments, shared with one another, that gave him strength before they returned to the Whickertons' home and were received by a small crowd of people. With her hand upon his arm, they gracefully accepted well-wishes and congratulations. Most of the guests were smiling while he could see apprehension and doubt as well as confusion and open disapproval on the faces of others.

The *ton* had come to call his new wife's family the *Wicked Whicker-tons* for it seemed that the whispers of scandal were never far off lately. Both of Christina's elder sisters, Louisa and Leonora, had caused somewhat of a stir before they had found their own happily-ever-after, and the news of how Thorne and Christina had come to be engaged had, of course, also spread among the *ton*, causing even more whispers. Yes, some very proper and sour old matrons refused to attend events if the Whickertons were present. Some had retreated, openly showing their disapproval of the family's rather eventful life. Yet most seemed far too curious to deny themselves the first-hand experience of witnessing the Whickertons mingle.

Fortunately, Lord Hartmore was the exception.

Thorne could not help but laugh at the thought of how silly everyone was behaving. These nonsensical rules governed everyone's life, and yet they held absolutely no meaning. No true meaning. No meaning governed by nature's laws.

To him, it was all very ludicrous.

The wedding breakfast was a rather intimate affair for Lord and Lady Whickerton had invited only family and closest friends. Thorne himself had only a few acquaintances in London and had therefore refrained from adding to the guest list. He knew no one in town whom he would wish to see at his own wedding.

Of course, all of his new wife's family was present. Thorne would not have wanted it any other way. After all, deep down, he was still hoping that one day, one day they would look at him and see family as well.

Today, however, he found them looking at him with caution. While the youngest, Harriet, smiled and laughed openly, the new Lady

Pemberton in particular seemed rather disapproving. Her gaze narrowed whenever it fell upon him and filled with deepest concern whenever it fell upon Christina. She truly worried for her sister.

Thorne could not deny that the thought troubled him. He had hoped that his wife's family would know that despite his humble upbringing he had grown into a decent man. He knew himself to possess numerous faults, of course. Nonetheless, he always thought of himself as someone who tried his best to do the right thing.

Perhaps with regard to Christina, he had been selfish after all. Could they sense it?

From across the room, Thorne watched his new wife speak to her two married sisters. All their faces held a look of concern as they whispered to one another. He could see Christina look up at him every once in a while before she would turn back to converse with Louisa and Leonora. He could not help but wonder what they were speaking of and wished the day would finally end so that they could be alone together and finally speak openly.

Something was bothering his new bride. Something was on her mind that plagued her. He had to know what it was, or he knew he would not find any sleep tonight.

"Welcome to the family." Christina's brother, Troy, stepped up to him, his words contrary to the look upon his face. His eyes were watchful, not unlike his grandmother's. However, no smile lingered upon his face. Instead, it rather resembled a scowl, something apprehensive and even slightly threatening in the way he was looking at Thorne.

Ignoring the slight hostility in his new brother-in-law, Thorne offered him a kind smile. "Thank you. I deeply appreciate all your family has done, and I hope that in the future we all shall be close." He glanced at Christina. "I know it would mean a lot to her."

His new brother-in-law followed his gaze before it returned to him. "It would, yes." Something in his expression softened; only a little, but it was there.

Still, a moment later, his lips thinned, and his jaw hardened as he took a step toward Thorne, his own blue eyes narrowed as they fixed Thorne with a somewhat menacing glare. "My sister might seem strong, dauntless even," he said very slowly, his voice so low that Thorne had to strain his ears to listen. "Yet there is a deeply vulnerable side to her. A side she herself is not even aware of for she has yet to see the ugliest side of the world."

Thorne nodded, finding his new brother-in-law's words to all but echo thoughts of his own.

"I am here to make it unmistakably clear," Christina's brother continued, "that if you treat her with anything less than absolute respect," his voice dropped into a low, menacing growl, "I will tear you limb from limb. Is that understood?"

Thorne would have been offended by his new brother-in-law's words had he not seen the fierce protectiveness and deepest concern that lingered beneath the man's hostility and his accusatory words. "You have my word," Thorne vowed solemnly. "I shall guard her happiness with my life."

For a long moment, the two men simply stood there, regarding one another, trying to make out the other's character. Then Christina's brother nodded slowly. "Good. I am glad to hear it."

Thorne knew that he would be tested, and he did not mind. Still, he could not help but notice that while his wife had a large family surrounding her, shielding her, protecting her, *he* had no one.

No one except for Samantha.

If only she could have been here today!

Chapter Twenty-Six

A HUSBAND'S CONSIDERATION

Christina was not certain whether she wanted the wedding breakfast to be over quickly or for it to last as long as humanly possible. She continued glancing in her new husband's direction, uncertain how the sight of him made her feel. There was still that fluttery response in her belly from his smile each time he caught her looking at him. Another part of her, though, somewhere centered near her heart, felt heavy and burdened and unable to step into this marriage with hope and expectation.

Sarah had not come.

Deep down, Christina was not surprised. Of course, Sarah had not come. Her parents would not have allowed her. Nevertheless, Christina had hoped to be able to speak to her friend. She had put it off for the past sennight, and now, it was too late.

All Sarah had asked was for Christina to tell her what it was she wanted; whether she wanted to marry Thorne or not; only Christina had not voiced her intentions either way. She had simply remained quiet, knowing that it was foolish to wait and expect life to sort itself out. Yet she had.

And now she was married.

Married!

Was that reason for joy or sadness? Oddly enough, it seemed both were applicable.

"Are you all right?" her mother asked gently, brushing a curl from her forehead and tucking it behind her ear. Her blue eyes were full of concern, determinedly held at bay so as not to worry Christina further. "You look..." She simply broke off; yet her meaning was clear. How could it not be?

Christina sighed, not knowing what to say. After all, she had not shared any of these thoughts with her mother. A part of her desperately wanted to while another feared that her mother would tell her unmistakably that, yes, she had been selfish, that she had betrayed her friend.

Sarah was simply too good a person to have said so. Of course, that did not mean that she did not feel it, that she did not think it. Was that why she had not found a way to escape her parents today of all days?

"I'm fine," Christina told her mother, willing a bit of a smile on her face. Still, the look in her mother's eyes told her clearly that she was fooling no one.

Her mother cleared her throat, her gaze momentarily falling from Christina's. "Is there anything...you wish to know? Anything you wish to talk about?"

As before, Christina could see apprehension on her mother's face. "It is not necessary," she replied, seeking to settle her mother's nerves. "I spoke to Louisa and Leonora, and I feel quite at ease." She inhaled a deep breath, seeing the doubt in her mother's eyes. "It is only Sarah I worry about."

"How so?" A frown came to her mother's face. "I thought you were doing this, marrying him, in order to ensure that she would not have to." She glanced over her shoulder at Christina's new husband. "Are you saying that is not the reason why you agreed to marry him?"

Christina closed her eyes, emotions within her warring with what to do. "At first, I thought so," she finally admitted, her eyes finding her mother's once more. "Now, I am not certain."

A hopeful smile came to her mother's face. "Is it possible that you have come to care for him?"

Christina bowed her head. "It is not only possible. It is highly likely."

To her surprise, her mother pulled her into her arms, a relieved sob leaving her lips. "Oh, I'm extremely glad for you, my child. You have no idea how much I worried for your happiness."

Christina embraced her mother, feeling some of the tension leave her body.

Releasing her, her mother stepped back, her hands remaining entwined with Christina's. "Then why are you concerned? If you care for him, you should be happy." Blue eyes searched Christina's face, incomprehension in them.

"He is a good man."

Her mother's frown deepened. "And that is a problem?"

"He would also have been good for Sarah." Christina shook her head as another wave of guilt washed over her. "Now, she is once more in danger of being married off to...anyone. Whatever happens to her now, it will be my fault!" Tears burned in her eyes, and she quickly blinked them away.

Her mother's eyes widened before she pulled Christina into another soothing hug. "Oh, my dearest Chris, you cannot think that. You—"

Christina pulled back. "But it is the truth. I know it to be." She shook her head and took a step back, unable to discuss this any further, knowing that she would break apart if she did. Never had Christina felt so powerless, yet so selfish at the same time.

"It is time for us to leave now," Christina told her mother before glancing at her husband across the room, his eyes upon her in a way that made her wonder if he knew how she felt. "It is time for us to leave."

Suddenly, Christina felt as though she could not bear her family's inquisitive glances a moment longer. They knew her too well. Indeed, never would she have thought that it could be a downside to having a loving family. A family who took an interest in her life. A family who saw how she felt. But right here, right now, it was.

She needed to get away.

"I suppose it may be time for us to depart, my dear," her husband's voice suddenly spoke out from behind her shoulder. She felt his fingers touch her elbow, asking her to turn and look at him.

Christina nodded, wondering if perhaps he actually knew what she needed in that moment. She looked up at him and saw concern in his eyes as they swept over her face.

Concern and confusion.

Indeed, he did not know what made her want to flee; yet he had responded to her need without a moment of hesitation. It made her like him even more, which was equally a blessing and a curse. Would she forever feel torn about him?

Although her family was somewhat reluctant to let her leave, Christina insisted. Goodbyes were exchanged and well-wishes repeated before the newlyweds made their way out the door and down to the pavement to where the carriage stood waiting...to take them home.

Home.

Before entering the carriage, Christina turned back and looked upon the townhouse she had called home her whole life. How strange would it be to live elsewhere now? Would she ever come to think of another house as her home? Right here in this moment, she could not imagine it to be so.

"It feels odd, does it not?" Thorne asked beside her, something knowing in his voice as though he understood her perfectly. "Sometimes places are just that, and sometimes places hold our hearts."

Her gaze moved from her old home to her new husband. "Have you ever left a place you considered home behind?"

He remained quiet for a moment, then slowly shook his head. "Not in the way you are right now." He held her gaze for a moment longer, then he offered her his hand.

Christina took it and allowed him to assist her into the carriage, strangely relieved that she would not be facing this new chapter of her life alone. Only he was a stranger to her, was he not? Then why was it that his mere presence seemed to calm her nerves and put her heart at ease?

It was late afternoon when the carriage rolled down the street toward her husband's rented townhouse. Christina could not help but wonder for how much longer they would remain in town. Thus far, she had not asked him of his intentions. How soon would he insist they return to Manchester? How much more time did he need to set his affairs in London in order?

"What are you thinking about?" Thorne asked into the silence lingering in the carriage. He sat across from her, his eyes watching her with a mixture of apprehension and curiosity. Was it possible that he felt not unlike she did herself?

Christina sighed and leaned back in her seat, allowing her eyes to shift to him. "I don't quite know. There's so much on my mind that I have trouble focusing on just one thing."

Her husband nodded. "I know what that feels like."

"You do?" Christina regarded him with a frown, wondering how many facets of her husband she had yet to discover.

A soft chuckle drifted from his lips. "Is that so unusual? Life is made up of so many parts, and I suppose it would be somewhat contemptuous to expect them to all line up neatly and not come rushing at one all at the same time."

Christina felt herself smile at him. "And what do you do when life rushes at you from all sides?"

He shrugged. "I try my best not to be overrun."

"And do you succeed?"

Again, he shrugged. "Sometimes." His eyes looked into hers as though he knew that there was more she wished to ask.

"And what do you do when life knocks you down? What then?" Never had Christina experienced it herself. Yes, that night, years ago, when her aunt had come to Whickerton Grove, her life had been... shaken. Yet it had not knocked her down, not in the sense it threatened to do now.

Thorne held her gaze, then leaned forward and rested his elbows upon his knees. "I get back onto my feet. What else is there to do? Of course, I suppose one could lie down and wait for death." A slow smile curled up the corners of his lips. "However, I've always found that to be a rather ineffective way to handle life."

Still smiling, Christina regarded him thoughtfully, wondering about the man she had married. "And what now? What are your plans? When will you—?" She swallowed. "When will we return to Manchester?"

Her husband opened his mouth to reply; however, in that moment the carriage pulled to a halt. "We have arrived, Sir," the coachman called from up on the box.

Christina exhaled a deep breath, then followed her new husband outside, accepting his arm as she lifted her gaze to her new, somewhat temporary home.

It looked like a house, a house like so many others. Would she ever look at it and feel differently?

"Should we go inside?" Thorne asked, his eyes once more upon her in that slightly unnerving way of his.

Christina nodded and allowed him to guide her inside. He quickly introduced her to his household staff before escorting her upstairs. Christina was somewhat surprised for she had expected to be shown up to her chambers by a maid perhaps or even the housekeeper. To her even greater surprise, her husband stepped into her chambers after her and then closed the door. "What are you doing?" she asked, unable to prevent herself from taking a step back. "Husbands are supposed to—" She broke off when she felt heat rush to her cheeks.

Thorne smiled at her knowingly. "Husbands are supposed to do what?" he asked teasingly as he slowly moved toward her.

Christina squared her shoulders, trying her best to ignore the pulsing heat that slowly sneaked up her neck. "Husbands are supposed to give their wives time to...prepare." Oh dear, had her voice truly trembled upon the last word?

The blasted man's smile grew wider. "Prepare for what?"

"As though you do not know?" Christina huffed out, her hands rising to settle upon her hips. "Do not tease me! It is rude and un-gentlemanly and—"

He stopped barely an arm's length in front of her. "I thought we had already established that I am not a gentleman." His brows rose in challenge as he looked down at her. "There is no need for you to be afraid. Yes, I am teasing you, but that is all." The humor left his face and was replaced by something most sincere, something that immediately chased away the nervous flutter in Christina's stomach.

"Then why did you step inside?" she asked, regarding him carefully.

She wanted to trust him. She wanted a marriage like her parents, like her sisters. Yet she had observed here and there, that although some women anticipated their marriage, their outlook changed after the wedding had taken place. It had sometimes made Christina wonder about how truthful people truly were during courtship and how many spouses woke up married to a stranger unlike the person they had thought to marry.

"You seem distraught," Thorne replied simply. "I have been waiting for a moment to speak to you, to ask you. What is on your mind? Is there something that worries you?" His eyes traveled over her face before finding hers once more.

Christina knew that she could not tell him the truth because if she did, then he would know. He would know that foolishly she had come to care for him while for him their marriage was nothing more than a business transaction. He might like her. He might find her amusing and appealing, but did he care for her? The way she was beginning to care for him?

Christina doubted it. "I have been wondering how soon I will need to say farewell to my family." She swallowed. "How soon do you intend to return to Manchester?"

A slow smile came to his face, filled with anticipation. "I have no intention of returning to Manchester."

For a moment, Christina thought she had misunderstood him. Yet that smile remained upon his face, his eyes expectant as they looked into hers. "You do not?"

He shook his head, and his hands reached for hers. His skin felt warm against her own, and she could feel herself draw in a slow breath as that odd shiver once more snaked down her spine.

"I know how close you are with your family," Thorne explained, her hands still resting within his own. "I have no wish to separate you from them. During the Season, I suppose we can remain in London. I have someone to oversee the cotton mill in Manchester."

"And when the Season ends?" Christina asked, feeling her pulse quicken for that time was only a few short weeks away.

His hands tightened upon hers, and the smile upon his face seemed to deepen. "I have bought an estate not a day's ride from Whickerton

Grove. I hope it will please you." His eyes were wide and fixed upon hers, full of anticipation as before, waiting, hoping.

Christina looked up at him, her own words momentarily lost as those he had spoken were absorbed into her mind and heart. "You did —? For me?" She felt tears begin to prick the backs of her eyes so touched and overcome was she by his thoughtfulness. "Why?" The word flew from her lips without thought. It was an old habit to doubt the good that came into her life.

His mouth curled up teasingly while his eyes narrowed slightly. "Are you saying you are displeased?"

Christina chuckled; she could not help it. "I am not. I'm merely surprised."

"You did not think me thoughtful?"

Christina tried to pull her hands from his, but he would not release her. "I know you can be thoughtful," she admitted freely. "However, it is rare for husbands to be *that* thoughtful."

Thorne leaned closer, his hands tightening upon hers and pulling her forward. "Husbands?" he asked in a throaty whisper. "Or gentlemen?"

Christina felt her breath quicken with every inch that was lost between them. "Are you saying there is an upside to not being a gentleman?"

He grinned at her. "I am pleased you grasped my meaning with such ease. That bodes well for us." His hands finally released hers but only to slide up her arms and then settle upon her back, urging her even closer into his embrace.

Christina looked up at him, suddenly feeling bold and...yes, dauntless. Had he not used that word for her before? "Are you expecting a happy marriage, *Sir*?"

He lowered his head to hers. "Fully," he whispered, and she could feel his breath against her lips.

Heat surged through her, and her knees once more began to feel unsteady as though no longer able to perform their task of holding her upright. "Are you planning on taking liberties, Sir?" she teased him, marveling at the ease with which the words left her lips.

Her husband chuckled as his gaze strayed to her mouth so temptingly close to his own. "Is it liberties if we are married?"

Christina longed for his kiss. Yet she could not help herself. "Is it your opinion then, that a wife has to submit to her husband's wishes no matter how she feels?"

He rolled his eyes at her in a slightly exasperated way, and a chuckle drifted from his lips. "Are you determined to twist my words for the remainder of our marriage?"

Christina grinned at him. "I must admit it is a tempting suggestion."

He returned her smile before the expression upon his face sobered. His eyes remained upon hers as his left hand once more slipped into her hair as it had the night before. "I would never take without consent."

Sincerity shone in his eyes; and Christina longed to hear it again. "Never?"

"Never," he vowed, holding her close. "You have my word." He leaned his forehead against hers, his breath fanning over her lips. "Trust me, Chris. I will not hurt you. Never. I'm not the man you once thought me to be."

Christina knew his words to be true. Indeed, she had robbed Sarah of a most wonderful husband. The thought was like a stab to her heart, and Christina almost groaned at the sudden sense of agony it brought. She felt herself being drawn into that dark place she had visited so often these past few days.

However, before she could succumb to it, something furious deep inside her roared loudly. *No!* Guilt and shame and regret had no place here! Not tonight!

Without thought, Christina pushed herself up onto her toes and claimed her first kiss as a wife.

As expected, her husband needed no persuasion. He responded to her kiss with the same passion that simmered in her own veins. She felt one of his hands in the back of her neck while the other remained on her lower back. His heart beat as fast as her own, a soft, yet powerful thud against her ribcage.

Thorne nibbled her lower lip, then deepened their kiss as his hands slid over her back. She felt a soft tug and then another and finally realized that he was undoing her laces.

Although curiosity shot through Christina's veins, urging her to allow him, somewhere in the back of her head, she remembered the conversation she had had with her sisters about a fortnight ago.

According to the law, Mr. Sharpe will have every right to consummate your marriage on your wedding night.

He will not force me.

How do you know? Yours is not a love match, and only a husband who loves his wife can be trusted to treat her with the necessary consideration.

"Wait," Christina whispered, pulling away. Her breath came fast as she looked up at him, then slowly shook her head. "I cannot."

A slight frown came to his face, and she could see no small measure of disappointment in his gaze. "You cannot?" he asked as his hands pulled her back against him. "Are you certain?" His head dipped lower and brushed a quick kiss onto her lips.

Christina once more pulled away, realizing that doubt remained. She wanted to trust him, but the truth was that he had not yet earned her trust...and she needed him to.

She wanted him to.

Never would she feel truly at ease with him, safe with him if she did not *know* that he would respect her wishes even if they went against his own.

"Not tonight," she told him, pushing his arms away. "I cannot."

Thorne inhaled a deep breath. "Are you certain you're not curious to experience those *unspeakable things* you've heard whispered for yourself?" He grinned at her.

"I *am* curious," Christina admitted, all but holding her breath. "But not tonight. It's too...too soon."

For a moment, he simply looked at her, and she was not certain what went on in his head. Then he sighed and smiled at her. "As you wish, *my dear.*"

Christina felt her whole body relax as her husband took a step back, that inconveniently endearing smile still upon his face. Indeed, he could be a gentleman if he wanted to!

As though to prove her wrong, though, he winked at her then and asked, "Do you want me to help you with your laces? I suppose I could lend a hand." A wide grin decorated his face as he lifted his hands as though to show that he was no threat. "It was merely an offer. Nothing more."

Unable not to, Christina returned his grin. "You truly are a most irritating man."

He chuckled. "So I have heard. Many, many times." With his eyes on her, Thorne inched toward the door that separated their chambers. "Although I have to say, *Wife*, you do not seem to truly mind."

Christina gritted her teeth to keep from laughing. "Is that so? Do you honestly believe you know me that well?"

Opening the door, her husband stopped on the threshold. "Every day with you teaches me a little something more. I cannot wait to see what tomorrow will bring. Good night, Chris." Again, he smiled that utterly infuriating smile.

Deciding that it was best to simply ignore him, Christina made to turn away, but then stopped when she found him looking back at her over his shoulder. "May I ask?" he inquired, a slow smile stealing onto his face. "Did I pass your test?"

Christina wanted to slap him! "You truly are the most irritating man I've ever met!"

He laughed. "So you keep saying."

"Because it is true. In fact, you seem to be becoming more irritating with each new day."

Thorne grinned at her. "And you like it."

"I hate it!" Christina insisted. Once more finding her hands settling upon her hips, she tried her absolute best to glare at her most impertinent husband.

"You just keep telling yourself that," he chuckled and then closed the door behind him.

Christina remained standing where she was, staring at the closed door and wondering how on earth she had come to be here. Her life had changed so drastically in a matter of weeks, and although she had done little else but think about all its implications day after day, a part of her still felt a sense of disbelief.

She was married!

She was married to Mr. Thorne Sharpe!

She was married to a man...she was beginning to care for. As irritating as he could be, he also made her feel...

Was there a word that would truly, fittingly describe this feeling of magical detachment? That sense that somehow she was not quite here? That she was floating and drifting? As though on a cloud?

Heaving a deep breath, she sank down onto the stool in front of her new vanity, her gaze still fixed upon the door through which he had left. Yes, he had honored her wishes although they had stood against his own. It was a reassuring feeling. Perhaps she was not wrong to trust him, to believe that when he said something he meant it.

Only a husband who loves his wife can be trusted to treat her with the necessary consideration.

Again, her sister's words echoed in her mind, and although Christina tried, she could not prevent an awfully besotted smile from sneaking onto her face. Was it possible? Could it be that he had shown consideration because at least a part of him had come to care for her? Was this not merely a business transaction for him, but perhaps something more?

Christina knew that *she* wanted it to be more.

But only the coming days would tell.

She hoped with all her heart that they would be happy ones.

Chapter Twenty-Seven

A TUMULTUOUS FAREWELL

The moment Thorne awoke the following morning, his gaze immediately moved to the door connecting his own chamber to that of his wife. He longed to see her and was halfway across the room, his hand lifted to knock, before he stopped himself. Perhaps he ought to give her more time to herself in order to settle in. He doubted she would appreciate it if he were to simply burst into her chambers early in the morning before she had any chance to dress herself.

Although he had to admit that the thought was appealing!

Yet in order to prove his dear wife wrong, Thorne refrained from acting upon that impulse and instead dressed himself and then headed downstairs for breakfast. A certain sense of unease lingered in his bones, and he found himself pacing the breakfast parlor until the door opened and Christina entered.

"Good morning, Chris," he greeted her, finding utter delight in this simple way of communication between them. No matter what she might honestly think of him, the beauty of their union was that they were able to speak to each other. "How did you sleep?" He could not help but wink at her, knowing that it would upset her.

Not because she truly was upset though, but simply because it seemed that she *wanted* to be upset with him.

And he had no intention of disappointing her.

"Oh, I slept quite well," she replied as she seated herself across from him. "You don't sit at the head of the table?" She glanced from him to the empty seat that should have been his.

Pulling out his own chair, Thorne shook his head. "I decided against it. I thought it would be more pleasant if we sat...closer together." He winked at her. "And I thought seating myself here would discourage you from choosing your own seat at the other end of the table. It would seem my predictions were correct."

Accepting a cup of tea, she looked at him curiously. "Does this mean I now need to be on my guard? To be manipulated by my own husband?"

He offered her a mock frown. "*Manipulated* is such an ugly word. I prefer to think of it as evidence that I simply know you better than you like to admit."

Instead of answering, Christina sipped her tea, a calculating look in her eyes as though she were adjusting her impression of him. "Do you have any plans for today?"

Thorne swallowed, hoping that today would not end in a disaster. "In fact, I do." He reached for his own cup, savoring the hot liquid as it flowed over his tongue. "As I told you last night, I have purchased a new estate, and I would very much like for you to see it."

Christina paused. "You wish to travel there today?" A slight frown came to her face, and he could see that she suspected that he was holding something back.

Which, of course, he was.

Thorne nodded. "Would you mind? Of course, if you like we can stop by at your parents' house, bid everyone farewell and extend an invitation for them to visit us at their earliest convenience."

Although her features had tensed at the thought of saying goodbye to her family, a small smile teased the corners of her mouth when he spoke of inviting them to their new home. "You would not mind?"

It seemed that perhaps he had not quite yet passed her test. "They are your family, and I hope that one day they will see me as family as well. Our home shall always be open to them."

That small smile upon her face slowly grew as she looked at him, her blue eyes beginning to sparkle in a way that warmed his heart. "Perhaps you are not as bad as I thought after all," she told him with a teasing look in her eyes.

"I will take that as a compliment," Thorne told her, grateful for the deeper meaning of those few simple words.

His wife nodded. "You should. You definitely should."

While Thorne's staff busied themselves with packing their belongings that morning, Thorne escorted his new wife to her family's townhouse. They had sent quick notes to Lord and Lady Barrington as well as Lord and Lady Pemberton asking them to meet them there as well.

Thus, the whole family was gathered when they arrived.

Thorne was well aware of the cautious looks her two married sisters cast in his direction, their eyes lingering upon their sister's face before turning to him. He saw questions in their eyes that whispered of concern, and he hoped that Christina would put their minds at ease once they had a chance to speak to one another.

Lord Whickerton and his son proved equally curious about how Christina had fared these past few hours as his wife. They were less direct in their approach; however, Christina's brother once more uttered a kindly phrased warning.

But a warning, nonetheless.

Knowing that their hostility toward him as well as their distrust stemmed from a place of deepest love for one of their own made it easier for Thorne not to feel offended. What he witnessed was loyalty and devotion, traits that were rare in the world and therefore, all the more precious. He knew it to be so because he could not recall ever having had anyone to stand by him the way Christina's family stood by her.

"Before you leave," the youngest Whickerton sister Harriet said to Christina, her green eyes slightly misted with tears, "I have something to give to you. I hope it will make you smile, and I hope it will make you remember me." She quickly slipped out of the drawing room and into the hall, only to reappear a moment later, a cage in her hand and a slightly ruffled-looking parrot within.

"Oh, you cannot be serious!" Christina exclaimed the moment her eyes fell on the feathered animal. "You must be jesting!" Lifting her hands as though in defense, she backed away.

Thorne frowned, looking from his wife to her sister and then at the parrot. "You don't like birds?" he inquired carefully, sensing a deeper meaning behind this rather unexpected gift.

Christina looked at him. "I don't like *that* bird!"

"Why not?"

Her jaw dropped in utter disbelief as though the reason should be obvious. He could see that she was all but searching for words to explain but could not discover any that would do her objections justice.

"His name is King Arthur," Harriet explained as she moved farther into the room holding the cage out to Christina. Her gaze moved to Thorne when she realized that Christina would not accept her gift. "He is a most loyal and watchful friend, and he will make you smile when you most need it." With another glance at Christina, she turned to him and held out the cage. "Please, take it with you. I know you shall take good care of him until I come to visit."

With another look at his fuming wife, Thorne finally took the cage, wondering if she would hold it against him. "Thank you for your...kindness, Lady Harriet." He looked at the ruffled-looking parrot, its ruby-red feathers shimmering and its eyes wide as it seemed to consider all those crowded around it. "King Arthur," Thorne mumbled incredulously. "What a...a fitting name."

Lady Harriet clapped her hands. "Yes, I thought so too."

Thorne was about to reply when the parrot suddenly stretched and turned its head. *"Pretty bird. Pretty bird."*

Thorne almost dropped the cage. "It speaks?"

Lady Harriet nodded eagerly. "Yes, he does. He's a most clever bird."

Looking around at his wife's family, Thorne spied expressions of suppressed laughter on almost every face. It would seem that the bird and Lady Harriet's devotion to it were a much-discussed topic. While she truly seemed to adore it, her family appeared to consider the bird a bit of a nuisance or at least a welcome source of amusement.

Thorne turned to look at his new sister-in-law. "Thank you, Lady

Harriet, for such a wonderful gift. I can see that he means a lot to you, and I promise that we shall take good care of him."

Fresh tears brimmed in Lady Harriet's eyes, and she swallowed hard. "Thank you," she choked out. "Thank you so much."

Turning to look at his wife, Thorne could see that Christina had finally realized the meaning of her sister's gift. While Christina might not like the bird, Lady Harriet was clearly giving away a dear friend, thus stating clearly how much her sister meant to her and how deeply she would be missed.

The two sisters embraced, tears running down both their cheeks. "You know I can't stand that bird," Christina whispered before pulling away and brushing the tears off her little sister's face. "However, I'm glad you're not giving me the toad."

Lady Harriet laughed, and then everyone else joined in. As though not wishing to be excluded, the parrot's head snapped up. "*The toad. The toad*," King Arthur squawked, a strangely serious expression upon his feathered face.

Thorne grinned. "I think I like him." That statement unfortunately earned him a somewhat incredulous look from his wife.

After another half hour of tearful embraces and warmest well wishes, Thorne finally escorted his wife into the carriage. To her dismay, he seated the parrot beside him before they turned to wave to her family as the carriage began to rumble down the street.

After turning a corner, Christina finally sat back in her seat as her eyes fell on their traveling companion. "I cannot believe she made me take the bird."

Thorne chuckled. "She clearly meant well. It is most obvious that she adores King Arthur."

His wife rolled her eyes. "Must you call it that?"

Thorne shrugged. "It's the bird's name. Why ever not?"

"It's such a silly name for a bird!"

"What would you call him then?" Thorne regarded the bird curiously, who in turn seemed to be regarding them with just as much interest. "What does one call a parrot?"

"I don't know." Christina threw up her hands. "Biscuits? It seems the only thing that blasted bird eats are almond biscuits." She leaned forward in her seat, a most serious expression coming to her face as she lifted her right forefinger. "But mind you, if they are just a tad too brown, *it* won't touch them!" Again, throwing up her hands, she sank back into her seat.

King Arthur turned his head from side to side and regarded Christina with a curious frown. "*Biscuits!*" He squawked. "*Biscuits!*"

Thorne laughed. "Perhaps you are right. Perhaps we should rename him." He glanced at Christina. "Do you think your sister would mind?"

"You honestly want to call him Biscuits? I was jesting!"

Thorne shrugged. "I cannot help but think that he likes the name. Perhaps he simply feels misunderstood."

"He's a bird! He can't feel mis—"

"*Biscuits! Biscuits!*"

Thorne laughed. "There you have it. I think he likes Biscuits."

Christina slumped back in her seat. "Very well. If you insist." She cast a pointed look at him. "He is your responsibility. I will not feed that thing."

Crossing his legs at the ankles, Thorne regarded her curiously. "Why do you dislike him so much?"

"You would, too, if you had to live with him these past few weeks." Sighing in a rather exhausted fashion, she briefly closed her eyes. "Of course, Harriet does not keep him in that cage all day. After all, a bird needs to spread its wings. And for reasons I cannot fathom that blasted bird always somehow ended up in my chamber." She sat up, her jaw slightly dropped as she stared at him, once again lost for words as she no doubt pictured the havoc Biscuits had wreaked upon her bedchamber. "Feathers everywhere! Honestly, the blasted bird should be bald. Where does he keep them? He shredded my best gown, and then he destroyed my—" Quite abruptly, Christina broke off. Her jaw tensed, and her gaze dropped from his as though she had been about to say something she did not wish for him to know.

Thorne frowned. "What did he destroy?"

Sighing, Christina shook her head. "Nothing. It was nothing." She cast him a forced smile and then turned to look out the window.

Although wishing to ask, to press her for more information, Thorne did not. He could tell from the way she had turned away that she would not volunteer anything further. Clearly, what had happened had deeply upset her. Yet Thorne could not imagine what the bird could possibly have destroyed that would have cemented Christina's opinion of him in such a way.

It had to have been something very, very dear to her.

But what?

Chapter Twenty-Eight

PINEWOOD MANOR

For the remainder of the day, they spoke little. Christina continued to look out the window as the carriage rumbled along, determined to ignore not only the bird, but also her husband. She was not truly upset with him, but his questions had unnerved her. She could not help but think of Aunt Francine and of what her aunt had given up in order to pursue her passion.

Christina knew she could never do so, and so she had decided long ago to pursue her passion in secret. Of course, her sisters knew of her fondness for writing stories. Yet her husband would not understand, would he?

By nightfall, they stopped at an inn, and Christina was relieved to see that Thorne procured them two rooms. Unfortunately, though, he carried the blasted bird's cage not into his own, but into hers.

"What do you propose I do with it?" Christina asked, tapping her foot in an annoyed gesture. She was well aware that she was overreacting; yes, wherever the bird was concerned she could not seem to help herself. Why on earth had Harriet insisted she take it? Was her little sister trying her absolute best to destroy her marriage before it had even truly begun?

Offering the bird a biscuit, Thorne then turned to grin at her. "I don't know." He shrugged. "Talk to him perhaps." He stepped closer, his eyes seeking hers. "Or you could talk to me."

Christina avoided his gaze, afraid that he would see too much. "About what? There's nothing to talk about. I've never liked my sister's pets, and she knows it."

His hand settled upon her shoulders, warm and teasing at the same time. "There's something on your mind," he whispered, his eyes once more seeking hers. "I can see it. Tell me, and I'll listen."

Christina shook her head and tried to step out of his embrace, but his hands remained upon her shoulders, keeping her in place.

"You can trust me," her husband whispered, and this time she did look at him.

"Can I?"

His gaze narrowed slightly as though he had not truly expected her to ask that. "Yes, you can. If there's anything on your mind that troubles you, please, share it with me. Is that not what family is for? Looking at yours, I know it to be true. As do you."

Christina could not deny that his words pleased her. She wanted to trust him, and she suspected that a part of her already did. Only this was a secret she had been keeping for a long time, a secret she had never intended to reveal to anyone outside of her immediate family. It carried a heavy weight, and she was not certain if he might not crumble under it. "I am tired," she finally said. "I wish to go to bed." She offered him a smile, feeling regret for failing to answer his request. He had sounded so honest, and yet Aunt Francine had once probably thought the same about her own husband as well.

Only to find herself to have been severely mistaken.

His hands fell from her shoulders; however, as she turned away, his hand caught hers and pulled her back—closer than before for his arms circled around her middle, reminding her of the night before.

"What are you doing?" Christina asked, trying her best not to succumb to that *unexpected* pull she was slowly beginning to *expect* whenever he stepped closer.

Her husband dipped his head no more than a fraction and looked into her eyes. "Don't pretend you don't know." He caught her chin between two fingers and urged her to lift her head. "May I kiss you?"

Christina knew what she wanted her answer to be; only she wondered if it would be wise. The day had been full of emotional challenges. She still felt close to tears whenever she thought back to her farewell to her family. Perhaps it would be wiser to—

"*Kiss you! Kiss you!*" the blasted bird suddenly squawked.

For a moment, they both tensed as though a shot had been fired nearby. Then her husband began to laugh. "I must say I like that bird. He sounds most intuitive."

Christina slapped him on the arm. "Oh, you're only saying that because you want to kiss me."

"Guilty," Thorne replied without hesitation. His eyes burned into hers, and his arm around her back urged her ever closer.

Christina sighed. "Oh, very well. But only one kiss. No more."

He chuckled, slowly lowering his head to hers. "Don't pretend you don't want this as much as I do."

"Well, I don't," Christina insisted, her voice ringing with insincerity even to her own ears.

"Yes, you do."

"No, I don't."

"Yes, you—"

"Oh, would you just kiss me?" Christina snapped, reaching up to pull him down to her.

"Happy to oblige," Thorne whispered against her lips.

"*Kiss me! Kiss me!*" the bird squawked again.

They both broke out into laughter. "I find the bird only repeats the most important things in life," Thorne remarked, casting a quick glance at the animal in question. "Good boy, Biscuit."

"We're not truly going to call him Bisc—?" Her question was cut short as her husband's mouth closed over hers.

Instantly, everything else vanished: all the sadness over her farewell to her family; all the annoyance with the bird; all the uncertainty that remained in her heart.

Her knees turned to water, and she sank into her husband's arms, allowing him to kiss her as he wished. As he had the night before. As she hoped he would for all the days to come.

Lifting his head, Thorne looked down at her, then once more

brushed his lips against hers. "I love kissing you," he murmured then lowered his head once more.

"*One kiss! One kiss!*" Biscuit squawked. "*No more! No more!*"

Stilling, Thorne closed his eyes before a slow smile began to spread over his face, giving him a disbelieving look.

Christina laughed. Yes, she would not have objected to another kiss. Far from it. Still, she loved the yearning expression in her husband's eyes even more. "I could not have said it better," she remarked, trying her utmost to regain a more serious expression.

Nevertheless, the smile upon her face would not be denied.

Thorne looked up and glared at the bird. "And after everything I've done for you, now you stab me in the back?" Shaking his head, he returned his gaze to her. "And you? Have you suddenly come to like the bird?"

Grinning, Christina shrugged. "What can I say? I suppose he's not as bad as I thought."

Thorne pinched her chin. "I remember you saying something quite similar about me not too long ago."

Christina shrugged. "I stand by what I said." She looked up at him and held his gaze, daring him to...

Do what?

She wasn't quite certain.

Exhaling a slow breath, Thorne slowly released her. He took a step back, and once more glanced at the bird. "Then I will leave you," he said with a smile. "Until tomorrow."

As the door closed behind him, Christina could not help but feel a stab of regret. She had wanted him to stay, and yet she had wanted him to go. He had honored her wishes, but, in truth, she had wanted another kiss. Still, she preferred it this way.

If in doubt, a gentleman would always act honorably, would he not?

Christina paused, remembering the countless times she had told her husband that he was, in fact, *not* a gentleman. When had she started to think of him thus? She could not deny that he did possess all the most admirable qualities of a gentleman. He might be of humble birth, but the respect and consideration he showed others could have fooled anyone.

Even her.

Christina smiled because she was glad for it, and that night, she slept a lot better than she would have thought.

The following morning, their journey continued in a more pleasant manner. Somehow, that ease between her and her husband had returned, and not even Biscuit's squawks managed to upset her as they had before. In fact, it often seemed the bird was on her side, repeating words and phrases rather to her husband's disadvantage than hers.

Still, when the carriage finally pulled into the drive of Pinewood Manor, Christina could not help but think that the look on her husband's face spoke of dread. He had seemed so eager before to show her the place he had bought for them; now, however, a dark cloud seemed to linger above his head.

"Are you all right?" Christina asked as he offered her his arm to help her alight from the carriage. "You seem...distraught."

He inhaled a deep breath, and then met her eyes. "Truthfully, there has been something on my mind I need to speak to you about; though, I could not seem to find the words nor the right moment to do so."

Christina felt something inside her tighten, like a noose around her neck slowly cutting off her ability to breathe. Was this what she had been waiting for? What she had dreaded to discover about her husband? That despite everything he had said and done, there was a part of him she ought not have trusted?

"Then tell me now," Christina urged him, knowing that it was always better to know than to be left in the dark.

Swallowing, he nodded, then turned to her and reached out to take her hands into his. "I told you that I had no family. That is true in a certain way. However—"

"In a certain way?" Christina interrupted, the noose around her neck growing tighter. "How can it be true in a certain way?" She pulled her hands from his.

The look upon his face fell as she retreated; yet she could see the determination to finally tell her the truth bright as ever in his eyes. "There is someone who—"

"Father! You have returned!" came a bright young voice that reminded Christina of Harriet's many, many years ago.

Shocked by the word she had heard, Christina slowly turned toward the front entrance and found a little girl of about five years rushing down the steps toward them. Her blond curls bounced up and down, and her green eyes shone as bright as her father's.

Christina staggered backward until her back was pressed against the side of the carriage, her eyes wide as she continued to stare at the little girl.

"Father! Is that her?" The little girl asked with a sideways glance at Christina before she threw herself into Thorne's arms. He hugged her tightly and lifted her into the air, swinging her in a full circle before setting her down once more.

"Sam, I want to introduce you to someone," Thorne said to the girl, holding one of her small hands in his. Then he straightened and turned toward Christina, and she could see the tension that once more marked his features. Despite the joy and ease with which he conversed with the child, dread still lingered. What did he fear she would do? Return to her family? Refuse to accept the child?

All these thoughts raced through Christina's head, and she was not quite certain which one of them broke her heart in that moment. She had dared to trust—despite her better judgment, despite all the rumors and whispers she had heard—and now she found herself burned.

"Sam," her husband said as he escorted the girl toward Christina, "this is my wife, Christina." He looked down and smiled at the girl before raising his gaze to Christina's. "Chris, this is my...daughter Samantha."

"Do not call me that!" Christina hissed, needing something, some reason to lash out at him without addressing the true issue that now stood between them. After all, the child was not at fault for her father's lies, and she would not say anything that might wound the girl.

"Welcome home," Samantha said, beaming up at her in a way that made Christina's heart ache even more.

Gritting her teeth, Christina tried to smile at the child, but knew that the expression upon her face was no doubt some kind of grotesque grimace. "Thank you," was all she managed in that moment before her eyes returned to her husband, aiming an accusatory stare at him—one he rightly deserved.

Kneeling down beside the child, Thorne took her hands and pulled her around to face him. "Sam, Christina needs a moment to truly arrive. It has been a long journey. We brought you a friend." He rose to his feet and then fetched the cage from inside the carriage. "This is Biscuit."

The girl squealed in delight and all but flung herself at the cage. "Oh, Father! He is beautiful! Can we truly keep him?"

Thorne nodded, then gestured to a matronly woman standing up on the stairs, one Christina had failed to notice before this very moment. "Mrs. Huxley, would you escort Samantha inside, please?"

The stout woman came forward and with a somewhat apprehensive look took the cage from Thorne's hands. Then she held out her other hand to the child and they vanished inside.

The moment they were gone, her husband turned to her. "Christina, I need to explain."

"Yes, you do!"

Chapter Twenty-Nine

AN OVERDUE CONFESSION

Thorne could have kicked himself. Of course, she was angry. She was angry and hurt. Anyone would be. Of course, he had known that this would happen, and yet he had remained silent. He had been a coward to not speak to her before now. It had been a mistake, a grave mistake.

Now, though, there was no changing that.

"I suggest we step inside." He moved toward her but took care not to step too close. "Then I will tell you all you wish to know. I promise."

Doubt remained in her blue eyes. For a moment, they lingered upon his face as though she was seeing him for the very first time. Then she gave a curt nod of agreement before stepping past him, ignoring his proffered arm and heading into the house.

Rushing to catch up with her, Thorne guided her into the drawing room, then closed the door. He was aware that she kept her distance from him, and he was surprised by how much it bothered him.

Yes, he ought to have told her. He had had countless chances, and yet he had not. In the beginning, he had been afraid that she would change her mind, despite her words, and refuse to marry him. Then, last night as well as this morning, Thorne could not help but think that if he told her now, she might not leave London with him. That she might return to her family who would no doubt grant her sanctuary.

Even from him.

Even from her own husband.

Of course, they would be right to do so. He was the villain in this, was he not?

Raking a hand through his hair, Thorne tried to find the words to say what needed to be said. His gaze moved to hers, and he found her watching him through narrowed eyes. "I can see that you're angry with me, and you have every right to be. But—"

"Where is her mother?" Christina snapped, her gaze moving to the door as though she truly expected another woman to burst in at any moment. "Is she here? In this house?" Her gaze narrowed even further as her jaw seemed to drop another fraction. "Is she your wife?" Her own words seemed to slam into her, and she took a staggering step backward, her eyes widening in shock.

In all honesty, Thorne had not expected this. These questions. "I have no wife," he blurted out stupidly, then shook his head. "I mean, of course, I do, what I meant to say was—" He broke off and inhaled a slow breath, trying his best to calm the wild hammering of his heart.

Lifting his chin, he took a step toward her, not daring to take another, and met her eyes, urging her to believe him. "You are my wife," he said softly and slowly. "You are the only wife I've ever had, and I ever care to have. There has never been another. I give you my word."

Christina remained silent, her wide blue eyes fixed upon his face. Yet he thought to see a mild softening of her features as though his words had brought her relief...if only a small measure of it. "Then... she's a bastard?" She all but flinched at the last word, and he could see her displeasure at hearing it leave her lips. "Where is her mother? Who is she?"

Thorne heaved a deep sigh. "In all honesty, I cannot say for certain. I've never met her."

Her gaze narrowed in confusion. "You've never met her? But how —?" She shook her head. "Would you care to explain this to me in a way I can understand?" A sharp tone came to her voice, and she uncrossed her arms, settling her hands upon her hips.

Thorne almost smiled for he liked that defiant expression upon her features. He moved toward one of the armchairs and gestured for her to sit in the other. "Please."

Christina shook her hand. "No, I cannot sit now. I am much too—" She broke off, spun around and paced a few steps back and forth. Then she once more turned and met his eyes. "Explain yourself."

Thorne nodded. "Although Samantha calls me Father," he began, sending a quick glance at the door to ensure that it was truly closed, "I am not the man who fathered her." He heaved a deep sigh as he remembered the day he had first laid eyes upon Samantha. "It was in the deep of winter. Snow covered the ground, and an icy chill lingered in the air when a knock sounded on my front door. I was about to retire and crossing the foyer at the time when I heard it. I went to open it," he blinked, and his gaze moved to settle upon his wife's, "and there she was, wrapped in a thin blanket, placed upon my doorstep."

A shuddering breath left Christina's lips as she stared at him, something achingly soft in her eyes, a feeling he remembered, a feeling that returned to him every time he recalled that first moment with Samantha. "Her mother left her upon your doorstep?" she whispered, utter disbelief in her voice.

Thorne nodded. "There was a note tucked into the blanket. It was no more than a few words, a few misspelled and barely legible words." Holding Christina's gaze, he took a step toward her, and this time, she did not retreat. "Life is hard for those who were not born to privilege. I try my utmost to be a fair employer and pay my workers a wage that allows them to live and not merely exist from day to day." He briefly closed his eyes as countless memories resurfaced of all the atrocities he had witnessed. "But I am one man, and there are many who simply do not care. Far too many people die every day because of something that could've easily been prevented. Parents work themselves to death, and children grow up in poverty, never knowing anything else. It is a sad world," he gritted his teeth until his jaw ached, "one that never fails to stir anger in my heart."

Tears misted Christina's eyes, and Thorne loved her for it. He loved that this very moment when she felt betrayed herself, when she had been hurt, she could still feel for others. Her heart was still able to show compassion. "It is why you came to London."

"It is," Thorne confirmed, remembering the moment he had come to realize that his own efforts alone would not do. "I tried to find Samantha's mother," he continued, linking his arms behind his back. "But I never managed to. I don't know who she was. I don't know if she still lives." A small smile came to his lips as a spark of joy shot through his heart. "I never...intended to keep her, but as I kept searching for her mother, day after day passed and eventually..." Looking at his wife, he shrugged.

Blinking back tears, Christina nodded. "You couldn't give her up," she finished for him. "She had already become yours."

Thorne inhaled a deep breath. "Yes, she had. So, I gave her my name and..." He paused. "I gave her my name, and yet the first time she called me Father, I..." He shook his head, looking at her. "Perhaps I was a fool for not seeing it coming. Why would she not call me *Father*? Nonetheless, I had not expected it. I should have. It is not those who bring us into the world we hold to heart, is it? It is the ones that stand with us every day through every trial." He rubbed a hand over his eyes, then pinched the bridge of his nose. "Honestly, I have never spoken about her to anyone. Not like this."

Emotions flickered in Christina's eyes; however, she remained where she was, the expression upon her face preventing him from stepping closer. "Why did you not tell me?"

The doubting accusation in her voice felt like a punch to the gut. "I don't know. I—"

"Yes, you do!" Something fierce came to her eyes as she took a step closer, pinning him with her gaze. "You do know. Be honest and admit to it."

Thorne gritted his teeth, his lower jaw moving back and forth as he looked at her. "I was afraid," he finally said, every fiber of his being revolting against the admission. In his world, weakness was exploited. It was the first lesson he had ever learned, and it still lived in his bones. "I was afraid you would change your mind and refuse to marry me."

Her lips pressed into a thin line before she nodded. "I know. You came to London to seek connections, to bring about change and improve the lives of those you feel responsible for." She turned away and walked over to look out the window. "It is a noble ambition and it recommends you. I know I misjudged you, but you should have told me."

Despite seeing only the back of her head, Thorne could tell that his lack of trust had wounded her. "I'm sorry. You're right. I should have told you. I wanted to, but I simply could not take the risk." He did not even dare picture a life without her by his side. Only a matter of weeks had passed since he had first laid eyes on her, and yet she had already become such an intricate part of his life that...the mere thought of her not being here with him sent a crippling agony through his body.

Thorne closed his eyes. When had he come to care for her in such a way? How could he not have noticed? Of course, he had been aware of her allure. There was something about her that drew him near. Something that made him seek her out. Something that made it hard for him to stay away.

From the first, he had known that he wanted her and no other. The choice had been easy. It had not truly been a choice. He had seen her, and he had known. Only the depth of his dependence upon her, upon her presence in his life, was shocking, nonetheless.

"I wish to be alone," Christina whispered, keeping her gaze fixed out the window. "Please."

Every fiber of his being told him to stay; yet a gentleman would comply, would he not? It would be the honorable thing to do. "Very well." He stepped back and moved toward the door, then stopped and looked back at her. "I will see to Samantha. Please feel free to go wherever you wish. This is your home as much as it is mine." He placed his hand upon the door handle. "I am sorry for the manner of your arrival here. I should've spoken to you before now. You have my sincerest apologies and my promise to do better in the future."

Thorne waited for another moment or two, hoping that she would turn around and look at him, that she would say something, anything.

But she did not.

With her back turned to him, Christina remained standing by the window, her eyes directed at the gardens outside or perhaps at something beyond.

Finally opening the door, Thorne left, hoping that his silence had not doomed them all.

Chapter Thirty
A NEW LIFE

S taring out the window, Christina felt tears slowly sneak their way down her cheeks. She clenched her teeth to keep the sobs that rose in her throat from spilling forth. She could still sense her husband standing by the door, looking at her, waiting.

For what, she did not know nor care. All she wanted was for him to leave.

When she finally heard the door close behind him, all her composure fell away. Her limbs began to tremble, and she sank down onto her knees as floods of tears spilled down the sides of her face. Why she broke down in such a profound way, Christina did not know. It made no sense after all. They had known each other a few weeks, no more. She could not possibly have come to care for him in a way that would see her heart in such danger because of a lie.

Only it was not the lie that pained her, was it?

Angrily, Christina brushed the tears from her cheeks, willing them to stop flowing. Unfortunately, they would not listen.

And so, she sat there, upon the floor behind the armchair and wept.

I was afraid you would change your mind and refuse to marry me. I should have told you. I wanted to, but I simply could not take the risk.

His words echoed in her mind no matter how hard Christina tried to shut them out. Yes, he had come to London for a reason. She could not fault him for that for he had proven himself to be a good man. He cared for others, and he was willing to go to great lengths to see them provided for, to see them treated justly. It was a noble ambition, and, yes, she *had* judged him wrongly.

Still, this realization walked hand-in-hand with another. She had fooled herself. Of course, she had not meant to do so. She had tried to be on her guard, to treat this union as a formal contract and nothing more. Most marriages, after all, were marriages of convenience. A contract beneficial to both parties. Unfortunately, somewhere along the way, Christina had allowed herself to care for him, to believe even that he might care for her.

Yes, they might suit each other. Their personalities fit, ensuring a pleasant union. He clearly found her appealing and enjoyed their teasing conversations as much as she did. But was that all?

For her, it went deeper.

To her great shame, it went far deeper.

For him, it did not. That much was clear now. Only moments ago, he had stated outright that he had been unwilling to risk losing her hand in marriage, to risk losing her father's connections.

It was not her he wanted. After all, only a few weeks ago he had been set on marrying Sarah. He did not care whom he took as his wife as long as said wife came with an introduction into London society.

Perhaps—

Christina froze when the sound of the door opening slowly drifted to her ears. Her breath lodged in her throat before she quickly reached up to brush the tears from her eyes. Yet there was nothing she could do about her reddened cheeks. Anyone who would look upon her would know that she had been crying. But who had come? Was it a servant? Her husband would have surely said something by now.

Pinching her eyes shut, Christina imagined the humility of being discovered by a servant in her current state, seated upon the floor, hidden behind an armchair, her face tear-streaked and her eyes puffy.

"Mama?" A pause. "Chris-Christina?"

Christina almost flinched at the sound of Samantha's voice. Yet it was the word she whispered that stole Christina's breath. The girl could not possibly be addressing her, could she? But who else was there?

Soft footsteps drew closer, and when Christina turned her head and lifted her eyes, she found herself looking into a hopeful little face that broke her heart all over again.

Samantha's green eyes reminded Christina of Thorne. Although she knew now that the girl was not his true daughter, Fate had seen it fit to strengthen their bond by such a resemblance.

The delicate smile that hung on her lips was full of longing. She looked down at Christina, waiting for her to...

...say something?

What was she to say? To a child she did not know? A child who had just now called her *Mama*? A child who was clearly in desperate need of a mother?

Yes, she was Thorne's wife and the girl was his daughter in every way that mattered; but did that mean that Christina was now her mother?

She closed her eyes and pinched them shut. This was all too much. Too much had changed in one day. Too much she had been unable to prepare herself for. Too much—

A soft weight descended upon her shoulder, and Christina's eyes flew open.

Samantha was kneeling beside her, her wide eyes watchful. "You look sad," the girl remarked, such youthful innocence in her eyes that stirred a memory of days long gone within Christina.

Swallowing, she once again tried to brush the tears from her cheeks. "I...I am overwhelmed," she told the child truthfully, unable to conjure a believable lie in that moment. Nor did she wish to. Too many lies had already been told.

"What does that mean?"

Christina exhaled a deep breath. No, she was definitely not ready to be a mother to a five-year-old girl. Yet it seemed that she did not have a choice. "It means that...that I do not know what I feel. A lot has happened, and I cannot seem to make sense of it." She shook her head, and a scoff almost left her lips. "I'm sorry. I'm afraid that didn't make it any clearer, did it?"

Seating herself next to Christina, Samantha crossed her legs under her skirts. "What has happened? Something bad?"

Christina folded her hands in her lap. "I had to say goodbye to my family," she told Samantha after a short pause. That much, at least, was true for the thought of her parents and siblings still threatened to bring fresh tears to her eyes.

Samantha nodded knowingly. "I'm always sad when Papa travels without me. I miss him then. Will your family come to visit us?"

"I believe they would like that," Christina replied, wondering if she even wanted them here now. They knew her too well and would instantly see what was going on. Although Grandma Edie was the one known to meddle in everyone's affairs, Christina's parents and siblings in truth were no better. They would all find reasons to get involved, thinking it their responsibility to see her happily settled.

Christina did not know if she was strong enough to bear a visit at this point. First, she needed to figure out how she felt about...all of this.

Samantha's little face brightened. "I would like to meet them. Do you have any brothers or sisters?"

Christina nodded, relieved to have been asked such a simple question. "I have a brother and four sisters."

The girl's eyes widened in awe. "That is a lot. I don't have any, but I always wanted to have a sister or even a brother. Perhaps now that you are here, I will."

Such hope rang in her voice that Christina momentarily forgot to be shocked by her words. She was still trying to regain her composure and think of something to say when a shadow fell over them. She looked up and saw her husband standing there, that wickedly twinkling look in his eyes clearly stating that he, too, had heard Samantha's heart-felt wish.

Christina wanted to sink into a hole in the ground.

"Here you are," he exclaimed, feigning surprise as he smiled at his daughter. "I thought you were seeing to Biscuit? Are you already bored with him?"

Scrambling to her feet, Samantha shook her head. "No, of course not. I love him." She glanced at Christina. "But I was curious. I couldn't wait." Her little teeth sank into her lower lip as she looked at Christina in a way that made her feel worse than she already did.

It made her feel like an imposter because Samantha was clearly considering her her new mother, and Christina could not have been any further from feeling like that herself.

"I understand," Thorne replied, brushing a gentle hand over the girl's head. "I believe he could do with a snack. Would you feed him? I've given Mrs. Huxley a few of the biscuits he is very fond of."

Samantha's face lit up, and she instantly darted away.

Withdrawing his eyes from his daughter, Thorne turned to Christina, then held out his hand offering to help her up.

With everything that had happened, Christina had completely forgotten that she was still sitting on the floor. A deep flush burned its way up her neck until it reached her cheeks, and although she accepted her husband's hand, her eyes remained firmly upon something other than him.

"Are you all right?" he asked, and she could sense that he was trying to meet her gaze.

Swallowing, Christina lifted her chin and then looked at him, trying her best not to flinch, not to be affected by the way his eyes looked into hers. "I am as well as can be expected."

He nodded. "May I show you to your chamber?"

"I would appreciate that," Christina replied, but then hesitated when he once more held out his arm to her. Her eyes rose to meet his; yet she did not know what she was looking for.

Thorne sighed, regret in his emerald eyes. "I wish we could go back to the way we were before." He held her gaze, and Christina could see that he would not walk away. Not without an answer.

Finally, Christina nodded. "Perhaps that would be best," she admitted, then accepted his arm. After all, what choice did she have? They were married. It was not something that could be undone. Her mother had warned her to choose wisely, and Christina thought that she had. Now, she was not so certain.

Only no regret would ever change what was, and so she would do well to make the best of things. Perhaps if she guarded her heart carefully, she could even find a little joy in this new life.

Chapter Thirty-One

THE DYNAMICS OF A FAMILY

wkward was the best word to describe the situation they suddenly found themselves in.

In all honesty, Thorne had not expected this. Admittedly, he had never once thought this far ahead. He had always worried about what Christina might do if he told her about Samantha before the marriage could take place. Yet the fool he was, he had never once considered what it might do to his marriage for her to find out after. Did she feel trapped? Did she have regrets?

Judging from the tense look upon her face these days, it was clear that she did. Thorne knew that some women could not accept another's child in their home. It had been the very reason why he had remained silent for so long.

Since Christina barely spoke a word to him or Samantha, her eyes downcast and distant, his own relationship with Sam stood in even starker contrast. As Samantha had never been one shy for words, she happily prattled on as she always did. The two of them conversed easily, and it made Christina seem almost like an outsider, as though she did not belong.

Did she feel it too?

Thorne did not know what to do about it. At first, he tried to include Christina in their conversations. His wife's replies, however, were rather monosyllabic. She clearly did not wish to participate.

Fortunately, Samantha did not seem to notice or perhaps she did but was determined to make her new mother like her. Of course, Thorne had noticed the longing looks his daughter cast in his wife's direction. He knew well how much Samantha longed for a mother. She had never been shy about sharing her hopes and dreams with him.

And so, he was not surprised to see Samantha take Christina by the hand one morning and pull her along to the stables. "Come. I want to show you the pony Father bought me. He is sweet and silly, and it tickles when he takes carrots from my hand." She giggled, completely oblivious to the reluctance upon Christina's face. "His name is King Arthur."

Christina's jaw dropped as she followed Samantha down the hall. "King Arthur? Honestly?"

Samantha blinked up at her. "Do you not like it? Father used to tell me stories, and I always wanted to be King Arthur and pull the sword from the stone."

Laughter fell from Christina's lips, and Thorne could not help but think that some of the tension suddenly vanished. "Yes, I've always loved the stories as well. However, I was surprised because Biscuit used to be called King Arthur as well. My sister gave him that name."

Samantha laughed. "Is that true? And how did he come to be named Biscuit?"

Thorne exhaled a deep, hopeful sigh as the two of them stepped outside and the door closed, cutting off their voices. Perhaps all would be well after all, he thought.

Perhaps.

In the coming days, Thorne often saw the two of them together, either in the stables or walking through the gardens. Although Christina had not yet returned to her usual self, he could see small changes within her. He knew it was Samantha's doing, and so he held himself back, giving them space and time, hoping that perhaps if he did not interfere, somehow everything would turn out all right.

A fortnight after they had arrived at Pinewood Manor, Thorne approached his wife's chamber after supper. He needed to speak to her alone, and throughout the day, Samantha had constantly been by her side.

After his knock, there was a moment of pause, and he wondered if she would invite him inside. Finally, he heard footsteps approaching from the other side of the door before it opened. Her eyes were slightly narrowed, confusion upon her face as she regarded him. "What do you want?"

"I wish to speak to you about something. May I come in?" He cast a look over his shoulder down the hall. "I do not wish to be overheard." Although Samantha was already in bed, one could never be entirely certain of the girl's whereabouts.

Thorne had always liked that about her spirit, though.

Christina hesitated, but then stood aside and allowed him in. "Is it something else you ought to have told me earlier?"

Thorne clenched his jaw, knowing that he deserved her distrust. "It is not." He closed the door behind him, then turned to face her. "I simply meant to inform you that I need to travel back to London for a few days. A few influential lords have agreed to meet me, and I need to take this chance to speak to them about the changes I would like to see."

The expression upon her face remained almost blank; yet she nodded. "I see."

Thorne hated this passivity in her. It was not who she was, and he would have liked to do nothing more than shake her awake, out of this trance. "Would you like to accompany me?"

Again, she did not answer right away, but looked at him as though the question he had put to her deserved careful consideration. "I believe it would be best for all of us if I remained here," she said without further explanation.

Thorne nodded. "Very well." This time, he hesitated, waiting, uncertain what for. Still, he did not wish to leave. It had been days since they had had a moment alone together, and he missed her. "Good night then," he finally said, seeing that she did not wish for him to linger.

"Good night," she replied and then closed the door behind him the moment he stepped out into the corridor.

Thorne hung his head, wishing he knew what to do, how to regain what they had once found. Had he only imagined the ease between them? Was it truly so impossible for her to overcome the lie he had told? It may not have been a lie in the strictest sense; but it had been an omission.

One he now regretted.

Deeply.

Chapter Thirty-Two

THROUGH THE EYES OF A CHILD

The moment the door closed behind her husband, Christina exhaled a deep sigh, then rested her head against its smooth wood. She had wanted him to stay; yet that simple desire had frightened her. She needed to guard her heart.

Perhaps it was for the best they spent as little time in each other's presence as possible. Many spouses did just that, did they not? Perhaps it was truly the best way to conduct a marriage that was born out of nothing more but mutual interest.

If she were to accompany him to London, they would spend hours in the carriage together.

Alone.

From what Samantha had told her, Thorne rarely took the child along when he traveled. Christina doubted it would be different this time. Perhaps she could have insisted on bringing the girl along. Still, Christina did not wish to see her family at this point. Her nerves were still too raw, and they would see easily how upset she was. No, it was best to wait a little longer, to let a little more time pass.

Perhaps in a few weeks, she would feel strong enough to face them.

Perhaps.

A few days later, Christina found herself standing in the front hall of Pinewood Manor, bidding her husband farewell. She had told herself to remain strong, to not show how much she wanted him to stay. Still, her hands trembled, and she could feel tears prick the backs of her eyes. What a weak fool she was!

"I shall miss you dearly, Papa!" Samantha mumbled as she hugged her father tightly. "Will you come back soon?"

Setting her back gently, Thorne smiled at her. "Of course, Sam. You know I cannot bear to stay away from you for long."

The girl giggled joyfully and once more embraced her father. "We shall both miss you so much."

At her words, Thorne looked up at Christina, a question in his eyes she did not dare answer but was afraid he might read upon her face. And so, she dropped her gaze and took a step back, willing her expression to harden lest he see how deeply his departure affected her.

"Will you run upstairs and wave to me from the window?" Thorne asked his daughter, who nodded eagerly, then dashed up the stairs as fast as her little legs could carry her.

Rising to his feet, Thorne turned to Christina, the look in his eyes as unnerving as when they had first met. Indeed, he did see far too much, and so she kept her gaze safely averted. "Will you change your mind?" he asked as he stepped closer, his eyes trying to look into hers. "Will you not come with me?"

Christina swallowed. "I do not believe that to be wise." Chiding herself for being a ninny, she finally lifted her gaze to meet his. "I believe some time apart will do us good."

Christina could not deny that looking into his eyes made her want to change her mind after all. There was something there, something that made her want to step forward and into his embrace.

Yet she did not.

She remained strong.

She needed to be.

Thorne nodded. "Very well then. Goodbye." As he turned away, she saw his jaw clench as though he was biting back words he desperately wanted to say. He proceeded down the stairs a few steps, but then stopped.

He stood there for a moment or two, not moving, not looking back at her.

Christina frowned, wondering what he was about. Had he forgotten something? Was he on the verge of saying more to her? Would he—?

He suddenly spun around, and the look in his eyes made her catch her breath. Long strides carried him back to her, his gaze determined and his jaw set. He reached for her then, his hands warm and possessive as he pulled her to him, pulled her into his arms. And then his lips closed over hers, and everything fell away.

As it always did.

He kissed her deeply as though trying to make a point. One arm remained slung around her middle while the other reached to cup her face, gently tilting her head so he could deepen the kiss further.

Christina had no strength to resist him, nor did she wish to. Those traitorous emotions once more sparked in her heart, urging her closer, urging her to kiss him back.

And then she did, and a low growl rose in his throat as he pushed her back against the doorframe, his mouth never leaving hers as they clung to one another.

"Papa!" Samantha's voice called from the top floor. "Will you be leaving soon?"

Reluctantly, he broke away, his breath coming as fast as her own as he stared at her, passion darkening his eyes. "I'll be off in a minute," he called up to his daughter.

Christina barely had time to regain even a sliver of composure before he moved closer once more, his eyes seeking hers mercilessly. "When I return," he whispered as his breath fanned over her lips, "we need to do something about...this. Us." He swallowed hard. "I have no intention of staying away from you for the remainder of our marriage."

Christina felt the corners of her mouth curl up into a smile. "Is that a threat? Or promise?"

Holding her gaze, Thorne returned her smile, something akin to relief upon his face, relaxing his muscles and giving him a more youthful and lighthearted expression. Still, the eyes that looked back into hers shone with passion yet to be acted upon, and he leaned down to whisper in her ear, "If you do not stop me, if you do not speak out loud and clear, the moment I return from London, you will be back in my arms." He stood back, and his eyes returned to hers. "*That* is a promise."

A teasing shiver danced down Christina's back as she held her husband's gaze. Even more than before, she did not want him to leave. She wanted him to kiss her again. She wanted...

He needed to go!

Her thoughts were far from clear, and she truly ought to think about this promise of his before accepting it in a moment of weakness.

"Have a safe journey," she told him, her voice far from steady. "I'll await your return."

For a long moment, they simply looked at one another, their breaths mingling as temptation urged them to act upon the desire they saw in each other's eyes.

Here.

Now.

"Father!"

Christina flinched as did her husband. Samantha's voice broke the spell, and she felt heat rising to her cheeks. His presence had once again made her forget everything around her. They were far from alone. Servants lingered in the corridors nearby. His daughter was upstairs out of sight, but not out of earshot.

Now, here was neither the time nor the place.

"I'm leaving!" Thorne called to his daughter, then he turned to Christina and gently reached for her hand, a teasing smile upon his lips. "Until I return," he whispered in a way that felt almost seductive before he placed a gentle kiss upon the back of her hand.

"Until you return," Christina echoed his words, suddenly feeling bereft of something the moment his hand released hers.

He cast her one last wicked grin and then hurried out the door and down the steps. Outside the carriage, he stopped and turned to look up at the window where Samantha was no doubt waving frantically at him. He returned her farewell and then climbed into the carriage, which immediately pulled away and rolled down the drive.

Christina knew that it was foolish; yet she remained in the doorway until not even a small glimpse could be seen of the carriage in the far distance.

"I shall miss him," came Samantha's little voice, sadness tinging every word. "I always do."

Christina looked down at the little girl and smiled at her. "I believe I will as well," she mumbled, not certain if that was wise. But wise or not, it seemed it was the truth.

Over the following days, Christina found herself doing exactly two things: either she spent her time with Samantha out in the gardens or the stables or even riding across the meadows on King Arthur and a beautiful mare Samantha had named Lady Marion, or she was all but lost in thought, replaying the last moment she had shared with her husband in her mind, recalling what he had said as well as the way he had looked at her, contemplating her options.

Yes, she knew that it would be foolish to hold a grudge for his omission. She still felt disappointment whenever she thought of it, yet what he had done was something she should forgive. In fact, it was the underlying meaning of that lie that pained Christina the most.

The thought that she meant little to him beyond his own ambitions.

Still, the more Christina thought about everything, the more she began to think that even though he might not love her, there still was something between them. She felt it every time he stepped into a room, every time he drew near, every time...he kissed her.

If she could not have love, maybe she could make do with passion. Was that not what he had referred to upon his departure? What had he meant when he said that she would be in his arms the moment he returned? Would he kiss her again? Would he...?

Whenever Christina thought of consummating their marriage, she could not stop a flush from rising to her cheeks. Yet she could not claim to be apprehensive. *Curious* was perhaps the correct word. *Tempted* as well. Still, she wished she knew him better in order to feel comfortable to share something so intimate.

"It's starting to rain!" Samantha yelled over the howling wind as they made their way back to the stables.

The day had begun in such a promising way, clear blue skies with not a cloud in sight. The sun's rays had seemed almost golden, their warmth pleasant and soothing and their brightness reflected in the soft glow of the fields and meadows.

Now, however, dark clouds rolled in, promising heavy rain to fall upon the earth and them alike. The soft breeze had turned into a howling wind, whipping Christina's hair into her face and making her squint her eyes as they found their way back. Samantha cast worried eyes over her shoulder at the dark horizon, a bit of unease upon her face. Yet she held herself tall and urged her pony down the small slope.

"We're almost there!" Christina called over the whipping wind, doing her best to smile at Samantha. While she could not rightly say that she had come to feel like a mother toward the girl, she had come to care for her. In fact, it was impossible not to care for Samantha.

The girl's bright green eyes had a way of melting her heart, no matter the resistance she put up. Samantha always spoke with such joy and trust, and the way she often turned to Christina was so natural, her little hand reaching for hers, that Christina found herself unable not to open her heart to her.

Together, they pulled to a stop outside the stables and slid out of their saddles. Stable boys came running to take the reins and see to the animals as Christina reached for Samantha's hand. "We better hurry or we'll get wet!" she called to the child the moment she felt a heavy rain drop land upon her cheek.

No more than two heartbeats later, the rain started to come down hard, and within moments, the two of them were soaked to the skin. Samantha shrieked and made to bolt for the house, but Christina held her back, laughter spilling from her mouth as she began to dance in the rain, urging the girl to do the same.

Samantha hesitated, her eyes wide as she stared at Christina. Then, however, all hesitation fell from her and she joined in. Her little booted feet splashed through the quickly growing puddles and they both twirled in circles, stretching out their arms and lifting their faces to the sky, eyes closed as the rain washed over them.

Christina could not remember the last time she had felt like this. It was a feeling that had been long gone, one of complete ease and freedom and weightlessness. It was a feeling she knew from her own childhood when life had been simple and beautiful and there had been no dark clouds upon the horizon.

Now, everything was complicated. Every step she took needed to be considered and contemplated, and she could never be quite certain where she would end. One wrong step, and then?

But here, now, in this moment, Christina forgot about all that. She looked at the little girl beside her, and together, they danced in the rain, laughing as they spun in circles, faster and faster until...

...they lost their balance and fell into a large puddle, mud splashing onto their riding habits.

"Mrs. Huxley will be mad!" Samantha called above the rain as laughter continued to spill from her mouth. "She will shake her head again the way she does!"

Pushing to her feet, Christina held out her hand to Samantha and helped the little girl out of the puddle. "Do not worry, Sam. I shall speak to her." She looked around at the soaked ground and the heavy rain still coming down. "This was fun, was it not? And well worth a stern look from your governess, don't you agree?"

Sam nodded eagerly, and then the two of them dashed toward the house and slipped inside through a back entrance. They removed their muddy boots but could not prevent their riding habits from dripping all over the floor. Maids appeared to quickly wipe up the water that once again collected in little puddles, and they made it halfway up the stairs before Mrs. Huxley came upon them.

As expected, the stout woman's jaw dropped open and she stared at them, first in shock and then in utter disapproval. "What on earth happened? You look—"

Christina exchanged a look with Samantha before turning to the girl's governess. "There's nothing to worry about, Mrs. Huxley. I suppose, we got a tad wet. Will you see to it that Miss Samantha has a bath before supper?" She looked down at her own riding habit and then turned to look at Samantha's. "Perhaps there is no use in trying to save these. A perfect chance to shop for new ones, wouldn't you agree?"

Grinning from ear to ear, Samantha nodded. "Will we go to London? To see father?"

Christina froze, but managed to maintain a smile upon her face. "At some point, we will. Right now, you need to warm up. I shall see you at supper." She looked after Samantha as the girl followed her governess to her chambers.

With her thoughts once more lingering upon her husband, Christina soaked in a bath of her own and then dressed for supper. Her mind and heart were still in an uproar as she headed down to the dining room. She tried her best to converse with Samantha, but found her thoughts straying time and time again.

When she finally fell into bed that night, Christina felt exhausted. Her limbs felt weak despite the soothing bath, and yet she could not deny that she had enjoyed the day with Samantha greatly. She had laughed in a way she had not in a long time, and remembering their little dance in the rain still brought a smile to her face.

"Perhaps all shall be well after all," she whispered to herself in the dark before her thoughts once more returned to her husband and the moments before they had last parted. They returned to their kiss, and as Christina fell asleep, she could almost feel his arms wrap around her.

Thunder rolled in the distance when Christina woke with a start. Her chamber was still dark, not even a hint of dawn visible through the windows. Nevertheless, awareness crawled over her skin, leaving goosebumps in its wake.

Someone was in her room.

"Christina?" a faint little voice whispered. A voice full of fear. A voice that was undoubtedly Samantha's.

Pushing upright, Christina swept her eyes over the room, seeing nothing but hulking shadows in the dim light of the silvery moon that shone in through the windows. Christina had never been one to draw the curtains for she had always loved the soft lights that still existed even in the deepest night. "Sam, is that you? Where are you?"

Out of the shadow near the door, a smaller one separated, and she could hear soft footfalls as the little girl slowly made her way over to Christina's bed. Her face seemed pale in the dim light, and her eyes were open wide as she kept turning her head from side to side as though afraid that something might come at her.

Christina quickly slipped from her bed and rushed over to the little girl, pulling her into her arms. "What are you doing here? Is something wrong with Mrs. Huxley?" Samantha's little hands and feet were ice-cold, and Christina quickly lifted her into her arms and carried her to the bed.

"No," Samantha replied as she snuggled up next to Christina under the blanket. "She is sleeping in her chamber."

"Then what are you doing here?" Christina asked as she rubbed the girl's arms and legs to bring back some warmth.

Snuggling deeper into Christina's embrace, Samantha whispered, "I didn't want her. I wanted you."

Those few little words whispered with such open affection and innocent trust warmed Christina more than anything else ever had. It reminded her of her own family, of the love they had always shared, of how safe she had always felt with them, knowing that no matter what there were people in her life who would always stand with her.

"You can always come to me," Christina mumbled before placing a soft kiss upon the girl's head. "We are family now, and I will always be there for you. I promise."

"You, me and Papa?"

Christina inhaled a deep breath. "Yes. All of us." Perhaps it was possible. Perhaps if they simply were to believe in it, it would be.

Perhaps.

"I had a bad dream," Samantha whispered near Christina's ear. "And I don't like the thunder. Or the shadows. It always makes me think there's someone in my chamber."

Christina held the little girl tighter. "I used to feel like that, too. I would often sneak into my sister's room, and we would huddle up in bed together when we were younger. We would tell each other stories and try to distract one another from being afraid."

"What stories?"

Christina paused, realizing that she had spoken without thought. "Oh, that is not important. We just made up things that...brought us joy, to chase away the fear." Always had it brought Christina joy to conjure stories out of nothing. To create worlds and people and creatures. To speak of heroes and villains, of great deeds and daring adventures.

"Can you tell me such a story?" Samantha asked, hope ringing in her voice as she pushed herself up onto her elbow and looked down at Christina. "Perhaps then I won't be afraid anymore."

For a moment, Christina was tempted to refuse her. It was a part of her life she had banished into the shadows long ago. Only the pleading look in the girl's eyes would not allow her. "Very well. If you insist."

Samantha smiled. "I do."

Snuggling back down, Christina stared up at the ceiling, Samantha in her arms, and let her thoughts wander. "Have you ever seen fireflies dance at dusk?"

Christina felt Samantha's head nod up and down. "Yes, I have. Far out by the woods and the lake."

Christina smiled. "Did you know that not all fireflies are truly fireflies?"

She could feel Samantha frown against her shoulder. "Then what are they?"

Deep happiness settled in Christina's heart, something warm and contented and heartbreakingly beautiful. She closed her eyes and inhaled a deep breath before breathing one simple word out into the dark, "Fairies."

In her arms, Samantha stilled, and Christina could all but feel a hum of excitement go through the girl's little body. Anticipation lingered in the air, and she knew without looking that Samantha needed to know more. "They live in a world all their own, out in the forests, in hollow trees and burrows. They live everywhere, unseen and safe, away from people for the most important rule, the very first one every fairy learns is to never show themselves to people."

"Why not?" Samantha whispered, and the fingers of her left hand curled into the fabric of Christina's sleeve. "I wish I could see a fairy. What do they look like?"

"They're small, very small," Christina whispered into the dark as memories of her own childhood resurfaced, a childhood full of stories and adventure. "Their wings are translucent, but they glow as bright as the sun. During a bright summer's day, they are well hidden, but in the dark, their bright light draws others near. That's why they often live where there are fireflies, to hide themselves, to remain safe from curious eyes."

"Has no one ever seen them? No one?"

Christina felt a most wonderful smile play across her face. "Well, once there was a young girl..."

Chapter Thirty-Three

A PROMISED RETURN

Thorne left London the very moment his last meeting with Lord Huntington ended. He had been away from Pinewood Manor and his family for more than a sennight, and he could not wait to return home.

Uncertain whether he had achieved anything meaningful, Thorne continued to replay the many conversations he had held during his stay in London again and again in his mind. Lord Whickerton had been most helpful in influencing others to listen. Unfortunately, not even his new father-in-law could work miracles. Most lords had other things on their minds besides safety regulations and healthcare needs for the common men, women and children. Few had ever laid eyes on a burn victim or someone with a missing limb. They could not imagine the life that others lived day after day.

To Thorne, it was frustrating to no end. To look into these men's bored faces and know that they spent their fortunes on frivolous things while others did not possess enough to feed their families. It was an unjust world, and Thorne always felt his anger stir whenever he stood up to fight for those who did not have a voice.

There were days when every thought of his that was occupied with something other than their plight felt like a betrayal. How could he laugh and enjoy himself when others suffered so much? How did he dare?

Nonetheless, there was not much Thorne could do. He could not change the world on his own. He needed others to join him. Yes, many had turned a deaf ear, but some *had* listened. Perhaps with time and repetition, he could secure their support and eventually bring about change.

It was his greatest hope for he knew not what else to do.

Yet this fight drained him for it often seemed impossible. It exhausted his mind and heart and even his body, and sometimes all he wanted was to forget about it and live in a moment of oblivion.

In these moments, the desire to return to his family pulled at him the strongest, to such an extent that he could barely resist. So, when Thorne left Lord Huntington's townhouse that night, he did not even return to his own. He mounted his gelding and urged it down the road leading out of London and into the country.

Toward Pinewood Manor.

Toward home.

And his family.

Thorne rode until it was too dark to see. Midnight was near when he finally came upon an inn, grateful not to have to spend a night on the road. Trudging up the stairs to his room, he lay down on the bed and closed his eyes. Although exhaustion pulled on him, his mind once more returned to the moment he had bid his wife farewell.

Countless times over the past sennight had he done so. Countless times had he relived that moment.

That kiss.

That look in her eyes.

Those words that...had given him hope.

Before he had left, an icy distance had been between them. He had felt it every day, uncertain what to do about it. More than once had he been close to confronting her. Yet he had not. He had felt guilty, knowing that Christina had good reason to distrust him, to punish him even for what he had done. He had lied to her and manipulated her into accepting his hand.

He ought not have done so.

Thorne also remembered *his* last words to her. *If you do not stop me, if you do not speak out loud and clear, the moment I return from London, you will be back in my arms.*

Would she? It was the one question that had all but tormented him this past week. Would she stop him? Would she tell him to leave her alone?

Or would she not?

Exhaustion finally closed Thorne's eyes; however, not long before dawn began lurking upon the horizon did he rise once more and head down to the stables to continue his journey.

Fortunately, on horseback, he was able to travel faster than they had by carriage the day they had first arrived. And so, Thorne found his gaze catch a first glimpse of Pinewood Manor no more than three hours after the sun had begun rising in the east. It was still early in the day, and he wondered if his wife was already awake. Was she already down in the breakfast parlor? Or was she still asleep in her chambers?

Eagerness burned in his veins, and he hoped with every fiber of his being that she would not refuse him. Thorne did not know what he would do if she did, but he feared he might perish.

Grateful for the stable boy who came running the moment he jumped off his horse, Thorne quickly climbed the steps of the front door and headed into the hall. Reuben appeared out of nowhere and offered a respectful bow. "Welcome back, Sir."

Thorne nodded to the old man. "Good morning. Is my wife already up?"

"I believe not, Sir."

Without another word or glance at his butler, Thorne climbed the stairs toward the first floor two at a time. A part of him felt foolish, even urged him to slow down, to remain cautious. Only he was unable to comply.

Large strides carried him down the corridor, his gaze fixed upon the door to his wife's chamber. Ought he to knock? Would she be furious with him if he simply burst in?

A soft chuckle drifted from his lips because he knew that she would be. Yet more often than not, it seemed that she *liked* being furious with him. He, too, could not deny that he loved her spirit, her directness, the way she offered resistance. It was almost a game between them, a game that had often enough ended in a kiss.

Would it today?

Thorne hesitated outside her door, but for no more than a second. He was willing to risk her wrath. He would rather she snap at him instead of denying him entrance. And so, he opened the door, quietly, and stepped inside.

Although not a sound drifted to his ears, the curtains were no longer drawn. Had she left them open over night? Or had she already risen without Reuben noticing?

Closing the door, Thorne turned toward the bed. He felt like an intruder, and yet he could not help himself. His gaze drifted up the covers, imagining her tempting body underneath, until they fell upon the small hand of a child.

Thorne blinked as his feet drew to a halt. "Sam?" he mumbled as he stared at his wife and daughter, snuggled in each other's arms, eyes closed and sleeping peacefully.

Always had he known that Christina would eventually succumb to Samantha's daring spirit and innocent laughter. Only *this* he had never imagined. Something had to have happened in his absence, and he wished he knew what that was.

He wished it could work for him and Christina as well. Perhaps if he asked, Samantha would share her secret with him.

For a long time, Thorne remained by the foot of the bed, his eyes drawn to them. Never had he seen them so peaceful, not even Samantha. The girl seemed to breathe more easily with Christina's arm wrapped around her.

A wide yawn suddenly stretched across the little girl's face as she turned in Christina's arms, her own stretching as slumber slowly fell away. Christina, too, began to stir as though sensing the girl was close to waking.

The moment Samantha beheld him standing by the bed, her eyes opened wide and then she suddenly surged upward. "Papa!" Jumping to her feet, she tiptoed across the mattress and then flung herself into his arms. "You're back!"

Thorne held her tightly, always amazed at the feeling that swept through him when those little arms wrapped around his neck. There was nothing like it.

Nothing.

Over his daughter's shoulder, Thorne saw his wife blink her eyes and then pushed herself up onto her elbows. Sleep still lingered upon her face, and she brushed a hand over her eyes before looking up at him.

"Good morning," Thorne greeted her with a grin when he saw a soft hint of red come to her cheeks. She inhaled an unsteady breath and then slowly reached out to pull the covers higher, almost up to her chin.

Thorne's grin deepened until his wife, finally abandoning the attempt to hide from him, pushed herself into a sitting position and met his eyes with an unflinching look of her own. "So, you have returned," she stated; something other than mere observation swung in her voice. It almost sounded like a challenge.

Thorne nodded, wondering if she remembered the words he had last spoken to her. The promise. "I have," he replied, wishing he knew if she could see the memory upon his face.

Setting Samantha back down onto the bed, Thorne looked at his daughter. "What are you doing here? I must say I'm quite surprised."

Samantha cast a warm smile over her shoulder at Christina, a smile that was full of shared memories and whispered secrets. "I had a nightmare," Samantha said, turning back to look at him, a hint of fear still in her eyes. "I was frightened, and so I came in here." And then all of a sudden, her face brightened in a way as Thorne had rarely seen it. "Christina told me a story about fairies. It was so beautiful. Did you know that fairies are all around us? They pretend to be fireflies to keep themselves safe."

Thorne returned her smile. "I had no idea. Perhaps you can tell me more about this after breakfast. You must be hungry." It was true, he did wish to know more about what had happened between his wife and daughter in his absence. At present, though, he could not deny that there was another matter on his mind.

Behind them, Christina was slipping from the bed and pulling on a robe. Her delicate hands moved swiftly to tie the belt before she walked around to the foot of the bed, her bright blue eyes coming to rest upon Samantha. "Perhaps you should go find Mrs. Huxley and get dressed. I admit I'm quite famished myself."

Jumping off the bed, Samantha beamed up at her. "Will you tell me more stories? About fairies?"

Smiling, Christina placed a gentle hand upon the girl's cheek. "Of course. Anytime you wish. Now, go and get dressed."

With her curls bouncing up and down, Samantha skipped from the room, a soft melody drifting from her lips as she continued down the corridor.

Following in his daughter's wake, Thorne moved toward the door... and closed it. Then he turned back around to look at his wife.

Her eyes were watchful as she regarded him. "What are you doing in my chamber?" Briefly, her gaze left his and darted to the door at his back. "You did not knock, did you?"

Thorne grinned at her. "How would you know? You were fast asleep." Reminding himself not to rush things, Thorne moved toward her slowly.

Her breath seemed to catch in her throat; however, her eyes remained upon his. "Is this a way for a gentleman to conduct himself? To enter a lady's chamber without invitation?"

Thorne chuckled, approaching another step. "Did you truly expect differently? Was it not you who told me repeatedly that I was *not* a gentleman?"

Her lips curled into the beginnings of a smile as she retreated a step. Fortunately, there was nothing timid or even fearful about her. She did not retreat out of concern, but...to lure him closer? "Gentleman or not, you have no right to be in my chamber." She retreated another step until her back came up against the right column at the foot of the bed.

Holding her gaze, Thorne ignored her words. "Is that so?" He watched her chin rise with each step he took, her blue eyes remaining fixed upon his. "Would you like me to leave?" he asked against his better judgment, knowing that he would come close to shattering if she were to order him away.

For a moment, Christina remained quiet; yet her gaze watched his approach with something more than interest. "I would like to know what you're doing in my chamber," she finally said when no more than an arm's length separated them. "Why are you here?"

Thorne could not help but think that she knew precisely why he was here. She knew, but she wanted him to say it. And so, he did. "I'm here to uphold a promise," he whispered as he slowly lowered his head to hers.

Her breathing quickened as she looked up at him, her lips slightly parted. "Are you a man of your word then?"

"Always," he whispered as he leaned closer still, his hands rising to settle upon her waist. He felt a shiver go through her as his hands continued to slide onto her back, pulling her into his embrace.

Time seemed to stand still as they stood there, their eyes locked, the distance between them shrinking incrementally as they all but drifted toward one another like two magnets unable to maintain the space between them.

"You were gone a long time," Christina whispered against his lips, her breath coming fast as her hands settled upon his arms.

"Too long," Thorne murmured, enjoying the tantalizing closeness between them. It was torture, and yet it was bliss at the same time. "Did you miss me?"

Her lips twitched, and he could see something utterly tempting spark in her blue eyes. They seemed to darken in a most alluring way, and he wondered if she was even aware of it. "Perhaps," she replied on a whisper, tilting her head upward another fraction.

Thorne grinned before his gaze darted to her lips. "Do you want me to kiss you?"

"A gentleman would not ask such a thing," she chided teasingly, raking her teeth across her lower lip in a deeply seductive, yet strangely innocent gesture.

Thorne chuckled deep in his throat. "I'm beginning to think that despite your words it is not a gentleman you want." He paused, then quickly dipped his head and brushed his lips against hers in a feather-light touch. "Is that not so? Admit it. You're beginning to like that I'm not a gentleman." He swallowed. "You're beginning to like—"

The breath lodged in his throat as he looked at her. He could feel his heart hammering in his chest and found himself surprisingly unable to finish what he had begun to say.

Her chest rose and fell with a deep breath. "You?" Christina half-asked and half-stated. Her fingers tightened upon his arms as though she wished to pull him closer.

Thorne was only too happy to comply. "Do you?" he whispered, brushing his lips against hers yet again.

"Never," she replied with a smile before she pushed herself up onto her toes and kissed him.

Thorne felt a low groan deep in his throat. "Never?" he asked and then kissed her again.

Her hands snaked upward, and he felt the tips of her fingers brush against his neck, then curl into his collar, tightening her hold on him. "Perhaps."

"Perhaps?" he teased, smiling against her lips.

"Perhaps a little."

Thorne slanted his mouth across hers and kissed her deeply. Then he lifted his head and looked at her. "A little?"

Her breathing came fast as she tried to pull him back down to her. "Or a little more." Her teeth once more dug into her lower lip. "Stop teasing me," she all but commanded, then kissed him as he had hoped she would.

Sinking into their kiss, Thorne reveled in the feel of her. Her skin was warm and soft even through the layers of fabric protecting her from his inquisitive hands. Still, the knot in the front of her robe quickly loosened, and his hands slid inside.

Christina gasped, and he felt another shiver run down her back. Yet she did not pull away nor demand he stop and act the gentleman he was not.

Nor had he any wish to be.

With each touch and each kiss, Christina grew bolder, her passion matching his in a way Thorne had not dared hope for. He was close to picking her up and moving this onto the bed when Samantha's voice echoed along the corridor. "Are you coming?"

Instantly, the two of them surged apart, both breathing heavily as they stared at one another in shock. A becoming flush darkened

Christina's cheeks before she quickly averted her gaze, a rather endearing, yet also somewhat embarrassed smile drawing up the corners of her mouth.

Briefly, Thorne closed his eyes and chuckled. "I love her dearly, but that girl has awful timing."

Reaching to refasten her robe, Christina grinned, her cheeks a blazing red now.

A moment later, the door flew open, and Samantha bounced in, dressed in a pale blue dress and her wild hair braided down her back. She looked from him to Christina and then frowned. "You're still not dressed." Confusion came to her eyes. "What have you been doing?"

Thorne had to clench his jaw to keep from laughing out loud for Christina's face seemed to darken with each inquisitive look Samantha cast in her direction.

"Are you well?" Samantha asked, squinting her eyes as she looked at Christina. "You look flushed."

Closing her eyes, Christina inhaled a deep breath, careful not to meet his eyes. Then she knelt down to speak to Samantha. "I'm quite well, dearest. How about you go on downstairs, and I promise I'll be quick. All right?"

Still frowning, Samantha nodded. "Very well."

"And take your father with you," Christina added belatedly before Samantha could once more skip out the door. "I have no need for him up here."

Thorne turned to look at his wife and saw her brows arch up in a teasing gesture. The red upon her cheeks was fading, and she once more stood tall and proud, meeting his eyes without the slightest hint of mortification. "Is that so?" he asked with a grin.

Christina nodded, her eyes sparkling with mischief. Then she stepped back to let him pass, careful not to allow him to come too close. "Indeed, your presence proves to be awfully distracting. If you stay, I believe I shall never make my way downstairs, and I admit I'm quite...famished."

"Come, Papa," Samantha exclaimed, taking him by the hand and pulling him away from Christina and toward the door. "I'm famished, too. She'll dress quicker without you here."

Reluctantly, Thorne followed his daughter. "And here I thought ladies could not make do without someone to help with their laces."

The look upon Christina's face told him loud and clear that she was not so innocent that she did not understand his meaning. The flush upon her cheeks returned, and she quickly averted her eyes. "I shall call for my lady's maid," she assured him once her gaze was steady again. "Do not trouble yourself, Sir."

Thorne cast her one last, longing look before closing the door behind him and his daughter. Nevertheless, the image of Christina, her blue eyes dark with passion and the belt of her robe undone, remained in his mind.

Indeed, they both knew what would have happened—could possibly have happened—if it had not been for Samantha's interference.

"I'm so glad you're back." Craning her little neck, Samantha beamed up at him.

Thorne returned her smile. "As am I."

Chapter Thirty-Four

HIDDEN STORIES

With a picnic basket slung over her arm, Christina made her way down the small slope into the meadow. The sun shone brightly, and she had to squint her eyes to spot father and daughter on the edge of the forest. The soft breeze carried their voices to her ears, but they were no more than a distant echo. She could not make out the words being spoken; all she knew was that they spoke with joy and laughter.

Wading through the tall grass, Christina marveled at how drastically her life had changed in only a few short weeks. Not long ago, she had not even known Thorne and Samantha existed. Then she had only known his name and the sight of him from across the ballroom. And now?

Now, he was her husband.

A smile came to Christina's face, and yet it was as always accompanied by a sense of guilt and shame. Yes, Thorne was now her husband, but perhaps he should not have been. Perhaps he should have been Sarah's husband. How easily could Christina picture her dearest friend here in the meadow, carrying a picnic basket for her new family. Such a life would have made Sarah happy, would it not? She would have been safe here, loved and cherished, away from her self-centered parents.

She would have been happy here.

"Look how high I am!" Samantha called from up in a tree. One hand was wrapped tightly around a thick branch while the other waved frantically, a wide rather triumphant-looking smile upon her little face.

Christina waved back. "Careful now, so you don't fall." She walked a few steps closer, then stopped and watched as Thorne directed Samantha's movements. He spoke calmly and with a voice that rang with conviction as though he knew with absolute certainty that nothing bad would happen, that Samantha would find her way back down to the ground safe and sound.

Of course, he could not *know*; nonetheless, it was that reassurance in his voice that seemed to make the world a safer place.

At least for Samantha.

Distractedly, Christina found herself staring at him. Although she had refused to acknowledge his appealing smile and wickedly tempting eyes before, now she could not. Now, she saw him for all that he was. He was not a gentleman, but a man who was kind and caring. A man who showed respect to those who deserved it. A man who was strong and who fought not only for himself, but for others as well. He was not one to close his eyes and ignore the pleas for help echoing around him.

Yes, he was not a gentleman, but he *was* an incredibly good man.

These last few days since his return from London, Christina had been all too aware of him. Whenever he stepped into a room, all her attention moved to him. It was as though the rest of the world was dipped in shadows while he stood in the light.

"Now jump!" Thorne instructed as he held Samantha's little hands within his own. She crouched on the low hanging branch, and with her eyes fixed upon his, she pushed herself off and jumped to the ground, his hands never releasing hers.

"Did you see that? Christina, did you see me jump?" Samantha exclaimed as she came racing over, her face full of joy and pride.

Shaken out of her thoughts, Christina cleared her throat before returning the little girl's smile. "Yes, I did. It looked quite frightening. Are you all right?" She set down the picnic basket and reached for the blanket within.

"Shall we set up over there?" Thorne asked as he came striding over. "Under the tree in the shade?"

His eyes looked into hers, and Christina felt her heart skip a beat. She quickly dropped her gaze and busied herself with the basket. "Very well." She lengthened her strides in order to put some distance between them; yet out of the corner of her eye she caught the hint of confusion that came to his face.

Of course, he was noticing her odd behavior. She was acting like a fool, like a coward. She had chosen this life, and now, she had regrets. She did not regret her choice, but that her choice had come at a price of someone she cared for deeply.

Oh, if only she could be happy here! If only she could give herself to this life! What would it feel like to truly live here in Pinewood Manor? To truly be Thorne's wife?

Stepping closer, Thorne took the blanket from her hands. "Are you well?" he asked, once more trying to see into her eyes. "You seem...not like yourself."

Christina quickly looked up at him and smiled. "I'm perfectly fine." Then she turned away and knelt down beside the basket. Out of the corner of her eye, she watched him spread out the blanket. She watched Samantha help to straighten the edges. Then she handed out the food to them both so they could place it in its center. She kept her hands busy and her eyes averted; however, before long all the work was done and her husband and Samantha settled onto the blanket, stretching out their legs.

"Will you not sit down with us?" Samantha asked as she reached for a pastry filled with marmalade. "Are you not hungry?"

Samantha smiled at her, then sat down next to the girl, careful to keep her distance from her husband. "I suppose not as hungry as you. However, I was not the one to climb to the top of the tree, now was I?"

Samantha once more beamed with joy before attacking the pastry in her hand like a hungry lion. "Will you tell us a story?" she asked with her mouth full. "What happened to the little girl after she ran away from home?"

Christina tensed, and her eyes involuntarily drifted to her husband. "Perhaps later." She could not quite say why she hesitated; however, she had never spoken to anyone about her stories. Only her family knew, and now Samantha.

"I would like to hear a story as well," Thorne said, his eyes lingering upon her face. She could see that he knew that she felt uncomfortable and that he was wondering why.

Still, Christina hesitated. Would he disapprove? Or would he not object as long as her aspirations never went beyond what was deemed appropriate for a woman? Or was this, perhaps, the solution she had been looking for?

Perhaps if he knew of her childhood dream of being a writer, if she could make him believe that she still intended to pursue it, he would prove himself unworthy of her. No doubt, he would tell her to forget about such aspirations and look toward home and family instead.

As Aunt Francine's husband had.

Perhaps then she would no longer feel guilty for robbing her friend of a good husband. Perhaps then her heart would turn from him, and she would be free to feel as she saw fit.

Christina heaved a deep sigh. "Very well." She tried to gather her thoughts, yet it had been a long time since she had spoken of her stories to anyone.

Samantha was different. She was a child, and her glowing eyes made her see everything in a different way. Adults were not like that. They were critical and judgmental, and their words had a way of slashing at one's heart.

With her eyes upon the little girl in front of her, Christina began her story. "It was already dark when Anna fled the house. She knew not where to go, but simply allowed her feet to carry her onward. A chilling wind blew that night, tearing at her hair and skirts as she stumbled through the tall grass. Her eyes were full of tears, and she could barely see the next step in front of her. Even without tears running down her cheeks, she would have been hard-pressed to make out anything in her vicinity. Dark shadows loomed, and the dim light that touched the world that night would not grant her safe passage."

Sitting completely still, Samantha stared at her, the bite of pastry in her mouth all but forgotten. "What...?" she tried to ask around the bite in her mouth, but then stopped, chewed a few times and swallowed. "What happened then? Did she get lost?"

Samantha smiled at the little girl. "She feared she would. She let her eyes drift over the land, but she could see nothing but shadows and darkness. She knew she could not go back home so she continued onward even though she did not know where to go."

Samantha scooted closer, her eyes wide, and the pastry in her hand squished in a way that marmalade dripped down from her fingers and onto the blanket.

"She walked and walked," Christina continued her story, careful to keep her eyes on the little girl. "Her legs began to grow heavy, yet she continued on. After a long while, she finally saw something in the distance."

Samantha drew in a sharp breath and clapped her hands together in joy. "Fairies!" The pastry was now hopelessly destroyed and clung not only to Samantha's hands but also to her dress and parts of the blanket.

Thorne chuckled, then rose to his feet. "You better wash before Mrs. Huxley sees you." He reached for a jug of water and urged Samantha to step off the blanket and hold out her hands. Then he proceeded to wash them until the child was reasonably clean once more. "Are you still hungry?"

Looking at her empty hands, Samantha nodded.

"Then I suppose you should eat before Christina continues the story," Thorne suggested with a smile, "for we do not have an endless supply of food, and if you continue to crush it in your hands in your excitement, we shall surely run out."

Nodding, Samantha complied and once more sat down upon the blanket and reached for a pastry. Thorne, too, returned to sit with them; however, this time, he seated himself far closer to Christina. She could feel his eyes drift over, lingering here and there, before she finally turned to face him. "Is something wrong?" she demanded, unable to keep her voice even.

Thorne frowned at her. "I was about to ask you the same thing," he remarked with a sideways glance at Samantha, who seemed to be rather oblivious at the moment for she chewed and swallowed and then took another bite. "You seem upset with me." He leaned closer. "What did I do?"

Christina's mouth opened, but no words came out for in truth he had done nothing. That was the problem, was it not?

"I'm finished," Samantha exclaimed before she rose and then seated herself in her father's lap. "Will you continue the story now?"

Grateful for the little girl's interference, Christina nodded. She kept her gaze upon Samantha's wide green eyes and tried her best to ignore the man who kept watching her with hawk's eyes.

The afternoon passed swiftly and pleasantly despite the tension that continued to linger in Christina's body. She kept stealing glances at her husband but could not be certain what he was thinking. She did not see disapproval upon his face, but rather confusion and the desire to understand.

She knew well how that felt for she longed for the very same thing. Never before had her own actions and thoughts confused her like this. Never before had she felt so at odds with the world and herself.

When it was time to head back, Christina mumbled an excuse, begging them to see to returning the picnic basket to Cook on their own. Then, before either one of them could object or ask for details, she rushed off.

Exhaustion lingered in her limbs for it was rather tiring to uphold this pretense. Yes, she was pretending. She was pretending to be upset with her husband. She was pretending to enjoy herself. She was pretending to *not* enjoy herself. She was pretending to...

Christina no longer knew. She stumbled ahead almost blindly and felt reminded of the little girl in her story who walked without sight but simply knew that she needed to get away.

Through a side door, she slunk into the house and somehow found her way into the drawing room. There she sank into an armchair, exhausted. She drew in a couple of deep breaths before she surged to her feet once more and began to pace, unable to sit still, her mind too full of thoughts. "What am I to do?" she mumbled to herself, feeling torn in two separate directions.

Although Christina had failed to write to Sarah and inform her of her decision with regard to marrying Thorne beforehand, she had somehow found the nerve to write to her after. A few weeks ago, Christina had finally penned a letter explaining how everything had happened and apologizing profusely for robbing Sarah of a decent husband. She was uncertain what she expected or hoped for; however, Sarah had yet to respond.

So far there had been no letter from her friend.

Nothing.

"What am I to do?" Christina once again mumbled to herself. Without Sarah's blessing, a dark cloud would forever be hanging over her marriage, over every moment. Despite Sarah's words, Christina could not help but think that her friend might be heartbroken after all. Before, she had not known what a wonderful man Thorne was...not until Christina had told her so. Was it possible that Sarah was unwilling to grant her blessing? Was that why she had yet to reply?

If only Christina had never...come to care for her husband! If only!

"Why can he not be the man I thought him to be? Why can he not be a scoundrel and a rake and a reprobate? Why?" She shook her head. "It would make everything so much easier." A frustrated growl rose from her throat. "Why do I have to like him?"

"*Like him! Like him!*" squawked Biscuit in the corner.

Christina flinched and spun around, staring at the bird. "What are you doing here?" she asked foolishly, cursing herself for not having noticed the bird's presence before.

"*Sam! Sam!*" Biscuit replied as though answering her question of how he had come to be there.

Sighing deeply, Christina turned away and stepped up to the window, resting her forehead against the cool pane. "What am I to do?"

"You could tell me what is going on," came Thorne's voice from the door, and Christina whirled around.

Standing there, he looked at her for a moment longer before pushing the door shut. Then he came toward her. "What happened?" he asked, those green eyes of his searching her face as though hoping to read the answer to his question there somewhere. "Why did you run off?"

Backing away until the window stopped her retreat, Christina shook her head. She could not think. Her nerves were too frayed. She needed him to leave. "It is nothing," she snapped, lifting her hand to stop him when he continued toward her. "Leave. I wish to be alone."

Slowly, Thorne shook his head. "Talk to me, Chris. Whatever is on your mind, has been there for days, weeks even. Do you honestly think it will go away if you ignore it?"

Christina bit her lower lip, tempted to confess everything, yet equally determined to keep him at arm's length.

"*Like him! Like him!*" Biscuit squawked.

Christina froze, feeling her eyes go wide as she stared at her husband, the bird's words—her words!—echoing in her ears.

Thorne stilled, his eyes darting to the bird before returning to watch her most carefully. And then she could see understanding dawn. A smile began to tease his lips before he took another step toward her. "Is that what it is?" he asked. "Are you afraid to like me?"

Christina continued to stare at him unable to say anything.

"Why?"

Chapter Thirty-Five

A HEART TORN

"Why are you afraid to like me?" Thorne asked as he regarded his wife.

Pale and looking utterly forlorn, she stood by the window, her eyes wide, reminding him of a cornered animal, frightened and desperately looking for a way to escape.

For days now, he had watched her. He had seen the torn look in her eyes but had failed to understand what had put it there. At times, she had delighted in his presence while at others the look in her eyes had dimmed the moment he had approached. To him, it had seemed as though she had been unable to make up her mind about whether or not she wanted him near her. Could it be that, somehow, she did care for him after all, but felt as though it was wrong of her?

Frustrated by her silence, Thorne closed the distance between them, his hands reaching to grasp her by the shoulders. He lowered his head and looked down at her face. "Chris, please! Tell me what is going on?" He inhaled a slow breath, trying his best to remain calm. "I can see…that you like me." She blinked, and her blue eyes rose to meet his. "I can feel that you like me. Why does that upset you so?"

An anguished look came to her eyes before she closed them and leaned forward to rest her forehead against his chest. "You're a good man," she mumbled, heaving a deep sigh.

Thorne continued to hold her by the shoulders, wondering if she would refuse him if he were to embrace her. "Is that bad?" he asked with a slight chuckle, seeking to lighten the mood.

With her forehead still resting against his chest, she nodded. "Yes, it's bad. Unbelievably bad."

Trying not to laugh, Thorne looked down at the top of her head. "All right," he said carefully, wishing he knew what went on in her head. "Would you mind explaining your reasoning? For I must admit that I do not understand. From the first, you criticized me for not being a gentleman. Honestly, I would think that you would rejoice at finding me to be a decent man, at least."

She continued to hide her face from him. "I stole her one chance for happiness," she mumbled into the folds of his vest, a hint of anger and regret in her voice, a voice that rang with exhaustion more than anything else.

Thorne frowned. "You stole whose chance for happiness? What are you talking about?"

A soft growl rose in her throat, and then she suddenly pushed herself away from him and lifted her chin, her blue eyes flashing. "Sarah's!"

"Miss...Miss Mortensen?"

Christina threw up her hands. "Yes, of course!"

For a long moment, Thorne looked at her and tried to see the many subtle emotions that danced over her face. There was more than anger and regret in her eyes. There was also warmth and hope; yet it shone like a light trying to fight its way through shadows, dim and hindered.

Biting her lower lip, Christina closed her eyes briefly. When she opened them again, she seemed a bit calmer. "I misjudged you," she finally said in a voice that held regret above all. "I thought you were a different man than you are. I thought...I thought you would harm her, make her unhappy. I thought she would not be safe with you."

Thorne frowned, still uncertain what precisely she was upset about. After all, if he had truly married Miss Mortensen, they could never have been happy together. The thought was ludicrous!

"I should never have interfered," Christina exclaimed on a sob. Her eyes suddenly filled with tears as she looked at him, slowly shaking her head from side to side. "If I had not misjudged you, if I had not thought her in danger, I would never have interfered. It was the greatest mistake I've ever made."

Thorne tensed at her words. "You... You regret marrying me?"

Christina nodded her head vehemently. "Yes!" Tears streamed down her face. "You could have been *her* husband; she would've been safe with you. She could've been happy after everything her parents have done to her. She deserves to be happy." Closing her eyes, Christina wiped the tears from her cheeks. "I thought I was helping, but I did not. I made things worse."

Thorne felt himself relax when he finally began to understand why his wife was so deeply distraught. At first, he had thought his fears confirmed, that she never wanted to marry him, that she truly regretted having done so. Yet that was not it, was it?

Reaching out, Thorne grasped her hands. "Look at me, Chris."

Blinking back the tears that lingered, Christina lifted her head. "I don't want to like you," she whispered, a hint of accusation in her voice as she looked at him. "Why couldn't you have been an awful sort of man?"

Thorne chuckled as his heart began to lighten. "I'm deeply sorry to disappoint you, my dear." He pulled her closer, wishing to comfort her, but also wishing to hold her. Her eyes held such sadness that it broke his heart. "I like you as well," he whispered, offering her a teasing smile.

Heaving a deep sigh, Christina tried to step out of his embrace. "That makes it worse." Still, a spark of something warm and appealing came to her eyes as though his words had pleased her.

Thorne frowned. "How so?"

Christina shrugged. "I don't know. But it does." Again, she tried to step out of his embrace, but he would not release her.

"Would you stop trying to get away?" Thorne demanded, tightening his hold on her.

"Then simply release me!" Christina snapped, flattening her palms against his chest as she tried to push him away.

To no avail.

"Not until you've heard what I have to say."

After another moment of futile struggling, she finally lifted her head and relented. "Very well. What do you have to say?"

Thorne inhaled a deep breath, hoping that what he had to say would not drive them further apart. An ordinary woman, he believed would look favorably upon the words he was about to speak; only Christina was far from an ordinary woman. "I would never have married your friend."

Staring up at him, she stilled. "But you...?" She blinked. "Why would you say that? You were speaking to her father. You all but told me that you intended to marry her!"

Thorne nodded. "I did. I did think that a mutually beneficial union would see everyone satisfied." He remembered well his rather innocent thoughts of marriage and all it might entail. Indeed, he had been foolish to believe that a marriage could ever be no more than a business arrangement. "I could see easily enough that she did not wish to marry me. I saw her pale face, and I saw her hands tremble. I am not an ogre. I would never have married a woman who looked at me and felt frightened." He shook his head slowly to emphasize his words.

Christina frowned; the pulse in her neck seemed to beat more rapidly. "But you said..." She regarded him more closely, her eyes narrowing. "You baited me. You said what you said because you knew it would upset me. You wanted to upset me! It was a game, was it not?" Again, her palms shoved against his chest.

Again, Thorne did not release her. "Yes, it was a game," he told her, lowering his head another fraction to look deeper into her eyes, "and I enjoyed playing it with you. Can you truly look at me and tell me that you did not?"

Christina's lips pressed shut, but the glare in her eyes seemed to dim...at least a little. "The day of my sister's wedding," she began, her eyes sweeping over his face, "it was no accident that you came upon me in the library, was it?"

Thorne shook his head, wondering why she would ask him so again. "It was not."

"Why? Why did you compromise me?"

Gritting his teeth, Thorne yanked her against him before his left hand traveled upward, traced the column of her neck and then slipped into her hair, cupping the back of her head. "Because I wanted you," he whispered heatedly, his head bent so low that the tip of his nose almost touched hers. "From the moment I saw you, I knew that I wanted you. I also knew that you would never agree to marry me, not with the way you were looking at me, the way you lashed out at me." His lips pressed into a thin line as he remembered the choice he had made a few weeks past. "Yes, I forced your hand, and I know I should not have." He shook his head, looking down into her wide-open eyes. "Still, I cannot say that I regret what I did."

Shocked speechless, Christina stared up at him, her breath coming fast. He could feel it tease his lips, tempting him, daring him to move closer still. The moment he dipped his head, though, she tensed and tried to pull away.

"You wanted me," she whispered breathless, her eyes still as round as before, "because my father—"

A sharp knock sounded on the door, and rather belatedly Thorne realize that voices could be heard from the entrance hall.

Reluctantly, he released his wife and took a step back. "Enter."

Reuben appeared and gave a quick bow. "Pardon me, Sir. You have visitors."

Still holding his wife's gaze, Thorne asked, "Who is it?"

"The Dowager Countess of Whickerton as well as Lady Juliet and Lady Harriet."

Christina blinked and turned away from him toward the door. "They are here?" she asked, utter surprise in her voice.

Reuben nodded. "Shall I see them in?"

Before either of them could reply, footsteps echoed closer, and the dowager's voice rang out loud and clear. "Oh, an old woman could die out here waiting for you to answer a simple question." She burst into the room, cast a kind smile at a rather befuddled-looking Reuben and then despite leaning heavily upon her walking stick hastened toward Christina. "My dear, how good it is to see you. My, you look splendid-ly." Yet Thorne could see her eyes narrowing as they swept over her granddaughter before moving to him.

"Welcome to Pinewood Manor, my lady," Thorne greeted her before his gaze rose to fall upon her two granddaughters, stepping into the room behind her. "We are most delighted that you have decided to pay us a visit."

The dowager chuckled. "Well, you are kind to say that." Her gaze moved over Christina's still red-rimmed eyes as well as the rapidly beating pulse in her neck before returning to meet Thorne's eyes. "It seems we have interrupted a most significant moment." Her brows rose in question.

Thorne swallowed, uncertain what to say. He turned to look at his wife, who in that moment stepped toward her grandmother and embraced her. "I'm so happy to see you, Grandma. It has been too long."

Hugging her granddaughter close, the dowager patted her back. "It certainly has, my dear." She pulled back and looked into her granddaughter's face, a kind smile upon her lips. "Now, I've heard that there is a young girl here who is to be my great-granddaughter. I insist to meet her this instant." Her smile brightened into something Thorne knew he would not forget for the rest of his life nor the words she had just said.

Deep down, he had always hoped to hear them.

Chapter Thirty-Six

HUSBAND & WIFE

Despite the precarious situation with her husband, Christina was relieved to see her grandmother. It was that way with grandparents and parents as well, was it not? They had a way of providing reassurance and comfort by simply being there, by offering a kind word and a soft smile. Nothing was resolved, and yet the world seemed a brighter place.

Casting a last look at her husband, Christina embraced her sisters and then escorted them all out into the garden where Samantha was picking flowers. The girl stared at them with wide eyes, then slowly moved closer, her gaze traveling from Grandma Edie to Juliet and Harriet. "Do we have visitors?" she asked, moving closer to Christina and taking her hand.

Christina smiled at her, but before she could reply, her grandmother stepped forward. "No, dearest, we're not visitors. We are family." Her eyes swept over Samantha, and Christina saw something deeply affectionate come to her grandmother's eyes. "I'm Christina's grandmother, did you know that?"

Samantha's eyes widened, and she shook her head, clutching the flowers in her hands tighter.

Grandma Edie chuckled. "I'm an old woman, but the good thing is old women get to be grandmothers." Her grin widened as she tried to lean down to Samantha as best as she could. "And now, I would also like to be a great-grandmother. Yours. Would that be all right?"

Samantha's little eyes seemed to be growing wider with each word Grandma Edie spoke. "You wish to be my great-grandmother?" she asked with such hope and longing in her voice that Christina felt tears prick the backs of her eyes for the second time that day.

Grandma Edie nodded. "Of course. If you agree, we shall be great-grandmother and great-granddaughter. Doesn't that sound marvelous?" She clapped her hands together, almost dropping her walking stick in the process. "In fact, I am quite certain I have never heard anything quite so wonderful. Have you?"

An enchanted smile spread over Samantha's face as she nodded her head. "You will be my great-grandma? Forever and ever?"

"Forever and ever. That is a promise."

The smile upon Samantha's face stretched so far that Christina feared the little girl's cheeks might hurt. "Do I call you great-grandma?"

Grandma Edie frowned a little. "Well, you may, of course. However, it does sound like a mouthful, does it not? If you wish, simply call me Grandma Edie," she glanced up at her granddaughters, "as Christina and your two new aunts do as well."

Samantha stilled. "Two new aunts?"

Christina sighed as she watched Samantha meet her new family. They were all delighted to see her and before long hugs and flowers were exchanged. Harriet quickly had Samantha giggling, chasing her across the lawn, pretending to be a wolf or a lion wishing to devour her.

Watching them, Grandma Edie chuckled. "Who knew you'd be the first one of my granddaughters to be a mother?" She gently patted Christina's hand.

"I'm not quite certain if I feel like a mother."

Grandma Edie squeezed her arm. "Don't worry. You will. You will." She looked at Samantha, squealing with delight as Harriet caught up to her. "You're already a natural at it. The child adores you and feels safe with you. That is all that matters."

Juliet heaved a deep sigh, her eyes wistful as she watched Samantha. "She truly is priceless."

Christina glanced at her oldest sister. More than once, she had found herself wondering why Juliet was not married. Somehow, her eldest sister seemed content being her grandmother's companion; yet there were moments when she did seem wistful, a longing expression upon her face when she saw mothers with their children or wives with their husbands.

The coming days passed in a cheerful manner and reminded Christina of her own childhood. The house was full of laughter and joy as Samantha darted from room to room always finding a playmate in Harriet and Juliet, even in Grandma Edie, who was never too tired to play tea party or read her a story. Samantha flourished under all the attention. She was truly a little girl made for a big family. Christina could only imagine her joy once the rest of her family arrived.

According to Grandma Edie, her parents wanted to travel to Whickerton Grove before paying them a visit. Of course, her father needed to see to their estate, and in truth, Christina was glad to not have them all arrive at once. Having Grandma Edie and her two sisters here was a good way of easing into things.

The only dark cloud upon the horizon was her husband.

Their conversation in the drawing room was constantly on Christina's mind. Whenever she saw him, even from a distance, her heart seemed to still in her chest, and even he appeared far from steady whenever his eyes fell on her. Yet Christina was hesitant to continue their conversation, for although Thorne had spoken with a passion about wanting her, she was afraid to allow herself to believe that he had desired her for more than her father's connections.

Indeed, he seemed eager for news from London, always disappointed when the day came and went without a message. He had spoken to her of his conversations with a number of lords her father had introduced him to. He had told her about his hopes for support.

Only when the day finally came that delivered a message to Pinewood Manor, it was not to her husband's liking.

Christina was not present when he opened the mail; however, she later noticed his absence for the remainder of the day. Usually, he was never far away, always nearby, playing with Samantha or speaking to her grandmother and sisters, his eyes often seeking hers as though waiting for some sign from her to approach.

That day, however, he seemed to have all but vanished. He only reappeared at supper time. Although he tried to be cheerful and attentive, Christina saw that he was in a sullen mood. Never before had she seen him so disheartened. She longed to know what had happened, yet she was not certain about approaching him.

Too many things still remained unsaid.

And unclear.

Grandma Edie, however, disagreed. "You ought to speak to him, Child," she said to Christina after Samantha had bid them a good night and headed upstairs with Mrs. Huxley. "He needs you."

Casting a careful look at her two sisters on the other side of the drawing room, Christina lowered her head to her grandmother's and whispered, "Do you know what news he has received?"

Grandma Edie shook her head. "I have an inkling; however, it is rather obvious that the man could use a shoulder to lean on." Her brows rose challengingly. "And you are his wife, are you not?"

Christina did not quite know what to say. Yes, strictly speaking, she was his wife. Yet their relationship was vastly different from the one her parents shared, the one she had observed all her life. "Ours is nothing more than a marriage of convenience. He wouldn't—"

Grandma Edie chuckled, trying hard not to allow the sound to grow too loud lest it drew her sisters' attention. "Have you failed to notice, my dear, that the man adores you? For the past few days, he's been skulking near you whenever he could, wondering how best to approach you. He's only been waiting for a sign from you to continue what you've obviously begun that day we arrived." She sighed regretfully. "I'm deeply sorry for interrupting you, Dear. Had I known, I would've been more patient."

Christina stared at her grandmother, feeling the heart in her chest skip and leap in an odd way. "He said that...I thought...I'm not certain if I..."

Grandma Edie placed a reassuring hand upon her arm. "Don't think too much, Dear. I know you're confused, but so is he. And he needs you right now."

Christina closed her eyes and scoffed. "I do not believe that to be true. He is so...self-sufficient. All that he does, all that he has accomplished already. He cares about so many people, and he has been doing his utmost to—" Again, she shook her head. "No, he does not need me. He does fine on his own."

Grandma Edie's hand tightened upon her arm. "Shall I tell you a secret?" she whispered, a wicked twinkle in her eyes. "Husbands are only ever as strong as their wives believe them to be." She chuckled. "But do not tell him that. Men are a shockingly fragile sort, always concerned with being strong, completely unaware that being weak has its advantages at times."

Christina could not help but smile. "Is that true?"

Grandma Edie shrugged. "In my opinion, it is. However, feel free to make up your own mind, Dear. Go to him. Today is one of the darkest days of his life. He fears that all he has been fighting for is lost."

Oddly enough, Christina had never thought of her husband as someone who feared anything. Nevertheless, it had to be true. Everyone feared something, was that not so? "Very well," she said to her grandmother and gave her a grateful hug. "I will tell you everything later."

Grandma Edie chuckled. "Oh, there will be no need. One look at you will tell me all I need to know."

Christina shook her head at her grandmother. "How do you do it? You always seem to know everything."

Her grandmother shrugged, grinning slightly. "That is an old woman's secret, one I shall not reveal to you this day. Now, go."

Slipping from the room, Christina crossed the entrance hall and headed toward her husband's study. Though, when she knocked and then opened the door, she found it to be empty. Where was he?

Hurrying from room to room, Christina found one after another deserted. Anxiety settled in her heart and grew with every step she took. Had he left? Had he perhaps gone back to London in order to... do something?

Eventually, she headed upstairs, peeked into Samantha's chamber and smiled when she saw the little girl sleeping peacefully. Closing the door softly behind her, she retreated to her own chamber, suddenly weary, and yet tense...and worried.

Opening the door to her own chamber, Christina drew up short when her eyes fell upon her husband standing with his back to her by the window. He did not move as she entered, nor did he turn and look at her. He simply stood there with his hands linked behind his back, his gaze directed out the window at the slowly darkening world.

"I've been looking for you," Christina said into the stillness of the room as she closed the door behind her. "Have you been here all this time?"

His shoulders moved as he heaved a deep sigh. "Is there something you need?" Fatigue rang in his voice; yet it was the ring of defeat that worried Christina most.

"I do not. I was concerned for you." Slowly, she moved toward him, wondering why he refused to look at her. "What happened?"

Thorne hung his head, and Christina felt reminded of how she herself had rested her forehead against the cool windowpane in the drawing room only a few days ago. Now, it seemed their roles were reversed.

Inhaling a deep breath, Christina took that last step, lifted her right hand and slowly—somewhat hesitantly—placed it upon his back between his shoulder blades. "Tell me what happened."

She could feel him draw in a deep breath before he finally turned around and looked at her. His eyes were dark pools, shadowed and guarded. "Why do you ask?"

Christina licked her lips, trying to make sense of the hint of anger she heard in his voice. Was it directed at her? "Because I wish to know. Because...you are my husband, and I am—"

Before Christina knew what was happening, she found herself in his arms. He all but crushed her to him, his mouth claiming hers and cutting off the startled gasp that escaped her.

Like a leaf tossed about by a strong wind, Christina was swept away by the strength of his need for her. Though passion undoubtedly simmered in his veins, Christina knew that it was something entirely different that had propelled him toward her. His heart ached—she was certain of it—and the way he clung to her, held on to her whispered of someone in need of comfort.

He kissed her fiercely, stealing her breath and rendering her legs all but useless. And Christina allowed him because she simply could not refuse him.

Nor did she wish to.

Only when his kisses softened did she draw back and look up at him. "What happened?" she asked yet again. "What news did you receive?"

Swallowing, Thorne bent his head and rested it against her own. "It is nothing," he whispered, his words echoing her own, which she had spoken the other day in the drawing room.

"It is not nothing," she insisted, placing a hand upon his cheek and urging him to look at her. "I can see your pain. Let me share it."

Her husband lifted his head and looked at her, his gaze slightly narrowed. "Why do you wish to do so? I thought you regretted marrying me." Bitterness swung in his voice, and Christina finally realized how deeply she had hurt him with her words.

Christina averted her gaze. "For Sarah's sake, yes." She looked up at him. "Never for my own."

His hands upon her tightened as his gaze grew in intensity, and his eyes held hers as though testing her words, afraid to believe them.

"Tell me what happened," Christina whispered yet again as her hands rose to cup his face. "Please."

Thorne sighed and then nodded. "I've received word from Lord Huntington." He swallowed, his jaw tense as though forcing out the words pained him physically. "He has discussed my proposal with his peers, and they have decided to think on the matter more thoroughly before committing themselves." A muscle in his jaw twitched. "With the Season at its end, he proposes to meet up again next year and discuss this matter further." He scoffed. "This matter!" He shook his head, his jaw gritted tightly.

Christina frowned up at him, uncertain what it was she was not understanding for clearly he looked displeased—to put it mildly. "Is that not good news?"

His eyes met hers, something sharp and steel-like in them. "It is a polite way of refusing me!"

Christina had to admit that lords and ladies often tended to speak without deeper thought, seeking to put those in their presence at ease and not considering what their words meant to others. Was it possible that Lord Huntington truly had no intention of supporting Thorne's proposal? Christina knew that it was not far-fetched. Still, she could not allow her husband to sink deeper into this sense of defeat. "Perhaps he means what he says."

"He does not," he growled, and she could feel the tension that held him in the arms that held her.

Christina lifted her chin, then grasped his and gave it a quick shake. "Then you'll convince him. Do you hear me? You'll convince them all."

For a seemingly endless moment, her husband looked down at her, something contemplative in his gaze. "What if I do not?" he finally said and bowed his head. "What then?" He swallowed hard and met her gaze once more, deepest sorrow visible in his green depths. "You have not seen what I have seen. I look at Sam, and I see other children like her, working day after day, their faces stained with dirt, their little backs broken." Tears shimmered in his eyes. "It is not right. Life should not be like this. Not for them, especially not for them."

Christina's vision began to blur as his words slowly drifted into her heart and made it ache. She could all but picture children like Samantha, their eyes no longer glowing, smiles long gone from their faces. Her husband was right. It was not the way it was supposed to be.

Seeing the defeated look in his eyes, Christina found herself reaching for him. As though she had done so a thousand times, her arms came around his shoulders and pulled him to her. She held him tightly, running her hands over his back and leaning her head against his.

He responded instantly, his heart beating fast against her own and his breath rushing over her neck. His arms pulled her closer, and for a long, long time, they simply stood there in each other's arms, seeking to give comfort as they contemplated what would happen should people like her father and brothers-in-law truly refuse to lend their support to this cause.

The thought was devastating, even to Christina, and she had not been the one who had spent her entire life fighting for it. She had only recently learned of something she should have seen long ago. Yet here she was, feeling a deep sense of responsibility grow in her chest. She needed to do something. More than that, she *wanted* to do something.

"I will help you," she whispered without another thought, knowing that it was the right thing to do. Perhaps together, they could mobilize the support that was needed.

Thorne pulled back and looked at her, a slight frown creasing his forehand. "Why? Because you're my wife?" A hint of disapproval swung his voice, and Christina knew that he worried she was doing this out of duty alone.

Nothing could be further from the truth.

She held his gaze, and her fingers curled into his shirt, holding him to her. "Yes," she stated in a voice that allowed for no doubt or uncertainty, "because I'm your wife, and I believe in you."

Her husband drew in a shuddering breath, and Christina could see that no one had ever told him so. No one had ever believed in him. He had always fought alone with no one to turn to and no one to lean on.

Grandma Edie's words echoed in her mind. *Husbands are only ever as strong as their wives believe them to be.*

Christina knew that her grandmother's words did not only pertain to husbands or men in general. It was true for everyone, was it not? Who would she, Christina, be today if not for the loving and unwavering support of her family? How would she have fared on her own?

The truth was, despite everything he had been denied, her husband had grown into a man anyone would be proud to know, to call husband or father or brother or son.

Holding his gaze, Christina gave his shirt a sharp tug, needing him to hear every word she was about to say, to hear it and believe it. "Yes, I believe in you." Her heart swelled with each word to leave her lips, and she could not deny the small shock she herself felt at knowing them to be true, hearing this utter conviction in her voice. Before this very moment, she had not known this was how she felt. "You truly are a good man, and I believe that you will see happen what you have set your mind to. I know you. You will not stop. You will not give up. You will convince them. You will see the change you long to see. I know it." A smile came to her face. "I believe in you. I do." A slight tremble shook her, and she inhaled a deep breath. "And...And I care for you. I tried not to, but it is the truth. I care for you very, very much."

Although disappointment still lingered, that sense of defeat was no longer the dominant emotion upon his face. The corners of his mouth twitched as Thorne looked at her, his eyes seeking hers, searching hers. "You care for me?" he whispered, and the corners of his mouth curled up into a smile, teasing as always, as she had known he would.

For a brief moment, Christina felt the urge to hide, to deny what she had said. But she refused. "I do." She nodded. "I do."

His hands reached up to touch her face. "I care for you as well," he whispered, tracing the tips of his fingers along the line of her jaw and then down the column of her neck before pulling her closer, her lips now no more than a hair's breadth from his own. "I have from the first moment I saw you."

Christina felt a most pleasant shiver dance down her spine. "I may have as well," she whispered, feeling his breath against her lips. "I was not supposed to. You were not to be mine, and yet lately I cannot help but wonder if I did what I did because..." She looked up at him, overwhelmed by everything that had happened these past few weeks, overwhelmed by the way he was holding her as though he never wished to let her go.

Thorne's breathing quickened, and a deep look of impatience came to his eyes. "Because?"

Christina licked her lips and decided then and there that she would not hide anymore. Never again. "Because I wanted you for myself."

A disbelieving smile slowly claimed his features. "You had no idea, though, did you?"

Staring up at him, Christina slowly shook her head. "I did not. Now, it seems so obvious." She blinked. "How could I have missed this?"

Chuckling, Thorne dipped his head and brushed his mouth against hers. "Perhaps if you had," he whispered, placing a kiss upon her lips, "you would have forced yourself to retreat out of respect for your friend. If you had, we might not be here."

The thought of Sarah still sent a stab of guilt through her heart; only Christina determinedly pushed it aside for in this moment, more than ever before, she wanted to feel something else. "Yet we are here," she whispered, gazing up at her husband as her hands slid up to link behind the back of his neck. "Now. Together."

His gaze darkened, and she could feel a change in his mood in the way his hands tightened upon her back. He bent his head then and kissed her, slowly, but thoroughly, and when his eyes found hers once more, she could see a question lingering in them.

Sinking her teeth into her lower lip, Christina held his gaze for another heartbeat. She felt nervous, a strange flutter in her lower belly; still, she had never felt so daring at the same time. "About those unspeakable things," she whispered with a teasing smile, uncertain how to continue. Her gaze, though, never wavered.

Thorne chuckled. "Do we have to call them that?"

"You have to admit, people do not speak of them," Christina pointed out, very much aware of the way her husband was watching her.

"It's much more fun to experience them," he whispered, grinning, before capturing her lips as though to prove his point, "than to merely speak of them."

Catching her breath, Christina returned his smile. "Is that a promise?"

A wicked grin came to his face that made her insides flip in a most tempting way. "It is."

"I'll hold you to it," she whispered against his lips before words became unnecessary.

Breathing, too, became secondary as they clung to each other, his lips devouring hers as his nimble fingers began to undo the laces of her dress.

Never would Christina have expected for this day to end like this, that she would find her husband waiting for her in her chamber, that she would find herself in his arms not long after. "Why did you come to my chamber tonight?" she whispered breathlessly.

His head rose, and his dark green eyes looked into hers. "Because I needed you." He kissed her again, then nibbled a path along her jaw to her ear. "Because I wanted you."

Christina gasped at the unfamiliar sensations her husband's touch elicited. "I'm glad you did," she gasped, running her hands upward and into his hair. "If you hadn't come to me," she pulled back and met his gaze, "I would have come to you."

Whether that had been true an hour ago, Christina did not know. However, it was now, and that was all that mattered.

A deeply heart-felt longing came to his eyes then, and he leaned down to place the most tender of kisses upon her lips, one that said more than a thousand words ever could.

"I might be falling in love with you," Christina whispered and threw every last shred of caution out the window, placing herself in her husband's hands.

After all, she trusted him. She did not know how it had come to be, but it had.

And she was glad for it.

Chapter Thirty-Seven

THINGS OF THE PAST

Cracking one eye open, Thorne peeked across the sheets at the other side of the bed. The moment his eyes fell upon his sleeping wife, a wide grin stretched across his face for what he had thought to be a dream had not been one after all.

Never before had Thorne been so pleased to wake up to reality. Never before had reality been better than the dream.

Darkness still lingered about the world as he looked out the windows, the edge of the forest a dim outline upon the horizon. For a reason he did not know, his wife seemed disinclined to close her curtains at night. Thorne wondered why that was.

Propping himself up onto an elbow, he looked down at her, her wild, golden hair almost glowing against the stark white of her pillow. Although her eyes were closed, Thorne knew them to be of the deepest blue he had ever seen.

"Are you watching me?"

He chuckled as her eyes slowly opened, and she looked at him, a teasing smile stretching across her lips. "How long have you been awake?" he asked, reaching out a hand to brush a soft curl behind her ear.

Rolling over to look at him, Christina shrugged. "A while." She pulled the blanket a little higher to cover herself, a touch of red coming to her cheeks. Her eyes held no discomfort or regret, though, and Thorne was glad for it.

"Are you all right?" he asked, tracing the tips of his fingers down her arm until he reached her hand and pulled it into his own, holding on tightly. "Any regrets?" He tried to ask the question lightly, yet he could see that she understood him well.

Her eyes were warm and comforting, and Thorne exhaled the breath he had been holding slowly. Still, her lips twitched in a bit of a wicked way. "Perhaps one," she said, trying her best not to smile and failing to do so.

Thorne laughed. "Do I dare ask?"

"It is not what you're thinking," she replied with a shake of her head.

Thorne frowned. "What do you think I am thinking?"

Grinning, Christina shook her head once more. "All I meant to say," she began, and the grin slowly faded from her face, replaced by something deeply caring, "is that I wish we had not wasted all this time. I wish...I had known from the start who we could be together."

Thorne nodded, pulling her hand to his lips and placing a soft kiss upon it. "I do as well. Still, I am glad we were able to take this chance." He watched her carefully. "May I ask you something? Something I've been wondering about for a while."

Her eyes narrowed slightly as she took note of the no doubt serious expression upon his face. "Ask what you will."

Thorne swallowed, hoping that she would not retreat from him. "It is about your stories."

Instantly, her hand tensed within his own, and he could all but feel an old instinct welling up inside her, an instinct to retrieve her hand, to put up a barrier between them. "What about them?" Christina asked, her gaze straying from his before it returned a moment later as though she had needed a moment to remind herself not to hide.

Giving her hand a gentle squeeze, Thorne sought her eyes. "You share them with Samantha, yet I cannot help but feel as though you do not wish for me to know them. Is that so?" His brows rose questioningly. "The day we picnicked near the woods' edge, you seemed reluctant to speak of them when Samantha asked you. It seems whenever I draw near, you'd rather not see them mentioned. Why?"

Sighing, Christina lay back down, and her eyes turned toward the ceiling as she inhaled a deep breath. "I swore never to speak of it," she said then, without looking at him, "at least not to my husband."

Thorne frowned, relieved that she did not withdraw her hand from his. "Why?"

For a moment, she turned her head to look at him, then sighed and returned her gaze to the ceiling above. "My aunt was an artist—she is an artist! Though, she was never allowed to be one. Women are often praised for their accomplishments; however, no one truly expects them or wants them to rise to fame, to stand out and succeed on their own, apart from their husbands."

Thorne listened quietly, seeing the torn expression he had observed before now clearly etched into her features.

"My aunt's husband was no different. Although they cared for each other—at least, I believe they did—he ultimately asked her to abandon her pursuits and see to their home and family. He did not understand her need to have something of her own, to follow that passion, that need to express herself." Closing her eyes, she inhaled a deep breath. "And so, she was forced to make a choice." Her head turned, and she looked at him, her blue eyes wide open, meeting his. "She left him and went to France. She gave up everything here, her home, her husband, her entire family, because she knew she could not betray who she was." A tear collected in her right eye. "I knew I could never give up my stories; yet I also knew I never wanted to have to make such a decision." A weak smile came to her lips. "I cannot imagine a life without my family. I could never leave them. I often wonder if she ever regretted her decision, if she ever found love again. Her husband is still furious with her. He is trapped in their marriage, without a wife and without an heir to his title." She sighed, unable to imagine such a life. "I sometimes wonder if he would have gone after her if it weren't for the war. I think he must know that she is in France." She closed her eyes and inhaled a deep breath. "I often wonder if she is happy, truly happy. Her letters only ever mention her art or they ask after us." She looked up to meet his eyes. "But can she truly be happy without her family? Without children? Was it the right choice for her?"

Moving closer, Thorne pulled Christina into his arms, placing a gentle kiss upon her temple. His fingers traced over her cheek, gently brushing away the tear that had escaped. "Look at me, Chris."

After a moment of hesitation, she finally lifted her eyes to his.

"I understand your aunt's decision," he told her, gently cupping her face and brushing his thumb over the tip of her chin. "We all need to be who we are, men and women alike. Those who love us will understand and never stand in our way." He paused, waiting for his words to sink in.

Christina blinked up at him. "What are you saying? Would you not object if I were to...write my stories down, even seek to publish them? Would you not be upset?" Disbelief rested in her blue eyes, not because of who she thought him to be, but because of something she had come to see as the truth long ago.

"I would be upset if you did not," Thorne told her earnestly. "It is who you are, and I would never want you to be someone you are not. It is you I wanted for my wife, not some kind of abstract version of you."

For a long, long time, her eyes looked into his as though she were waiting for something that would disprove his words. "Do you truly mean what you say?" She reached out a hand and placed it on the side of his face. "It would not bother you? You would not hold it against me?"

"Do not be so hesitant to ask for the very thing you yourself promised me freely and without restraint. Was it not you who said you believed in me? Who promised me her help and support? Who said that I needed to hold the course because eventually I would succeed?" A mock frown came to his face as he smiled down at her. "I do not quite recall who said all those wonderful things. Could it have been you?"

Christina chuckled. "You can be quite childish at times."

He laughed. "I will see that as a compliment. After all, nothing and no one is more precious than our children."

Smiling, Christina shook her head. "You truly are not a gentleman," she whispered, reaching up to pull him down to her, "you are a far, far better man than that."

"And you are an exceptional woman," he whispered, brushing his lips against hers, his heart warming at her words. "I've always thought so. From the very first." He grinned at her. "And I've never been known to be wrong. Not once."

Rolling her eyes at him, Christina laughed; yet the sound was cut short when his lips claimed hers anew.

Never had Thorne dared to dream of such a life. A wife he loved and a daughter he adored. He had been happy being Samantha's father before. Now, though, it seemed as though everything was falling into place.

Thorne delighted in seeing Samantha with Christina as well as her newfound aunts and great-grandmother. They all doted upon the child, and he could see that Samantha was always meant to be part of a large family. She blossomed in a way he had never seen before. Her exuberance and joy knew no bounds.

When the rest of the Whickertons arrived a fortnight later, Samantha was beyond herself with happiness. At first shy, clinging to him or Christina, she peeked out from behind them, her wide eyes sweeping over Lord and Lady Whickerton as well as the rest of the siblings and their respective spouses.

Yet each and every one of them made an effort to lure the little girl out of her shell, to gain her trust and to win her heart, and before the first day was out, a distant observer would never have guessed that Samantha had not grown up with all of them from the very beginning.

"She's a darling girl," Lady Whickerton exclaimed, hugging Christina tightly. "You're so very fortunate."

Christina exchanged a look with Thorne before smiling up at her mother. "I know. I am so very fond of her already." Her face darkened a little. "It..."

Thorne watched Lady Whickerton squeeze her daughter's hand. "Yes?"

Christina's eyes once more wandered to him, and he could see restraint there, reluctance to speak of what was in her heart for fear of hurting him.

Offering her a smile, Thorne wanted her to know that beyond everything else it was important for them to be honest with each other.

Relief came to her eyes before she turned back to her mother. "I cannot help but wonder if how I feel for her is different from the way I would feel toward a child I've brought into this world myself. It is a thought I cannot seem to shake lately." She glanced up at Thorne, and he saw a slight blush come to her cheeks.

Lady Whickerton smiled at her daughter. "Oh, my dear, do not worry. A mother's heart does not distinguish." She looked up at her husband. "And neither does a father's."

Stepping up to his wife, Lord Whickerton placed a hand on the small of her back. "Your mother is right, my dear. Blood does not matter. Love is born out of something else. It is *being* a parent that matters most."

Her parents smiled at one another in a way that gave Thorne pause. It made him wonder because the look in their eyes suggested that they spoke from experience. Had either one of them ever loved a child that was not their own?

"Thorne," Lord Whickerton exclaimed, turning to him, "or do you object to the familiarity of first names?" A bit of a grin came to the man's face.

Thorne chuckled. "Not at all, my lord."

"Then call me Charles, will you?" He clasped a hand on Thorne's shoulder, and they walked a few steps off the terrace and down into the gardens. "I've spoken to Lord Huntington once more."

Thorne stopped in his tracks and turned to look at his father-in-law.

"We've agreed upon another meeting a month from now at Whickerton Grove," his father-in-law explained, a kind smile upon his face. "Invitations to all those interested in your cause have been sent. I've already received a few confirmations. Does that suit you?"

Exhaling a deep sigh, Thorne nodded. "It does, yes." Utter relief swept through him, and he felt the sudden urge to embrace his father-in-law. The time for that had not yet come, though. Still, he could imagine that, perhaps a few years down the road, Christina and

Samantha would not be the only ones he loved and considered family. "Thank you. Thank you very much for all your help and support."

Again, Charles clasped his shoulder and gave it a warm squeeze. "Thank you for bringing this matter to my attention." He sighed deeply. "You're a good man, Thorne, and I'm glad to see my daughter so happy."

"She's wonderful," Thorne told his father-in-law, knowing that he meant every word. "I consider myself most fortunate that she agreed to marry me."

Charles laughed. "It seems *someone* smiled upon you."

Thorne frowned as a suspicion snuck into his mind. "Who?"

His father-in-law's brows rose mockingly. "My mother, of course."

"She told you? She told you that she came to me?"

Charles nodded. "I admit, I was not pleased when I first heard of it. Yet she's always had a way of...meddling in others' affairs. Fortunately for her, her matchmaking efforts have never gone wrong. At least, not that I know of."

Thorne laughed. "I have yet to thank her."

"Does Christina know?"

Thorne shook his head, knowing that secret to be the only thing that remained unsaid between them. "Your mother made me promise not to say a word, at least not, until she saw it fit to free me from that promise."

Shaking his head, Charles sighed deeply. "I shall speak to her."

"Thank you. I admit I do feel awful for keeping this from Christina. I hope she will not hold it against me."

Charles chuckled. "Feel free to blame it on my mother. After all, she's at the root of this. She generally is." Laughing, he slapped Thorne on the back. "Come, let's walk a bit and discuss the meeting ahead."

Thorne nodded, eager to return to his wife and set things straight between them.

For good.

Chapter Thirty-Eight

A MOTHER'S RETURN

Seated at his desk, Thorne looked up from his papers, his gaze drawn to the window where his new sister-in-law, Harriet, was once more galloping off into the distance.

On her own, no less.

Smiling, Thorne chuckled. By now, he was well aware that the Whickertons did things their own way. Most parents of the *ton*, he supposed, would have objected to their daughter riding off without a chaperone of some kind. However, Lord and Lady Whickerton—Charles and Beatrice!—strongly believed that not only their son, but also their daughters had the right to make their own choices.

As well as their own mistakes.

Thorne promised himself that he would grant Samantha the same rights, the same freedoms, the same choices. After all, how would he have felt if he had been forced to live his whole life directed by others, dependent on other people's whims?

No, it was unimaginable.

A knock sounded on the door to his study before Reuben stepped into the room. "I beg your pardon, Sir. You have...a visitor." The old man's lips thinned in a rather disapproving way. "She insists on speaking to you."

Thorne frowned. "She? Did she give a name?"

"A Mrs. Miller." Reuben's lips thinned even further, and Thorne could see that the man spoke with great reluctance.

Rising to his feet, Thorne stepped around his desk, his gaze fixed upon his butler, trying to understand what had raised the man's disapproval in such a way. "I cannot say that I've ever heard her name."

Reuben swallowed hard. "Mrs. Miller claims to be...Miss Samantha's mother."

Thorne's jaw all but dropped as he stared at his butler. "Pardon me?"

Reuben cleared his throat. "Mrs. Miller insists on speaking with you regarding her...daughter."

All of a sudden, the clock situated upon the shelf to his right seemed to tick with a loudness it had not possessed before. Each second seemed to crawl by with agonizing slowness as Thorne continued to stare at Reuben. He could feel every muscle in his body pull tight, every breath accompanied by a sense of almost painful dread. Why now?

Ever since he had found Samantha upon his doorstep, Thorne had wondered about the child's mother. He had spent months trying to find her. Yet eventually he had given up, certain that he never would. Samantha had become his, and his alone.

Now, after years of it only having been the two of them, they had found a family to call their own. Christina was his wife, and slowly, step-by-step, she was becoming Samantha's mother.

Thorne loved seeing the two of them together. He loved the way Samantha turned to Christina, snuggled into her side or reached for her hand, her eyes glowing with trust and love, the same way they did when she looked at him. Through Christina's stories, they had found a way to one another, often huddled up together in the evenings, Samantha's head resting upon Christina's shoulder as Christina continued her tale of the fairies that lived out in the forests.

The glow upon his daughter's face never failed to make Thorne pause in his step whenever they sat in this manner and his little daughter listened, listened most carefully, and imagined. He could see it in Samantha's eyes. Christina's words drew her away from the here and now, allowed her to dream in a most wonderful way.

Samantha looked utterly happy and at peace in these moments, and Thorne could not help but fear what her mother's sudden reappearance might do to his daughter's life.

"Shall I send her away, Sir?" Reuben asked, a hard look in his eyes.

Thorne cleared his throat, willing his thoughts back to the here and now. "No. Please, send her in."

"As you wish," Reuben replied, that same disapproving tone still in his voice as he withdrew.

Thorne listened to the echo of his footsteps receding. He all but held his breath as silence once more stretched from one moment to the next. And then, his ears picked up the sound of footsteps coming closer. Not only one pair, but two.

Indeed, Thorne could not say what he had expected; however, when Mrs. Miller stepped into his study, he could not help but stare. His eyes swept over her pale face, searching for similarities between her and his precious daughter.

Her pale blonde hair was pulled back into a neat bun, giving her angular face an even sharper edge. He could see that she was thin, frail even. Her skin was pale to the point of concern, and she seemed in desperate need of a good meal; in fact, several of them. Her linen dress looked faded and washed so often that its color had been lost. The hem was frayed, and he could see holes along the seam of her sleeves.

"Mr. Sharpe," Mrs. Miller addressed him in a faint voice, her blue eyes wide as she attempted a courtesy, "I am so grateful you agreed to see me."

Thorne gestured for Reuben to leave them alone and then turned to the young woman. "Mrs. Miller, I presume." His gaze swept over her face, trying to determine what had brought her here after all this time. "What can I do for you?"

Wringing her hands, the woman met his eyes hesitantly. "Is my daughter well?" She dropped her gaze to her hands before looking up at him once more.

Thorne tensed at her question, finding himself displeased to hear another speak of Samantha as their daughter. "She is well."

Mrs. Miller's face softened, and a deep sigh left her lips. "Thank you. Thank you for taking care of her all these years. I am most grateful to you."

A thousand questions assailed Thorne along with a thousand thoughts he did not dare dwell upon. "Why did you leave her upon my doorstep?" he asked in a voice that was far from friendly. "How could you set her down and simply walk away?" With his eyes fixed upon her, he took a step closer. "I had people looking for you for months." He shook his head as the disbelief of those early days returned to him. "How could you simply leave her?"

Tears welled up in Mrs. Miller's eyes, and she wrung her hands in a way that made the sinews stand out white, even more so because of her frailty. "I could not think of another way," she sobbed, her thin frame trembling almost violently. "I did not wish it, but it was the best I could do for her."

Thorne closed his eyes and inhaled a deep breath, seeking to calm the turmoil in his own heart. Until this moment, he had not been aware of the anger he had harbored toward her. "Why?"

Her mouth opened, but no words came out. Instead, she suddenly seemed to sway upon her feet, her face paling to such an extent that Thorne jumped forward and grasped her by the elbow. "Perhaps you should sit," he said steering her toward one of the two armchairs under the window. Then he turned and poured her a glass of brandy. "Here, drink this."

Breathing fast, Mrs. Miller accepted the drink and took a small sip, coughing as the liquid burned down her throat.

Thorne sat down in the armchair beside her, his eyes returning to search her face.

For a long moment, Mrs. Miller stared down at the glass in her hand. Then she sat back and lifted her chin. "When she was born, my husband had just died in a mining accident," came her frail voice, choked with tears. "And I...I have a son. His name is Owen, and he is seven years old. He..." Once more, she looked down at the glass in her hands. "He is sickly. He has been since the day he was born. His legs... He...He cannot walk." She looked up at Thorne, and large tears rolled down her cheeks. "He needs me. He needs me in a way that..." She shook her head, fatigue marking her features. "I did not know what to do."

Thorne heaved a deep sigh as the woman's words snaked their way into his heart. Indeed, was she not one of those he sought to protect? Thorne knew it to be true when his gaze returned to her. He tried to push aside his own emotions and to look at her with untainted eyes. Yes, her life was a struggle. Even before her husband's death, Thorne doubted that the family had been well provided for. On her own, however, Mrs. Miller had been unable to support herself and her children. Yes, it had been a reasonable choice for her to leave her daughter with him. A choice she had made to protect the child she already had as well as the one she had just brought into the world.

An impossible choice, but a choice, nonetheless.

"I am deeply sorry for your loss as well as your struggles," Thorne said gently, still at odds about how to feel. It seemed there were two different people within him: the father who sought to protect his family and the man who had spent years fighting for the plight of those who did not have a voice. "May I ask? What brings you here today?"

Mrs. Miller swallowed, then reached up to brush away the tears. "I came to see her, and..." Her gaze fell from his as she bit her lower lip. "I came to ask for your help." Almost fearfully, she peeked up at him through lowered lashes. "My son... He..."

Thorne rose to his feet and moved a few steps away before turning around once more. "What is it you're asking?" he inquired, unable to banish that odd sense of dread or perhaps foreboding that still lingered. He could not explain it, yet neither could he rid himself of it.

Inhaling a deep breath, Mrs. Miller pushed herself out of the armchair. She seemed unsteady, her hands stretched out for balance, and Thorne wondered when she had last eaten. Then, her eyes returned to him, and she crossed to where he stood. "I am asking for your help," she said softly, forcing a smile onto her face. Then she lifted her hands and placed her palms upon his chest, her face lifted toward his. "Of course, I'd be more than happy to repay you for your efforts."

An icy chill crawled up Thorne's spine as he stared down at her upturned face. His stomach twisted and turned, and his hands reached out to grasp her wrists, to remove her hands from his person. "Mrs. Miller, I must insist—"

The sound of someone clearing her throat drew their attention toward the door, and Thorne found himself looking at his wife, her blue eyes narrowed and her jaw tense as she glared at them. "How dare you?"

Chapter Thirty-Nine

MRS. MILLER

Never in her life had Christina felt quite like this, quite so shaken, so furious, so disappointed, so...

Not even the night Aunt Francine had come to Whickerton Grove could measure up to how Christina felt when she saw another woman in her husband's arms. The way they stood close, her eyes looking into his and his hands holding her to him.

"Christina!" Pushing the woman aside, Thorne hastened toward her. "I can explain."

Christina shrank back as he tried to reach for her. "Can you?" she challenged, glaring at the other woman, wondering who she was. How could she have been so mistaken?

Her husband exhaled a deep breath, and she could see that he fought to remain calm. "Yes, I can." His voice was hard, unburdened by guilt. He stepped toward the door and gestured for her to follow. "Mrs. Miller, I shall return shortly." Then his gaze moved to Christina. "Come with me."

Christina's jaw hardened, and she was ready to refuse him. However, before she could, his hand clasped around her arm and pulled her along, shutting the door behind them.

Out in the corridor, Christina tried to dig in her heels, but her husband dragged her along until they were a good distance from his study. Then he spun around to face her. "I can see what you're think-ing, and I assure you that you're wrong."

Christina laughed. It was an almost hysterical sound, and she hated herself for breaking apart like this. "Am I? How can there possibly be a reasonable explanation for why she was in your arms?" She shook her head, backing away.

Coming after her, Thorne pulled her toward him, his eyes vibrant in a way she had never seen before. "She was not in my arms," he hissed against her lips. "She..." His eyes closed briefly.

"What?" Christina demanded.

Her husband exhaled a slow breath and then looked at her, a strange sense of mortification in his eyes. "Truth be told, she...she offered herself to me."

Christina felt sickened. She tried to pull free of her husband's grasp, but he would not release her. "Why? Why would she do that? Who is she?"

Thorne's gaze softened, and a hint of sadness came to his face. "She says she...is Samantha's mother."

Christina froze as though she had suddenly turned to a block of ice. Her husband's words rang in her ears, and yet she could not seem to make any sense of them. "Her mother?" she gasped. "How can that be?"

Thorne shook his head. "I cannot be certain. She says she left her on my doorstep out of need. Her husband died, and she had another child, a sickly child, to see to."

"Why is she here now? After all this time?" Feeling her pulse thud-ding in her neck, Christina was grateful for the way her husband's hands held onto her. Although she had only met Samantha several weeks past, Christina could not help but feel terrified by the thought of another woman sweeping in to take her place in the little girl's life. Yes, she had struggled with becoming Samantha's mother, but deep down, Christina realized in that moment she wanted to be her mother. She had been uncertain, but she did want to be Samantha's mother.

What now?

"Then why would she...offer herself to you?" Christina asked with a snarl, torn between a sense of compassion for the woman's plight as well as a feeling of deepest jealousy burning itself through her veins. Had this woman come here to take away not only her daughter but also her husband?

To Christina's great annoyance, an irritatingly pleased smile slowly spread over her husband's face. "Are you jealous?" he whispered, urging her closer against him.

Christina set her hands against his shoulders and tried to push him away, but to no avail. "Do not flatter yourself. I have every right to be upset that—"

"Of course, you have every right to be upset. In fact, I cannot deny that I am most pleased that you are. You—"

"You are *my* husband!" Christina exclaimed, uncertain why she did so. After all, it would only fuel Thorne's delight with her reaction.

He grinned. "And you are *my* wife." The next moment, he dipped his head and kissed her, making it unmistakably clear that she was not the only one staking a claim.

For a long moment, they clung to one another, one fierce kiss becoming another, before their hearts slowly began to calm. "What will you tell her?" Christina demanded, her eyes challenging him to answer correctly.

Thorne chuckled. "You're most adorable when you're jealous, Chris. It suits you."

Christina slapped his arm. "Be serious!"

After inhaling a deep breath, his face began to sober. "Of course, I will not accept...her offer. I don't know what you think you saw, but the only reason I grasped her arms was to remove her hands from my person. That is all." His deep green eyes held hers, needing to know that she believed him.

Sighing, Christina nodded. "Very well." A deep breath rushed past her lips, and she was surprised by the sense of relief she felt at knowing that her husband desired no one but her.

A warm smile came to Thorne's face, and he reached up and touched her face in an utterly gentle gesture. "You believe me?"

"I believe you," she whispered in reply before her hands grasped him by the lapels and tugged him closer. "Don't make me regret it."

"Never."

Christina heaved a deep sigh. "What now?" she whispered, casting a look over her shoulder at the door toward her husband's study. "Are you certain she's Samantha's mother?"

Thorne frowned, and Christina could see that the possibility of an imposter had never before entered his mind. "I had not thought of that. She seemed so...so sincere in her emotions." He cleared his throat. "Perhaps you're right. Perhaps I should at least, for Samantha's sake as well as our own, have someone look into her story, confirm that she speaks the truth."

"I believe that to be a wise thought," Christina agreed before a slight frown came to her face. "Do you hear that?"

Her husband stilled. "That is Samantha's voice, is it not?"

Christina strained her ears to listen. "Not only hers. It's coming from the front hall." Slipping from her husband's embrace, Christina hurried down the corridor, her feet carrying her closer to the voices, her husband's echoing upon the parquet floors behind her. Was there another child in the house?

Stepping into the hall, Christina pulled up short when her eyes fell on Samantha as well as a little boy seated in a chair near the entrance. Two footmen stood nearby, their eyes never leaving the child as though they had been instructed to watch him. "Who is that boy?" Christina asked, turning around to look at her husband.

"I believe he is Mrs. Miller's son," Thorne replied to her question, apprehension upon his face. "She said his name was Owen."

Together, they stood at the edge of the hall and watched the two children. Were they truly brother and sister?

Christina could not say that she saw a particular resemblance. However, the same could be said for her and Leonora as well as Harriet. The three of them looked vastly different from one another, and yet they were sisters.

"Why do you only sit there?" Samantha inquired as she eyed the boy curiously.

Owen's lips thinned, and his brows drew down in a disapproving frown. "I can't walk," he snapped, his voice hard.

"Why not?" Samantha inquired undeterred.

"Because I can't."

"That's not a good answer," Samantha replied as her eyes swept over his legs. They were thin and oddly bent. "Have you ever tried?"

Owen crossed his arms in front of his chest, a look full of hatred filling his eyes. Christina suspected that the child had been teased and mocked about his inability to walk all his life.

"Would you like to come to my tea party?" Samantha asked, a wide smile coming to her face. "I can bring the tea here. You don't have to get up."

The boy's lips pressed together as though he wished to say something but knew it would not be wise. Still, pain lingered upon his face, and Christina knew that if he truly were Samantha's brother, they could not simply send them away.

She turned to look at her husband. "We need to know if they truly are who they claim to be."

Thorne nodded, then turned his gaze from his daughter and Owen to her. "I agree. I'll hire someone to verify her story. In the meantime..." He trailed off, a question in his eyes.

Christina sighed. "They can stay, but only under one condition. Until we know for certain who they are, they are simply our guests. If she does not agree to this, she must leave."

Her husband nodded. "I'll speak to her." He held her gaze for a long moment, then turned and walked back toward his study.

For a moment, Christina remained and looked at the closed door through which her husband had vanished. She wondered what was happening inside, and a part of her tensed. A part of her wanted to hurry after him and assure herself that nothing untoward was happening, that he remained true to her. Only another part of her reminded her that there was no need, that she could trust him.

Christina smiled. "I can, can I not?" she whispered to herself. "He's a man of his word." More than that, he cared for her, did he not?

More than once, he had said that he *liked* her. He had yet to speak of love, but there had been moments when Christina had all but seen the words in his eyes. Yes, she could trust him because he cared for her.

Because he did not want anyone but her.

A warm feeling settled in Christina's belly and chased away the last of the lingering chill Mrs. Miller's arrival had brought upon her.

"Mama, will you come to our tea party as well?" Samantha suddenly called from across the hall.

Christina almost flinched. How odd was it that in the very moment that Samantha's mother had returned for her, the little girl had chosen to bestow that title upon Christina? Was it a mere coincidence? Could it mean something?

Whatever the answer, Christina could not help but smile. Her heart warmed and danced with joy, and she knew that no matter what happened from this day onward, she was now and would forever be Samantha's mother.

Perhaps not the only one.

But looking into Samantha's eyes, Christina knew that she did not mind. She wanted her daughter—her daughter!—to have everything. To feel loved and cherished. To be full of joy and see nothing but beauty in the world. These were the thoughts of a mother, were they not?

"I would love to," Christina answered her daughter and then strode forward to greet their newest arrival. "You must be Owen?"

The boy glared at her. Only she could not help but think that deep down he did not wish to. He was merely protecting himself because the life he had led thus far had taught him that it was necessary.

"Sam, will you ask Cook for some milk and biscuits? After all, we have a guest."

Samantha's face brightened. "Of course." In an instant, she dashed away, always eager to sneak into the kitchen. It was a happy place for her for Mrs. Norris, their cook, doted upon the little girl and more often than not sneaked her a little treat.

"Let us help you into the drawing room, mmh?" Christina smiled at the boy, then gestured to another footman. "Would you carry him inside, please?"

The boy's lips thinned further, but he did not object as the footman picked him up as though he weighed nothing—which by the looks of him he most certainly did —then placed him in an armchair in the drawing room next to Biscuit's cage. He looked almost frighteningly thin, and once or twice as they waited, Christina thought to hear his little stomach rumble loudly.

The moment milk and biscuits arrived, Owen's eyes widened, and he licked his lips, no longer able to maintain that look of furious indifference upon his face.

"Please, eat as many as you like. There is enough for everyone," Christina told him, handing him a plate filled with biscuits. "Milk?"

With his mouth stuffed, the boy nodded. He seemed younger now that he was no longer on his guard, distracted by the needs of his body. He ate and ate, barely speaking a word, but listening intently as Christina and Samantha began to converse with the girl's dolls.

"*Biscuits! Biscuits!*" squawked Biscuit, his feathers ruffed that he had been overlooked.

Grinning, Samantha hurried over and handed him one of his beloved almond biscuits. "There you are. Enjoy!"

"*Enjoy! Enjoy!*" Biscuit squawked, then bent his head to nibble on his treat.

Christina watched Owen carefully out of the corner of her eyes and promised him and herself in that moment that no matter the result of Thorne's investigation, she would ensure he would always be well-fed. This was what her husband was fighting for, was it not? It was the memory of children like Owen which haunted him at night, was it not?

Indeed, it was wrong for some to have more than they could ever need while others did not even have enough food in their bellies. This was the world they lived in. The world they had been living in.

But no more.

Thorne was right.

Things needed to change.

Chapter Forty

DOUBTS

Thorne could not deny that it felt strange to have Mrs. Miller and her son in the house. Although the woman had instantly agreed not to reveal her identity to Samantha, Thorne could not help but think that something eluded him, and so he kept watching her most carefully.

As did everyone else.

As the Whickertons rarely kept secrets from one another, Thorne and Christina had not hesitated to share what had happened with the rest of their family. They too seemed torn between compassion and distrust. It was the way of the world, was it not? Of course, there were always those who deserved support and kindness while it was also true a deceiving mind often hid behind tearful eyes and a charming smile.

The only ones who seemed unaffected by the tension that lingered were the children. Thorne was relieved to see that Samantha delighted in their new visitors, particularly the boy. Although Owen was rather taciturn and somewhat hostile, Samantha did not seem to care. She was her usual exuberant self, sharing her toys freely and always ensuring that Owen could participate in her games despite his inability to walk.

"Look at him," the dowager countess chuckled as she stood beside

Thorne and Christina at one end of the terrace, watching the children play at the other end. "She's wearing him down, is she not?"

Thorne looked down at her and smiled. "She has been known to do so." He grinned at his wife.

Christina nodded, a warm glow in her eyes as she looked at Samantha. "Yes, she has a way about her."

"Any news?" The dowager countess inquired, looking from her granddaughter to Thorne. "Is her story confirmed?" Her gaze moved to the bench on the side of the terrace where Mrs. Miller sat and watched her son, an equally warm smile upon her face as well. Thorne could not help but think, though, that something tense lingered in her eyes. Was it only the uncertainty of her situation? Or was it more than that?

"Not yet" Thorne replied when Reuben stepped out onto the terrace.

"Pardon me, Sir." He hesitated for a moment before Thorne nodded to him to continue. "I'm afraid I have been unable to recover the silver letter opener from your study. Of course, I will instruct everyone to keep an eye out for it."

Thorne nodded, and the man disappeared.

"A letter opener is missing?" the dowager inquired with narrowed eyes. She looked at him for a moment before turning her gaze to Mrs. Miller.

"I'm afraid so," Christina answered for him. "We do not wish to point fingers, but, of course, the thought has crossed our minds as well. After all, she was alone in the study the day of her arrival at Pinewood Manor."

Thorne sighed. "I do not wish to believe it, yet a part of me understands." He wondered what he would do if he were unable to put food in Samantha's belly. How far would he go to see her fed?

The answer was: to the end of the world if need be.

⁓

Over the next couple of days, Samantha continued to draw Owen out of his shell. The pinched expression upon his little face showed clearly that he was on his guard, that he did not wish to be included in her games or at least that he did not think it wise to allow himself to be included. Every now and then, though, he could not help but crack a smile, something almost lively dancing in his pale eyes. There was a yearning there for the life Samantha called her own, a life he had never known and was afraid to want.

"She never truly speaks to Samantha, does she?" Harriet observed as she and Christina strode through the tall grass beyond Pinewood Manor's gardens. Her gaze remained upon the little girl as she chased ahead toward the forest line, Mrs. Huxley as well as Mrs. Miller and her son following upon her heel.

"Not that I have ever observed," Christina replied as her gaze moved from Mrs. Miller to Samantha and back. Of course, the woman always tended most diligently to her son, presently pushing the bath chair they had fashioned so that Owen could leave the house without being carried. That pinched expression upon his young face seemed to lessen whenever they stepped out of doors, when the wind brushed over his head and the sun touched his skin.

In these moments, the serious, most earnest little boy almost looked like a true child again.

"Don't you find that odd?" Harry asked, a slight frown drawing down her brows as she watched the frail, young woman carefully.

Christina shrugged. "I cannot say. I cannot imagine what it must feel like to give up your child, to spend years without her and then to see her again." She heaved a deep sigh. "We haven't told Samantha. I keep wondering if we should, but what if Mrs. Miller did not tell us the truth? What if there's a lie in her story somewhere? A lie that could hurt Samantha?"

A wide smile came to Harriet's face. "You truly do sound like a mother," she commented, wrapping an arm around Christina's shoulders and giving her a quick hug. "You're trying to protect her. There is nothing wrong with that." Her gaze once more moved to Mrs. Miller. "Your husband's investigators have not yet discovered anything that would prove her story untrue?"

Christina shook her head. "Quite frankly, they have not yet found anything, nothing that would prove her story true or untrue." She shook her hand. "I do not know what to make of this. But I suppose you're right; I think I would feel better if Mrs. Miller tried to reacquaint herself with Samantha. I cannot help but think that she does not genuinely care about her. And if that is so, then why is she here?"

Harriet nodded in agreement. "It seems the only thing she cares about is her son. Did she not say she had come to ask for help?"

Heaving a deep sigh, Christina nodded. Indeed, regular meals had done both of them well. Although Mrs. Miller still looked frail, she seemed stronger these days. As did Owen. Was it truly the only reason why Mrs. Miller had come? Did it have nothing to do with Samantha?

Christina did not know what she was hoping for. Only it was not her decision to make. All she could do was wait and see what would happen.

Chapter Forty-One
HIDDEN IN THE TALL GRASS

Thorne strode down the corridor, crossed the drawing room and stepped outside onto the terrace. His gaze moved to his wife, who sat with her family outdoors, enjoying the warm summer's sun. He paused before approaching her, ensuring that Mrs. Miller was not within earshot. In fact, he could not see her or the children anywhere, not even down in the gardens below.

"Is something wrong?" Christina asked as she stepped toward him. "You look concerned." Behind her, the rest of her family stopped conversing and turned their attention to him as well.

Thorne met his wife's gaze. "Where's Mrs. Miller?"

Christina's gaze turned down to the gardens and then to the meadow beyond. "She and Mrs. Huxley took them for a walk. Why?"

Thorne shook his head. "It is nothing. Truly." His gaze rose and briefly settled upon his father-in-law's before returning to his wife. "So far, my investigator was able to confirm that Mrs. Miller's husband died a few years back in a mining accident. However, it appears that Mr. Miller died not five years ago, around Samantha's birth, but rather a year before that."

"A year before her birth?" Leonora asked with a concentrated frown as she glanced from her husband to her mother. "Then he cannot possibly be Samantha's father, can he?"

Grandma Edie shook her head. "No, dearest, he cannot." She turned her eyes to Thorne. "Did she say that her husband was Samantha's father?"

"Not specifically," Thorne replied, trying his best to remember what precisely Mrs. Miller had told him. "As far as I can recall she merely said that he died before Samantha was born, indicating that life had become much harder for her, especially with a sickly child to take care of."

"Still, she lied," Harriet stated vehemently, looking from one family member to the next. "She may not have stated outright whether or not Mr. Miller was Samantha's father; however, she did say that he died shortly before her birth. Therefore, she lied." Her eyes moved to meet Thorne's. "Why?"

"Perhaps," Juliet, the eldest Whickerton sister, began tentatively, her gaze somewhat elusive as she spoke, "she was afraid he would think ill of her if he knew she had given birth to a child out of wedlock." Her eyes moved to her mother and then to her grandmother. "It could be as simple as that, could it not?"

Louisa nodded. "Jules is not wrong. People can be very judgmental, and she had no way of knowing whether you," she met Thorne's gaze, "would grant her request for help if you had known."

Louisa's husband, Phineas, cleared his throat, a contemplative look upon his face. "To be clear, does it matter to anyone here whether Mr. Miller was Samantha's father or not?"

Everyone shook their heads.

"Then there is no need to discuss this further," Phineas concluded. "What we do need to ascertain is Mrs. Miller's reasons for coming here, and, of course, whether or not she truly is the girl's mother."

Thorne sighed. "I cannot yet answer that definitively."

"Should we not confront her?" Leonora's husband, Drake, suggested with raised brows. The man never said much, but when he did speak, it was worth listening. "She lives in your house," he continued, his gaze meeting Thorne's, "has access to your child, and yet you know near to nothing about her. All you do know is that she lied to you."

Thorne nodded as did many of the others. "He's right," Troy, the

Whickerton's only son, agreed, a tense expression upon his face. "Far be it for me to judge her for anything she might have had to do in order to survive; however, we need to make certain that she is not a threat to this family."

"Yes, we do," Thorne concluded, glad that he had shared the bit of news he had received with his new family. It felt good to be able to discuss these matters and have others weigh in, offer their counsel as well as their support. "I shall speak to her this instant." He stepped away and headed down the steps into the gardens.

"I'll come with you!" Christina called and then rushed to catch up with him. A warm smile came to her features, and she slipped her hand into his. "She's my daughter as well, is she not?"

Her skin felt warm and comforting against his own, and Thorne held her hand tighter. "She is, and she's lucky to have you." Quickly, he pulled his wife behind a tall growing bush and gave her a quick kiss. "As am I."

Christina smiled in a way that made his knees go weak. "And don't you forget it." She tugged him onward. "Come. We'll settle this here and now, and tonight we'll sleep better for it."

Rushing along, Thorne chuckled. "Sleep?"

Teasingly, his wife rolled her eyes at him. "Perhaps I truly ought to have heeded the many warnings that were whispered to me about all the unspeakable things to be found on a husband's mind such as yourself."

Thorne laughed, then picked her up and twirled her in a quick circle. "Oh, do not pretend they're not on your mind as well. I know you better than that, *Wife*."

Racing each other to the end of the gardens, Thorne once again experienced a moment of disbelief. The way his life had changed in such a short time sometimes still amazed him. Never had he been this happy, this carefree; and sometimes, he worried that it might all only be a dream.

Was he asleep? Did a woman like Christina not truly exist? Had he dreamed her up? If someone were to wake him and he were to open his eyes, would she still be here?

Then she flung herself into his arms, and he felt her heartbeat

282

against his own. Her lips claimed his, and he returned her kiss with a desperate fierceness. If he was indeed dreaming, he never wanted to wake again.

"You're an awful distraction," Thorne mumbled against her lips before kissing her again. "At this pace, we'll never reach them before nightfall."

Christina chuckled. "Perhaps we'll meet them halfway." She pushed out of his embrace, then grasped his hand and tugged him along as she strode out of the gardens and into the meadow.

Thorne's gaze swept over the small slope that led down to the forest's edge. The sun still stood high in the sky, yet the dark red glow whispered of the day's end. A mild breeze blew, and the tall green stalks swayed gently as though they were dancing. He could hear the sound of crickets and birds and...

His feet pulled to a halt as his ears strained to listen. "I cannot hear them," he mumbled as his eyes flew over the forest's edge.

"What is it?" Christina's concerned face appeared in front of him. "Is something wrong?"

"I cannot hear them," Thorne said yet again, his voice stronger now, louder, needing her to hear him. His eyes met hers. "Where are they?"

Christina spun around as she, too, searched the wide expanse of land around them. "Perhaps they headed into the forest."

"All of them? Even Owen with his bath chair?" He grabbed her hand, and together, they raced down the small slope, their eyes continuing to sweep over the land.

Something cold, almost icy began to snake its way down Thorne's spine. He could not explain it. Although he did not know what it was, it had the power to raise the hairs in the back of his neck. Something was wrong. Something had happened. Somehow, he knew.

Somehow.

"Samantha!" Christina called, her hand holding his with a tightness that spoke of her growing concern. "Mrs. Huxley!"

Silence met them.

Nothing, but silence.

"Where could they be?" Christina exclaimed as her eyes turned to him, and then moved to search their surroundings once more. They slowed their steps, still wading through the tall grass when Christina suddenly stopped. "There!" Her hand shot out, and her finger pointed westward to a spot near the forest.

Thorne squinted his eyes, and in the moment the tall grass stalks swayed to one side, he thought to glimpse one of the back wheels of Owen's bath chair.

His upended bath chair.

Together, the two of them raced forward, their hearts beating almost out of their chests. "Owen!" He heard his wife call as they pushed forward.

Indeed, as they drew closer, Thorne could see the bath chair lying on its side, the back wheel slowly turning in the wind.

Christina dropped to her knees as she reached the chair, and Thorne saw Owen lying on the ground, his eyes closed and a bruise growing on his forehead. His wife's hands ran over the boy's face, then reached to check his pulse. "He's alive," she whispered, her breath coming fast, and her eyes were wide with fear. She looked up at him and then craned her neck. "Where are the others? What happened here?"

Thorne stood up tall, and using his hand to shield his eyes from the setting sun, he allowed his gaze to sweep over their surroundings. At first, he could not see anything beyond the endless sea of swaying grass. Then, however, his gaze touched upon something else.

He surged forward, large strides carrying him closer to the forest's edge where he found Mrs. Huxley, lying on her back, a bleeding wound upon her head. He tried to rouse the woman, but she was out cold. Yet her pulse beat strong.

Shaking his head, Thorne rose to his feet once more. He could not imagine what had happened here. Had someone attacked them? Where were Samantha and Mrs. Miller? Were they somewhere nearby? Hidden in the grass?

"One of us should go get help," Christina stated as she came walking over. "We will need help to take them back to the house." Her hand settled upon his arm. "Where could she be?" Her blue eyes were wide and full of fear.

Thorne shook his head. "I don't know. But we will find her." His gaze lowered to meet his wife's. "Head back and alert your family."

Christina nodded, then paused. "Perhaps you should go. I suppose you would be faster than me." She looked down at her skirts, knowing that they would hinder her movement.

Thorne shook his head. "Whoever did this might still be nearby. I'm not leaving you alone here. Go." He squeezed her hand, and she nodded.

Then Christina raced back toward the house as fast as she could.

"Samantha!" Thorne called his daughter's name, trying his best to remain calm. It would serve no one if he lost his head, least of all his daughter.

Remaining alert, he slowly moved along the forest's edge, trying to spot anything that might give them a clue as to what had happened or where Samantha and Mrs. Miller had gone. Had they been attacked as well? Or had they been able to flee?

Thorne paused and looked back over his shoulder to where Owen still lay in the grass. He could not help but think that Mrs. Miller would not have left her son behind. Whatever else she might have lied about, he did not doubt that she loved her child dearly and would give anything to see him safe. Why then was she not here?

Chapter Forty-Two

A LITTLE BOY'S HEART

Never in her life had Christina felt this kind of fear. She had been concerned, worried, fearful even. Yet nothing had ever compared to this feeling of dread, of panic that had settled in her stomach. On top of that, her heart hurt. It physically hurt whenever she thought of Samantha, and tears would well up in her eyes again and again. Still, tears were of no help, and so Christina brushed them away determinedly.

The moment her family saw her return, they had known that something was wrong. They rushed forward to meet her, barely allowing her to explain before they continued onward to the meadow where Thorne waited.

Her brother carried Owen back to the house while Phineas and Drake took turns carrying Mrs. Huxley. They all searched for further clues but found nothing.

"There's nothing left for us to do here," her father said to Thorne, putting a hand upon his shoulder. "We should return to the house and wait for Mrs. Huxley to wake. Perhaps she can tell us what happened."

Thorne's jaw tensed painfully, but he nodded.

Fortunately, Mrs. Huxley began to stir the moment Drake stepped back into the drawing room and set her down upon the settee. A low moan rose from her lips, and she pinched her eyes shut.

Christina squeezed her husband's hand, then rushed forward. Juliet placed a wet linen cloth upon the woman's forehead as Christina sat down next to her, gently taking her hand. "Mrs. Huxley? Can you hear me?"

The woman drew in a trembling breath and tried to open her eyes. "What happened?" she whispered weakly, her eyes blinking fiercely against the bright sunlight streaming in through the windows. "Where am I?"

Christina squeezed the woman's hand reassuringly. "You're at Pinewood Manor, Mrs. Huxley. Do you remember what happened? Where is Samantha?" Christina could barely contain her anxiety; yet she knew it would do no good to rush the woman.

Mrs. Huxley blinked and looked up at her. For a moment, it seemed as though she had no notion of what Christina had spoken. Then, however, her face seemed to pale. "A man," she gasped, and her hand tensed upon Christina's. "There was a man."

Thorne stepped forward. "Did you know him?"

Mrs. Huxley tried to shake her head but flinched at the movement. "No. But...But Mrs. Miller did."

Cold dread settled in Christina's stomach, and she looked up at her husband, knowing that he felt the same. She could see it in his eyes. His hand settled upon her shoulder, for comfort as much as support.

"How do you know?" Thorne asked gently, yet the pulse in his neck beat wildly. "Did she say his name?"

"No," Mrs. Huxley moaned, her eyes closing once more.

"What did he look like?" Thorne inquired, and Christina could feel his hand upon her shoulder tighten.

Around them, the room had fallen deathly quiet, everyone watching and listening, afraid to breathe a single word.

"Tall," Mrs. Huxley breathed weakly. "Scar on his forehead. Disheveled clothing. Called...her...Ellen." A long breath left Mrs. Huxley's lips, and she slipped back into unconsciousness.

For a moment, no one said a word. Then Drake stepped forward. "We need to speak to the boy. He may know who that man was."

Rising to her feet, Christina nodded. "He is still unconscious," she mumbled, looking across the room at the small child her brother had settled on the other settee. "We don't know when he will wake. If he will awaken in time to—" Her words broke off as her heart clenched painfully.

Instantly, her husband's arms came around her, holding her tightly. "We'll find her," he whispered, his jaw set determinedly. "We will get her back."

Her father stepped forward then. "Troy, can you take Mrs. Huxley upstairs? Juliet, see to her, please. I've already sent for a doctor." Troy and Juliet nodded. "Where could they have gone?" His gaze moved to Thorne. "Is there a place near here where he could've taken them?"

Silently, Troy and Juliet moved. While Troy picked up Mrs. Huxley, Juliet held open the doors for him. Then they were gone.

Christina looked up at her husband and saw him hang his head. "I'm afraid I do not know these lands." Indeed, they had only just moved to Pinewood Manor, hoping to find a home here for their family. It was a beautiful place, but they had yet to meet neighbors and acquaint themselves with the lay of the land.

Suddenly, Harriet jumped to her feet. "I know someone to ask!" she exclaimed, then rushed toward the door, barely sidestepping Grandma Edie as she hobbled back inside.

"What else is there to do?" Leonora mumbled, moving closer to Drake, who slipped an arm around her shoulders and pulled her tight against him. "We have to do something."

"There's nothing to do but wait," Thorne sighed tensely, casting an impatient look at Owen. "Perhaps when the boy wakes, we shall find out more."

Phineas took a step forward. "Should we not search the surrounding area?"

"Yes, I believe that would—" Louisa began, but broke off when Grandma Edie suddenly rapped her walking cane onto the floor repeatedly.

Everyone stilled and turned to look at her.

"I just thought you'd like to know," she began, lifting her cane and pointing it toward the settee where Owen lay, "that the boy's awake."

Everyone whirled around, only to see that Owen lay as still as before, not even a muscle twitching.

"How do you know?" Louisa inquired as she stepped closer, slightly squinting her eyes as she observed the boy. "He looks as before."

"Are you saying he's pretending to be unconscious?" Phineas inquired as he stepped up to look over his wife's shoulder.

Christina stilled as she looked across the room at the little boy. She remembered the hard look in his eyes the day they had arrived. He had learned to protect himself, always fearful, always distrustful. Who knew what had happened today? Was he afraid that he would be blamed? That his mother would be blamed?

"Would you give me a moment alone with him?" Christina said gently, looking from her husband to her siblings and parents. "I wish to speak with him."

Although reluctantly, they all nodded and then one by one took their leave. "We shall be right outside," Thorne said loud enough for the boy to hear. He squeezed her hand and gave her a nod of encouragement.

When the door finally closed behind all of them, Christina moved over to the settee and pulled up a chair. "Owen? Would you please look at me? I promise you have nothing to fear. All we want is to find Samantha and your mother."

For a long moment, the boy lay completely still. Yet Christina thought to see a slight tremble go through him.

"I know you must be afraid," she whispered, gently placing her hand upon his frail shoulder. "Did you know that man? Do you think he would hurt your mother?"

His eyes were pinched shut, but a single tear forced its way out and rolled down along the bridge of his nose. Then a soft sob escaped his lips.

Christina moved to sit on the settee with him and reached out to brush her hand over his head, careful not to come too close to his bruise. "Please, tell us what you know, and I promise you that we shall do everything we can to protect your mother."

His teeth sank into his bottom lip, and then he finally blinked his eyes open and looked at her. "You promise?"

Christina nodded. "I promise. You have my word. Whatever happens, I will do what I can to ensure that she is safe."

Inhaling a deep breath, Owen then pushed himself into a sitting position. The movement brought pain to his head and he flinched. Christina rose and brought over the bowl of water, then dipped a small cloth in and placed it upon his head.

Owen sighed when the cool cloth touched his forehead. "His name is Sullivan," he said quietly, lifting up his hand to keep the cloth from sliding from his forehead.

"How does your mother know him?" Christina asked gently, torn between obtaining the answer she needed as quickly as possible and treating this boy with a kindness he had never known but deserved. "He's not your father, is he?"

"No." A shadow passed over his face. "Father died not long after I was born."

A soft whooshing sound suddenly drew Christina's attention, and she turned to see Biscuit fly across the room and then settle upon the back rest of the settee.

Owen flinched in fright, his eyes wide as he stared at the bird seated so close to him. "What's that?"

Christina smiled at him reassuringly. "He is Samantha's pet. You do not need to worry. He is very friendly." She swallowed and turned back to the boy. "How does your mother know this man? Can you tell me—"

"*Not her mother!*" Biscuit squawked. "*Not her mother!*"

Christina stared at the bird, remembering the many instances when Biscuit had repeated words before, words he had heard someone say. Slowly, she turned her head to Owen, and the look in his eyes told her all she needed to know. "Samantha is not her daughter, is she?"

Owen's head sank. "She did not mean to lie, but she did not know what to do." He swallowed, and another tear snaked down his cheek. "I'm old enough to help, yet I cannot do anything. I'm a burden to her. Because of me, she is forced to accept Mr. Sullivan's help so we can survive." His little hands balled into fists. "And he...he demands something in return."

Christina gritted her teeth, wishing she were unable to imagine what precisely Mr. Sullivan demanded of Owen's mother. The little boy's misery broke her heart, and she understood that it had been nothing short of desperation that had brought Mrs. Miller to their door.

If only they had known the truth.

"What does he want with Samantha?" she asked, placing her hand upon the little boy's clenched fists. "Do you know where he could've taken them?"

Owen shrugged. "I do not know. Mother came here to get away from him, but he followed us. The other day, she saw him at the edge of the forest, but bade me not to say anything. She talked to him and asked him to leave, but he would not." Shy eyes rose to meet hers. "He said he had an idea, one that would make us all rich."

Christina tensed, disgusted with people who were only out for money. She knew that once she had thought her own husband to be such a man. She could not have been more wrong!

But what were they to do now?

"She pleaded with him not to take Sam," Owen continued, tears now running freely down his cheeks. "He wouldn't listen. He wanted her to come, too, but she refused." Christina moved to sit beside Owen, gently pulling him into her arms. "He said he would kill me if she did not."

Christina could barely suppress the curse words that were at the tip of her tongue. Anger burned in her veins, and she held the boy tighter, willing herself to remain calm. "Thank you for telling me all this. Thank you, Owen."

If only it would do any good.

Chapter Forty-Three

UNEXPECTED HELP

A lways had Thorne thought of himself as a patient man. Now, he knew that that was not the case. Like a caged lion, he paced the front hall, his hands balled into fists, his mind restless. His thoughts continuously strayed to Samantha, trying to picture her, where she was, what she was doing...what was being done to her.

"Do you believe all this is part of some kind of elaborate plan?" Troy said to everybody around. "Is it possible that she planned this from the beginning?"

Thorne stopped his pacing. "I do not believe so."

"Why?" Louisa inquired, her eyes narrowed as she leaned into her husband's side.

Thorne shook his head. "I do not believe she would leave her son behind. It doesn't make any sense. Whatever she's doing, she's doing for him." Again, he shook his head. "She would not leave him behind."

Drake cleared his throat. "If that is the case, then we are waiting here for nothing. If Mrs. Miller was not part of the plan, then I doubt her son knows anything of worth."

Phineas nodded. "I agree. We should be out there looking for them."

"Looking for them where?" Leonora threw in, her gaze moving

from one to the next. "They could be anywhere. We don't even know which direction they went."

Again, silence fell over the hall, all their faces taut. Each one of them felt the crushing weight of this immobility forced upon them. They needed to act. They *wanted* to act; only they could not. What were they to do?

An eternity seemed to pass until the door to the drawing room finally opened, and Christina stepped out. One look at her face told Thorne that whatever she had learned from the boy would not help them in recovering Samantha.

Still, he was relieved to hear that Mrs. Miller had not betrayed them. At least, Samantha was not alone with that man. With Mr. Sullivan. At least, someone was with her.

"Does that mean we are to expect a ransom note soon?" Troy asked looking from Thorne to his father. "If he wants money, he will not harm the girl."

They all nodded; yet Thorne could see that they all knew that sometimes things went wrong. Not every plan panned out. Sometimes someone got hurt.

At the sound of horses approaching, Thorne turned to look over his shoulder and out the window. He stilled when he saw Harriet pull up short and jump off her mount, closely followed by an unknown man. He was dressed well and had the bearing of a lord.

A moment later, the door flew open, and Harriet rushed inside. "Have you learned anything new?" she asked, looking from one to the next.

"Nothing that would lead us to Samantha," her father replied, stepping forward, a slight frown upon his face that deepened when his gaze moved beyond his daughter to the man entering after her. "May I ask where you have been?" His brows rose before his gaze once more traveled to their visitor.

Harriet offered her father a soft smile. "I went to fetch someone who can help." She looked over her shoulder at her companion and waved him forward. "Jack."

Thorne could not help but think that *Jack*—whoever he was—was a most unlikely man to be found at Harriet's side. In everything she did, she was wild and untamed, always ready to break with convention, an easy smile upon her lips and her cheeks flushed by the many adventures that seemed to continuously cross her path. *Jack*, on the other hand, appeared rather stoic and serious and proper in the way he stood in the hall, his shoulders squared and his chin lifted in an almost haughty way. For all intents and purposes, he looked like a true aristocrat, someone who could not be bothered to care for anything or anyone outside of his own personal sphere.

Yet he was here.

Harriet's parents turned their attention to the newcomer, and Thorne could see her father's gaze sweep cautiously over the unknown man in their midst. "May I ask your name, *Sir?*" A hint of displeasure swung in his voice, and Thorne could imagine that once all this would be resolved—successfully!—Harriet would find many questions put to her by her parents.

Their visitor's brows drew down, in part in confusion; nevertheless, a hint of anger momentarily lit up his eyes as they moved to Harriet, a question there as well as a hint of reproach. Then he cleared his throat and turned his attention back to Lord Whickerton. "I apologize. I was under the impression that your daughter had informed you of our acquaintance." Again, his dark gaze moved back to Harriet, that same hint of reproach in them as before.

Completely unperturbed by the dark look in the man's eyes, Harriet shrugged, a wickedly teasing smile upon her lips. "A girl has to have her secrets," was all she said to that.

Shifting rather uncomfortably upon his feet, their visitor decided to ignore his *acquaintance*'s inappropriate behavior and proceeded to introduce himself. "I am Bradley Jackson, Duke of Clements. My ancestral home is less than half an hour's ride from here."

Thorne could not recall ever having heard of the Duke of Clements; however, the Whickertons seemed to be familiar with the name, a hint of intrigue coming to their faces.

"I do not wish to be rude," Thorne began as the fear that lingered in his bones began to grow more painful with each moment that passed; "however, there is a most dire situation that requires our attention." He looked from his father-in-law to the Duke of Clements. "Is there any way you can help us locate my daughter?"

The duke nodded. "I believe I can."

Thorne drew in a sharp breath, and he could feel his wife's hands tensing upon his arm. "How?" he asked, striding forward.

Clearing his throat, the duke turned to him. "Over the past few days, I have repeatedly discovered tracks of someone slinking through the forest between Pinewood Manor and Clements Park. Judging from the damage the man has inflicted upon the vegetation, I assume it is someone not used to maneuvering through the countryside."

Thorne exchanged a quick look with his wife, her eyes as wide as his own. "Do you know where he is now?"

The duke nodded. "Provided he has not yet moved on, I assume you will find him in a small rundown hut not far from here. However, I suspect he will move on in the morning. It is not a place one lingers."

Thorne felt his heart almost beat out of his chest. "Can you lead us there?"

The duke gave a quick nod. "Of course."

"Thank you," Christina told the duke with a grateful nod. Then she looked to her family. "Who will join us?"

Every one of her family nodded in agreement, their faces determined as they stepped forward. "Oh, no," Phineas interjected though, placing a staying hand upon Louisa's arm. "You are not going."

A thunderous expression came to her face. "You cannot tell me what to do! Who do you think you are?"

Phineas grinned at her. "In case you have forgotten, my dear, I am your husband, and I swear I will tie you to the bed if you attempt to follow us. Not today. Not in your condition."

Louisa glared at her husband as the rest of her family began to stare at her with wide eyes. "Your condition?" her mother mumbled, slowly stepping toward her and reaching for her hands. "Are you with—?"

"Yes, I am," Louisa replied with a roll of her eyes. Then she turned an accusing gaze to her husband. "Thank you for ruining the surprise!"

Still grinning, Phineas feigned a formal bow. "You are most welcome, Lulu."

Louisa huffed out an annoyed breath, then began to wave her hands in a shooing gesture. "Go! Now! You can all congratulate me upon your return. Now, go and fetch back Sam." She turned and grabbed Phineas by the lapels. "You will pay for this later," she whispered under her breath, a wicked grin coming to her face.

"Oh, I'm counting on it," Phineas replied, then placed a quick kiss on her lips before hurrying out the door with the others.

Touched by this simple, and yet profound moment between Louisa and Phineas, Thorne turned to look at his wife. After Christina exchanged a few words with Grandma Edie and Juliet, who would remain behind with Lady Whickerton—Beatrice!—to see to Mrs. Huxley and Owen, she was about to head out the door as well when Thorne reached out and held her back. As he pulled her closer, she looked up at him with wide questioning eyes. "I love you," he whispered then, wondering what had made him wait so long to admit how he felt for her. "You know that, don't you?"

A wide smile came to Christina's face. "I had hoped," she whispered, her hands reaching up to touch his face. "I believe I love you as well."

Thorne felt his heart begin to sing with joy, and he quickly pulled her into a tight embrace. "Let's go and get our daughter back," he whispered into her ear before standing back and then planting a quick kiss upon her lips.

With eyes as bright and blue as a summer's sky, Christina looked up at him, then nodded, her jaw set in determination. "We will find her. We will find her, and everything will be all right again."

Thorne grasped her hand, and together, they rushed outside.

Chapter Forty-Four

INTO THE WOODS

The sun was beginning to set as they thundered down the path toward the forest. Christina could see the duke upfront in the lead, closely followed by her husband as well as her brother.

The wind whipped her hair about, and she turned her head to brush it behind her ears. Her gaze fell upon Harriet and Leonora, leaning low over the necks of their horses as they chased after the others. Drake was not far from his wife's side while Phineas and her father brought up the rear.

Harriet grinned at her as their eyes met, and Christina wished she could ask her sister how on earth she had met the duke. They seemed like day and night, and yet Christina could not help but think that, somehow, they had gotten to know each other well. How had this happened? Where had she met him?

In truth, that seemed to be the one question with a rather straight-forward answer. After all, had Harriet not ridden out these past few weeks without a chaperone again and again? Sometimes, she had been gone all afternoon, only to return late, exhausted, but with a wide smile upon her face. Had she always gone to meet him?

The odd thing was that the Duke of Clement seemed...almost annoyingly proper. No matter what Harriet did or said, he seemed to disapprove. When Christina and her sisters had mounted their horses alongside the men, his gaze had swept over them before he had turned to Harriet and whispered, "You and your sisters are joining us?"

Harriet had simply laughed. "Does this truly surprise you, Jack?"

Christina had not failed to note that the duke tensed every time Harriet referred to him as *Jack*. She suspected that it was not the nickname itself, but rather the familiarity it inspired that displeased him. After all, it was not proper for her to call him by a nickname.

Upon reaching the forest, they slowed their horses allowing them to pick their own path through the thicket. "How much farther?" Thorne asked the duke up ahead.

"This is uneven terrain," the man replied, casting a calculating gaze over his surroundings. "Yet it is the straightest path. I expect we shall reach the hut by nightfall."

Christina felt her hands tense upon the reins. "I hope she's all right," she mumbled, not daring to consider what they would do if she were not.

Pushing her mount up next to Christina's, Harriet said, "She will be fine." The tone in her voice held utter certainty. "She's tough and resourceful and she knows that we will come for her."

Christina smiled at her sister. "How can she know that?"

Harriet frowned. "How can she not? We are family. Of course, we will come for her. It's what family does."

Christina held out her hand to her sister, and Harriet took it, squeezing it reassuringly. "Thank you for all your help," Christina said to her sister. "I don't know how we could have possibly found her without…" Her voice trailed off as her gaze drifted to the front of the little group where the duke rode beside her husband.

Harriet chuckled. "Well, I have long since suspected that there is a very persuasive upside to unconventional means."

Staring at her sister, Christina laughed. "What on earth does that mean?"

Harriet merely shrugged.

"How did you meet him?" Christina whispered, urging her mount a little closer to Harriet's.

A bit of a secretive grin came to her sister's face. "Oh, that is a long story. I will tell you all once we have Sam back at Pinewood Manor, safe and sound."

"I'll hold you to that."

As the sun slowly dipped behind the horizon, the path grew more treacherous. Darkness began to linger, and they could barely see their hands in front of their eyes. Christina could not say whether or not the moon shone overhead because of the thick foliage of the trees shielding them, but equally keeping them in the dark.

The duke stopped and jumped off his mount. "From here, we will have to continue on foot." Only he did not move onward. Instead, he knelt down, and after a small while, Christina saw sparks flying. He lit four torches and handed three of them out to the other men: one to Thorne, one to Troy and one to Phineas.

Beside Christina, Harry chuckled. "Of course, he wouldn't think to hand me one."

Slowly, they continued onward, deeper into the forest. Christina was worried that they might simply walk past the hut in the dark; yet by the time she was close to giving up hope, she spotted a soft glow in the distance. "There!" she exclaimed, pointing in between the trees. "There's a light there."

Everyone stopped to look. "Is this the hut?" She heard Thorne ask, his voice tense and full of fear as well as eagerness to reach Sam and finally bring this awful day to a successful end.

"It is," the duke confirmed, then he stepped toward them as they all gathered around him in a circle. "We should split up and approach from all sides." In the dim light of the torches, his gaze came to rest upon Harriet before it moved to Christina and Leonora. "I suggest the ladies remain behind with the horses."

All three of them instantly shook their heads. "I will not remain behind," Christina stated vehemently. "She's my...daughter. She's my daughter."

Again, the duke's gaze fell on Harriet, and Christina could not help but think that something unspoken passed between them before he nodded and then gestured for the others to follow.

As the duke had suggested, they split into four groups. While Thorne and Christina approached from the front, Drake, Phineas and

Leonora turned to the right. Her father and Troy circled around back whereas the duke and Harriet proceeded to the left. They moved as quietly as they could to not give themselves away before they would be in position around the hut.

As they drew closer, Christina could make out muffled voices. With each step, they grew louder until a shriek tore through the night.

Beside her, Thorne tensed, his free arm reaching out to clasp hers before he swiftly pulled her behind him. "That was not Sam," he muttered under his breath, casting a quick glance at her over his shoulder.

"Mrs. Miller?" Christina whispered. "Who else could it be?"

A loud bang echoed through the forest as though someone had tossed something heavy across the small space of the hut. Christina flinched, holding onto her husband's arm, before they continued their approach, eyes fixed on the dim glow shining out through the hut's window.

Step-by-step, they moved closer, and Christina cast her gaze from left to right, taking note of two other torches proceeding forward as well. She could not make out the people holding them, but at least she knew they were there. Only her father and Troy were hidden to her by the hut in their path.

"Where is she?" A male voice filled with outrage suddenly hollered from inside the hut. "What did you do?"

"Nothing," came Mrs. Miller's fearful voice, now unmistakable. "I do not know where she is. I was asleep like you."

Again, the sound of objects being flung about reached their ears, and Christina tugged on her husband's arm, looking up into his eyes.

Thorne looked back at her with the same tense and contemplative look in his eyes. For a moment, they remained where they were, uncertain about what to do. Had Samantha somehow slipped out of the hut? Was she no longer there?

"I will go after her!" thundered Mr. Sullivan's voice once more. "If I cannot find her, I will—!" His voice broke off the moment he flung open the door and his gaze fell on their flickering torch.

For a moment, time seemed to stand still as they stared at one another, the contours of Mr. Sullivan's body illuminated in the door frame by the soft glow inside the hut.

As far as Christina could tell, he was a tall man, but haggard, not unlike Mrs. Miller. His clothing was disheveled, and a wild beard grew upon his face.

Out of the corners of her eyes, Christina could see the other two torches inching closer to their position. The duke and Harriet as well as Drake, Phineas and Leonora had to have noticed that the door had been flung open and that a confrontation was at hand. But where was Samantha?

Mr. Sullivan's eyes opened wide as he took note of the number of people slowly collecting in front of the hut. For a moment, he seemed uncertain of how to react. Then, however, he suddenly reached back inside, and a moment later, pulled Mrs. Miller out and in front of him. "Stay back!" he yelled, then whipped out a blade and pressed it to her throat. "Stay back or I will bleed her dry!"

Christina flinched, and her gaze darted to Mrs. Miller, her face even paler than usually, her eyes wide as she clutched at Mr. Sullivan's arm.

Beside her, Thorne straightened. "I have come for my daughter!"

Mr. Sullivan scoffed and pressed the blade deeper into Mrs. Miller's flesh. "You can have her for a price! But you must leave first!" The hand holding the blade seemed to tremble, and Christina worried that she might not be able to keep the promise she had made to Owen.

"I will not leave without my daughter!" Thorne said loud and clear, his voice far steadier than the arm under Christina's hand. "Show her to me! I will not move from this spot until I know that she is well!"

Christina felt her heart almost beat out of her chest. A part of her urged her to throw caution to the wind and just dash ahead and into the hut. Yet if Samantha was still in there...

But was she? If she were, would Mr. Sullivan not be threatening her instead? Where could she be?

Christina let her eyes sweep over her surroundings. In the dark, though, she could make out truly little. If indeed Samantha was nearby, would she not have already shown herself to them?

Frustration swept through Christina's body when she suddenly paused. Her gaze lingered upon the torch to her right, no closer than before, but still a good bit away. Phineas was holding it, and Leonora stood at his side. Drake, however, she could not make out in the dark surrounding them. Where was he? Christina could not imagine he would leave his wife's side in such a moment.

"You will leave," Mr. Sullivan hollered, "and you will wait for my instructions. If you do not, I will kill this harlot right here on the spot." He chuckled deviously. "And your daughter shall swiftly follow."

Christina held on tightly to her husband's arm as her gaze continued to search for Drake, her eyes squinted. She saw the trunks of tall-growing trees, interspersed with bushes and ferns. An owl hooted its objection to their disturbance of an otherwise peaceful night when...

Mrs. Miller made a choking sound, her mouth opened and closed as though she wished to say something. Mr. Sullivan, however, jerked the knife deeper into her flesh until he drew blood.

Christina turned away from the sight before her as the duke's voice echoed through the night. "If you harm her or the child, you will not leave this forest alive. I suggest you choose wisely."

Christina stilled as she saw something move in the dark. Her eyes squinted further, and she caught a glimpse of Drake's tense face, a good distance from where he ought to have been. He stood shrouded in darkness, his head slightly bowed, and he seemed deep in concentration. His hands moved swiftly in front of him before he finally stood back, straightened his shoulders and lifted his chin. Then Christina saw him lift his right arm and point it at Mr. Sullivan. She gasped when she saw a pistol in his hand. What was he doing? Did he truly intend to shoot the man? What if he hit Mrs. Miller?

And then Christina remembered something Leonora had once told her in confidence. Something that suggested that Drake knew well how to hit his mark. He had been in countless duels and always come out the victor. He was an excellent marksman...who never missed.

Christina could only hope that was true.

And then a shot rang out, and Christina was not the only one who flinched.

Chapter Forty-Five

A FLICKERING LIGHT

Thorne all but felt the shot reverberate within his bones. His body jerked, and he stared at where the bullet had torn through Mr. Sullivan's throat...only inches from Mrs. Miller's face.

Without a thought, he thrust the torch into Christina's hands and then dashed forward as he watched Mr. Sullivan's eyes widened in shock, his hand tensing upon the blade while his other clamped around Mrs. Miller's arm. The man's legs were giving out as blood flowed from the wound in his throat.

Out of the corner of his eye, he saw Drake charging forward as well. Yet Thorne reached the few steps leading up to the door first. Vaulting toward the man who had kidnapped his daughter, Thorne grasped his arm before the knife could dig any deeper into Mrs. Miller's throat. He twisted the blade out of the man's hand as Drake grasped the woman's arms and pulled her away.

Mr. Sullivan went down like a felled tree, his eyes wide as his breath gurgled with blood, then ceased.

"Where is my daughter?" Thorne yelled as he knelt down and grabbed the man by his shirt front. "Where is she?"

"She...She's not here," panted Mrs. Miller, her face pale as she clutched one hand to the cut on her throat. Drake's hands were still holding her upright before he reached into his pocket, pulled out a handkerchief and handed it to her.

Thorne surged to his feet. "Where is she? What did you do?"

Christina came bounding up the stairs, the rest of her family following close behind, her eyes wide, fearful as she rushed to his side. "Sam?"

Thorne shook his head and turned to Mrs. Miller. She pressed Drake's handkerchief against her throat and then drew in a careful breath. "He fell asleep," she whispered, casting a hesitant look at the body at her feet. "He had bolted the door, but there's a small window in the back. I helped her slip out and told her to run."

Thorne breathed a sigh of relief; yet it was a premature reaction, was it not? After all, his daughter was far from safe. She was out in the forest at night all by herself. Where could she have gone?

"I'm so very sorry for what happened," Mrs. Miller sobbed, exhaustion repeatedly closing her eyes as she fought to remain conscious. "I never meant for this to happen. I never thought he would ever do such a thing." She shook her head, a deep frown coming to her face. "He was so angry and kept muttering, '*He said this would be easy*'. He threatened my son, and I—" She suddenly froze before her free hand shot forward and grasped Thorne's jacket. "How is he?" Fear stood in her eyes: the same kind of fear Thorne felt in his own heart. Fear for her child. "Is he a-alive?"

Thorne nodded, grateful to be able to put the woman's fears to rest. "He is well. He has a bump on his head, but he is well."

Closing her eyes, Mrs. Miller almost went down as her knees gave out. "He is well," she mumbled over and over again as Thorne held her. "I'm so sorry. I didn't know what to do. I didn't know..." Tears stood in her eyes as she looked at him and then at Christina. "I'm so very sorry."

Drake stepped forward then and eased the shaking woman out of Thorne's arms. His gaze met Leonora's, and she nodded, moving toward him. Settling the softly sobbing woman into his wife's arms, Drake then headed back down the few steps and looked from the duke to Phineas, to Troy and then to his father-in-law. "The girl slipped out the back. Let's fan out and find her."

The others nodded and did as he had instructed, their torches held high as they began calling Samantha's name. Harriet joined in.

Thorne brushed a hand over his face before he, too, headed out.

"Wait!" Christina called, hastening to catch up with him. "I'll come, too."

Together, they walked through the darkened forest, their torch illuminating the path ahead. "We should move to the back of the cabin!" Thorne called to the others. "For she slipped out the back window." Murmurs drifted to his ears, and he spotted the others turn in a similar direction, the soft glow of their torches pointing them out. "If she's nearby though," Thorne whispered to his wife as she clung to his arm, "why is she not answering?"

For a moment, Christina remained silent. Then she looked up at him. "We don't know how long ago she slipped out the window, how much ground she managed to cover." She inhaled a deep breath, one that rang with hope. "Perhaps she simply cannot hear us."

Thorne nodded, his eyes sweeping from side to side and down to the ground as though he were afraid he would accidentally step on her. Where could she be? His gaze drifted to the horizon...or to where it should be. The night was far too dark, not even a sliver of light granted by the night sky as it lay hidden from them by the thick foliage of the forest. Only their torch illuminated the next few steps ahead. Where could she be?

Suddenly, Christina pulled up short, and he jerked to a halt as well, turning around to look at her. "What is it?" he asked as he held the torch higher to see her face.

In the warm orange glow from the torch, he could see a strange look come to her face. It was somewhat hesitant, and yet he recognized the whisper of awe that touched her eyes. "Fairies," Christina whispered, and the corners of her mouth tugged upward as though she wanted to smile.

Thorne frowned. "What?"

Her eyes moved to him, and this time, she did smile. "Fairies." Her right arm stretched out and pointed up ahead, her eyes following. "Look!"

Moving his attention from his wife to the terrain up ahead, Thorne paused, for a moment confused as to what she was pointing out to him. What had she seen? There was nothing there but darkness. He was about to turn back to her and ask for an explanation when he paused.

Up ahead, in the far distance, he thought to see...a light. Not only one, but many. They were dancing, fluttering about like...fairies. "Fireflies."

"Yes!" Christina exclaimed beside him, her arm squeezing his ever tighter. "In the dark, she would've seen them, would she not?" She looked up at him, and he turned to meet her eyes. "Perhaps she remembered my story."

Although he was fearful to allow it, Thorne could not help the hope that surged through his heart at her words. "Perhaps she went in that direction. Come." Pulling his wife closer, he held up the torch, and together, they moved toward the dancing lights.

Chapter Forty-Six

A TIMELY REUNION

Christina's heart beat wildly in her chest as she kept her gaze fixed on the small flickering lights. They looked precisely the way she had always imagined them, precisely the way she had spoken of them to Samantha. More than once, her daughter had asked her to repeat that story of a young girl who had gotten lost in the forest, who had run away from home because of a misunderstanding, only to find that she did not know the way back.

And then the girl had stumbled upon a place where fireflies danced at night. She had been drawn there by the light, only to find that what she had thought to be fireflies had been fairies instead.

In Christina's story, the fairies had led the young girl home again and helped reunite her with her family. Had the sight of these lights reminded Samantha of that story? Had she seen them and then walked toward them?

Moving slowly, the two of them found their way through the thicket of the forest. The farther they moved along, the more her heart began to beat with impatience. Eventually, though, the thicket grew thinner, and they were able to walk with greater ease, finding their way around trees, left and right, until they stepped out into a clearing.

No more than a sliver of moonlight shone overhead: yet it reflected upon the still waters of a small lake. Tall trees grew on the opposite side of it, and Christina drew to a halt when her gaze fell on countless little lights dancing upon its banks.

Never in her life had she seen anything more beautiful. Was it possible that Samantha was here?

Slowly, they made their way along the edge of the lake, their eyes sweeping over the little lights nearby. "Samantha!" They took turns calling, though it felt wrong to disturb the silence of this place. "Samantha!"

"What if she's not here?" Thorne asked, his voice tense and full of fear. "What if she went a different way?" He raked a hand through his hair, his jaw clenched as his eyes continued to search their surroundings.

Christina could not explain it, but, somehow, she was certain that Samantha was nearby. Her gaze swept over the many lights and began to linger where a couple of them seemed to cluster together. Slowly, she moved closer, her gaze dropping to the ground, running over the tall grass toward an old, gnarled oak tree. She felt a tug upon her heart as though something was urging her to keep going, to move closer.

And then she saw her.

Curled up into a little ball, Samantha lay at the base of the tall tree, two of its large roots seemingly circled around her as though trying to hold her, shield her. Fireflies danced above her head like a marker, pointing their way to the most precious treasure they had ever known.

"Thorne!" Christina called in a hushed voice, slowly moving closer, her eyes fixed upon Samantha, her own breath evening out as she saw the little girl's chest rise and fall in slumber. "Thorne! She's over here!"

In a flash, her husband was beside her. She could almost feel his relief as they both fell to their knees beside their daughter. Tears stood in his eyes as he reached out a careful hand to place it upon her shoulder. Christina, too, felt the need to reach out, to feel her warmth and know that she was alive, that she was well.

Their eyes met in the dim light, and they breathed out as one. "We found her," Christina whispered, reaching out her other hand toward her husband, who grasped it with a smile.

"Your story saved her," he whispered, his eyes glowing in the soft light emitted by the dancing fireflies around them. "She knew to come here because of the story you told her."

Christina's eyes misted with tears, and they both looked back down at their daughter the moment Samantha slowly began to stir. Her eyelids began to flutter, and her little arms and legs began to stretch. "Papa?" She blinked, and then opened her eyes.

Thorne smiled down at her. "We're here. We're here." His hand settled upon her shoulders as he waited patiently for her to wake up fully.

Samantha blinked a couple of times before a wide smile spread across her face. Then she surged upward and threw herself into his arms. "Papa! The fairies brought you to me."

Christina laughed, a deep sigh following as she watched father and daughter. Thorne pinched his eyes shut as he held Samantha close, savoring the moment, only too aware of how close they had come to losing her.

Looking into her father's face, Samantha frowned. "Why are you crying?"

Thorne wiped the tears from his eyes. "I was worried we wouldn't find you," he whispered gently, brushing a curl behind her ear. "Are you all right? That man..." He swallowed hard. "Did he hurt you?"

Samantha's nose crinkled, and a slight shiver went through her. "I did not like him. He was very mean. But Ellen told him not to hurt me, and when he fell asleep, she lifted me out the small window and told me to run." Her eyes moved to Christina, and she held out her hand to her.

Christina grasped it gently, surprised how warm her skin was. "And then you came here?"

A small smile flickered over Samantha's face. "I did not know where to go. Everything was dark. I almost went back." Her smile stretched wider. "But then I saw the lights, and I knew it had to be fairies." She squeezed Christina's hand. "I remembered your story, and so headed toward them." She lifted her gaze to look upon the little flickering lights around them. "Are they not beautiful? And they brought you to me." Again, she looked at Christina. "I always knew your story was true. Always."

Thorne chuckled, still hugging his daughter to his chest. "I suppose that seals it."

Christina frowned. "What do you mean?"

"What I mean is," he reached out and grasped her free hand, "that after such a glowing review, you have no choice but to publish, to share your gift with the world and delight more children with it." Warmth rested in his eyes as he looked at her. "Do not hide talent like yours."

Christina felt her heart pause in her chest. "You cannot mean that." She shook her head, and suddenly felt like that thirteen-year-old girl once more who had eavesdropped upon her aunt's conversation with her parents that night long ago. It had shaped her in more ways than she could have foreseen in that moment, and yet her grown self counseled that she was the master of her own fate after all. She was not her aunt, nor was Thorne the same man as her aunt's husband had been. They were who they were, and they needed to make their own decisions.

Free of the past.

"Of course, I mean that," Thorne confirmed, his hand squeezing hers for reassurance. "Don't you think I would delight in boasting about my genius wife, capable of creating such wonderful stories?" He grinned at her in that way of his.

Christina stared at him, not daring to believe. "You truly would not object? You truly mean that—"

"I always mean what I say. Still, ultimately, it is your decision. Do what makes you happy because that is precisely what I want for you. To be happy."

Samantha had been looking back and forth between them. Now, she joyfully clapped her hands, a wide smile upon her face. "Does this mean more stories?"

They both laughed. Then Christina nodded. "Yes, I suppose it does." She hesitated for a moment but then leaned forward and whispered, "Truth be told, I have countless notebooks still at home, filled with story after story."

Grinning at her, Thorne leaned closer as well. "Truth be told, I thought you might."

Together, the three of them laughed as the fireflies continued to dance around them.

Chapter Forty-Seven

TRUTH BE TOLD

T he house was silent as Thorne left his study. Shadows clung
to every corner, and he could not help that eerie feeling that
crawled down his spine. The dark reminded him of the
previous night as they had gone after Samantha, and he wondered if it
would forever be thus.

No sound drifted to his ears as Thorne began to climb the stairs to
the upper floor. Everyone had retired to their chambers, exhausted
from the events that had transpired not long ago.

Thorne smiled at the memory of how the Whickertons had
welcomed Samantha back. All of them had feared for her, and all of
them had rejoiced at her return.

She was one of them now.

As was he.

It was a feeling like no other, and Thorne was most grateful for it.
Samantha and he had always been a family from the first, but it felt
wonderful to have others to join in their lives, in their joy as well as
their sorrow.

Others to count on.

Others to turn to.

Others to love.

Thorne knew that Mrs. Miller longed for the very same thing. She loved her son beyond hope, but it was only the two of them. It made life hard for her and for Owen as well.

After they had returned to Pinewood Manor, Mrs. Miller had shared with them the details of how she had learned of Samantha's existence. It had been by sheer happenstance.

Only a few months ago, Samantha's true mother had passed away after a long illness. Mrs. Miller had been the one to tend to her in her final days. They had never known each other well, and yet Samantha's mother had spoken to her of the little babe she had left upon Thorne's doorstop all those years ago. Tears had stood in her eyes as she had spoken of her precious child and the longing she had felt for her all this time.

Only life had prevented them from ever knowing one another, and Thorne wondered how things might have gone differently if she had not simply left Samantha but come to him for help...for the both of them. How would life be different?

He would never know.

Mrs. Miller had meant to free herself of her dependence upon Mr. Sullivan. By pretending to be Samantha's mother, she had hoped to gain entrance into Thorne's home. She had been the one to take the silver letter opener as well as a few other things, wanting to begin a new life with her son.

One where she did not have to fight to put food in her son's belly day after day. She had seen a chance, and she had taken it.

And then Mr. Sullivan had found her.

Only it seemed that Mr. Sullivan had not acted upon his own voli-tion. *He said this would be easy.* The words Mrs. Miller had heard him mutter again and again continued to echo in Thorne's head, and he wondered if perhaps there was still someone out there who was a threat.

If only he knew; yet what he did know was that although Mrs. Miller had made mistakes, she was another victim of this world. She was the kind of person whom Thorne had sworn to fight for, to protect.

After all, he felt absolutely certain that he himself would not have acted differently had it been Samantha's welfare at stake; and so,

Thorne had assured Mrs. Miller that she and her son would always be safe from now on. He would make certain of that. And he would travel to Whickerton Grove in a few days in order to meet with other lords of the realm and seek to persuade them to work with him to improve living conditions for those who suffered most.

"You have yet to speak to her, have you?" came Grandma Edie's voice before she hobbled into the light a moment later, her pale eyes seeking his.

Thorne drew to a halt, surprised to see her. "I thought everyone was abed."

The old woman chuckled. "I was waiting for you."

"Why?"

"To release you from your promise." Her gaze held his, and she nodded slowly. "You have yet to speak to her?"

Thorne bowed his head. "I've tried," he admitted, lifting his gaze once more. "I've said as much as I dared, but I wonder how she will feel when she learns the truth."

A warm smile came to Grandma Edie's face. "She will not close her heart to you, of that I am certain." Lifting her cane, she pointed at Christina's door. "Go and speak to her. Sleep will not be yours until you do." Then she cast him a last smile and hobbled away.

Thorne inhaled a deep breath, knowing that she was right. He approached his wife's door, and then knocked, hoping that she was not yet asleep.

Thorne was surprised that her bid for him to enter came quickly, the sound of her voice muffled by fatigue. Was something keeping her awake as well?

Stepping inside, Thorne found her standing by the window, gazing out at the darkened lands. She turned to him then, a soft smile upon her lips. "I had hoped you would come to me." She breathed in deeply before her gaze moved down to a sheet of parchment clutched in her hands. "I received a letter from Sarah today."

Thorne had been about to move toward her, but now paused. "Is she angry with you?" he asked, sensing that something was not right. The look in her gaze held something vulnerable, but a spark of anger seemed to simmer in her veins, held at bay by sheer will alone.

Christina closed her eyes. "I've been blind not to see it." She shook her head slowly. "I always knew how egotistical her parents were, and yet" her eyes opened and she looked at him, something deeply apologetic in her gaze, "I never thought they would go to such lengths. Never."

A sense of worry snaked up Thorne's back, and he stepped toward her, pulling her hands into his own, the sheet of parchment still clutched in them. "What is it? Tell me." He searched her eyes, feeling his unease grow.

Christina swallowed hard, and her lips pressed into a hard line. For a moment, she seemed close to losing her temper, but then managed to rein it in at the last second. "Sarah wrote to warn us." Her jaw tensed.

"Warn us? What do you mean?"

She pulled her hands from his, the sheet clutched in one fist. "She overheard a conversation between her father and someone she did not know. From what she could gather, she fears that her father might be attempting a kidnapping."

Thorne felt the blood in his veins turn to ice. "Sam."

His wife nodded, tears misting her eyes; only the pulse in her neck still hammered angrily. "Yes, Sam." Her lips pressed into a thin line before she inhaled a deep breath and spoke. "What happened was my fault. If I hadn't—"

Thorne grasped her hands. "No! Don't do this! Don't do this because it isn't true!"

"But if we hadn't gotten married—"

"Then Sarah's father would have hurt someone else in order to get what he wanted," he told her vehemently. "This is not your fault." He pulled her into his arms and held her close. "Sam is fine. She is fine, and she will be for all the days to come." He smiled down at her, equally shaken by the thought of any kind of harm befalling his little girl. "We will make certain of that."

Christina nodded, her blue eyes aglow with a fierce determination that reminded Thorne of a mother bear. "Yes, we will." She inhaled a deep breath and stepped back, her gaze once more drifting down to the crumpled sheet. "Sarah wrote that she had to bride a maid to smuggle this letter out because her father forbade her to write to me."

"There," Thorne said, sensing how deeply the loss of Sarah's friendship had weighed upon his wife's heart. "You have your answer, do you not? She was never angry with you or upset, was she?"

A tentative smile came to Christina's face. "No, she wrote that she wishes us all the happiness in the world."

"She is a good friend," he said with a warm smile, relieved to see his wife breathe easier.

Her face lit up. "The best friend there ever was!" She heaved a deep breath. "I wish there was something we could do to help her. Perhaps...Perhaps Grandma knows a way." Placing the letter upon the small table by the window, she stepped toward him, a hesitant smile upon her face. "She is awfully meddlesome, if you haven't noticed yet; however, her plans usually work out. Perhaps...she'll be able to think of something."

Gritting his teeth, Thorne breathed in slowly, bracing himself for what was to come. Would she be furious with him once he told her the truth?

A slight frown came to his wife's face as she looked at him, her eyes watchful—not unlike her grandmother's. "I cannot help but think that there's something on your mind and has been for days." Her blue eyes searched his. "Tell me."

Thorne heaved a deep sigh and then once again reached for her hands. "It is true," he said, pulling her closer to him. "There's something you don't know. Something I promised not to tell you."

A frown came to her face. "Promised whom?"

Thorne could not help the smile that spread over his face. "Your grandmother."

Christina closed her eyes and laughed. "Why am I not surprised?" Her eyes searched his. "What did she do? What did she persuade *you* to do?"

Thorne held his breath. "She persuaded me to compromise you in the library that day."

The look upon his wife's face told him loud and clear that his answer was not what she had expected. "What?" Her mouth dropped open, and she stared at him in disbelief. "Why would she—?" She pulled her hands from his and took a step back. "What are you saying?"

Thorne ran a hand through his hair. He hated the renewed distance between them; yet he knew that he deserved it. He had lied to her. He had kept something vital from her, and she had every right to be angry with him.

"Did she make a deal with you?" Christina asked all of a sudden, anger darkening her voice. "You needed a wife with connections, and everyone knows how much she loves to meddle and match-make. I've seen it with my sisters and with my cousin even. Of course, she meant well. She always means well. But..." Her voice trailed off as she shook her head, staring at him in a way that broke his heart. "You took away my choice," she whispered with a trembling voice. "I know how much it means to you to help those who cannot help themselves. However, I never thought you would go that far."

"That is not what happened nor is it why I agreed to marry you."

Christina scoffed. "Agreed to marry me? To compromise me is more like it."

Thorne clenched his teeth, reminding himself of what the dowager had said to him the day she had sought him out and made this rather astounding proposal. "Yes, I compromised you." He stepped toward her, his gaze seeking hers. "But you let me."

Her eyes widened. "I—?"

"You let me!" Thorne stressed, refusing to release her gaze. "You could have walked away, but you did not. You *chose* not to."

Clamping her lips shut, his wife stared at him.

Thorne took her reaction as an invitation to continue on and explain himself further. "Your grandmother came to me and said that she had taken note of the way I kept looking at you. Somehow, she knew how I felt about you even then." A shuddering breath brushed past his wife's lips. "She said that she believed us to be a good match, not with regards to title and fortune, but in the one way that truly matters."

Watching his wife most carefully, Thorne slowly reached out his hands and once more grasped hers. At first, he thought she would pull them away. He could feel the urge to do so in the slight twitch of her muscles. Yet she did not. She allowed him to touch her, to hold onto her.

"She told me of her plan," Thorne continued, "and ensured that I would receive an invitation to your sister's wedding reception."

Christina closed her eyes. "I never honestly thought it could have been her. I always wondered who had invited you."

Thorne inhaled a deep breath, his fingers tightening upon hers. "She never meant to force your hand, but merely to force you to make a decision."

Her eyes opened and looked up into his. "A decision? About what?"

Thorne gave her a small smile. "About me."

Frowning, Christina shook her head. "About you? But why would she think—?"

Thorne shrugged. "I'm not certain. She said you would know."

Chapter Forty-Eight

HOW IT ALL BEGAN

C hristina was still staring up at her husband as her mind drifted to something her grandmother had once said to her. *Hatred does not stem from nothing.*

Swallowing hard, Christina then drew in a slow breath. She remembered well how furious she had always been the moment her gaze had fallen upon *Mr. Sharpe*. She had thought herself furious because of his intentions toward her friend, yet recently, she had come to realize that perhaps it had been more than that.

Blinking, her gaze focused. "She knew that I cared for you even before I did," Christina whispered, overcome by the thought that if her grandmother had not interfered, she might never have found herself married to the man she loved.

A soft smile played over Thorne's face. "She said it was to be your decision," he told her gently, his warm hands holding hers. "She said that if you truly did not care for me, you would leave upon finding yourself alone with me in the library. You would know that you would be compromised if you did not." He pulled her closer, and one arm slipped around her middle. "She said even if *you* did not, your heart would know what to do."

Christina sighed. "She was right. I suppose my heart did know. I do remember thinking that I needed to leave, and yet I could not. Something kept me there." She smiled up at him. "You."

Her husband's arm tightened around her as his other hand slipped into her hair, and then he was suddenly kissing her. Kissing her the way she had wanted him to even on that day in the library.

"You cared for me even then?" Christina whispered, searching his eyes, needing to know if it was the truth. "Truly?"

Thorne nodded. "I could've accepted a marriage without love so long as both parties were willing, were not bound by love elsewhere." He shook his head, a hint of disbelief coming to his eyes. "Then I saw you, and everything changed in that moment. I don't think I realized it then, but it did."

Christina rested her forehead against his chest and breathed in deeply. Then she lifted her eyes to his. "I wish she had simply come to me! Why didn't she simply come to me? She could have told me what she suspected, what she thought instead of—"

"Would you have listened to her? Believed her?"

"No! Of course not!" The words left her lips without thought.

Thorne grinned, his brows rising meaningfully. "I know it feels awful to be manipulated even if it was done for one's own good. Still, I am grateful for what she did. You must admit if she had not, you would never have agreed to marry me, would you?"

Slowly, Christina shook her head, knowing her husband's words to be true. "I would not." The thought was frightening.

Devastating.

"Will you forgive me then?" Thorne asked, regret mingling with the knowledge that he had done right in his green eyes. "I never meant to deceive you, but I'm glad I did nonetheless."

Christina could not help but smile. "Very well. I forgive you, but only this one time. Do not make it a habit to deceive me for I will not stand for it." She chuckled.

"I wouldn't dare," Thorne whispered, then lowered his head to hers. He brushed a soft kiss onto her lips. "I promise."

Christina reached up to touch his face, feeling the soft stubbles upon his chin after a day of upheaval. "I know I should not be angry with her, but I am."

Thorne smiled at her, gently running his knuckles along the line of her jaw. "I don't think she'd mind. She does what she deems right, unafraid to suffer the consequences."

Christina laughed. "She knows that I'll not be angry with her for long. I simply cannot."

"She's a hard woman to be furious with, is she not?" he asked chuckling.

"You have no idea," Christina replied. "Perhaps she simply does so because life is not adventurous enough for her." She frowned. "I wonder what she might be planning next."

"While I don't think she dislikes adventure, I do believe she does what she does out of love for you. You and your siblings."

Christina rolled her eyes as a sense of foreboding came over her. "I still have three siblings, who are yet unmarried." She cocked an eyebrow at her husband. "Do you think we should warn them?"

Thorne laughed. "I'm afraid it wouldn't make a difference."

"You're probably right."

Leaning down, her husband rested his forehead against hers. "Do we need to speak of your grandmother any further?" He grinned at her in a temptingly wicked way.

A tingle chased itself down Christina's spine at the suggestive tone in her husband's voice. "What other topic did you have in mind?" she replied teasingly.

Claiming her lips, he kissed her deeply. "Something rather unspeakable."

"Unspeakable, you say," Christina murmured as she pushed herself up on her toes to return his kiss. "That does sound intriguing."

"It does, doesn't it?" Thorne whispered against her lips before he suddenly swept her into his arms.

Christina shrieked as her feet left the floor, then clamped a hand over her mouth, afraid her family might overhear.

Thorne chuckled. "They're asleep," he told her, carrying her to the bed.

"As we should be."

Again, a wicked grin came to his face. "Later."

Christina could not argue with that. After all, she would be a fool to do so.

Epilogue

A few weeks later

"Open it! Open it!" Samantha squealed as she clapped her hands together excitedly, hopping up and down. Her eyes remained fixed upon her father as he did his utmost to pry open the wooden box.

Christina felt her teeth dig into her lower lip, feeling the same sense of impatience bubbling under her skin.

Thorne groaned as the lid refused to yield. "One would think treasure lies within." He gritted his teeth and tried again.

"It *is* treasure!" Samantha exclaimed, and Christina wanted to hug her little girl for her unfailing devotion.

Then the lid sprang open, and Samantha jumped forward, climbed upon her father's desk and peered into the box.

Inside, cushioned by a bed of straw, lay a handful of leather-bound copies of Christina's first book.

Her heart jumped at the sight!

"May I have one?" Samantha exclaimed, looking up at Christina with wide, glowing eyes. "Please!" Her little hands reached for the topmost book, then paused as she waited for an answer.

Christina smiled at her. "Of course. Choose whichever one you like." She watched as Samantha gently lifted a book from the crate, all but cradling it in her arms, her little eyes sweeping over the gold lettering on the cover.

A Fairy's Tale.

Without removing her eyes from the book, Samantha headed toward the door. "I need to show this to my dolls. They will love it. I'm certain. And Owen, too." Awe swung in her voice, reminding Christina of the bond that had developed between them in no small parts because of this story.

Indeed, that which she had once thought to be a hindrance to her happiness had now proven to be a beautiful connection between her and her family.

Christina was proud.

Proud of herself.

Proud to find herself part of a family who supported one another without hesitation, without doubt. And her husband was now one of them. He had proven himself to be worthy of her trust, and she no longer worried that he was the one now in possession of her heart.

"It is a remarkable achievement," he whispered beside her, one arm moving to wrap around her shoulders as they stood gazing down into the crate. "I always knew I would do well, but to have found a wife of such literary talent..." He looked at her and grinned. "Only an extraordinary man like myself could have procured her hand in marriage."

Christina laughed, then slapped him on the arm. "You're impossible! Are you never serious?"

Thorne turned to look at her, pulling her closer. "I find life much more interesting when I'm not." He leaned in and pressed a gentle kiss to her lips. "However, I've come to realize that there is one key ingredient to my happiness."

Christina lifted her brows. "Do I dare ask what that is? Your ego perhaps? Or—?"

"You," he interrupted with a grin before he pulled her into his arms and kissed her once more. "You and Samantha and even that somewhat unusual family of yours." He cleared his throat and turned to look at the desk. "Speaking of which, there's a letter here for you." He handed her the sealed envelope, and Christina immediately recognized her sister's handwriting.

"Juliet?" She frowned, then broke the seal. "I must admit I did not expect to hear from her. As far as I know, she accompanied Grandma Edie to a friend's estate for the remainder of the summer." She unfolded the letter, and her eyes dropped to the page.

Dearest Christina,

I'm writing in haste for I need your help as I do not know what to do. It may be nothing, nothing more than a rumor, or it may be a grave situation indeed.

Grandma Edie and I are still at Rosemere Hall. Only this morning a visitor arrived from London, who brought with him a most disconcerting rumor. Apparently, people are whispering that our youngest sister has run off to Gretna Green with Lord Burnham. Is she not with you at Pinewood Manor?

Christina felt her fingers tense upon the parchment. "Oh, Harry," she mumbled under her breath as a cold chill raced down her spine. After all, Harriet was not at Pinewood Manor and had not been for some time.

"Are you all right?" came her husband's voice. "You look pale." He moved closer, and Christina gestured for him to read the letter along with her.

Please write back with the utmost haste. I do not wish to alert our parents to the situation if there is nothing to be concerned about if this is truly nothing more than a vicious rumor.

Nevertheless, I am concerned. Although Harriet has always been unpredictable, this does not seem like something she would do. Has she not always proclaimed she would never marry?

I pray that she is with you safe and sound at Pinewood Manor. However, if she is not, Grandma Edie insists that you inform the Duke of Clements of the situation immediately although she refuses to tell me why.

Your devoted and most anxious sister,

Juliet

"Lord Burnham?" Thorne asked, turning to look at her, a deep frown upon his face. "The name does not sound familiar. Who is he?"

Christina shook her head, still staring at the letter, her mind racing to make sense of everything. "A mere acquaintance, nothing more." She turned to look at her husband. "I do not understand. Why would Juliet think Harriet to be here? She left for Whickerton Grove a fortnight ago."

"Perhaps it is nothing more than a mere misunderstanding," Thorne counseled, placing his hands upon her shoulders. "You should write to your parents and ask about Harriet's whereabouts."

Still feeling somewhat dazed, Christina nodded.

"Odd," Thorne remarked as his gaze once more shifted to the parchment in her hands. He sighed. "Honestly, I'd begun to think that perhaps she and the duke..."

Looking up at him, Christina nodded. "I did as well. I was surprised when she left so abruptly." She shook her head, hating the confusion that seemed to linger in every corner.

"Do you believe they quarreled?"

Christina shrugged. "I suppose it's possible. Still..."

"Harriet is rather the impulsive sort," Thorne stated carefully. "Do you think that perhaps she fell head over heels in love with Burnham?"

Christina could not help the grimace that came to her face. "I can't imagine it to be so. She never seemed partial to Lord Burnham, no matter how hard he tried to impress her." Again, she shook her head. "No, Harriet would not run off and get married. Not her!" She lifted her eyes to her husband's. "Something is wrong. Something is very wrong."

Taking her hands, Thorne nodded. "Sit down and write a letter to your parents as well as the duke. We'll see them delivered within the day." He squeezed her hands gently. "Then we shall know more."

Nodding, Christina sat down at his desk and quickly reached for parchment and quill. "Oh, Harry, what did you do?" Yes, Harriet had always been daring, but she had never been foolish. If she truly wished to run off to be married, she would leave a note. She would not disappear without a word and put them all through hell.

Christina was certain of it.

Then what had happened?

THE END

Thank you for reading *Once Upon an Irritatingly Magical Kiss*!

Be on the lookout for the next story about Harriet and her duke!

If you want to read more about the Whickerton family, make sure to check out *Once Upon a Devilishly Enchanting Kiss* (Louisa's story), *Once Upon a Temptingly Ruinous Kiss* (Leonora's story) and *Once Upon a Kiss Gone Horribly Wrong* (Anne's story).

Harriet's story will be released on October 14 in *Once Upon a Devastatingly Sweet Kiss*, which is now available for pre-order! Get your copy of this opposites-attract Regency romance where an untamed lady and a proper duke are put to the test when they fall in love against all odds.

Also by Bree Wolf

THE WHICKERTONS IN LOVE

LOVE'S SECOND CHANCE SERIES: TALES OF LORDS & LADIES

ALSO BY BREE WOLF

FORBIDDEN LOVE NOVELLA SERIES

About Bree

USA Today bestselling and award-winning author, Bree Wolf has always been a language enthusiast (though not a grammarian!) and is rarely found without a book in her hand or her fingers glued to a keyboard. Trying to find her way, she has taught English as a second language, traveled abroad and worked at a translation agency as well as a law firm in Ireland. She also spent loooong years obtaining a BA in English and Education and an MA in Specialized Translation while wishing she could simply be a writer. Although there is nothing simple about being a writer, her dreams have finally come true.

"A big thanks to my fairy godmother!"

Currently, Bree has found her new home in the historical romance genre, writing Regency novels and novellas. Enjoying the mix of fact and fiction, she occasionally feels like a puppet master (or mistress? Although that sounds weird!), forcing her characters into ever-new situations that will put their strength, their beliefs, their love to the test, hoping that in the end they will triumph and get the happily-ever-after we are all looking for.

If you're an avid reader, sign up for Bree's newsletter on www. breewolf.com as she has the tendency to simply give books away. Find out about freebies, giveaways as well as occasional advance reader copies and read before the book is even on the shelves!

Connect with Bree and stay up-to-date on new releases:

 facebook.com/breewolf.novels

twitter.com/breewolf_author

instagram.com/breewolf_author

bookbub.com/authors/bree-wolf

Printed in Great Britain
by Amazon

24559963R00199